'Shades of Sarah Waters…irresistible'
The Guardian

'Compelling'
–Sarra Manning, *Red* magazine

'A bawdy, romping affair … '
The Times

'This is one hell of a read'
The Sun

'A saucy bodice-ripper'
The Metro

'A fun, explicit romp with real stakes that will have you
trying to finish this book in one sitting'
Stylist

'This tale of 18th century debauchery unfolds in the
tradition of *Fanny Hill*'
Lovereading

Wray Delaney is the pen name of Sally Gardner, the award-winning children's novelist, who has sold over 2 million books worldwide and been translated into 22 languages. She lives in London and this is her first adult novel.

An ALMOND for a PARROT

WRAY DELANEY

ONE PLACE. MANY STORIES

HQ
An imprint of HarperCollinsPublishers Ltd.
1 London Bridge Street
London SE1 9GF

1
First published in Great Britain by
HQ, an imprint of HarperCollinsPublishers Ltd. 2016

A catalogue record for this book is
available from the British Library

ISBN: 978-0008-18253-3

Printed and bound in Great Britain by
CPI Group (UK) Ltd, Croydon, CR0 4YY

For my mother, Nina Lowry.

The third female circuit judge to be appointed in England, she sat for twenty years at the Old Bailey. For her service she was given the Freedom of the City of London with the right to drive a flock of sheep across London Bridge. She has yet to do so.

A remarkable woman, who I'm very proud to call Mum.

Fleet Marriages

One of the most disgraceful customs observed in the Fleet Prison in the seventeenth and eighteenth centuries was the performance of the marriage ceremony by disreputable and dissolute clergymen. These functionaries, mostly prisoners for debt, insulted the dignity of their holy profession by marrying in the precincts of the Fleet Prison at a minute's notice, any persons who might present themselves for that purpose. No questions were asked, no stipulations made, except as to the amount of the fee for the service, or the quantity of liquor to be drunk on the occasion. It not unfrequently happened, indeed, that the clergyman, the clerk, the bridegroom and the bride were drunk at the very time the ceremony was performed.

Appendix VI, The Newgate Calendar

Chapter One

Newgate Prison, London

I lie on this hard bed counting the bricks in the ceiling of this miserable cell. I have been sick every morning for a week and thought I might have jail fever. If it had killed me it would at least have saved me the inconvenience of a trial and a public hanging. Already the best seats at Newgate Prison have been sold in anticipation of my being found guilty – and I have yet to be sent to trial. Murder, attempted murder – either way the great metropolis seems to know the verdict before the judge has placed the black square on his grey wig. This whore is gallows-bound.

'Is he dead?' I asked.

My jailer wouldn't say.

I pass my days remembering recipes and reciting them to the damp walls. They don't remind me of food; they are bookmarks from this short life of mine. They remain tasteless. I prefer them that way.

A doctor was called for. Who sent for or paid for him I don't know, and uncharacteristically I do not care. He was very matter of fact and said the reason for my malady was simple: I was with child. I haven't laughed for a long time but forgive me, the thought struck me as ridiculous. In all that has happened I have never once found myself in this predicament. I can hardly believe it is true. The doctor looked relieved – he had at least found a reason for my life to be extended – pregnant women are not hanged. Even if I'm found guilty of murder, the gallows will wait until the child is born. What a comforting thought.

Hope came shortly afterwards. Dear Hope. She looked worried, thinner.

'How is Mercy?' I asked.

She avoided answering me and busied herself about my cell.

'What does this mean?' she asked, running her fingers over the words scratched on a small table, the only piece of furniture this stinking cell has to offer.

I had spent some time etching them into its worm-eaten surface. An Almond for a Parrot.

'It's a title for a memoir, the unanswered love song of a soon-to-be dead bird. Except I have no paper, no pen and without ink the thing won't write at all.'

'Just as well, Tully.'

'I want to tell the truth of my life.'

'Better to leave it,' she said.

'It's for Avery – not that he will ever read it.' I felt myself on the brink of tears but I refused to give in to them. 'I will write it for myself. Afterwards, it can be your bedtime entertainment, the novelty of my days in recipes and tittle-tattle.'

'Oh, my sweet ninny-not. You must be brave, Tully. This is a dreadful place and…'

'And it is not my first prison. My life has come full circle. You haven't answered my question.'

'Mercy is still very ill. Mofty is with her.'

'Will she live?'

'I don't know.'

'And is he alive?'

'Tully, he is dead. You are to be tried for murder.'

'My, oh my. At least my aim was true.'

I sank back on the bed, too tired to ask more. Even if Hope was in the mood for answering questions, I didn't think I would want to know the answers.

'You are a celebrity in London. Everyone wants to know what you do, what you wear. The papers are full of it.'

There seemed nothing to say to that. Hope sat quietly on the edge of the bed, holding my hand.

Finally, I found the courage to ask the question I'd wanted to ask since Hope arrived.

'Is there any news of Avery?'

'No, Tully, there's not.'

I shook my head. Regret. I am full of it. A stone to worry one's soul with.

'You have done nothing wrong, Tully.'

'Forgive me for laughing.'

'You will have the very best solicitor.'

'Who will pay for him?'

'Queenie.'

'No, no. I don't want her to. I have some jewels…'

I felt sick.

'Concentrate on staying well,' said Hope.

~

If this life was a dress rehearsal, I would now have a chance to play my part again but with a more favourable outcome. Alas, we players are unaware that the curtain goes up the minute we take our first gulps of air; the screams of rage our only hopeless comments on being born onto such a barren stage.

So here I am with ink, pen and a box of writing paper, courtesy of a well-wisher. Still I wait to know the date of my trial. What to do until then? Write, Tully, write.

With a hey ho the wind and the rain. *And words are my only escape.* For the rain it raineth every day.

Chapter Two

To Make a Hasty Pudding

Take a quart of milk and four bay leaves, set it on the fire to boil. Beat up the yolks of two eggs and stir in a little salt. Take two or three spoonfuls of milk and beat up your eggs and stir in your milk. Then with a wooden spoon in one hand and the flour in the other, stir until it is of a good thickness but not too thick. Let it boil and keep stirring then pour it in a dish and stick pieces of butter here and there. You may omit the egg if you do not like it but it is a great addition to the pudding and a little piece of butter stirred in the milk makes it short and fine. Take out the bay leaves before you put in the flour.

Written in Newgate Prison
September, 1756

I would like to make myself the heroine of this story and my character to be so noble that you could not help but be in love with me. Perhaps I should portray myself as an innocent victim led astray. But alas, sir, I would be lying, and as I am on the brink of seeing my maker, the truth might serve me better.

Feathers and dust. Let me try to tell you my truth as seen through these two green eyes, not just the one eye that is always blinkered in favour of its owner. Forgive me if I don't throw myself into the most saucy parts of my life first – like all seductions, it is the undoing of layers that makes the moment the greater by anticipation. Haste is always a lover's downfall. Whether that be the same with my story only the telling of it will show. I would like to make you laugh, to see that smile that curls across your lips. Laughter is by far the better remedy for all life's ills. Our days are measured too often in woes and too seldom in humour, which is a pity, for what is this world if not a farce, a comedy of follies performed without rehearsal, a stage waiting for a strumpet to tell her tale? So let me start, sir, before the clock runs out of hours.

~

Is it breeding that makes us what we are, or the muck we are born into, be that of a stable or a palace? Perhaps it is a smattering of both – and in my case, mingled with a sprinkle of magic. My father – if he really be my father – was one Captain Truegood, who gave up the Seven Seas to become a merchant in bricks. Finding that, like bread, bricks cannot be done without and like bread they are needed daily, soon he possessed more money than his feeble senses knew what to do with. His wealth enabled him to purchase an accomplished wife from a noble family, whose fortune had dwindled to little more than a title. My mother was seventeen when the contract was signed, and I can only imagine the disappointment of the marriage bed. Captain Truegood, no doubt drunk as was his way, made a hasty pudding of me. My mother's sentiments upon such pitiless passion I will never know, for no sooner had she seen my face, than she decided very sensibly to depart this world. If there was misfortune in my life it was, I suppose, not to have had the sense to follow her, but once I made my arrival there was little I could do but grab life by the dairies and live it to my best advantage.

What philosophical thought my father had about his nine months of marriage and subsequent widowhood, he never said. But Captain Truegood was a man of few words and those that came to him came through the grape and the grain, only to be distilled into ill-thought-out mumblings and ill-thought-out doings.

My father had no interest in me other than to see me at first as a great nuisance and later as little more than a chamber-maid. I will skip-hop over the inconvenience of my infancy for it is the general belief that nothing of value is to be remarked upon in the early stages of a female's life, unlike that of the male. Several writers have deemed the early years of a young man to be of such momentous importance that they have even recounted the circumstances pertaining to the time before the sperm meets the egg. All I will say is that my father begat me and my father promptly forgot me.

My first conscious memory is of the large wooden table in the kitchen. I spent most of my younger days hidden under it, keeping out of sight. That table was the centre of my world, the only solid thing in a house built on sand. I imagined its legs turning into roots that burrowed deep into the earth. No matter what else might befall me, the table would remain unmoved by fortune's wheel, a constant, like Cook.

Cook as good as brought me up; half-baked me, as she would say. Having no children of her own and little understanding as to what infants might need, for guidance she relied on her cookbook as if she hoped to find the method for the growing of children, just as there were recipes for every other kind of slaughtered meat. I'm not certain that she fully understood the recipes for she told me she believed reading was nothing to do with letters. Recipes, she said, were weighed in words and words were weighed in time. As with so much that Cook said, this meant little or nothing to my green ears, but I would often fall asleep to the rhythm of Cook kneading bread, rolling pastry, cutting meat.

Did I long for my mother? Yes. Of a need for love, all children who haven't known one put the absent parent into a cabinet of angels – or fairies, as in my case. The only place I felt close to my mother was the blue chamber. I knew her spirit had long escaped the house in Milk Street but the walls of her room held tight to her memory. I would talk to her about my many frustrations and ask why it was that my father had so little regard for me. She was wise enough never to answer, but I would always find solace knowing her to be listening like a benign angel.

I much preferred the company of servants to that of my father's chuckle-headed friends whose delights mainly seemed to be pinned on wine, peppered by the gaming tables. The world beyond our house was to me but a small theatre seen through shuttered windows. The comings and goings of the players were all such a narrow view of the great metropolis allowed. They were accompanied by the changing scenery of the seasons, signalled more by the fashions than anything nature had to offer.

I never liked the house. The furniture was heavy and given to chattering, or so I believed when little. The worst offender was the grandfather clock. It stood on the first floor landing, an immovable exclamation mark, its face as large as the moon without any of the illumination. Its chimes called to the dead more than to the living. The grandfather clock's quarrel was with a young boy by the name of Samuel. In tick-tock talk, it would say:

'What-have

'you-to

'show-for

'your-self

'young-Sam?'

I told Cook there was a boy trapped inside the clock. The thought of it gave me nightmares. Cook, who had to share a bed with me, soon lost patience at being woken by a terrified child, and without my father's permission took the key to the clock from his study.

'There,' she said, as she opened the clock. 'You see? It's empty. A pendulum and two weights, the sum total of time.'

I could say nothing. For there crouched a small boy of about my age, his hands over his face. I never spoke about the clock again and neither did Cook.

As the outside world was forbidden to me, I organised the interior of our house into the streets and alleyways of the city I didn't know, of which I had only heard Cook speak. The main staircase was Gin Alley; at the top of the first flight was the step I called the Coffin-Maker, for it groaned every time I stepped on it. The seventh step from the ground I called Dead Drunk for it wobbled like my father in his cups.

The problem of how to avoid them tied me up in knots until it occurred to me that the simplest remedy would be to learn how to fly. To that end I took to practising, at first by jumping off a chair. I was deeply disappointed to find I was unaccountably earthbound. I thought I needed more height to achieve my goal, and so it was that one morning I stood on the top landing and threw myself off. As I hurtled downwards, I realised I was about to land flat on my face on the stone floor and I willed myself to stop.

I stopped.

I hung in the air on an invisible step, and it was then I heard Cook scream. I landed with a bump. Cook hit me with her wooden spoon.

'What are you about?'

'I'm learning to fly,' I said.

'Well don't. You can't. So there.'

Strange to say that after that I never could do it again. Perhaps I had never done it at all. I wonder what would have happened if Cook had told me that my other notions were impossible, but she didn't and I came to believe that everyone must see the world as I did.

Once a week, Mrs Inglis would call on Cook. Mrs Inglis was a large lady with a face so folded with jowly flesh that it resembled an unmade bed. She always seated herself in the chair near the stove where she would pull up her petticoats and rest her feet on a stool. Her legs were blotched and itchy. Sighing, she would say what a trial it was to be old and who would have thought it would have come to this pretty pass. Cook would sit opposite and they would chinwag away the woes of the world into a bottle of gin.

Mrs Inglis always brought with her a sickly child of about thirteen. She would stand beside Mrs Inglis's chair but not once did Mrs Inglis talk to her.

'Back in the days…' as Mrs Inglis loved to say. 'Back in the days, I ran a good school, I did. I had good girls, such good girls. I never let anything untoward befall them – could have done, earned a little extra on the side. It would've been legal, but I never. Was it my fault, what happened?'

'No, Mrs Inglis,' Cook would say. 'Let's think on something merrier.'

Then they would start on the gossip.

If I thought it odd that the girl should be so ignored I said nothing as long as she stayed by the chair and didn't come near me.

One day, while Mrs Inglis blabbered fifty to the dozen about nothing, or nothing I understood, the girl joined me under the table.

'How old are you?' she asked.

I was five at the time.

'Are you hiding from the gentlemen?'

'What gentlemen?' I said.

'The gentlemen who take you on their laps and ask to see what shouldn't be shown. Pretty Poppet they call me.'

I didn't like the way Pretty Poppet spoke and asked Cook why Pretty Poppet came all the time.

'Because some griefs you never rise above,' she said.

Mrs Inglis continued to visit and while time passed Pretty Poppet didn't age. I decided it would be pointless to say anything more to Cook, for surely both she and Mrs Inglis could see her just as well as me.

So it was that out of the rubble of neglect I slowly grew with a head full of recipes and ghosts.

Chapter Three

Three events stand out in the sea of sameness and have become magnified in my memory. Each in their way forecast the future and, although I didn't know it, gave me a glimpse of what my life might hold.

At eight years I was employed to clean the downstairs parlour – a gloomy, wood-panelled chamber that appeared to vanish into the darkness. Mr Truegood and his friends would meet there in what my father loosely called the Hawks' Club. Its members were gunpowder-blasted mumpers, broken-limbed soldiers, sham seamen and scaly fish, all of whom had long left the shores of sobriety. Here they sang their bawdy songs, gambled and drank well into the night until they could see the silver of their dreams in the bottom of a pewter mug.

The following morning it would be my job to bring a semblance of order to the chaos. I would find the chamber shuttered and through the shutters urgent pinpricks of light would show a yellow, wheezy fog that hung mournfully in the middle of the room, smelling of stale tobacco and defeat. I would polish the round wooden table, sweep the floor and lay the fire. This chamber in its various states of debauchery was my storybook. The main character the table itself, the empty plates and broken wine glasses spoke the lines and gave away the players of last night's revelry. Among all the clutter lay treasure forgotten by these fuddled-headed gentlemen. A button, a snuffbox, a pipe in the shape of a man's head: I would stash them away, pirates' gold waiting to be reclaimed.

One wintry morning I opened the shutters and saw, propped upright by the side of a chair, a wooden leg with a scuffed shoe attached to it. The leg was so finely carved and painted that for a moment I thought it to be made out of flesh and bone. I didn't fancy touching it, so left it where it was and set about my work. My heart as good as stopped when I discovered a dead man sitting in the chair by the fireplace. He had his eyes wide open and was staring at me, his face whiter than Cook's flour. I was about to call for help when his hand shot out and took hold of my arm. My cry was swallowed back down upon itself.

'Who are you?' asked the dead man.

'Tully Truegood,' I replied, feeling my legs to be made of marrow jelly.

All his features were delicately rendered, each with a point to them. His hooked nose ended in a point, his chin jutted, even his ears appeared more pointed than the few ears I had seen before. I had no idea what an elf might look like but from the stories that Cook had told me I imagined that the dead man's face couldn't be so dissimilar from those of fairy folk. His eyes were set back into his face, his lip but a thin bow, his tongue the arrow. I saw now why I had thought him dead for his face was painted white and his almond-shaped eyelids had another set of eyes painted on them so that when they were closed they appeared open. The whole effect was most disconcerting.

'Captain Truegood has a daughter,' said the man. 'Then you are the answer to the riddle. How old?'

'Eight.'

'Is there any more wine in that bowl, Miss Truegood?' he said.

'I think so.'

'Then fetch me a glass and my leg, if you would be so kind, before the devil takes it to dance a jig.'

The moment he spoke, all my fear of him dissolved into excitement. Having concluded that he was a character from a fairy tale, I was no longer afraid. Up to then most of my days had been humdrum to say the least; so much so that I was scarcely conscious of which month it was. I had lately in my childish wisdom fallen into a gloom at the thought that time might have forgotten me altogether, that I would never be pulled into the adult world. Perhaps the dead man was here to do just that.

Once he had his painted leg back, he rolled up his breeches and I watched, fascinated, as he attached and strapped the wooden limb to his stump. When he stood and dusted himself down I was surprised by how tall he was, and that his clothes were colourful, his coat being striped. He squared his wig in the mirror.

'You are no hen-hearted girl,' he said, and whistled.

I could not for the life of me see why he needed to whistle, but then, from the darkest part of the parlour, appeared a little white dog.

The dead man watched me as he clicked his fingers. The dog, obeying his master's command, danced on his hind legs. Thrilled, I knelt, clapping my hands as the little white dog came to me and I held him in my arms as he licked my face. It made me laugh, and I closed my eyes and relished the feel of that soft tongue. When I opened my eyes again the dead man and his dog had gone. For a long while I wondered if I had conjured them up and if I had conjured the boy in the grandfather clock for there was no other explanation for the appearance of any of them. Perhaps everyone could do it and it was nothing to wonder at. I thought to ask Pretty Poppet next time she came with Mrs Inglis, but Mrs Inglis didn't come again; she had been taken to the Fleet Prison for unpaid bills.

I tried to ask Cook; but she huffed, and said, as she always said when there was no answer, 'Butter and salt.'

I count my life as having begun that day, the day I saw the little white dog. All before that I consider to be nothing more than an audition for the main play.

~

The second event took place when I was nine. The boot boy, who was twelve, told me he loved me and wanted to see what lay under my skirts.

I, being innocent, replied, 'Petticoats.'

'No,' he whispered. 'I want to see what is there after you have lifted them aside.'

If this was what love was, it seemed a trifling thing to show him, and being curious as to what lay in his breeches, I agreed, if he would unbutton himself.

I remember a pink plug tail that hung down and that I wasn't much impressed. But a bargain being a bargain I duly pulled up my petticoats and was surprised to see the way the small shrivelled plug tail became all perky and stood engagingly to attention. After that I don't think I saw him again, and lost all interest in the rising and falling of such a small drawbridge.

By now my father had become attached to the whorehouse and addicted to the gaming tables so that his considerable fortune began by degrees to diminish. As it depleted, so did his servants, until there was only Cook and myself to run the house, and it was in these very diminished circumstances that the third event took place.

I was twelve when I was married.

~

Ah, sir, I see now I have your full attention. My unexpected wedding took place one Friday in the middle of the night. My father, roaring drunk and mighty out of temper, came all bellowing, sail flapping, into the chamber I shared with Cook. She, poor woman, did her level best to guide the Captain's sinking wreck into a safe harbour.

'No, sir, leave the girl alone,' she said.

But Captain Truegood was set on his course and neither the cook nor the devil was about to stop him. He was persuaded that he should at least wait downstairs until I was dressed.

Sleepily, I put on my threadbare clothes, Cook put my hair into a cap and thus attired in the plainest of styles I went to join my father in the hall. Two sedan chairs and their porters were waiting. I could only think of the mess they had made of the white stone floor and wondered if my father had need of me to clean it after he and whoever his guest was had departed.

To my astonishment it appeared that the second sedan chair was for me and for the first time in my life I was to be allowed out of the house. Where I was bound I had no idea and could not ask my father, for Captain Truegood had not left off his shouting at one and all to make haste. I remember the journey vividly, though having no knowledge of the city I had been born into I cannot say where I was taken other than it was a tall house where a great number of people were gathered within. Most lined the stairs. They were a motley crowd made more merry by the gin. Captain Truegood, still roaring, waved his stick about, clearing lovebirds from the stairs for each couple seemed very free with one another.

'She's a bit on the young side,' said one woman.

'Do you know what you're about?' another asked me.

'Let me pass, madam,' thundered Captain Truegood, who, having hold of my hand, near as dragged me to the first floor and along an ill-lit corridor. Only when we were outside a door did he stop. Fumbling in his pocket, he took out a mask and told me to put it on.

'All you need do is say, "I consent", nothing more. Do you understand?'

Not waiting for an answer, my father, swimming in wine, threw open the door and, tripping on the carpet, nearly capsized altogether. He was saved by a minister of the church.

The chamber we had arrived in was empty but for a minister and a gentleman in a fine wig who appeared to be as drunk, if not more so, than my father.

'You are late, sir,' said the gentleman.

He was dressed in a grand style in a brocaded coat. With him was a black spider of man who scuttled to a curtain at the end of the room where he seemed to take instructions and papers from someone before returning to the side of the grand gentleman.

I knew that I was to be married, but which of these unpleasant-looking men I would have the honour to call husband I couldn't say. The whole idea of being married was one I had given little thought to, but remembering my father's words, I said nothing until I couldn't help but speak. The room was in such darkness that for a moment I wasn't sure what tricks the light played: for seated behind the minister was a shrivelled-up woman dressed in the dustiest of clothes.

'Who is that?' I asked.

The minister turned and seemed shocked to see her there. 'That,' he replied unsteadily, 'is my wife.'

'Then, sir,' I said, 'I am afraid she is dead.'

The remark was greeted with laughter, not from the minister or my father or his pissed acquaintance but from the folds of a curtain. A young gentleman, also wearing a mask, stepped out into the light and stood beside me.

'Of course she's dead,' he said, his words slurred. 'Marriage is murder.'

Whether or not the minister heard I wasn't sure, but much to my father's fury it made me giggle. Everyone was drunk except me and the minister, and I wasn't sure how sober he was. Surely, I thought, a wedding this soaked in liquor could never be considered binding.

The minister raised his eyes to the high ceiling as if hoping to find a god to calm him and said, 'My wife has been shown to me this night. It is a sign to remind the living of the passion to be found in life and the brief amount of light there is before everlasting darkness.'

'On with the thing, sir!' shouted my father.

'This is no time for ghosts,' said his brocaded friend.

The minister, somewhat shaken, went on, though every now and again he glanced uneasily behind him to where his dead wife sat watching.

The wedding service consisted of nothing more than the

young gentleman and myself giving our consents and signing the papers that the black spider eagerly put before us.

And that was that. I never saw my bridegroom's face, nor was I informed of his name, nor the purpose of such a hasty marriage. Cook told me the next day that my husband had gone to join the navy and I need think no more about it.

'With luck,' she said, 'you will be a respectable widow by the time you're fifteen.'

I mention these three events only because by the time the years had chased the child in me away I saw all too clearly how the upturned cart of my life was settled. I was destined to live out my days emptying my father's chamber pot and serving him his meals. This may well have been my fate, but it was at this very low juncture that the tide changed in my favour.

Chapter Four

My father was to remarry.

When I heard the news that I was to have a stepmother I was completely flummoxed. I could only assume that this lady, whoever she was, must be wealthy and my father had tricked her into believing she was marrying a respectable merchant. There seemed no other explanation for her acceptance of such a foolish proposal.

By this time, I was sixteen and had by degrees taught myself to read from cookbooks, discarded newspapers and the salacious pamphlets that Captain Truegood regularly purchased. It was in one of the newspapers that I had first come across advertisements by gentlemen for wives and occasionally by women in want of a husband. I made up one I thought my father might have written if he had resorted to writing to the paper in search of a wife. I read it out to Cook and it tickled her fancy no end.

An Invitation To The Ladies.

A captain who left the Navy to become a merchant finds himself shipwrecked on dry land with a wet whistle that can never be satisfied. Losses and crosses have reduced his fortune to no more than his wardrobe, a diamond ring, a gold watch and an amber-headed cane. In addition to the above he has a flaxen full-bottom, flea-ridden wig befitting a man of his age and position. I plead to the generous ladies of the cities of London and Westminster: SAVE ME. Letters to be sent to Truegood, Milk Street at Cheapside.

Cook told me only three days before the wedding that my stepmother-to-be had two daughters of about my age. That went some way to explain her decision to marry. Perhaps she wasn't wealthy after all and was in search of respectability. Between you and me and a four-poster bed, there was little to nothing to recommend my father.

On the day of Captain Truegood's nuptials he, was surprisingly sober and dressed in his flaxen full-bottom wig and his best suit of clothes. He stood in the hall clutching his amber-top cane, tapping it on the barometer and bellowing as if there was a house full of servants, not just Cook and myself.

'Everything is to be shipshape,' he roared. 'I am off to be married.'

No one replied, only the front door groaned as it was closed.

There was a wonderful peace to our house, as there always was the moment the captain left. I could almost hear the walls let out a sigh and settle back to relish their bricks, bones and plaster conversations. It was at these moments that the house became bearable; the quiet peace of it, the enticing smell of fresh bread wafting from the kitchen. I thought I would have the best part of the morning to enjoy the silence before Captain and the new Mrs Truegood returned.

'Do you think…' I asked Cook. She had just taken a batch of fresh-baked rolls from the oven and I was putting them on a wire rack to cool. They smelled so good that my mouth watered and I slipped one surreptitiously into my apron.

'I saw that, miss. Now put it back.'

Reluctantly I did as I was told and she huffed.

'Do you think – '

'I try hard not to,' interrupted Cook, stuffing a fowl.

'Do you think that my father will tell my stepmother that she has a stepdaughter?'

Cook was never a great conversationalist and my question was greeted by a grunt, which I took to mean 'no'.

I sighed. I had asked as I was certain that it would come as something of a shock to my father's new wife for I doubted that he had told her of my existence. The reason, I supposed, was that he had so long persisted in treating me as a servant that he must have felt it to be the truth. Quite why he saw me in this unfavourable light I have never fathomed. I didn't think for a moment that my stepmother's discovery that I had sprung from Captain Truegood's loins would go in my favour.

'Do you think I will be asked to leave?'

'Leave where?'

'Leave here.'

'What? You buffle head, of course not. What would you do?'

'Be my own mistress,' I said, 'for I am determined not to be beholden to a man – especially one like Mr Truegood.'

'I have no time to listen to this stuff and nonsense.' Cook softened. She took one of the rolls and handed it to me. 'Help yourself to butter then go and see if the canaries are still alive.

I'll call you if I need you. And try to bring some reason into that muddled head of yours.'

All that was left of the grand furnishings in the blue chamber was a four-poster bed. The chamber smelled of oranges and cloves just as it always had done. When I was little I would sit at the table with Cook, my fingers hurting as I pushed cloves into the orange flesh, releasing its puff of perfume. I felt cross at the idea of anyone else occupying this chamber, removing the veil of my mother's ghost by their presence.

I opened the shutters and sunlight showed up the shabbiness of all within. It was only in candlelight that the chamber had any pretence to grandeur. I took the cloths off the two cages, pleased to see that the canaries were alive, and put them in front of the window where the birds started to sing, their bright yellow in such contrast to the blue.

Satisfied that all was as it should be, I resigned myself to the fact that I would no longer be able to come here. I took a last glance at the antechamber. The only piece of furniture there was my mother's full-length looking glass.

I decided then that this was perhaps the only opportunity I would have to take stock of my figure. I had read somewhere that an accomplished young lady should be able to play a musical instrument, speak French fluently and dance. I could do none of the above. The writer also said that a good figure and a pretty face could outshine all these achievements.

My father, in his drunken wisdom, had decided not to waste his money on my education. He strongly believed that knowledge gave women the wrong ideas and made them a nuisance to their husbands. I cannot tell you how much I longed to be in charge of my own destiny. Never again did I want to be beholden to another soul. I had lived sixteen dull summers subjected to the tempestuous seas of my father's ill-spent fortune and if I was ever allowed to have a life I did not want to be held prisoner by another man's purse strings. In short, I was determined to earn my own way in this topsy world.

If there was a time for an honest appraisal of my assets, surely it was now, there being no one else in the house apart from Cook. I undressed and for the first time stood as naked as Eve before the mirror and studied myself in the long glass. I had rounded ivory globes that sat well, but I thought were a little too large for such a trim waist, though they did have pleasing rose petal nipples. I had a flat stomach, and a dark, soft covering of downy fluff hid my Venus mound. As for my shoulders, they were not too bony, more soft as was the fashion of the day. Those at least I thought were passable. My legs I decided were shapely. I had fine ankles and slender wrists, all of which I put down to being in my favour. But my face was the greatest disappointment. I could tell I was not destined to be a beauty. It was long, as was my neck; my nose, alas, seemed snubbed. I had thick eyebrows that met in a bow in the middle and lips too full. My teeth I deemed to be my only asset worth a mention: they were neat and white. I felt the whole composition had been put together in a clumsy, ill-thought-out manner. The portrait was framed by thick, unruly hair of a mouse-coloured hue. The only striking quality about my looks, or so I thought, was the colour of my eyes. They were green and my skin alabaster, which was not due to any design but by the mere fact that I had hardly seen any sunlight since the day I was born.

The front of me being thoroughly weighed and found wanting, I had turned my attentions to my bottom, when to my utter horror the door to the antechamber opened and there stood a gentleman in the finest clothes I had ever seen. Such was my embarrassment to be discovered this way that I daren't look up and neither did I think to find my shift to cover my modesty. Instead, head bowed, I stared at his riding boots.

'Madam, pardon me,' he said, as calmly as if he had found me fully dressed. 'I did not mean to intrude upon your toilette. I am looking for Captain Truegood.'

'He has gone off to be married,' I said. 'No one is at home.'

'And who do have I the honour of addressing?'

'Tully Truegood, sir.'

Daring myself to look up, I was struck dumb by his appearance, for he was not only most handsomely dressed but possessed a face which, unlike mine, seemed to have been put together with great thought, and a certain knowledge of how good features and a strong jawline and a straight nose could make a girl weak to the knees.

I must have gone white, or whiter still, for he helped me to a chair then went in search of port wine. I found my shift and hurriedly, if unsteadily, put it over my head.

He re-entered the chamber with a glass and, smiling, said, 'Madam, I prefer you as you were for you have been blessed with a figure that is a delight to look upon.'

He handed me the wine and I drank it down in one great gulp.

'Thank you, sir.'

'I will come back,' he said, 'when your father is at home.' He bowed and went to leave.

'Who shall I say called, sir?'

He didn't reply. And then to my amazement he came back

into the room and lifted my face to his and kissed me. Having never been kissed before I was uncertain as to what I was supposed to do. He wasn't, and before I knew what had happened my mouth was full of his tongue and a part of me that had never ached before felt as if it might die if something wasn't done to soothe the yearning.

He pulled away from me so suddenly that I felt bereft and without a thought to modesty I put my arms round his neck. Laughing, he untangled himself from me and undid the ribbons on my shift so that it fell once more to the floor. He stroked my face. His fingers were long and elegant, and slowly they went down my neck, over my breast, and circled my nipples, which had the effect of making them hard. His hand caressed my stomach and wherever his fingers went they seemed to waken the flesh of me that before had been fast asleep. He touched the inside of my thigh and then up into the soft purse of my Venus mound.

I should have been outraged and I was not, just ablaze with longing – for what, I didn't know. I felt certain that I was about to find out, but he took his hand away.

'Don't give that sweet, white rose of yours to any stranger,' he said. 'Wait for your husband to come and claim it, and more besides.'

'I don't think he ever will,' I said.

He smiled and kissed me once more. 'Oh, he will. Believe me, he will.'

And with that he was gone.

I tried to compose myself but the ache in me was so terrible and all of it stemmed from between my legs. I wondered if I was ill with a fever but could not think of any remedy. How long I sat there in that bemused state I could not say. At length

I was startled into action by the sound of a carriage pulling up outside our house and the noise of people arriving. Hurriedly, I dressed, my cheeks still on fire.

I went down the stairs and stopped on the first floor landing from where I could see all the people in the hall without being seen.

Quite a party had arrived and I could not fathom which of three elegantly dressed ladies was my stepmother for all were so beautifully turned out. But it was not the sight of the exotic plumage that unsettled me: it was the tall, thin man with a wooden leg coming in with my father. His face was bleached of colour as I remembered it and behind him came the little white dog. I held tight to the banister for there was a whooshing sound in my head and the taste of iron in my mouth. The little dog discovered my hiding place, ran up the stairs and jumped up, asking to be lifted from the ground.

My father, upon entering the hall and seeing me, gave me a look and, if looks could be fired from pistols, that look would have killed me.

'This way, madam,' he said, and guided one of the ladies into the parlour where Cook had laid the wedding breakfast.

It was then that I was overtaken by a most strange occurrence that I put down to the unusual excitement of seeing the one-legged man again. He whistled to call the little dog back and winked at me, showing his painted eye. The whooshing sound in my head said he had seen right through me, that he knew about the gentleman. I was standing on the Coffin-Maker's step and in my hurry to move on I must have tripped, and it felt to me as if my clothes were wings, unravelling from me, and I had taken flight. The one-legged gentleman's face appeared to become detached from his body and floated nearer to me and at that moment I saw the stairs rise, felt myself falling into them, and fortunately remembered no more.

Chapter Five

The general view of stepmothers is that they are cruel, with only one intention: to promote their children over and above their husbands' hated offspring. This turned out to be far from true in my case. If it wasn't for the arrival of my stepmother I dread to think what would have become of me.

When on the day of the marriage I fell down the stairs and passed out, it seemed to be for only a matter of moments.

I couldn't have been more mistaken, for I woke to find myself neatly tucked up in bed on soft pillows that I never knew we owned, in a room with furniture I had never seen before. I couldn't think how I came to be there in a fine cotton nightgown with lace at its edges. Such wanton luxury made me wonder if I had died and was in heaven, for there seemed no other rational explanation for these radical changes. Alas, that lofty thought lasted less than a minute. There was a clatter outside, the door flew open and there was Cook, carrying a tray.

'So your ladyship is awake at last,' she said, coming in with all the grace of an overfed turkey.

'Where am I?' I asked.

'Where you have been since the day you were born – in your father's house in Milk Street.'

Unless my eyes were playing tricks with me, I would swear

that Cook looked cleaner. She was wearing a white linen apron and there wasn't the usual smell of rancid fat about her.

I was muddled and was on the point of questioning her when the strikingly elegant woman who I remembered seeing in the hall came into the room.

'That will be all, Martha,' she said, dismissing Cook.

Martha. It was shocking to learn that Cook had a name, for as long as I had known her, she had been just plain Cook.

Cook dropped a curtsey, which my father had never had the luxury of receiving, and left as a gentleman in a purple velvet coat with a sprig of lavender in his lapel entered the chamber.

'This is Doctor Ross, Miss Truegood,' said the elegant lady. 'It is due to his good care that you are still with us.'

Doctor Ross had a face that could reassure the dying that they had a lifetime to live. He smiled, gently took hold of my wrist and leaned towards me, his breath smelled vaguely of mint. He looked into my eyes, felt my forehead and pronounced that the fever had passed and I would live.

Had the world fallen on its head and got up the wrong way? This was all a fuss about nothing. Before I could be stopped I climbed out of bed only to realise my mistake for my legs were not quite as determined as my will to stand upright.

The doctor smiled again, caught hold of me and helped me back into bed.

'You are lucky that nothing was broken,' said the elegant lady, who I assumed must be the new Mrs Truegood.

'Why should anything be broken?' I asked.

'Because you fell down the stairs and had a fit.'

'Then I must have ruined your wedding breakfast. I am so sorry, madam. It has never happened before and it will never happen again.'

She laughed. 'We all hope it will never happen again, my dear. But far from ruining the wedding feast you saved us from eating a rotten fowl that no amount of butter in the world could disguise as being edible. If you had to choose a day to have a fit, why, you couldn't have chosen a better.'

None of this made any sense at all.

'How long have I been here?' I asked.

'Ten very worrisome days.'

'What was my ailment?'

'A brain fever,' replied Dr Ross.

Mrs Truegood propped me up on the pillows and, as foolish as it was, I burst into tears, for never could I remember such care being taken of me, even if anyone had thought I might need it.

She leaned forward and said softly, 'Things will change for the better, Tully. I may call you Tully?'

Muddled was altogether too gentle a word to describe my feelings at that moment. I was completely befuddled. All that had been before was swept away. Was it possible that this was the new order of things?

Dr Ross's prescription was bed rest. I lay half sleeping and half dreaming of the gentleman's visit and my mind having nothing else to occupy it I began to wonder what lay in a grown man's breeches and how that joined together with my small mound. In fact, I could hardly think of anything else. The memory of the way his fingers had touched my skin sent a delicious tingle right through me. I tried to think what a plug tail might look like when it belonged to a man and such was my imagination that I found my body would readily ignite and I had no idea how to put out such a persistent flame. I grew fearful that I might still indeed have a fever.

The only release from these worrying thoughts was the company of my two new stepsisters who took it in turns to keep me entertained, and I began looking forward to their daily visits.

Never had two sisters been more different in character and looks. Though they claimed to be around my age, they were much more sophisticated and worldly than I. Hope had eyes that giggled into life and the most infectious laugh. She knew just how to dress her curvaceous figure to the best effect, wearing her corset tight so that her breasts sat engagingly high and, surrounded by Belgian lace, were shown off to their best advantage. A dainty dish that I thought a fine gentleman might relish. She had the skin of a fresh peach and only on close inspection could you see that her face was painted and any blemish hidden behind moon and star-shaped beauty spots.

She would come after breakfast and tell me the changes that had been brought about while I had been lost in the world of sleep. At first I thought there could be no other reason for her visits but to find entertainment in my ignorance, for she knew so much of the world and the ways of society. She read to me from newspaper gossip columns about balls and assemblies, Ranelagh Gardens and the opera. But once she realised I knew nothing about such things she settled for more domestic topics.

'Queenie has had the blue room papered with birds of the wildest imaginings.'

'Queenie?' I said. 'Who is she?'

'Oh, I mean Mama – it's our affectionate name for her,' said Hope. 'All the old drapes are taken down.'

'Did Cook do that?' I asked.

'Cook!' The very idea made her burst into fits of laughter. 'Can you see her balancing on a ladder? No – fortunately, our servants came with us. My dear, what a state the whole house was in. I do believe Mama has taken Mr Truegood by the ankles and shaken him into action.'

The idea that anyone – let alone a woman – might have that power was an intoxicating thought.

'Mama insists that Martha's time could be better spent than seated beside the fire turning the spit. Yesterday a wheel and pulley was put up and a turnspit dog purchased just for that purpose.'

'Oh my word,' I said, 'what magic.'

'No,' said Hope, 'it's what all sensible kitchens have.'

It took me a little while to trust Hope. I waited, wondering if she would turn on me once finding a weakness, and use it for cat and mouse games. In that I did her much wrong, for I can honestly say that Hope hasn't a mean bone in her body.

I once asked her if there was anyone she didn't like, and she said, 'Tully, if you don't like someone, stand out of their way and let them pass.'

Hope had wisdom and, as I discovered later, was furiously loyal. She never wasted her words on false promises, but I did not know that when she told me that the dressmaker was to call. I could hardly believe it for I had only ever worn second-hand clothes that Cook bought for me in Long Lane market. I had mended my stockings and my shift so many times that they were only good for rags. The very notion of having a dress made for me was too giddying for words. After all, clothes cost money – and that was one thing my father was loath to part with when it came to me.

'Then, when you are completely recovered, you will come out with us in the carriage,' Hope continued. 'The doctor said that it was the lack of fresh air that brought on your fit.'

I secretly thought it had a lot more to do with the gentleman visitor.

Mercy, unlike Hope, had a boyish figure and was taller than her sister. She could not be described as beautiful, more handsome, her face had an altogether sterner profile and at first I thought that perhaps she hadn't taken to me, or saw me as a foolish, fluff-headed girl. She never said as much as Hope and sat quietly studying me. But by degrees I began to realise that Mercy's soul ran deep and when she spoke it was very rarely of ribbons and tittle-tattle. She would read to me, and that's what I looked forward to the most, for the story she read was about a woman who against the odds survived on her wit and a knowledge of just what took a gentleman's fancy. I couldn't imagine that the gentleman visitor would have left Moll in the blue chamber.

By late April, spring had taken hold; birdsong filled the morning and a golden light the afternoon. The dressmaker had indeed come and, under Hope's guidance, I was fitted with new bodices and petticoats and a round gown. It had sleeves of about three-quarter length with lace flounces at their ends, the fabric stiff and embroidered with small flowers. My bosom sat high, pushed up by the tightness of the stomacher, and Hope made sure that the kerchief designed to go round my neck for decency showed as much of my assets as modesty would allow.

The first time I wore my new gown, Hope dressed me. I still felt surprisingly weak, but was pleased finally to be in an upright position, helped in no small part by the tightness of the bodice and the stiffness of the petticoats and fabric. At least it anchored me to the ground. I caught a glimpse of myself in the mirror as Hope pinned up my hair under a lace cap.

It was that afternoon that Mrs Truegood asked to see me in her chamber. The fact that the house now had servants and that doors were opened and closed and visitors ushered in and out without fuss made me feel vulnerable. I had little confidence that my new clothes would save me. Perhaps they were no more than wrapping paper for a parcel, a sweetener before being sent to another house.

~

I found my stepmother sitting at her dressing table and was much taken with the alteration of the room, for although the skirting was still blue, the walls had undergone a transformation and were filled with birds of paradise sitting on impossibly thin branches of trees. Above the windows, which before had only had the luxury of shutters, there was now a confectionery of fabric. The furniture was no longer oppressive but light and spindly, crafted no doubt by fairies. Before I could think of the right words to describe how pleasant the room now seemed, Mrs Truegood told me to stand in the light. My fears returned.

'Please, madam, don't send me away,' I said. I felt tears pricking my eyes.

'Why would I do that?' she asked.

It was only then that I realised there was another person in the chamber, a sombre-looking gentleman, all in black, wearing a full-bottom wig. His face resembled a pig's bladder, inflated and ill defined. Only his nose stood out, heavy and bloated with wine. The tip of his pink tongue flicked across his lips as he studied me.

'This, Mr Quibble,' said Mrs Truegood, 'is Miss Truegood, my stepdaughter.'

'Are you sure, madam, that this is the girl – there has been no mistake?'

'Quite sure, sir.'

'What is her age?'

'She has sixteen summers, sir.'

'Why does the gentleman ask about me?' I whispered to Mrs Truegood.

Mr Quibble cleared his throat. 'I am a lawyer representing a gentleman of means who has asked me to make enquiries about Miss Truegood's eligibility.'

My heart took a leap. The fates must be on my side. They must be, for they had brought forth the gentleman from the blue chamber. Who else could possibly have any interest in me? I blushed to remember that he had seen me in my birthday suit and hoped that he had not told Mr Quibble about our indecent meeting. The lawyer walked round me then went to the far side of the chamber and squinted at me as I had seen my father do in front of a painting.

'Can you dance?' he asked.

'No, sir.'

'Have you had any education in etiquette at all?'

'No, sir.'

'Can you read and write?'

'A little, sir. Not much.'

He thought for a long while and then said, 'Hmm. She has an interesting face,' as if this wasn't quite what he was searching for. 'Pretty it is not.'

'I agree,' said Mrs Truegood. 'But I believe she may have something more than just the passing cloud of youth. I think she may have beauty. As I am sure you are aware, Mr Quibble,

I have only recently married and I find my husband has somewhat neglected his daughter.'

'So she has no education?'

'A little.'

These two seemed to be playing a game of tennis and I the ball. Mr Quibble's tongue flicked across his top lip again.

Mr Quibble stood and, by the buttoning of his coat, disciplined his ungainly shape.

'In her present state,' he said, 'she is far from suitable and needs to be brought on quite considerably.'

'It can be done, Mr Quibble,' said my stepmother. 'She is a bright girl and has a compliant nature.'

He gave a quick bow and left.

Mrs Truegood took my hands and pulled me down beside her.

'Tully,' she said, 'on the day of the wedding, a gentleman called at the house. Do you remember?'

How did she know about the gentleman? Did I say something unguarded in my fever?

'Yes,' I said, 'I remember but I don't know who he was. He didn't leave a name.'

'Did anything happen, Tully, when he was here?'

'No, nothing,' I lied, not knowing the lanes and alleys by which such a lie is lost. I feared I had given myself away for my cheeks had gone to fire.

'Come now,' said Mrs Truegood. 'Did he make any proposals to you? He took no advantage of finding you here alone?'

My silence was an insufficient answer.

'Tully, I am asking if you are still a virgin.'

Chapter Six

Virgin Eggs, from *Being White, Un-soiled*

Boil half a pint of cream and as much milk with a
bit of lemon peel, sugar and a pinch of coriander
seed, and reduce it to half; when it is almost cold,
mix some sweet pounded almonds with it, two or
three bitter ones, and five or six yolks of eggs. Sieve
it into the table dish and bake it between two slow
fires as a cream.

The new Mrs Truegood not only knew her mind but spoke
it to such great effect that the house became well run and my
father's days took on an order that before they had lacked. The
main meal of the day we ate together, and for the first time I
was allowed to sit at the table rather than wait upon it. I stood
in awe of my stepmother, never suspecting that all was but
a masquerade and that the play had purpose: the conclusion
of the drama would be my marriage. Her designs for Hope
were further on, for Hope was already engaged to Mr Sitton.
He was a jolly, portly gentleman who by all appearances was
besotted with Hope. Unfortunately, his widowed mother did
not share in his affections. She let it be known that she would
rather be dead than see her son married to what she called
'that woman'. I could not see any objection to the match and

believed Hope to be far too young to be called 'that woman'. I thought it a harsh way to describe my stepsister.

Mr Sitton was so incensed by his mother's pious opinions of his fiancée that for a time he seemed quite downcast. He announced at one supper that he was at his wits' end to know how to bring his mother round and proposed that he and Hope should be married in secret and let the rest go hang.

'My dear Mr Sitton,' said Mrs Truegood, 'I strongly disagree. The marriage will take place with your mother's blessing or not at all for love isn't food enough to keep one alive. And if you were cut off from your money, why, what would become of your table?'

Now there was one thing Mr Sitton loved perhaps a little inch more than Hope and that was food, and even in the height of his argument he could see that it would be hard to survive without vittles, no matter what Mr Shakespeare had to say on the matter of love being a hearty meal.

'I promise, madam, I will do nothing in haste.' He looked imploringly at Mrs Truegood and said, 'But I cannot wait – we cannot wait – longer than six months to be married.'

And by the longing smile he gave Hope it struck me that he really was in earnest.

'Six months?' said Mrs Truegood. 'That is far too long. Three and you will have Hope as your wife, sir, with your mother's blessing.'

Generals, I am told, prepare for battle, but I doubt if any general had taken as much pain planning a campaign as did Mrs Truegood. Every detail was considered for she was a formidable enemy.

We started to go to church on Sundays. My father had a pew which gathered more spiders than worshippers and had remained empty for more Sundays than ever it had been full. When we arrived, there wasn't a person in the congregation who didn't turn and look at Mr Truegood, his new wife and his very handsome stepdaughters. Our presence encouraged much whispering and I heard some unkind words. I could not think why such things should be said.

The parson was an exceptionally dull man who spoke not plainly. His sermons were long and the point, if there was one, was often tangled in a knot of coughs and splutters. I think he was trying to cure everyone of their sins by boredom. He seemed to dwell a lot upon the weakness of the flesh and the ruination of morals by wanton lust. By the look of his six squashed-nosed children, I could well imagine little joy to be had in the conception. Every Sunday his poor vase of a wife sat trying to pacify her screaming infant and I felt that I too might scream if I had been born into such a family. Whenever the infant fell quiet the parson would raise his fist and bring it down with such thunderous effect on the pulpit that the baby would start up all over again. In short, a more miserable-looking family would be hard to imagine and I didn't bother to try.

Instead, in the hour and a half of the unmitigated sludge of his sermon, my mind would wander free of restraint back to the moment I had met the gentleman in the blue chamber. I delighted in thinking what might have happened if he hadn't left so abruptly. The thought of those sweet fingers and what further pleasures they might have brought me started a fever without a cure so that by the time the sermon was over my cheeks would be apple-red. The foolish parson, who always smiled at me, his eyes glancing down at my kerchief in hope of seeing my breasts, would inform Mr Truegood that I was a devout daughter. My father was not at all certain what kind of daughter he had. He made no comment, usually because he was put out of sorts by all the preaching and furious at any man keeping him from his dinner and a good port wine.

Fortunately, Mrs Truegood was far too particular to allow any holy spirit to make a dent in her plans. She was only there to be seen, not to be moved. I will confess to being very naive. I was not brought up in a Christian way and wasn't much impressed by all I heard. If God was the head of the family, I thought he was a dull man indeed and, like my father, appeared to have a morose sense of justice ruling under the reign of chaos. It seemed unfair that we were all born in sin for how on earth were we to get out of it? And was there really much point? For according to this parson, and the one who had married me, life was but a flickering flame blown out by no more than a draught. If that was so, I was determined to enjoy all such a fragile existence had to offer.

Two tutors were employed to educate me, or as Mrs Truegood said, 'To bring me on.'

I had no idea what that meant and Mrs Truegood would not elaborate on the subject except to say it was essential that I was brought on if I was to amount to anything. She had used the word 'essential' about the spit-roast dog, telling Cook that a spit-roast dog was essential if her cooking was to amount to anything half decent.

Mrs Coker, my elocution tutor, was a fine lady, exceptionally tall and made taller still by her wig. She floated, or so it seemed to me, rather than walked through the house. Her skin was remarkably smooth and she told me she kept wrinkles at bay by pulling certain threads of her hair tight and pinning them to her scalp before she put on her wig. She wore many patches on her white face and Mercy said she looked like a ghost.

When I told Mrs Coker that I had never been out of the house and barely knew how Milk Street connected with the rest of London, she was genuinely shocked. She questioned me about my life and how I had retained my humour when confined to the house. She concluded that the only way I had managed was by the gift of a vivid imagination. Every word she used was an island in its own sound; her words never ran carelessly into another, each was protected by a moat of silence.

'Language is music,' she declared.

I was lucky then to have a good ear for a tune.

The turnabout in my fortune was so sudden and so giddying that I could not fathom what my stepmother must have said to my father that he had become generous in his care of me.

Chapter Seven

Hodgepodge of All Sorts of Meat

Take an earthen pot, well scalded, and put into it four pounds of the loin of mutton, two pounds of filleted veal, one partridge, two large onions, two heads of cloves, one carrot and a quart of water; put a paste made of flour and water round the cover to keep in the steam; place this pot within another somewhat larger, and fill up the vacancies between the two pots with water; let them simmer or stew for seven or eight hours, taking care to supply the outer pot with boiling water so that the meat in the inner pot may be constantly stewing; when done, sift the broth through a sieve, let it settle, and then sift a second time through a napkin; serve the meat and the broth together in a terrine.

My other tutor, Mr Smollett, was an earthbound weasel of a man whose nose caused him no end of trouble, as did his pious beliefs, all being equally irksome. He arrived every morning clutching a prayer book to his pinched-in body. No doubt, as a boy, he had been told how tall a man should grow and when finding himself beyond the mark, felt obliged to shrink the difference into his shoulders.

He seemed to be only concerned with the vices that were to be discovered at the theatre and the coffee house, so that as well as being pinched in body, he was pinched in mind. By degrees it became clear to me that Mr Smollett was nothing more than a hypocrite, for, behind all his condemnation of the city of sin, I could tell the level of excitement the subject brought him to by the dribbles that fell from the end of his troublesome nose.

After a while I could read fluently. Books I liked, but I was bored with all that dull Mr Smollett had to say and I wasn't paying much heed when one day he announced he was going to talk on the cause of all evil in the world. I think this may have been brought about by my exceedingly low-cut bodice. Mrs Truegood had told the dressmaker to accentuate my natural assets and the effect of my assets on Mr Smollett resulted in a lecture on the electrical influence of the female root on the male root. For the first time Mr Smollett had my undivided attention.

'I will endeavour to explain,' he said, 'but I am sure it is beyond your comprehension.' Seeing that his speech wasn't received with the usual posy of yawns he carried on. 'The male root can grow to between seven and twelve inches long. The top is carnation in colour, softer than a petal to touch. At the base there are two globes, bound to the stem of the root. The outside of the bags is wrinkly and covered with a kind of down, much resembling the hair on a beard of corn.' He paused, then with his chest puffed out, said, 'But as soon as this magnificent root is under the influence of the female root, it rises itself to become as stiff as a poker and remains so until the electrical fire is spent, which is known by a plentiful eruption of glutinous matter.'

'What about the female... root?' I asked.

Sweat salted his forehead and his cheeks went claret. He took out his kerchief and blew his nose so hard that his wig became somewhat lopsided.

'The mouth and the whole appearance of the female root is often covered with a bushy kind of hair,' he said, his eyes never leaving my assets. 'It is a broad root within which a hole is perforated. The hole contracts or dilates like the mouth of a purse. To look at it you would never imagine that you could put anything into it at all, let alone a male root. But upon travail, it will dilate so much as to receive a rolling pin.'

After this pretty speech, Mr Smollett suddenly excused himself from the chamber. He came back adjusting his breeches, somewhat calmer.

I hoped he might talk further on the matter. He didn't, though henceforth his attitude towards me became more familiar. He would insist that I sat on his lap while I read to him. That way, he said, it would be easier for us both to see the words. Being a good girl I did as I was told. I could feel the root of him go poker hard. I didn't find it without interest and would have been more engaged if its owner hadn't repulsed me quite as much Mr Smollett did.

There had been many sea changes in the house since my father had remarried, and he grew to doubt that he was still the captain of his ship. Mrs Truegood insisted that new linen mattresses were bought and the old, moth-worn, flea-ridden mattresses be burned. My father almost choked at the very notion, but one look from my stepmother shipwrecked any complaints he might have harboured. She also stated that wives and husbands who slept in separate beds had healthier nerves and stronger spirits than those who slept together. My father roared like bedlam and fell to swearing, but all for naught. His new wife remained unmoved and, deaf to his pleas, ordered a drink be made for him of sage, rosemary and sarsaparilla, which she said was good for a troubled temperament.

So it was that Mrs Truegood kept to her own set of rooms and my father reluctantly to his, and never the two did meet so it seemed to me, for I would have heard the floorboards creak and I never did.

My lessons with Mr Smollett continued and my curiosity – nay, I will call it hunger – to know more about roots would have led me into ruin if Mercy hadn't taken it upon herself to save me.

I had slept so long with Cook, and was so used to her snores and farts and the smell of the sheets, that I found my new bed a little cold and was delighted when Mercy asked me to share hers. She said it was too wide, and Hope had her own bedchamber as she was to be married and consequently needed time alone.

The first night, I found her half undressed while her maid folded her clothes. Mercy's bedchamber smelled of oranges and had a bookcase full of novels. She was not in the least bit shy to be seen half naked. She had next to no bubbies at all on her boyish figure.

'I sleep on the right,' she said, 'with a pistol under my pillow.' I must have looked truly alarmed, for she burst out laughing. 'No, no, of course I don't, you noodle.'

She kissed me on the cheek and said she was pleased to have my company. In the nights that followed we often talked, or she would read to me. Before she blew out the candle she would turn and kiss me goodnight.

No one had ever shown such tenderness to me before and, for reasons I couldn't fathom, with each of her kisses not so much an ache but more a curious itch began to trouble me. I lay in the dark and wished my body wasn't such a riddle to me. One night everything changed.

I remember waking from a nightmare. I dreamed that a man whose face I couldn't see was trying to push me into a chamber. He threw the door open and inside were three women, tied by their hair to three metal rings that hung from the ceiling. I pulled away from him and I found myself falling down an endless stairwell.

I must have shouted out in my sleep for I woke to find the candle alight and Mercy looking down at me.

'It's all right,' she said and kissed me gently on the lips. 'It's a nightmare, nothing more.'

She put her arms round me and held me to her, rocking me. I found myself returning her kisses and with each peck the ache became stronger until I was desperate for relief from it. Mercy asked if I felt calmer and all I could do was nod. She blew out the candle, turned over, and promptly fell to sleep. I lay wide awake, certain I must be ill for the surely the ache shouldn't have returned at Mercy's kiss. A terrible thought occurred to me that I was truly sick and there was no cure. I stared into the darkness, sobbing, as lost as midnight. Mercy stirred once more and asked sleepily what was wrong.

'Mercy, I think I have a fever,' I blurted out.

'Oh, no, my dear,' said Mercy, hurriedly relighting the candle. 'What is the matter?'

'I have a terrible ache!'

'Where?' Mercy asked.

I couldn't tell her, I was too embarrassed.

'Where?' she asked again.

'In between my legs.'

'Show me,' she said.

I bunched up my nightdress so it was above my waist and pointed to my Venus mound.

Mercy fell back on the pillows in a fit of giggles. 'My dear Tully. That is quality, so it is.'

'What do you mean?'

'When did this ache of yours start?' she said, struggling to compose her face.

With eyes half closed and pulling my nightgown up further so that it hid my face, I made her promise not to whisper a word to any soul as to what I was about to tell her.

'It started with the gentleman visitor.'

'Oh sweet Lord. What gentleman?' said Mercy.

I peeled back the nightgown from my eyes, for her voice had lost all its humour. I told her how the gentleman had found me as naked as the day I was born and how he had kissed me and how his fingers had the effect of making my body flame.

'I thought it must be love. It seemed the only rational reason for the ache. But when you kissed me just now on the lips the same ache came back, so you see I think I must be ill.'

Mercy tried to stifle a laugh.

'It's not amusing,' I said.

'You are a noodle,' she said. 'You're not ill. You're as healthy as any other full-blooded female. Perhaps more so than others.' She pulled the nightgown from my burning cheeks. 'Shall I show you the remedy for your ache?'

'Is there one?' I asked.

'Yes,' she said and kissed me, her tongue sweeter by far than that of the gentleman in the blue chamber, and her fingers more gentle. My whole body ignited on the point of bursting into flame. Her mouth by degrees – and such delicious degrees – found their way to my globes and stayed there while her hands progressed further down in between my legs, which she gently parted. Her finger then went into my wet purse and found the spot of all my ache, a hard pearl which she attended to with such care that I thought I might go wild if there wasn't some release. My whole body started quaking and I felt I could endure it no more when, to my utter surprise, there was an explosion followed by the most exquisite sensation and the ache burst into a thousand fragments of joy. I let out a cry as a flood of warmth and glory filled me, and all was peaceful.

Without thinking or even considering the right and the wrong of what had taken place, I put my arms round Mercy and kissed her.

'That,' she said, stroking my hair, 'is the remedy for your ache.'

~

I woke to find that I was curled up in Mercy's arms and that she too was naked. She had a flat stomach and her Venus mound was covered in a lush bush of black foliage. Waking, she looked at me and kissed me and asked how my ache was.

I smiled. 'Better. But still there.'

'So is mine,' said Mercy.

She opened her legs and, taking my hand, guided it down to the spot and kissed me with such longing that I felt my ache return with a vengeance. Afterwards, I told Mercy what Mr Smollett had said about the root of all evil. She said she had never heard anything quite so silly, and was a far better tutor in every way than dull Mr Smollett. Shortly after this, Mr Smollett and his root vegetable came to a pretty pass, which proved to be a good thing for I would have been obliged to use force to deter him if it had gone any further.

Like the boot boy, he suddenly declared his undying love for me.

'Mistress Truegood,' he said, 'I am on fire.' And he took hold of my hand and placed it firmly on his vegetable patch.

I said nothing but decided that come feathers and dust this would be the last lesson I had with Mr Smollet.

'You want to see the root of all evil,' he cried. 'I know you do. You want to feel the passion that cannot be denied.'

And before I could say that due to Mercy I was now in a much better position to wait a while, he had quite undone himself to reveal a rather disappointing upright carrot.

'Mistress Truegood, touch me,' he pleaded.

'No thank you,' I said, 'I would rather not.'

'Please,' he said, grabbing hold of his small root. 'Put me out of my misery.'

The door to the chamber burst open.

'Happily, sir,' came the stern voice of Mrs Truegood.

I watched fascinated as the carrot shrivelled and became only good for compost.

'You will leave this instant,' said my stepmother.

And to my delight, Mr Smollet and the root of all his evils did just that.

But having seen my tutor's shrivelled vegetable made me realise that there was something missing from Mercy's love-making, something I longed to experience: not Mr Smollett's root of all evil, more a man who possessed a true pole of pleasure.

Chapter Eight

Riddle for the Ladies

In what do good housewives take delight
Which though it has no legs will stand upright?
At the end it has a hole, it's stiff and strong;
Thick as a maiden's wrist and pretty long.
Yet women love to wriggle it to and fro
And take delight to watch it grow.
By giddy sluts it is sometimes abused
But by good housewives, rubbed before it's used.
Now tell me, merry ladies, if you can,
What this must be that is a part of man?

You may think, sir, that I was corrupted by a wicked stepsister. But I was by far the keener player, by far the most inquisitive, the one who most desired to understand the joys to be found in our pleasure gardens. The new delights Mercy showed me made me look forward to bedtime, for I was still a prisoner of Milk Street. Mercy and the pleasure she brought were my only form of escape. In my body I began to find another land that held another treasure.

Not being worldly-wise, I had no inkling of the intrigues that lay behind my father's new marriage. I couldn't for the life of me see why my stepsister Hope would want to marry Mr Sitton, for she was exceedingly pretty and Mr Sitton could not be called handsome, being beetle-browed with a chin that had lost the will to stand away from his neck. In my humble opinion there was little to recommend him apart from what he stood to inherit upon his marriage: a newly-built house in Grosvenor Square and another in Chelsea, forty-one servants and three carriages. I thought that if I was Mr Sitton I wouldn't have dallied a moment in making Hope my wife. But Mr Sitton belonged to a banking family that was extremely careful in all matters financial. There was no end of to-ing and fro-ing, made many times worse by his irksome widowed mother who held more than the purse strings of her only son.

As we lay in bed one lazy morning, I asked Mercy if Hope couldn't find an altogether more agreeable husband with a more agreeable mother. Mercy burst out laughing.

'No,' she said, and kissed me before she climbed out of bed. She stood naked, silhouetted against the window, the spring light illuminating her ivory skin. She had a very fine figure and I somewhat wished mine was not so full of curves, for I liked the lack of them in her and the way it all was so pleasingly joined together. Her downy, dark bush, unlike mine which was hardly there at all, marked well the point of all desire.

'Mrs Sitton,' said Mercy, pulling the bedclothes off me and tickling me until I could bear it no more, 'Mrs Sitton wants her only son to marry into another wealthy family. And Hope is not wealthy.'

Catching my breath, I persisted. 'Then why doesn't Hope find someone else?'

'Ninny. She doesn't want anyone else and you are far too

young to know the half of it or truly understand the value of a vintage wine.'

Genuinely, there was so much that I didn't understand. So great were the vacant spaces in my knowledge that sometimes I despaired that I would ever amount to anything and would remain a fluff-head of a girl.

'I want to learn about love,' I said.

She kissed me again. 'It will be my pleasure to teach you.'

Her lessons riveted me as Mr Smollett's and Mrs Coker's had not, and by degrees I became less modest in both thought and deed.

Mrs Truegood employed a dancing master for me – a Monsieur Le Choufleur. He came with a fine reputation. To begin with I thought Monsieur Le Choufleur quite splendid, for he wore tight satin breeches that showed off his assets to such enchanting effect that I may well have forgotten myself if it hadn't been that my stepmother supervised the lessons, fearful, no doubt, of more unwanted instruction on horticulture.

'The thing that baffles me,' I told Mercy, 'is what part a root vegetable plays in this game of love.'

'My sweet virgin,' said Mercy, laughing, 'that isn't my speciality, but when the occasion arises it will be plain for you to see.'

The occasion arose sooner than expected.

It was his eyes that in the end put me off Monsieur Le Choufleur. He had the appearance of a dog in need of a meal and, over the weeks, he came to look starved and struck dumb by a tragic melancholy for which there was no remedy.

After my lesson had finished one afternoon, I returned to my bedchamber and was seated at the dressing table, trying on the pretty pearl earrings that Hope had kindly lent me, when one of them fell to the floor and disappeared behind a fabric screen. I was on my hands and knees, looking for it, and so was hidden from view when the door opened and my maid came in with Monsieur Le Choufleur. I thought I should stand and ask them what was the meaning of this when the meaning became all too clear, for my maid was kissing Monsieur Le Choufleur. This I could see for I had a perfect view of the proceedings due to a fortuitous rip in the fabric of the screen. The maid was not young and had a full figure, and I wouldn't have imagined for a moment that the dancing master would have been interested in that abundance of flesh.

She locked the chamber door and asked if sir would be needing any assistance with his breeches. I had left it a kiss too late to announce my presence and decided instead to satisfy my curiosity.

My maid had undressed Monsieur Le Choufleur to reveal a most glorious pinkish parsnip that rose and leaned towards her. Such a noble sight – nobler by far than its puny owner. A blue vein ran to its tip and she gently stroked it. Monsieur Le Choufleur undid her stays and her breasts were so large they would have filled a market basket. The sight of them was too much for the dancing master. He went at them as if he was a babe in arms and the effect was to make that noble parsnip grow to a prize vegetable. The maid wasted not a moment in pushing him onto the bed, climbing on top of him and settling herself upon the root.

The dancing master, displaying his skill in manoeuvring his partner, rolled her over so her carriage – and a very fine one it was – was open to him. Placing his hands on her backside, he thrust in his root up to the hilt. They set to and both let out a cry of joy. I was somewhat startled to hear my dancing master shout, 'Oh, Miss Tully, my love!', which must have been disappointing for my maid, whose name was Prue.

Seeing such a sight and the pleasure it gave both parties, I had happily acquired the knowledge of how a male and female root join and there seemed nothing evil in the union whatsoever.

The next day, Monsieur Le Choufleur wrote to say he was indisposed and didn't feel able to continue the dancing lessons. All that was left of him was a small stain on the bedcover.

'It seems, Tully,' said Mrs Truegood, 'that you have had quite an adverse effect on poor Monsieur Le Choufleur.'

'Was it my dancing?' I asked.

'I think that it might have accelerated his condition. Did you not realise that he had become besotted with you?'

'No,' I said, which wasn't the full truth.

'Well, then. If ever a man again tries to tell you what he feels about you through dance, I can rest assured that he is wasting his time.'

A week after Monsieur Le Choufleur left, a parcel arrived. Inside, wrapped in far too much paper, was a book with a note written by my dancing master. 'You are made for love,' it said.

Intrigued, I sat down in the drawing room to read it. I was pleasantly surprised by the novelty of its illustrations: women all undone, no hoops or stays to hinder entrance to their pretty little gardens while the men possessed wonderful upright roots. Both male and female embraced each other in the most joyous of ways. My senses were inflamed by such glorious visions.

I was left wondering if there were men in this world who really boasted such male roots as were engraved there. Not the dancing master nor the boot boy and most decidedly not Mr

Smollet possessed anything as fine. These vegetables, I thought, were much exaggerated by the artist whose imagination had perfected what nature had failed to enhance.

I think it was this book more than what I had witnessed between my maid and the dancing master that made me long for adventure. At night my dreams had to do with the stranger in the blue chamber and none of them was at all decent. I dreamed too of being a great actress, well versed in the art of lovemaking. I felt I had spent too long waiting in the wings for my cue to enter upon life's stage.

The spring weather was no help. It made the frustration of being indoors harder to bear for we were confined to the house in Milk Street, forbidden to go out in society until the matter of Hope's marriage had been settled.

The dancing master's book afforded me many hours of pleasure, more than the learning of his steps had done, and I kept it well hidden, certain that if Mrs Truegood should see it, it would be forbidden. I did show it to Mercy and Mercy showed it to Hope, who thought it hilarious and insisted on taking it to show Mr Sitton. Very sensibly, he came every morning to our house, I assumed to avoid his disagreeable mother. He would take his hot chocolate with Hope in her bedchamber and be there until the morning was all but gone. Weddings, I was told, take much organising. I was convinced that my delightful book would never be returned and I was wishing I could remember all the images when Hope came to my bedchamber.

She handed me the book with a smile and said, 'Thank you. Mr Sitton was most amused.'

Sensing that this might be an opportune moment, I asked if the illustrations weren't a little overstated for surely no man owned a root as enormous as that given to the gentleman on Plate Nine. The illustration showed a man with his breeches undone and his male root hard as a cucumber and he about to thrust it into the female root of a large, naked lady. She was bending over, her bottom as big as a full moon.

'What is all this nonsense with vegetables?' asked Hope.

I told her about Mr Smollet and what a small carrot he had. I wanted to tell her about the dancing master and the maid, but I thought it might be too shocking.

'You have seen a very poor specimen,' she said. 'I can assure you Mr Sitton is very well endowed in that department.'

'You mean you have done this?' I said, finding the illustration on Plate Twenty that showed to perfection the ecstatic effect the male root had upon the female.

'And more besides,' she whispered. 'You did not suppose that Mr Sitton and me merely *enfiler des perles*?' I did not speak French and could only guess at what she meant. She smiled. 'There now. Do you think me quite without morals?'

'No,' I said. 'Though it wouldn't matter to me if a man had fifteen houses if his asset was as small as Mr Smollet's. I would never wed him.'

'Oh, Tully!' exclaimed Hope. Then, laughing, she said, 'I am so glad I have a perfect ninny of a stepsister.'

Chapter Nine

I believed Mrs Truegood would be mortified if she knew the truth of what was going on under her roof. I thought she might not recover from the shock of knowing that Hope was having more than hot chocolate with Mr Sitton and that I was having much more than a bedtime kiss from Mercy.

Mr Crease, the gentleman with the painted eyes who owned the little white dog, was an advisor to Mrs Truegood. She had made a formidable enemy in Mrs Sitton, who had no intention of letting her son marry Hope. 'Not while there is flesh on my bones,' she stated in one letter. She had a very strange way of writing and the image left me wondering if anyone, even a dog, would be interested in the flesh on her bones for she looked as if all the marrow of enjoyment had been well and truly sucked out of her.

Mr Crease and his little dog arrived every morning after which footmen and letters went to and fro between Milk Street and Grosvenor Square. Perhaps only Mr Crease's dog knew that Mrs Sitton was holding the winning card in that mean hand of hers.

One morning, Mr Sitton didn't call on Hope but instead a letter was delivered by one of Mrs Sitton's forty-one servants. It said that Mr Sitton had been called away on business. There was no doubt as to the author of the letter: it had been written by the bag of bones that was Mrs Sitton. Hope was heartbroken and said she knew she would never see Mr Sitton again.

On hearing the news, Mr Crease closeted himself with Mrs Truegood, leaving his little dog pining outside the door to her chamber. I couldn't understand why Mr Crease didn't let the dog in as his cries were quite heartbreaking. I asked Mercy the name of Mr Crease's dog.

She looked at me strangely and said, 'Why do you ask?'

'I just wondered.'

'And I wonder where Mr Sitton has gone.'

The significance of Mr Sitton's sudden absence meant nothing. My question, I thought, did. 'But what is Mr Crease's dog called?' I asked again.

'His dog was called Shadow because he would whine if he was ever parted from Mr Crease.'

What did Mercy mean by speaking of the dog in the past? Surely she should say his dog *is* called Shadow? Had he died in the night?

'Do you think it is odd that Mr Sitton didn't call before he left town?'

To tell the truth I had not being paying much attention to the daily ups and downs of Hope's marriage plans.

'Tell me about Shadow,' I persisted.

'He was the most famous little mongrel that ever lived.' Still that uncomfortable past tense. 'Mr Crease and Shadow performed all over Europe for emperors, kings and queens. Mr Crease would lay down a pack of cards in a circle round Shadow, each one a letter of the alphabet, then invite someone from the audience to ask a question. The little dog would cock its head as if he was listening and then solemnly put a paw on each card and spell out a word. What he had to say had more wisdom than many men speak in a lifetime. After Shadow's death, Mr Crease became too despondent for anything but gambling and whoring. Then one night he fell off his horse on Hampstead Heath. By the time he was found the following morning there was nothing the surgeon could do for his crushed leg but saw it off.'

'But he still has Shadow,' I said.

'Don't be a ninny,' said Mercy firmly. 'The dog died ten years ago.'

'But I see Shadow every day.'

'Enough of this nonsense,' said Mercy, more sharply than she had ever spoken to me before. 'I think you must be seeing ghosts.'

I went to ask Cook if she had seen Mr Crease's dog.

'Dog? The only dog I know about is that one up there,' said Cook, nodding at the spit-roast dog going round and round in his wheel. 'And it has a foul nature.'

She wasn't a woman to go over her words and she had no intention of putting any more meat on her answer.

I tried to speak to Hope.

'Tully,' she said, 'what nonsense is this? Mr Crease doesn't have a dog.'

She was looking so sad that I said, 'Perhaps it's best just to get married as I did, without any fuss.'

'Are you determined to vex me?'

I told her how I had been wed at twelve and to that day had no idea who my husband was.

'Is this another story in a similar vein to that of Mr Crease's dog?'

'No,' I said. 'Both are true.'

Hope told me to leave her alone so to pass the time I set about making a pack of cards with the letters of the alphabet on them. Shadow, a wig on legs, trotted into the drawing room, sniffed each card then looked up at me as if waiting for a question.

Kneeling down, I asked, 'When will Hope be married?'

Placing a paw on each card he spelled out 'SIX YEARS'.

Impossible, I thought. Perhaps my question was too difficult. I tried another. 'Will Mrs Sitton ever give her consent?'

The little dog spelled out 'NO'.

I was about to ask another question when I heard someone behind me and Mrs Truegood said, 'Tully, what are you doing?'

I turned round to see my stepmother looking perplexed.

'I wanted to see how clever Shadow is,' I said standing up. 'But his answers are puzzling.'

Just then, Mr Crease came in and Shadow went straight to him, wagging his tail. Mrs Truegood let out a small scream.

Her voice no more than a whisper, she said, 'Crease, what trickery is this? Stop it this instant.'

'I can assure you, madam,' he said, 'this is not my doing. I thought I was the only one able to see Shadow. But Tully has a gift. She saw him when she was but a child and again at the wedding breakfast. Even I can't do what she can. She has the power to make him visible to others.'

I didn't understand and I understood less as Mrs Truegood backed towards the door.

'Crease, stop this,' she said again with more urgency. 'Whatever conjuring tricks you may have developed, sir, you should not be meddling in the black arts.'

'Madam, do you want me to ask him a question?' I asked for surely they were making jest of me.

'No!' She paused and stared at me as if I was a stranger, then said, 'Yes.'

'When will Mrs Sitton agree to the marriage?' I asked.

Shadow spelled out 'NEVER'.

Mrs Truegood put her hand over her mouth. 'Where is Mr Sitton?' she said slowly to the dog.

'AT SEA,' he spelled out.

The door opened, Hope entered and saw Shadow. She let out a most terrible scream and the little dog hid under a chair, while Mr Crease picked up my cards and handed them back to me.

'Go to your chamber, Tully,' said Mrs Truegood. 'Stay there until I call for you.'

She ushered me from the room. I felt wretched for I hadn't meant to displease her in any way. Whatever I had done, I knew it was serious. That night, Mercy did not come into our bed and I felt I was being punished. Prue brought me a tisane, I drank it, and the bedroom door, for the first time, was locked.

I woke the following morning with a throbbing head and knew even before I was fully conscious that something was wrong. The house had a quietness to it, the bricks holding themselves tight together, bracing for the storm within and the rain without.

I went to dress, only to find that all my fine clothes had vanished right down to the last stocking and pin. All that was left was the rag of a dress I had been wearing when Mrs Truegood first came to the house. All calmness left me. I tried to open the door but found it still locked.

It was noon by St Mary-le-Bow on Cheapside when Cook opened the bedchamber door. The silence was broken by my father bellowing at the top of his voice in the way he had before matrimony had tamed him.

'Cook! More wine, woman!' he shouted. 'What's wrong with you?'

'Where's Mercy? Where is everyone?' I all but screamed.

'Gone,' was all she would say. 'Gone.'

Chapter Ten

Tarts, The Common, or Country Fashion

Take a fresh cream cheese, made the preceding day, or only made five or six hours before; mix a bit of butter and a few eggs with a little salt; make the paste pretty thick, and the top the same; bake it without glazing the top crust or border.

I could not make head or tail of what had happened and why my stepmother and stepsisters had vanished. Surely Mercy wouldn't have left me behind?

Only three of Mrs Truegood's servants remained and I begged them to tell me where she had gone, but they ignored my pleas. I asked for my clothes back but one of the footmen said my things had not been touched.

'Then where are they?' I asked and to that there came no answer.

They gathered together all that belonged to their mistress and departed, taking the yellow canaries too. I decided I would follow them but my father took the precaution of locking all the doors after they'd left.

'Don't think that you have any sympathy from me,' he bellowed. 'You have brought this on yourself.'

'How? Please tell me how?' I said, but he would not.

Perhaps, I thought, Mrs Truegood had spied on Mercy and me and been so horrified by what she had seen that she had taken her daughters away.

I hoped that Cook might have some inkling as to what had passed but she seemed to know nothing.

'And my clothes are gone,' I said.

'The master had me sell them this morning,' she said. 'All hope is gone.'

'And Mercy, too,' said I.

'Butter and salt,' she said. 'Butter and salt.'

'What does that mean? You always say it and it means nothing.'

'Butter and salt in the right proportion means a good life. Too much salt and all is ruined.'

Like so much of what Cook said, this only possessed a pepper grain of sense and brought little comfort.

Until Mrs Truegood had arrived, my life had been filled with nothing more than half-formed dreams, but never had I felt as desolate as I did then. The memory of the handsome stranger was now but a patch of blue sky vanishing among thunderous clouds. And the thought that I would never see Mercy again near broke my heart.

It was not long before the house went to rack and my father to ruin. Cook fell back upon her grubby apron and untidy ways. Even the spit-roast dog had vanished along with all the other conveniences and Cook whiled away the hours turning the spit, roasting and burning the meat in equal measure. Thirsty work, she said, that was only eased by gin.

Many times I thought of running away but my father took to being my jailer with more vigour than he had ever shown when a merchant in bricks.

I once read that when Vikings faced defeat in battle they set their ships ablaze. Mr Truegood must have read that too for he seemed determined to cast himself upon the bonfire of bankruptcy. Never one to miss out on pleasures he reinstated the Hawks' Club. His wayward, sea-salty friends reappeared to help him light the fuse to his inevitable ruin. Like it or not, and I can assure you, sir, I liked it not, I was dragged down into the ashes with him.

The taste for such luxury as Mrs Truegood had shown me had spoiled me for all else. I had lived less than three months in the light and the rest of my days rolled out before me in a never-ending line of chamber pots filled with my father's shit.

Summer crept along, heating up the streets, heating up the house. Everything was stagnant apart from the hornets' nest in the attic where I had been ordered to sleep with Cook as before. What, I asked myself, would happen if I stood very still in the blue chamber? Would life pass me by altogether until I turned to dust? I missed Mercy. What hurt the most was the thought that I had meant nothing to her. That alone was a splinter in my heart.

There was no money for meat and vittles, there was no money for wine. There was no money for the removal of the hornets' nest. Cook and me had to move out of the attic. It had become unusable, filled with the incessant angry whirling of hornets' wings. It came to symbolise everything that was rotten in our house.

The merchants soon refused to give my father any more credit. He only minded about the wine merchant. It was in want of alcohol that he sent Cook to hire some clothes for me so that we might see the wine merchant together. The thought of being out of the house raised my spirits no end and I saw it as a chance of escape. Before leaving I had had the wit to snatch up the book my dancing master had given me. But Mr Truegood kept his hand on my arm with the ferocity of a crab. There being a customer with the wine merchant, we walked back and forth outside shop until Mr Truegood was certain there was no one else inside but the wine merchant.

'Tell him...' he said as he pushed me at the door, 'tell him to deliver the wine and you will be the payment.'

My only hope was that the dancing master's book might have some currency. The wine merchant sat behind his counter, an owl in an ivy bush, so woolly was his wig. He had the startled look that owls have when light is shone upon them.

'Not another bottle until my bills are paid,' he said. 'One way, or another.'

He eyed my assets, which the ill-fitting gown showed immodestly well. I had a nasty feeling that 'another' would have a Mr Smollett approach attached to it, and I put the book on the counter and asked if it would pay a part of the bill. The wine merchant sighed.

'I have prayer books from all the drunks in London. I don't need more.'

But he opened the book and stopped. On the front page was an illustration that had arrested me when I first saw it. It showed a woman undone, her pretty breasts all pert, her nipples pointing up to heaven, her legs lusciously parted, and between them was her maid, kissing that most tender spot. It made me sad to remember how Mercy was so expert in this.

The wine merchant's eyes widened and he cleared his throat. Quickly I took the book back.

'Forgive me, sir,' I said and made to leave. 'It was foolish to ask.'

Outside I could see my father, his face red with rage, waving his arms and shooing me back.

'Not so hasty,' said the wine merchant. 'If you would show me the book again…' I could see where this was leading. A customer tried to enter the shop and the wine merchant said firmly that it was closed. 'I will take the book in lieu of payment this time, Miss er, er…'

'Truegood,' I said, handing him the book.

'The book and one kiss. But if the old devil runs the bill up again I will take from you the pleasure to be found in… in… this illustration.' He showed me Plate Three. It was without doubt the dullest of all the illustrations to be found there: a man flattened out on top of his lady, his breeches round his ankles and only a small part of his carrot inside her. He looked in ecstasy; she looked bored.

I agreed to the wine merchant's terms. So this was what it was to be a whore.

'Seal the bargain with a kiss,' he said.

I had never kissed an owl before but I imagine the wine merchant and an owl might have more in common than either would have expected. I pulled away for want of breath. He still didn't let go and his hand found its way under my skirt and petticoat and I having nothing on that would stop his hand from further roaming it went straight to the point.

I eased myself away and left the order for the wine on the counter.

'When he has drunk this,' said the wine merchant, 'I will be needing proper payment.'

I left him smelling the tips of his fingers.

By the time the wine had run out my father had gambled everything away.

It was the morning that the grandfather clock was removed that marked the end of my time in Milk Street. I had forgotten all about seeing the small boy trapped inside until Cook mentioned it.

'Do you remember when you saw the boy inside the clock?'

'Did you see him too?' I asked, for she had never said.

'I don't know. It was so long ago. Perhaps...'

Two servants turned up with a cart to take away the grandfather clock. My father, drunk and maudlin, showed them upstairs to where the clock stood.

'Handsome,' said one of the men.

The other opened it to take out the pendulum and the weights and he was there, the small boy, curled up, cowering, waiting to be hit.

I held my peace, my heart beating, then my father said, more to himself than to anyone else, 'I used to hide in there when I was a lad, to keep out the way of my father's temper.' He stopped, moved back in surprise, and was saved from falling over the bannister by one of the men.

'Careful now, sir,' he said.

'Did you see that?' my father asked. 'Did you see that?'

I had seen.

'See what?' said the other man.

My father looked at me. 'Did you see?' he said. 'Did you see the boy?'

'Yes,' I said, 'I did.'

'It was me,' shouted my father. 'It was me – Samuel. Me...'
His eyes filled with tears.

Now, wouldn't that make a rounded tale, sir, if finally my
father had become regretful of how he had treated his one
and only child? Perhaps in a pantomime such tales run round
that way. Not in this one, I assure you.

Chapter Eleven

Fowls in a Plain Way

Prepare the fowl for roasting and make a sauce with the liver, parsley, shallots, a bit of butter, pepper, salt and a little basil; stuff the fowl with it, and roast it wrapped in slices of lard and paper. When three parts done, take off the paper and lard-baste it all over with yolks of eggs beat up with melted butter, sprinkle crumbs of bread over it, in abundance, and finish the fowl to a fine yellow colour. Make a sauce with a bit of butter, one chopped anchovy, a few capers, a little flour, two spoonfuls of broth, nutmeg, pepper and salt; form a liaison like a white sauce and serve it under the fowl.

That evening, Mr Truegood held the last of his parties. He had been drinking his sorrows away most of the afternoon and by the time his gambling companions arrived, whatever rational thoughts his head might have possessed had long been pickled.

He shouted down to the kitchen that I was to serve his guests tonight and, if I didn't, then the dress, the stockings and the rest of the clothes he had hired for me would be returned to Mrs Phelps' shop. I knew well that come high tide tomorrow they would be gone anyway. When the bailiffs arrived to take Mr Truegood to the sponging house, at least Mrs Phelps' clothes would be returned in a better state than I had found them. I had spent a great deal of time cleaning and mending the dress. The lace edging being good for nothing but cobwebs I had carefully removed it and wore the dress plain. The stomacher I laced tight causing my bosom to be pushed up high.

I had never before had to serve my father. It had always been Cook's job, and mine was to clean up after him. Now I seemed to have inherited both ends of the leaky old donkey. If Cook had been conscious it might have helped, but she was out cold by the fire, a tumbler of gin beside her.

'Tonight,' declared Mr Truegood, 'I will win it all back – every penny.'

'Perhaps, sir,' I said, 'it would be best to leave off the cards.'

'Who are you to tell me what to do?'

Seeing he was set to gamble away what little was left of nothing, I said no more.

The ragtag members of the Hawks' Club turned up and sat crouched over their cards with such expression as if their very life would be judged by a winning or losing hand.

'He is late,' said a card player.

'He will be here,' said my father.

I went to the kitchen for more wine and brought up as well a board of ripe cheese that I had picked two maggots from, and bread on the cusp of turning green. Candles are a luxury that the bankrupt can ill afford and therefore the chamber had more of the dark about it than the light. So dark it was in fact that I did not at first see the newcomer seated at the card table. His clothes showed that he was a dandy and spoke of wealth that shone bauble-bright.

My father had started well and won ten guineas but, being born a fool, was determined to stay true to his origins and with the next hand lost all he had gained.

'Come, I will play again,' said my father.

'With what, sir?' said the dandy. 'It appears to me you have nothing left to gamble with.'

'I have that, sir,' said Mr Truegood, pointing at me. 'Thirty guineas is the rate for a virgin and she has never been touched.' He lowered his voice. 'Pox free, I promise you.'

'If she is a virgin that goes without saying,' said the young rake.

I thought this is how slaves must feel when they are brought to the market. My would-be seducer never once looked in my direction but with a shrug of his shoulders he agreed.

I didn't want to stay and watch my fate being decided by such a hopeless gambler as Mr Truegood and was edging towards the door when he growled, 'Stay where you are.'

The other gamblers became quiet when Mr Truegood lost his bet and with it his daughter. He rose, unsteady on his feet, and stood near the fire staring at the coals.

'Take her,' he said. 'But thirty guineas doesn't include her clothes. I will need twenty-six pounds for them. Are you willing to pay extra?'

'No,' said the rake. 'The bet was Miss Truegood's virginity, not her clothes.'

'Leave them upstairs,' said my father to me.

'But what am I to wear?' I asked.

He shrugged. 'You won't be needing them.'

I turned to the rake to see if he had any opinion on my garments. He said nothing.

My father's friends sat round the gaming table studying their wine glasses as my father rejoined them.

'Go and change,' he said. 'Make haste. I'm sure the young gentleman doesn't have all night.'

I stayed where I was, aware of the anger that was growing in me, and stared at Mr Truegood. If he wanted his clothes he could have them here and now. I started to undress.

'What are you doing, girl?' he said, looking at me in horror as I unlaced my stomacher, took off my dress, my petticoat and my chemise, letting each item fall to the floor. 'Have you no modesty?'

'Have you no morals?' I replied. 'If you are willing to gamble away my maidenhead, what use, sir, is modesty to me?'

I stood naked apart from my stockings and my shoes. Even in my rage I knew that the small heel gave me height and my anger made me taller than I had ever been before. The young rake was now standing, and I saw a smile cross his face.

One of Mr Truegood's sea-shanty friends said to the rake, 'You're a lucky man – she's a beauty. I will pay you double – treble – if you will sell her to me.'

'She is not for sale, sir,' he replied.

I was furious with my father. I'd had enough of this unbearable man, of his mean, stingy ways, of his neglect.

'You have treated me, your daughter, as nothing more than a servant,' I said, picking up the clothes. 'Here, take the stinking rags.'

I threw them onto the card table, scattering aces and queens.

'You are no daughter of mine,' shouted Mr Truegood. 'You

are a bastard. Your mother duped me. When I married her you were already aboard.'

The revelation was a flash of the most brilliant blue ever to have appeared in such an ill-lit room. It liberated me instantly from any obligation to this obnoxious man. I picked up the wine I had brought from the kitchen and went up to Mr Truegood. His face was blotchy, his lips pursed, his glazed eyes near bursting out of his head to see me so brazenly standing there.

I poured the whole bottle over his wig.

He was too drunk to do anything except stare at me, wine dripping off his lips, his chin and down on to his grubby stock. He didn't resist as I took the house keys from his pocket.

'You are mad, you will end your days in Bedlam,' he said.

'I am mad,' I said. 'Mad with rage at you.'

'What a bottom she has,' said one of the rum gamblers.

'And what duddies,' said his companion. 'Milksoft sweet they are.'

Ignoring them, I went up to the rake.

'You can't go out like that, girl,' Mr Truegood managed to mutter. 'You're not decent.'

I turned back to him and spat in his face.

'I would call you a dog but that is an insult to a noble creature. You, sir, are nothing but a turd in the gutter of humanity.'

And with that I left the room. At the front door the stranger gave me his coat and I put it on. And so I finally left the house in Milk Street as near naked as when I had first entered it.

My fury was such that I hadn't taken in the young man. It was only when we were in the carriage that he burst out laughing. It was a laugh that could belong to no one other than Mercy.

'Did you really not recognise me?' she said.

I was still so red-raw with rage that I couldn't quite believe it was she. I looked her in the eyes. There was no mistaking my Mercy.

'You were spectacular,' she said.

'Why didn't you take me with you when you left? Why did you leave me in that house to rot? Not one letter, not one word – nothing!' For the first time tears welled in my eyes. 'Let me out of this carriage,' I demanded and tried to push her away. 'Tell the coachman to stop.'

As I put my hand on the carriage door she pulled me towards her. Stronger than me by far, she held me tight. There was no doubting she made a very fine gentleman, but I was too furious to be still and did my best to free myself, to little effect.

'If you had any care of me,' I said, fighting back molten tears that burned my cheeks, 'you wouldn't have deserted me.'

'Come,' Mercy said softly, stroking my face. 'Let us not argue. At least I rescued you. Or rather you rescued yourself – I merely opened the door and lent you my coat.'

Her very touch awoke all desire. Anger, passion, all is one and all have much the same effect. Mercy kissed me. Her kisses turned my anger into an ache.

'I won you, remember,' she said, laughing.

Her hand slipped inside the coat and down to the place she knew well. At that moment I cared little if the whole world saw us. Mercy lay me down on the velvet seat of the coach and I gave in to desire.

She kissed my neck and my breasts and said, as she parted my legs, 'I am very pleased that I've won such a beauty.'

'So so am I,' I said as her tongue found its way into my purse.

With the rock of the carriage and Mercy's lips upon me I all too soon reached that most wonderful of sensations.

A sprinkle of silver fluttered across my eyes and, unable to help myself, I arched my back and cried out, 'Thank God that shit is not my father.'

Chapter Twelve

If I possessed any skill with a pencil I would draw you a picture of the mansion in Lincoln's Inn Square but instead you will have to content yourself with my words and, there being more words than colours to be found in a paintbox, I have riches indeed to play with.

It was a grand house with tall windows on the ground and first floors. Two columns framed the portico and another two embraced the front door, over which was set a half-moon fanlight. If you believe as I do that houses have their own personalities then this one by design stood alone, independent of its neighbours which looked on decidedly envious. If that didn't mark it out as different, its gated drive did, as did the lights that shone from every window.

'My lady,' said Mercy, taking my hand and leading me into a marbled hall.

It was layered with plaster dust. A small forest of ladders leaned against the walls and the rolling staircase was swathed in dust sheets. Even the chandelier had a huge fabric bag covering it and the whole place smelled of paint. I wasn't sure if the interior was being put together or pulled down for everything was in such a pickle.

'Who lives here?' I asked, pulling back, not knowing where Mercy had brought me.

'I do,' said Mercy.

I was completely flummoxed.

From upstairs appeared a footman. It was impossible to tell whether his wig was powdered or thick with dust.

'What will they think of me?' I asked, as he came down towards us. 'I am stark naked under your coat.'

'You look beautiful. And it matters little what anyone thinks – there is no need for modesty here.'

I longed to ask her what she meant but Mercy left me after the footman had shown me to a drawing room that opened on to a fanfare of well-proportioned rooms. Like the hall they were mainly covered in dust sheets, and a scaffolding of wood rose to a platform near the ceiling which was half painted. I craned my neck to look up and realised that in part it depicted deliciously wanton women, their lovers still only in sketch form, winged creatures who possessed majestic machinery larger by far than those to be found in the dancing master's book. The whole thing spoke of yearning and the want of satisfaction.

I was so taken up with all that I'd seen that it was several minutes before I caught sight of myself reflected back at me. In the mirror that hung over the fireplace was a most indecent young lady. Quickly, I buttoned up Mercy's coat so that at least I appeared to possess a modicum of propriety. I had wiped the dust off the mirror and was making a hopeless attempt to coax my hair into better shape when I saw her.

'Feathers and dust!' I said aloud.

The sight of her sent a shiver through me. Pretty Poppet looked anything but pretty.

'What are you doing here? Who let you in?' I said, sure she shouldn't be there.

Before Pretty Poppet could reply, Mrs Truegood entered the room. She was dressed in a low-cut gown and I was astonished to see her so little concerned with modesty. On her cheek she wore a crescent moon and a star was painted above her eyebrow. The effect of her paint and patches – in fact the effect of her whole bearing – had more to do with Lady Midnight than the respectable merchant's wife she had been in Milk Street. I dreaded to think what had befallen my stepmother in such a short space of time that she was now living in this derelict house.

She ignored Pretty Poppet and, disregarding my appearance, pulled a dust sheet off a chaise longue and said, 'Come, Tully, sit down, my dear.'

Why did no one ever speak to the girl?

'First,' said Mrs Truegood, 'I must humbly ask your pardon for the deception, though I assure you I had sincerely hoped to find you a husband before a morsel of the truth escaped.'

I couldn't think of what to say. I feared that Mercy's coat would fall open and, ignoring my stepmother's request, I stayed with my hand resting on the mantelpiece, desperate to be touching something solid. The scenery of my life seemed to be changing fast and so far it had proven to be but an ill-conceived picture on a painted cloth.

'I should introduce myself. My name is Queenie Gibbs. Your father owed me a great deal of money and I knew I was never to see a ha'penny of it, so I conceived the idea that he would repay me in another way. Mr Sitton had set his sights on marrying Hope, but the obstacle to the match was his mother. If my plan was going to work we needed respectability – hence I went through with a sham marriage.'

Pretty Poppet had perched herself next to Queenie on the chaise longue.

'He isn't my father,' I said. 'Just as you aren't my stepmother. I expect you are going to tell me that Mercy and Hope aren't your daughters.'

'No, they're not. I must appear most cruel. Forgive me. My plan may well have worked if it hadn't been for Mrs Sitton. I had underestimated a mother's desire to protect her child.' Pretty Poppet moved closer to Mrs Gibbs, who rang a little bell on the side table and a man dressed all in grey entered. 'Refreshments,' she said.

I wasn't sure if she was addressing the man, Pretty Poppet or me. I was very hungry and quite thirsty.

'Yes, please,' I said.

Queenie Gibbs leaned back. 'When I think about it, my dear, the whole plan was a failure before it even had a chance to be my greatest success. Mr Truegood, never a quiet drunk, blurted out my intentions to one of his scurvy friends who, for a good sum, soothed those burning ears of Mrs Sitton with the truth. She had her son bundled off against his will on a ship for America, thereby securing the family's mean little name and considerable fortune.' She sighed. 'When Crease's dog answered my question and spelled out the words "AT SEA", I knew I'd failed.'

'It is a terrible pity for Mr Sitton. I am sure the water will not agree with him one jot,' I said, still trying to adjust my picture of my stepmother to fit this woman, Queenie Gibbs.

'It's by the by. Tully, believe me when I say I truly wanted to do right by you and I would have stayed to find you a suitable match. But when I learned from Hope that you had been married at twelve and that the marriage held fast, I lost all patience with Mr Truegood – even more so when he refused point-blank to tell me the name of your mysterious husband, or the reason he had married you off at such an unnecessarily young age.'

'A debt,' I said. 'It could only have been in want of money.'

'Indubitably. Thank God those marriages have been abolished. They have ruined many a family.'

'I don't want to go back to Milk Street,' I said. 'Could I stay here?'

Mrs Gibbs stood and walked to the window. 'In all honesty this is not the place for you.'

'Why not? I could be a maid.'

'Do you know how much a maid earns?' she said. 'Five pounds a year.'

To me that seemed a fortune. What I could do with five pounds a year.

'I would be happy with that,' I said. 'I could help you run the house.'

Mrs Gibbs laughed. 'Who do you think owns this house?'

'I don't know.'

'I own this house. And it is in the process of being made into one of the finest brothels the metropolis has to offer.'

I stumbled over the thought.

'I will explain. I grew up in poverty in Covent Garden. A flower girl, I climbed up society's rickety ladder – man by man. In other words, I made my money as a prostitute. I also happen to have a mind for business and I was determined never to go back to where I came from. This, my dear, is a house of pleasure. I do not need more servants, I need experienced ladies of easy virtue, exotic birds to delight rich gentlemen.'

'I could learn to be an exotic bird.'

'No!' said Pretty Poppet.

Queenie surely must have heard her but she didn't look round.

'How much do you think Mercy and Hope earn?' she asked

As I'd assumed they were ladies, I hadn't thought for a moment that they earned a penny, and, blushing, I said so.

Mrs Gibbs's answer stunned me.

'Mercy earns six hundred pounds a year, Hope, about four hundred. Without, that is, all the little gifts – the jewels, the clothes.'

It was incredible. Mrs Gibbs was talking of unimaginable sums. It had never occurred to me that a woman could earn so much.

'Did Mr Sitton know all this?' I said, sounding as pious as the parson on Sundays.

She laughed. 'Yes, Tully. He had been Hope's particular for a long time – and he loved her.'

There was a knock at the door. I rather hoped this was the refreshments, for I needed longer to convince Queenie that I was in earnest when I said I wanted to learn to be a lady of pleasure.

It was Mr Crease who came in, his peg leg thudding on the floor and, without a 'Would you mind?' or a 'May I?', he dragged a dust sheet off a spindly chair and sat down. He seemed to glance at Pretty Poppet.

'I always said you were no hen-hearted girl,' said Mr Crease to me. 'Mercy told me. I should think the Hawks' tongues were lolling at the sight of you in all your glory.' He stopped and studied me. 'Is Shadow with me?'

I couldn't see the dog and said so. The door opened again and in came the man, who I now realised was the butler,

carrying a tray of sweetmeats and a bottle of champagne.
Shadow was behind him. He ran to his master, wagging his
tail. The butler nearly dropped the champagne when he saw
the little white dog.

Mrs Gibbs said sharply, 'That will be all, Mr Pouch.'

'Ads bleed,' said Mr Crease. 'How do you do it, Tully?'

'I don't know,' I said. 'I honestly don't know.'

'Have you brought back any other spirits?' Mr Crease
asked.

I didn't want to tell him about the grandfather clock. Why
I could see my father as a small boy was a puzzle, so I shook
my head.

'I think you have, Tully,' said Mr Crease, and he looked
again at Pretty Poppet.

'Crease,' said Mrs Gibbs, 'I'm not sure about this.'

'I am,' said Crease. 'Queenie, imagine what a spirit-seer
could bring to my performance.'

'Am I a spirit-seer?' I asked. 'But can't everyone see them?'

Mr Crease ignored my question. 'Is there anything about
Queenie?'

'No, Crease,' said Mrs Gibbs, seemingly unaware that Pretty
Poppet was standing next to her, resting her head on her
shoulder.

This, then, was the crossroads. I closed my eyes and waited.
I opened them only when Queenie let out a terrified cry. Everything was the same except that Queenie was death-white
and even Mr Crease seemed to have lost his tongue. They were
both staring at Pretty Poppet.

'Shall I sit on your lap, sir?' she said to Mr Crease. 'Shall l
wriggle your fancy? I jiggle it well.'

'Oh, Poppet! Poppet, my darling little girl,' said Queenie,

a sob in her voice. 'Stop, don't say that. I can't bear it.' She stretched out her hands to the girl. 'I wish I could have saved you.'

'Mother,' said Pretty Poppet, 'don't rattle your bones. I'm long gone.'

She walked to the door and disappeared.

'I'm sorry, Mrs Gibbs,' I said. Queenie had tears in her eyes. 'I didn't mean to upset you.'

Mr Crease said quietly, 'Tully, what you do is extraordinary: you bring back the dead to the living. Queenie, we have to keep her here – for her own safety if nothing else.'

Queenie looked at me and beyond me with such longing, then reluctantly said, 'Welcome to the fairy house, Tully.'

Chapter Thirteen

Of Candied Sugar

Candies are different sugar works which are served to garnish dessert fancies; they are of many different kinds, made with any sort of fruit, though all are made much alike.

This is the age of deception, of wigs, paints and patches, where all that nature has generously given mankind is no more than a base canvas in need of enhancement. Most of us hide behind the painted visage, very few are seen for who we really are. This, sir, is my naked account. I stand before you as I am. Have a little more patience, for you are about to make your entrance on this stage to play a greater part than ever I would have supposed. I will try not to trip over myself in my haste to give you your overture, for first I must set the scene. You met me when the curtain had already risen and the show begun. You never knew what went on backstage to make it appear seamless, even magical. Let me tell you of my transformation; it was not as simple as it appeared.

~

I had imagined that Mercy would share my bed again now that we were once more under the same roof. Every night I waited, she didn't come and I didn't understand why not. She wasn't unkind, never said she no longer wanted me, but there was an aloofness about her that hadn't been there when we were in Milk Street.

'Will I see you tonight?' I asked her on one occasion.

'No, I am otherwise engaged,' she said, and kissed me.

In her wig and her fine suit of clothes, she looked the perfect young dandy. I longed for it to be as it once had been between us. Her distance upset me more than I had words to say. I felt my position at the fairy house was no more secure than a child's loose tooth hanging in her gum. This was a whole new world to me and if I was flummoxed by Mercy then I was even more confused as to where I stood in relation to Queenie. As a stepmother she had been kind and solicitous in her care of me but here in the fairy house she, like Mercy, was preoccupied. I thought I knew the reason for the change in Queenie, if not in Mercy. It was on account of the appearance of Pretty Poppet.

I asked her who Mr Quibble was, and if it was he who had spent all that money on my lessons.

'Tully,' said Queenie, 'I paid for your lessons. As for Mr Quibble, when he came to see me about you, I understood he was acting on behalf of a suitor. If I'm honest, I distrusted him. But that is all over and done with and best forgotten.'

To my surprise it was Mr Crease who was the kindest to me in those early days. He gave me time for my spirit, as he called it, to settle into the fairy house before we started to work together.

I had been there less than two weeks when Queenie surprised me with a small dinner party held in my honour. It took place in her private chamber, which she called the rookery. The rookery was painted midnight blue with tiny gold stars thrown all over it. The furniture too was gilded and the effect of the decor was to make you feel that you were inside a jewellery box. Tonight the room was glowing with the honey gold light of a hundred beeswax candles.

~

Hope's skin was dusted white, her cheeks blushed rose, her gown cut so low that the tops or her nipples showed. Her hair was set high, her ringlets decorated with flowers, and I could well see why a man might lose a fortune to spend one night with her.

Mercy wore a banyan embroidered with artichokes, red high-heeled shoes and a cap hiding her hair. Of the three of them, Queenie was the most sober in a sack back gown and a lace cap upon her head. Champagne was served to us in tall, fluted glasses then, when we were all seated, Queenie gave a little speech.

'Tonight each of us will tell you, Tully, a story of our own choosing. Each in its way will tell you more about us. All I ask is that you don't judge us too harshly for no one is born a whore; circumstances more often than design cause us to trip and fall on an unseen step.'

Soup was served in the best china and I, loving a story, could have happily dined on words alone.

Hope went first:

'I was raised by my aunt and uncle who ran a haberdasher's shop in Bath. My aunt, a follower of Wesley, with a cruel mis-understanding of the Bible, never forgave me for being pretty.

According to her Bible, vanity belonged to the devil and all artificial enhancement was an abomination that led man from the path of righteousness. This sentiment was strange indeed when all my uncle's customers were courtesans, harlots and whores who spent liberally of their money, thinking nothing of ordering ribbons and lace bows by the box. It was due to their extravagance that the business flourished.

'For my part I worked and slept in the shop. My education came from studying those fine ladies and their fashions. The more I watched the more determined I was to become like them for they had a freedom that virtuous wives could rarely claim.

'By sixteen I longed to be rid of those hypocrites my aunt and uncle and be my own mistress. The opportunity presented itself when I was noticed by a Mrs Gaye, who had come from London to spend the summer in Bath.

'Suffice to say that Mrs Gaye as good as bought me from my aunt and uncle to be her companion, or so she told them. She told me that if I was compliant she would take me to her bawdy house in London where, she insisted, I could make a small fortune for I had been blessed with a face and a figure to flatter it. She spent a fair sum of money in having me dressed and showing me off at the assembly rooms. It was there that I caught the eyes of two very handsome young gentlemen who were only a little older than me, and I much enjoyed their compliments.

'Mrs Gaye could not have been more pleased, and that night she informed me that the two brothers, both lords, and a year apart in age, had each of them taken a fancy to me, but only one could have the honour of claiming my maidenhead. Being true gentlemen they said I was to choose and, far from feeling flustered, I felt nothing but excitement at the thought of earning my ticket out of that wretched town.

'The following day we went to their house and were shown into a most elegant drawing room. In the past I had only visited such a house as this to deliver parcels, and there was I being served tea by a footman in white gloves. We waited until a servant came to say his lordships wished to speak to Mrs Gaye and I was left on my own although I could make out voices from the adjoining room.

'When Mrs Gaye returned she told me how the game was to be played. She said it was unusual, but as long as I had no scruples she felt the thing would turn out very well. For the first time I felt genuine anxiety. I could not imagine what she meant. Before I had a chance to ask a bell sounded and the interconnecting doors were pulled back to reveal a black velvet drape that screened the room beyond.

'I looked to Mrs Gaye, she smiled and assured me that I would find everything to my liking. Then, taking off my kerchief so that my bosom was more on show, said, "Never has a fair maiden been more blessed for the purpose of the day."

'Still there was no sign of the brothers. The servant closed the shutters and the room fell into darkness. Candles were lit and only when the servant had left did I see at my eye level two round holes in the velvet drapes. I really had no idea what to expect when through the holes appeared the most perfectly formed male appendages. Just the sight of them excited me beyond anything I could have imagined, both round tipped and pink with a pleasing thickness to them. I thought they looked quite edible.

'"What do I do now?" I asked Mrs Gaye, and she, never short of imagination, whispered into my ear then left. In that

time the two appendages had become disappointingly limp.
I touched the tips of both and was pleasantly surprised at
how soft they were, and found that once touched they both
immediately resumed the upright position. I could not make
my choice and said so. There came no answer and, feeling that
these two maypoles were mine to play with, I kissed both.
Then feeling a little braver I did as Mrs Gaye had instructed
and took the tip of one into my mouth. I was delighted by the
taste and the extraordinary sensation that it sent through my
body. The other one fell a little, sensing that I hadn't chosen
him. Sad to see such a fine maypole lopsided, I kissed its soft
tip, licking the dew that lay on its surface, and, finding it
not at all unpleasing, my tongue licked it again. There was
a groan from behind the curtain and I jumped backwards. I
had completely forgotten that these two marvellous pieces of
machinery belonged to anyone.

'The servant reappeared and, as if it was nothing more
than tea being served, announced that the choice was made.
He took me upstairs to a bedchamber and the elder brother
entered, wearing a long dressing gown. It flapped open and I
recognised him by his maypole which sat among a glorious
bushy mound of dark hair. He came to me, kissed me and
slowly, taking great delight, he undressed me until I stood as
nature intended, an Eve to his Adam. He led me to the bed
and there lay beside me, stroking and kissing every part of
me until I was as much on fire as he was and all the while
the maypole waited to be danced around. I touched it and
tenderly he asked if I would kiss it once more. I did and my
hand instinctively found its way to the two globes that rested
at the root of him. I was now kneeling, my backside bare and
upright. I became aware that someone else was on the bed, his

fingers finding the spot that I had made only recent discovery of, now caressing it and opening me up.

'He held on to my hips and guided his sweet weapon up into the folds of my purse and, successfully finding the passage, slowly pushed the tip of his engine deeper into me. My mouth was still round the elder brother's maypole, my tongue performing a minuet on his tip, and so it was we all three were lost in transportations of pleasure until we found exquisite release. And I had found my release from Bath.

'I never went to Mrs Gaye's bawdy house. She had performed her role. A month later, being the mistress of two of the most delightful and eligible dandies, I was taken to London, set up in a house with servants and given the heady sum of one hundred and fifty pounds a year. I can truly say that for two years never had a woman been more satisfied in bed or better exercised in the arts of Venus than I was.'

The soup plates were cleared at the end of Hope's story and all questions barred.

'This, Tully,' she said, 'is just an hors d'oeuvre.'

Chapter Fourteen

After the main course was served and eaten, Mercy sang a song for me, which she said was story enough:

I took her about the middle so small
And laid her on the green;
And in tying of her Garter,
The like was never seen.
She opened her legs so wide
That I slipt in between.
Sing fall down, lay her down, down a, down a good.
And in tying of her Garter,
She lost her maidenhead;
I care not a pin for that said she,
It stood me in little stead.
For oftentimes it troubled me,
As I lay in my bed.
Sing fall down, lay her down, down a, down a good.
And when I had had my will of her,
I took her up again;
I gave her kisses twenty,
And she gave me the same;
Then she away for Highgate,
And I for London town.

Sing fall down, lay her down, down a, down a good.

'More,' I said. 'Oh, sing us more.'

'No,' said Mercy. 'Only fools are full of humour and wit and I have little of either, but I have a present for you.' She rang the bell and a servant brought in a tall dome wrapped in paper. 'Open it,' she said.

I had never had a present in my life, and I'm ashamed to say that I burst into tears.

She kissed me on the lips and said softly, 'Don't be a noodle.'

Once the paper was removed, I stared at it at first in wonder and then became perplexed for it was a birdcage, and in it a white parrot with cheeks of lime green sat on a perch, swinging back and forth.

'This is for me?' I said and opened the cage door.

'Careful, Tully,' said Hope, 'it could fly away.'

Mercy said nothing. The moment I put my hand in the cage I knew the poor bird was dead.

'There's no need to worry. It will never fly,' I said, closing the cage door and feeling more disappointed with my gift than I should have.

'It has been stuffed and preserved,' said Mercy. 'I had it sent from Paris. The great courtesan Madame Eugenie has one.'

I wasn't sure that I wanted this stuffed bird whoever had one, but nevertheless I thanked her. It felt to me that Mercy was trying to say something with the cage and its lifeless inhabitant. I put the cage on the floor and wished she hadn't given it to me.

Queenie started her story:

'By chance I was a flower girl, by chance I was deflowered and by chance I did well. But youth doesn't last for ever and

I wasn't going to end in the gutter sucking on the gin bottle, the tit of mother's ruin, as I had seen many do before me.

'With the money I had saved I opened my first bawdy house just off the piazza at Covent Garden. I kept clean girls and for several years I made a good living. My mistake was that I accepted IOU notes. Your father – or not your father – fell into the category of those who didn't pay in cash and owed me a healthy sum of money. I had more of those notes from him than from any of my other customers.

'One night the house was broken into by a party of rakes, bursting with more wine than a pig's bladder. They demanded that each should have one of my gals. I said not unless they could pay. Not one of them had a farthing on him and, furious at being denied, they took to breaking all they could see. A neighbour called for the constable and I was arrested for running a disorderly and indecent house. The gentlemen too were arrested but, one of them being an earl, they were released.

'The judge was not so lenient towards me and he sent me to Newgate. I tell you this for a tuppence worth of tar, it is not a jail any man or woman wants to be in. The only way to survive was to pay handsomely, and I did just that for a clean cell and all the other trappings. My jailer was a greedy bastard. He wanted money all right, but he wanted what lay under my petticoats and I wasn't showing *him* my garter. In my heyday I was a high-class whore, not one that a cheap, poxy bastard of a jailer could afford – as I told him.

'He said he had ways to make me reconsider and I took that to mean he was going to take me by force.

'I put up a terrible fight the night he came for me. He dragged me from my cell and took me through the stink of that babbling Tower of Babel down to where the air was even more putrid. He opened a cell door and threw me in. I remember thinking that only my father had ever treated me as badly as this and if the jailer touched me again I would kill him just as I should have killed my father. Even whores have their pride, Tully.

'"You'll be screaming to be let out," he said as he locked the door. "Tomorrow you'll wish you'd been nicer to me. A night spent in here has sent grown men mad with fear. In the morning you'll be the same."

'"Never," I shouted. "I have courage – blood red courage!"

'His footsteps and his laughter disappeared. Gradually I became aware of a pile of rags moving across the floor. I wasn't about to let a heap of rat-infested rags have the better of me. I stood up tall and said, "I am Queenie Gibbs of Covent Garden and I am not afraid."

'A face emerged and a cold sweat came over me for I was looking into two staring, lifeless eyes. I bent down, lifted the rags from this half-dead man and gave him a little of the gin that I kept in my petticoats for warmth and courage. I helped him to sit up. It took me a moment to realise that the eyes were painted on the creature's eyelids. His real eyes were as black as a jailer's night, his face white. Once unwrapped, I could see that his clothes were filthy but of quality. He didn't say a word, and I thought, well, neither will I. So he sat there on the stone floor and I stood. It was blooming freezing.

When finally he spoke it made me jump.

'"Do you like the dark, madam?" He said it slowly as if each word caught on his throat.

'"On the whole," I said, "I prefer the light – the better to see my companions."

'Instantly the cell was illuminated. I kept hold of my nerve and he watched me.

'"Is that to your satisfaction, madam?" he asked.

'Refusing to be impressed, I said, "A bed, chairs. A table perhaps."

'What I tell you now is no fib. In a moment that cell had a bed, a table and chairs that would have graced a fine house. I burst out laughing and thought, either I have jail fever, or this man is a sorcerer of exceptional talent.

'He asked if I would help him to a chair on account of his only having one leg.

'"If we have to sit here," I said, "let us have wine and bread."

'And there on the table was a loaf of bread and a carafe of wine.

'I took a mouthful, thinking it would be air, but that night we became as pissed as lords. I lay down on that bed of fine linen too drunk to reason – something I don't usually do – and woke to find the sorcerer aroused and, having no objections, willingly let him take me.

'Now here's the rub: I have had many lovers, some fitted me better than others, but I'd not had one like him. I have more trouble than some to reach that melting moment and often it eludes me altogether. He took his time, waiting for me. Never had I reached it with more abandon than I did that night.

'In the morning the cell was back as it was and my companion gone. I asked the jailer who he was; I even paid him to tell me but all he would say was that the devil was in Newgate Prison and I had spent the night with him.

'After my stint inside I decided to sell the bawdy house and travel to Paris – I had enough money to do it with some style.

'There I was invited to the house of an old lover and after

dinner we went to the theatre to see a magic show. There was no one there who was anywhere near as spectacular as the man I had shared the cell with.

'My host whispered that the next act was a Mr Crease, that he had been one of the greatest magicians of his day, but when he lost his dog Shadow, he had lost his gift.

'The moment I saw him I knew he was the man I had spent the enchanted night in Newgate with. He was taller than I remembered and most beautifully dressed in a long coat of dusty green and pinks. My host was right. The show was disappointing for there was none of the magic that I had witnessed in the cell. But I sent my card backstage and asked if Mr Crease would call on me.

'I had gone to bed when my maid woke me to tell me that a gentleman urgently wanted to see me. I went into the sitting room and to my surprise Crease was there.

'"Forgive me, madam," he said. "You saw a mundane show tonight. I work better with a private audience. I have no desire to perform in public but the truth is I need the money."

'I offered him tea and he said it was unnecessary. His stiffness in manner I presumed came from his concern to find me in that city and a fear that I might let slip where I had met him. I assured him he had no need to worry and his secret was safe with me as I hoped mine was with him. I had started to say some silliness when he stopped me.

'"I am not of this world," he said. "And I little trust those that are. I love them even less. You are different. Why are you different?"

'"I do not know," I replied.

'"Did you believe in the bed, the chairs, the wine, our love-making?"

'I told him that I did, that I had tried to find him but with no success.

'"Do you believe in me?" he asked.

'I said I did.

'"Then," he said, "you must give me every last penny you own, for if you are to build your fairy house you will need a king's ransom."

'As I had never told him my dream I asked him to explain himself.

'"You want to build a brothel that is the most unique in London, with the finest decor, the finest chef and the finest courtesans. Are you brave enough to take the gamble?"

'And here's the strangest part: I gave him everything I possessed, including my jewellery. Only when he had left did I realise I hadn't asked him what I was gambling on. I waited twelve days, by which time I believed myself truly ruined. I couldn't even pay my hotel bill and felt myself to be a royal fool. Just when I was at my lowest, my maid brought me a parcel. I opened it to find more money than I had ever seen before.

'I stood up, shaking, speechless, as Crease entered the room.

'"Shall we build the fairy house?" he asked.'

Chapter Fifteen

That night after the dinner party I lay meditating on all that I had been told.

My bedchamber was decorated with hand-painted wallpaper and the exotic flowers and twisted vines on a smoky pink background made the room feel lush.

It struck me as strange that Queenie had never once mentioned Pretty Poppet, and I couldn't but wonder why, for it was clear that the girl was her daughter. Hope's story, I thought, was the best. I wished that I might have as much good fortune as she, and thinking of all the delights that can be found in the flesh made me long for Mercy to come to me in my four-poster bed. There, together amid the duck-egg-green drapes, we might imagine we were landing on some far distant island. Surrounded by sleep, she would perhaps tell me her untold story.

My stuffed parrot had no option but to be wide awake. It appeared to be watching me. I wanted to ask Mercy why she had given it to me; I wanted more to hear her story, which I was convinced she was saving for me alone. At every creak and squeak I told myself she was just outside and at any second she would open the door and all would be well again. I heard the clock chime midnight and decided that I would go to her. I tiptoed along the hall and thought to enter her room through the antechamber. It never occurred to me that there might be someone else there.

The door to the bedroom being open, I saw the golden moonlight spilling over a naked nymph. Her flaming red river of curls rippled over the pillows and kneeling above her on the four-poster bed wearing only a man's shirt was Mercy. Protruding from the shirt was the most magnificent piece of machinery, carved like the one on Plate Twelve of the dancing master's book. I remembered it was called 'A Virgin's Delight'. Mercy took off her shirt and I could see that the contraption was tied prettily to her, and the sight of it brought on an ache in me. I should have turned and left, but I was tied to the spot – by curiosity? By jealousy? I know not.

Mercy caught sight of me and, despite my presence, bent over the lovely nymph, kissed her mouth, her neck, her ivory globes, and then parted the nymph's legs, rubbing the tip of the machine on her Venus garden. When the nymph arched her back, Mercy thrust her pretty machine deep into her. In and out and in and out, and in until the nymph let out such a cry that I knew she had reached that divine moment.

Now was the nymph's turn. She undid the ribbons, took the contraption off Mercy and, caressing her, rolled her onto her back, parted her legs, then kissed her all the way down to the mark and stayed there. Mercy turned her head from side to side before she too died away in pleasure.

I ran off, heartbroken, and cried myself to sleep.

I woke the next morning determined not to tell a soul what I had seen. I would swallow my hurt. Let my toes turn green and fall off, I wouldn't say a word.

But the moment Mr Crease looked at me with his painted eyes he said, 'So it's finished.'

'What's finished?' I asked.

'Mercy and you.'

Tears welled up and I told him everything. His face remained hard.

'Good,' he said, 'I will have your undivided attention. Your instruction will start after lunch and I don't want another tear from you.'

Hope found me near the back staircase, sobbing. She took my hand and led me to her chamber.

'Ninny-not, what is the matter?'

And although I had made up my mind to tell no one else, for fear of my toes really turning green, I couldn't help myself.

'Mercy doesn't love me any more,' I blurted.

Hope laughed.

'There is no humour in it,' I said.

'Yes, there is. Tully, you, my sweet virgin, are made to be loved and to be loved by men not women. I know that and, more important, Mercy knows it. It is only you who hasn't realised it yet.'

'Who was she – the woman Mercy was with?' I asked

'She is called Mofty. Unfortunately for her, she is married to a rake who enjoys pulling the wings off beautiful butterflies.' Hope took my hands. 'You have been locked away, my ninny-not, and understand little of the hypocrisy of this world and its masks. Mofty's husband, Victor Wrattan, is a professional gambler and a notorious libertine who is renowned for beating the spirit out of his women. As handsome as they come on the outside and as black as the devil on the inside. Mofty was married to him at sixteen and has the scars to show it. Her survival is in no small part due to Mercy. But while we were at Milk Street she suffered badly.'

'Why doesn't she leave him?'

'Money, or rather the lack of it. She had a handsome dowry when she married the dashing Mr Wrattan, but, of course, every penny of it went to him and she has been left with nothing but the crumbs from his table.'

'Then how does she afford Mercy?'

'She doesn't, Mercy doesn't charge her. I believe Mr Wrattan is enjoying himself elsewhere at present.'

'What happened to Mercy's other ladies when she was in Milk Street?'

'They just had to wait. Queenie told everyone she had family business to attend to.'

I sighed. The thought that I had lost Mercy hurt me deeply.

'Do you miss Mr Sitton?' I asked.

'Very much,' she said.

'Why did you want to marry him? After all, you have your independence.'

Hope smiled. 'Tully, how long do you think my face will shine in all its glory for?'

'For ever,' I said. 'Can't you wait for him to return?'

'I do not share your optimism. My looks will fade, alas, and with them my charms. Unless I have some security I will have little to live on apart from my reputation and I have seen too many whores end their days in the Fleet having spent a small fortune on fripperies. I don't wish to be one of them. Come, my love, smile. A broken heart is a whore's downfall, the ruination of many a good courtesan. I will get over mine just as you will get over yours. My advice, Tully, is in future keep your heart in a cabinet, lock it up and hide the key.'

Chapter Sixteen

To Make an Orange Fool

Take the juice of six oranges and six eggs well beaten, a pint of cream, a quarter of a pound of sugar, a little cinnamon and nutmeg. Mix all together, keep stirring over a slow fire till it is thick then put a little piece of butter and keep stirring till cold, and dish it up.

I have not really done justice to Mr Crease. My drawing of him I feel might be too sketchy. It is important for all that follows that he should be better painted. He was the most contrary of men and his temper more unpredictable than the weather. For all that, his skill as a magician was second to none. Every illusion he performed was done with a grace that his everyday life lacked for he possessed an abrupt manner and said what he thought without the inconvenience of worrying if what he thought might offend. Fools he tolerated moderately well.

That first disastrous rehearsal took place in the long gallery on the third floor, the last of Queenie's undecorated rooms. Here was a broken mirror, cobwebs, dust and little more except two chairs. Mr Crease started to talk about the show that he was going to perform at the masquerade ball on the opening night of the fairy house.

'We will start with the setting,' he said, and he closed his eyes so that only his painted eyes could see.

By degrees the chamber began to change slowly into an elegant garden. The floor became grass and gravel, and in the distance the sunlight sparkled on a fountain. Orange trees grew in huge terracotta pots, the scent blew gently in the breeze.

I clapped my hands in amusement.

'More, more,' I said and it all vanished – every blade of grass, the fountain and all the orange trees.

'Never do that again,' he said sharply. Then changing his tone, he asked, 'What was missing from the garden?'

'Nothing. It was perfect.'

'There were no people. That is what I want you to do.'

'You mean like Pretty Poppet?'

'No,' said Mr Crease. 'Best leave her alone. Try someone else.'

'Who?'

He didn't answer.

I was pleased when at least I managed to bring Shadow into the room.

Mr Crease ignored his little dog and said, 'Ads bleed, is that the limit of your powers? Is that all you can offer me? Is your imagination so stifled by preconceived ideas? Is it solely reliant on rational laws of probability?'

'I suppose it is,' I said.

'What a whimsical, pathetic thing you are,' said Mr Crease. 'I am bored with your conventional, feeble mind. It is always elsewhere. So far I have seen nothing that makes me inclined to waste my gifts on you.' He walked to the door. 'You have the skill of a clodhopper. A street magician might amuse me better.'

'You haven't shown me how to do anything,' I said. 'How am I to learn if you don't show me?'

'You think there is a recipe for this?'

'It would help.'

'If you were a cheap street magician I might show you a few tricks but I would never insult the word by calling it "magic". Where do you think your power lies?' I had no answer. He came back to me and put his finger in the middle of my forehead and then on my stomach. 'It comes from within. You believed in Shadow and the power of that belief pulled his ghost through, made him visible to others. You did the same with Pretty Poppet. My fear, Tully, is that your gift is born out of nothing more than naivety. The minute you said to yourself, "This isn't possible, this isn't rational, this defies gravity," it was no longer possible. Today I believe I am seeing the tail end of a childish gift and if that is the case I dust my hands of you.'

I felt so angry my cheeks went to flame.

'You mightily misjudge me, sir. And you are no help whatsoever. How should I conjure ghosts out of thin air? Tell me?'

He walked out the door and slammed it behind him.

I remembered the dark days I lived through in Milk Street, for perhaps there is nothing darker than when you have found sunlight only to see the shutters closed and to be imprisoned in the abyss again. Did I have the power? Had I really said to myself it was impossible so many times that it had become impossible?

Again that night I didn't sleep, but lay awake wondering if

Mr Crease could be right. When I was a child I believed everyone could do what I could do. That much is true. I believed it with an unquestioning passion. Perhaps that was what was missing: belief, passion.

After breakfast the next day I left the dining room and reluctantly made my way up to the long gallery, taking with me Mercy's present for want of company. I started to talk to the stuffed parrot as I waited for Mr Crease.

'I would much prefer that you were alive. At least then you might bring me some comfort and help, perhaps, in proving my worth to Mr Crease. Did you note, dear, dead parrot, he has a very good set of teeth? "Boozey." Well Boozey, is that what you were called? Why? "A sailor named me long ago. Wing white in blue sky, my feathers knew the wind and the ways its breath blew."'

I was so lost in what I took to be a one-sided conversation that I didn't hear Mr Crease come in.

'What is the name of your parrot?' he asked, making me jump. He was standing right behind me.

'Boozey,' I said. 'Though where that came from I haven't an angel's feather of an idea.'

'A good name,' said Mr Crease. 'Does the parrot recognise it?'

'The parrot is dead.'

'So is Shadow. Who captured the parrot?'

'A sailor.' I thought I might as well make use of what had slipped into my mind.

'Where?'

I shrugged.

'Parrots come from jungles far away,' said Mr Crease. 'Where a lushness of foliage grows.'

As he spoke, foliage grew out of the walls of the long gallery, a tangle of woody vines hung down, leaves sprouted, soft as a baby's skin, stitching themselves over each other, hungry for the light. Butterflies, paint pots on wings, flew among the branches, as the plaster ceiling disappeared into a blue sky. An opera of birdsong echoed round us. A snake slithered on its belly into the undergrowth. Heat filled my senses and the perfume of exotic flowers was so heady I felt giddy. All this Mr Crease appeared to have at his command.

Forgetting about what was possible or impossible, I called 'Boozey', for surely if anyone should relish this landscape it would be my dead parrot. I called again and felt a feathery wind by my ear and saw his white shape fly past.

'Boozey, where are you my beauty?'

Far off someone else was calling, and before us appeared a thin reed of a man dressed in sailor's clothes.

He stood in a small clearing, a machete in his hand, his head tilted to the sky, listening to its cry, following the movements of the parrot until it came to rest on his outstretched hand. His face lit up.

'There you are, my beauty,' he said. 'I won't have you served up for the captain's dinner. Here, I've peeled you an almond.'

And he fed it with unexpected delicacy to the small beak of his great love.

With a click of Mr Crease's fingers everything disappeared and the parrot was back on his perch, unmoving, lifeless. There was not a sign of what had been before. Convinced I had played no part in the magic that had unfolded before me, I gazed defiantly at Mr Crease.

He stared at me, silently tapping his cane on the floor.

'You are right,' I said. 'My gift belongs to childhood. I

couldn't do anything like that. I wouldn't know how to go about such imaginings – after all, I have spent my life imprisoned with only fleeting glimpses of the outside world. I have never seen a jungle, never seen a forest, never seen a river. I don't know what a street magician can or cannot do. I am, as you say, miserable, predictable and mundane. I didn't ask to be your apprentice and – '

Mr Crease interrupted me. 'We are finished,' he said.

I picked up the cage and went to my chamber with tears in my eyes, convinced that my time at the fairy house was over. I told myself that I didn't care and packed what little I had. I was itching to see the world. But when I opened the chamber door the maid was standing there.

'Mr Crease says I am to dress you and he wants you downstairs before the clock strikes the half-hour.'

I looked at the clothes she was holding.

'Those are a young man's clothes,' I said.

The maid wisely kept her peace. Only when I was dressed and a short bob wig and a hat firmly placed on my head did she say, 'You make a handsome lad.'

The quality of the clothes alone made my heart stop pounding. Surely if Mr Crease was to have me thrown onto the streets he wouldn't have me dressed in such expensive finery?

I found him by the front door brushing plaster dust off his hat.

Weaving between the ladders I went to him and said, 'I beg your pardon, sir. I spoke out of turn.'

'Never apologise to me,' said Mr Crease. 'I don't give a fuck.'

Chapter Seventeen

To be outside the fairy house, to take gulps of air that had not stagnated in closed chambers, felt to me to be freedom enough. I didn't ask Mr Crease where we were going, just enjoyed feeling my leather shoes upon the ground, my stride free of skirts. The novelty almost made me forget the morning's disaster. Mr Crease said not a word.

I thought myself a sailor who had after a lifetime at sea been cast up upon a strange shore. So lost was I trying to make sense of this brave new world that I walked on not realising that Mr Crease had stopped.

'Listen to me,' he said. 'What do you think happened in the long gallery?'

I was at sea once more. 'You created it all,' I said without confidence, for in most of Mr Crease's questions there was a catch.

He slapped me across the face and at that moment I hated him wholeheartedly.

'Do you need to be so cruel? What, sir, is the purpose apart from your own pleasure?'

'It is you who are being cruel. You are crueller by far to yourself than ever I am to you. Put aside the hatred you feel for me and listen. Listen.'

I held my head up high and bit my lip.

'When I came to the long gallery this morning I had decided there was no point to the exercise and I had told Queenie as much. You didn't hear me enter but neither did you look at the cage for if you had you would have seen the parrot come alive. You would have seen it cock its head to one side, you would have heard it tell you its name and who it belonged to. Instead, you were thinking that you had failed, that you hadn't anything magical to show me. It is your lack of belief in what you do that causes your gift to be erratic.' I stared down at my shoes. 'Look at me.' He jerked up my face to his. 'You are a natural shaman. If you were a man you would know it and your conceit would be unbearable. Instead I find this gift in an uneducated girl who doesn't believe in her own talent and who is obsessed with being bedded.'

It was, I thought, most probably the only compliment Mr Crease would ever pay me. In that I was wrong.

'Come along,' he said. 'First, we go to Covent Garden and then I want you to see what a street magician does.'

At the piazza he pointed out St Paul's Church. 'Here, at the altar of sex, the congregation is praying: will he want me, will he fuck me, will he pay me. Welcome to the arsehole of sin where anything you want can be yours for a purse of gold.'

We walked on under the arcade which afforded some shade to the women there, dressed in their bawdy finery. Already the day was hot. Shop windows flashed past in a daze of glittering, eye-catching baubles. A street musician, leaning against a column, sung a ditty:

> *'The king asked the queen*
> *The queen asked the king...'*

The queen was hiding in the shadows and I wanted to stop and find out what she had to say on the matter, but Mr Crease was walking with such a purpose that stopping was no part of it and we left the musician behind. A girl approached us, her face so thickly covered in white paint that her age was well hidden. Letting her shawl fall off her shoulders she showed a pair of pert breasts. Mr Crease brushed her aside.

'I'm clean,' she shouted after us.

At the end of the colonnade, Mr Crease stopped suddenly. I near tripped over him.

'The musician,' he said, 'tell me about him.'

The musician as far as I could see was counting his takings. I didn't know what to say. Mr Crease closed his eyes so that the two painted ones stared at me. He pushed his finger into the middle of my forehead.

'Use that eye, that eye alone. Try again. What do you see?' He tapped his cane on the ground.

'But surely you can see it too,' I said. 'As I think can everyone else. It would be impolite to draw attention to the situation.'

Mr Crease banged his cane on the ground. 'See what?'

I sighed. It seemed so silly to have to point it out.

Taking a breath, I said, 'His wife is standing in the shadows.'

'And?' said Mr Crease.

'And she is dead. Full of holes.'

'I would say stab wounds.'

'Yes. You can see her as well as I. It is nothing remarkable.'

I watched as two ladies passed by the musician who took off his hat and bowed. They too must have seen her for they let out the most terrible screams. The musician, startled, turned round and began to shout.

'Go away, woman! Don't reproach me – I never killed you.

Are you trying to drive me mad? Why do you torment me?'
Then, even louder than before, he began to sing, 'The king
asked the queen, the queen asked the king...'

By now a crowd had gathered round him. Mr Crease
manoeuvred me into the sunlight.

'You see,' I said, 'I was right not to point it out.'

'Ads bleed,' he replied. 'You are either a simpleton or a
genuis. Don't you understand what you can do? You and I
can see the dead woman. No one else can until you make her
visible to them. Even I can't do that.'

'Is everyone blind then?'

I thought about this revelation as we walked across the
square. I had never seen so many people all gathered in one
place. Was I really to believe that not one of them could see
what I could see?

'It's not just the dead,' I said, stopping Mr Crease. 'I saw a
boy called Sam in the grandfather clock at Milk Street and so
did Mr Truegood. He told me that was him as a child. What
does that mean? And if I can see the dead then tell me, why
could I never call my mother back?'

Mr Crease's voice was softer. 'Because her spirit is free.'

'How do you know that?'

A sedan chair was fast making its way towards us through
a field of rotting vegetables.

'Later, Tully, we will talk of this. Not now.' He moved me
quickly out of the way and into a coffee house.

Inside, men of all ranks were sitting at tables and the smoke
was so thick that it hung in a grey cloud above their heads.
Mr Crease pushed through the crowd of gaudy muckworms,
until he found who he was looking for – a robust man, every
inch of him made of muscle and spoiling for a fight.

'Mr Bird,' said Mr Crease. 'Sit,' he said to me and I pulled a chair close to the table.

'Three bowls of Politician's Porridge,' called Mr Bird to the serving girl, the only other woman there.

Mr Crease half closed his eyes as he lit his long white pipe.

'Who's the lad?' said Mr Bird.

'My apprentice,' said Mr Crease.

'To be trusted?'

Mr Crease nodded. 'Is it true that Bethany has left her keeper?' he asked as three bowls of coffee arrived.

'True as a Sunday,' said Mr Bird.

'Found her in bed with his footman?'

'Discovered them in a very interesting position that left little doubt as to the point of the exercise they were performing.'

'Have you anything more for me?' he asked and put a purse on the table. Mr Bird put his hand out to take it but the purse moved and no matter how hard he tried he couldn't catch it.

Observing this, the dandy at the table opposite said, 'That is some trick, sir.'

He had with him a small box and inside was a canary that seemed to be dead.

'What else have you heard?' asked Mr Crease, ignoring the comment.

'I heard some news this morning,' said Mr Bird. 'Fresh as baked bread it is.' He did not have an easy way with a story, being given to taking the longest route and disdaining all short cuts. 'The gentleman you was asking about is as dead as a plump turkey. Murdered, found with his throat slit. Not a pretty picture.'

'I need more than the obvious.'

'Of course, Mr Crease, and I am on my way to finding it out if you would just have the kindness to let go of the purse.'

I wanted to ask who had been murdered and might well have done so had I not seen you walk into that unmemorable sea of chattering faces and lopsided wigs.

Wait, wait. I should conjure an orchestra so that it might herald your entrance, the audience standing to give you a round of applause in anticipation of the performance to come. When the rope is round my neck this memory is the one I will hold tight, the moment I saw you. What a striking young gentleman you were: your eyes sky blue, lips generously made for kissing, your nose that of a Roman god. Your enviable hair was your own which was considered most unfashionable yet it suited you handsomely – powdered grey, tied with a black bow, more elegant than the white wool bush that most men had ill fitted upon their heads. Several stared at you for your clothes – a soft, dove-grey jacket and silver waistcoat – were finely cut. It occurred to me that you were used to your entrance causing a stir.

~

I felt Crease's cane on my shin as if he knew what I was thinking. He looked up and seeing who had caught my attention he stood.

'Mr Fitzjohn,' he called. 'Mr Avery Fitzjohn, if I am not mistaken.'

The young gentleman, Avery Fitzjohn, smiled and made his way towards us. I kept my head low for fear that my burning cheeks might give away my indecent thoughts.

'Mr Crease,' he said. 'It is good to see you, sir. A long time – and you still recognise me.'

'Join us,' said Mr Crease. He handed Mr Bird the purse. 'Ned, find out what you can and meet me at the house.'

Mr Fitzjohn rested his hat on the table and took Ned's seat. Mr Crease ordered more coffee.

Close to, this young man was even more desirable than he was at a distance, his face so well drawn.

'The boy all gone, the man appears,' said Mr Crease. 'What brings you back to the metropolis?'

I had never heard Mr Crease talk in such a civil manner to anyone apart from Queenie.

'My return is due to my uncle being very ill. And I have other business. Tell me, is it true that Queenie is opening a new house?'

'Indeed she is,' said Mr Crease. 'The fairy house – a brothel like no other the metropolis has to offer. It will open with a most spectacular masquerade ball.'

'Then I have returned to London at exactly the right time. I always said that the old rogue, my uncle, must be good for something. In that I was right. If it was not for him, I would still be in Paris.'

'What are you doing there?' asked Mr Crease.

'I'm studying to be a physician. I have to do something with my days other than look decorative. After all, I am not destined to inherit a title or a fortune so I might as well inherit some knowledge.' Turning his blue eyes on me, he said, 'What is your name?'

I didn't know what to say but Mr Crease said quickly, 'This is Master Thomas, my apprentice.'

'Well, Master Thomas,' said Mr Fitzjohn. 'Do you always keep sixpence behind your ear?'

Instinctively, I put my hand to my ear and a sixpence rolled onto the table.

Mr Crease was amused at my astonishment.

'The only trick you ever taught me, Mr Crease,' said Mr Fitzjohn, 'and I have never forgotten it. I use it to intrigue the ladies.'

'Master Thomas,' said Mr Crease, 'what trick do you have to show my friend?'

My heart sank as I dearly wanted to impress Mr Fitzjohn. Then it came to me.

'Sir,' I said nervously, 'I think there is a bird under your hat.'

'Under my hat?' said Mr Fitzjohn.

'Yes, sir.'

'I doubt it,' he said and looked at Mr Crease, who shrugged.

Cautiously, Mr Fitzjohn lifted his hat. There stood the canary. It started to tweet.

The young dandy whose dead canary it was had paid his bill and was making his way out of the coffee house with the box. I knew that the moment he reached the door the spirit of the bird would fly to freedom.

'*Touché*,' said Mr Fitzjohn. 'I can see you are a worthy pupil. Alas, I possess no such skill.'

The bird took flight and he turned and watched as the slash of yellow disappeared into the grey.

'Magicians and physicians have more in common than either would like to acknowledge,' said Mr Crease.

'Dammit, you are right, sir. We both deal in the impossible: the illusion that death can be bargained with.'

Through the window I could see the dandy looking into the

small box that contained his dead canary. He threw it away in disgust. Mr Crease saw him too.

Mr Crease stood and bowed to Mr Fitzjohn. 'I will have an invitation sent to you. Where are you staying?'

I knew then that if I could choose who I would give my virginity to, I would with all my heart choose you. Hope was right. You made me realise that what I longed for was not a tied-on virgin's delight but the real thing.

Chapter Eighteen

Sheep's Tongue in Paper

Cut braised tongues into two pieces and put round them a forced meat made of fowls' livers, or any sort of poultry, with the yolks of hard eggs, sweet herbs, a little suet or beef marrow, pepper and salt and a few fine spices. Pound together; roll them up in paper, first rubbed with oil or butter; either broil or bake them slowly, and serve dry or with the sauce.

To my delight, Avery Fitzjohn walked out of the coffee house with us.

'Where are you off to?' he asked Mr Crease above the voice of a street-seller calling his wares.

'My name, your name, your father's name, your mother's name.'

'Bartholomew Fair,' said Mr Crease. 'Come with us.'

'I would dearly like to but I have a lawyer to see, so, sir, I bid you good morning.'

I turned to watch him go and in doing so bumped into the street-seller. There was a terrible clang as the alphabetical posy he was holding fell to the cobbles. I bent to pick up the marking irons and much to my embarrassment found that Mr Fitzjohn had stopped to help.

'Allow me, Master Thomas,' he said, smiling.

When all the letters had been given back to the street-seller, I thanked him and hurried to catch up with Mr Crease. Only when I was sure Mr Fitzjohn was out of sight did I ask Mr Crease who he was.

'A very interesting young man.'

'And...?'

But Mr Crease had nothing further to add. We walked on and I began to flag. To my relief Mr Crease hailed a hackney carriage.

I was delighted by the novelty and had just settled myself inside when, looking out through the window's metal grille, my heart near stopped. A little way off, staring at the hackney carriage, was the gentleman from the blue chamber.

'Mr Crease, there was a gentleman who came to Milk Street the day of Mr Truegood's wedding to Queenie. He is standing over there.'

'Where?' asked Mr Crease. But the gentleman in question appeared to have vanished. 'Are you sure it was him?'

'Yes,' I said as we bumped along. 'No. I don't know.'

We arrived outside a tavern in the midst of a huge crowd. If chaos wanted to show herself in all her disarray then she could not have chosen a better occasion than Bartholomew Fair. People were packed as tight together as in a barrel of eels. I was almost overcome by the smell of sweat and roasting pig.

'If we become separated,' said Mr Crease, who I could hardly hear above the squealing of catcalls, the squeaking of penny trumpets and the thunder of kettle drums, 'this is where we will meet: here at the King's Head.'

Inside the tavern it was as busy as outside but slightly cooler for the shade. Mr Crease fought his way through until he found two seats by the window on the second floor. He ordered *coloquintida*, a small beer, which never having tasted before I thought odd, but not unpleasant. From the window we could just see one of the stages. An actor strutted about in tinsel robes and gilded buckskin. A magician took to the stage and I watched and was disappointed by all I saw him do.

'That,' said Mr Crease, 'is a buffoon who thinks he's a magician conjuring up tricks for other buffoons to watch.'

I was surprised by the heavy handedness of the magic. Every trick performed could be seen it for what it was: a cheap fraud.

'That isn't magic,' said Mr Crease and ordered more beer. 'It couldn't even own the word. You asked me a question.'

I had all but forgotten. The sight of Avery Fitzjohn had put it out of my head.

'I did. I wanted to know how it was I could see the boy in the grandfather clock although Mr Truegood wasn't dead.'

Mr Crease closed his eyes so that his painted eyes could see into me.

'It was said by Mr Shakespeare that one man in his time plays many parts, his acts being seven ages. Mr Truegood's haunted boyhood was a part he had never been able to let go. It happens often that the living are more haunted by their pasts than they are by the dead who, like your mother, on the whole have somewhere else to go.' Changing the subject, he asked, 'Is that gentleman you thought you recognised anywhere about?'

'No,' I said.

'Drink up then.'

Outside, we were caught up in the crowd. We swam rather than walked past booths and theatrical stages, stalls selling

hobby horses, singing birds, toy dogs, and all that shimmered and shone. I, no more than a magpie, was unable to take my eyes from the gaudy trappings on sale. I looked round and realised Mr Crease was well ahead of me. I tried to break free of the forceful tide and that was the cause of my misfortune. I lost my wig and my hat and instead of concentrating on the whereabouts of Mr Crease, I tried to retrieve my possessions. It was too late – they were trodden into the mud and shit, as good as lost for ever. Now I could no longer see Mr Crease. He was neither to the front of me nor to the back, and I found I was being jostled into a large booth. I was trying to extricate myself when a candle lit up the stage and a curtain was pulled aside for a harlequin to announce that the play was called *The Devil of a Duke*. The crowd clapped.

Intrigued, I stayed to watch. One character acted the drunk and reminded me more than I liked of Mr Truegood. The heat in the tent was too much and I made my way out. There, my eyes accustomed themselves to the bright sunlight but I still couldn't see Mr Crease. I realised that without my wig and hat my disguise was undone.

'Have you paid?' said a man who was standing by the opening.

I hadn't a penny on me. 'No,' I said, 'I haven't.'

It was then that I felt a hand holding tight to my arm.

'Oh, Mr Crease,' I said, turning round. 'I thought I'd lost you.'

And I looked up, not into Mr Crease's face, but into the eyes of the gentleman from the blue chamber.

What followed shook me badly and made me wonder about those two rogues, Fate and Destiny, who daily play piquet with our lives without one jot of concern for the consequences. It is

terrible to think that all our hopes and dreams are in the hands of these two swindlers. I thought myself to be so insignificant a mortal that they would not tamper with my days in any way; in that I was proved decidedly wrong. There you see, sir, that the shallow shores of my mind have shells on them; whether there be pearls I cannot say. But I dally.

The gentleman from the blue chamber quickly paid the man.

'Here,' he said, 'take this and be done with it.'

In the sunlight the gentleman was certainly handsome but where Mr Avery Fitzjohn's face was open I could not say the same for this gentleman. What had I been thinking to cast him in such a romantic light?

To my surprise he again took hold of my arm and addressed me by my name. 'Miss Truegood, I insist that I escort you home. My carriage is at your disposal.'

There seemed something mighty untoward in his design, even to my feeble brain, and instinctively I tried to pull away. It was then that I seemed to wittingly or unwittingly conjure up Pretty Poppet. The gentleman saw her too and wavered. In that instant I broke free and ran, breeches being better suited to running than petticoats. I heard my would-be abductor, not far behind, curse and call my name. Pretty Poppet guided me, weaving in and out of the crowds. She lifted the flap of one of the smaller tents and, terrified of being caught, I ducked inside.

My heart was pounding so fast that I didn't concern myself with the interior of the tent or who it might belong to but kept my eyes on the opening. Through it I could see the gentleman searching the booths.

'Come away from there and be seated,' said a voice behind me.

I turned to see a woman, heavily made-up, sitting at a small dressing table. Her hair was near gone, apart from a wisp, and a wig stood on a stand.

'He will not come in here,' she said. 'You are safe with me.'

I didn't feel as certain as she did.

Further in, the tent was full of clothes of the most glittery kind and they smelled of warm wax, paint and sweat.

'Sit down and let me know you.'

I sat beside the actress and she took hold of my hand and looked at my palm. I felt rather shy and awkward.

'Thank you, madam, for letting me hide here,' I said. 'I'm sorry, it is most rude of me to have barged in uninvited.'

She waved my apology aside. 'What do you wish for?' she asked.

It was such a surprising question that I didn't have an answer ready. 'Nothing,' I said.

'Do not waste a wish on nothing,' she said as I looked at the entrance of the tent again. 'What do you wish for?'

I wasn't in the mood for games. 'Are you sure he won't find me here?' I asked.

'Quite sure. Now tell me. I am curious to know: what does a young girl dressed as a boy wish for?'

To stop her asking any more questions I said, 'I wish to be my own mistress. But really, I cannot concentrate on this – I think I am in danger.'

She looked at my palm again. 'You are Mr Crease's apprentice,' she said.

That took my breath away. 'How do you know?' I asked.

She laughed. 'Do you not recognise me, young lady?' She placed the wig on her head.

'Mrs Coker!' I said, amazed. 'I never supposed my elocution teacher to be an actress.'

'And I never supposed I'd see my pupil dressed as a boy. We have managed to surprise one another. Come now, play the game. I will grant you your wish. It will help you make your fortune.'

'But I haven't wished for anything.'

'You have been wishing since the day you were born. A pearl hand is what I will give you.'

'What's a pearl hand?' I asked, my eyes still on the tent flap.

'If you do not find out for yourself, come and see me again,' she said, 'and I will tell you.' With that she turned her attention to the mirror and powdered her nose. 'Beware of Captain Spiggot, for he is no friend of yours.'

'I don't know any such captain,' I said.

'You will do,' she said.

A dwarf wearing a jester's cap entered the tent.

Mrs Coker stood up as tall as I remembered her. Somewhere outside a band began to play. The dwarf preceded her through a flap at the far end of the tent and up steps that led to a stage.

Mrs Coker whispered, 'Now, go home as quickly as you can.'

Chapter Nineteen

Pike in the Form of a Dolphin

When the fish is gutted and scalded make a few incisions on the back and sides; rub it over with salt and coarse pepper, marinate it in oil with parsley, shallots, one clove of garlic, and two laurel leaves. Tie it on a skewer in the form of a dolphin, bake it in the oven, basting now and then with some of the marinade. When done, drain it off and serve with whatever sauce you please.

I pushed a little way through the crowd but then glanced back as the dwarf banged a drum to silence the audience. He announced that the play they were about to see was called *The Fairy Godmother's Wish* and the leading role was to be performed by Mrs Coker. Instead of going home as quickly as I could, I stood there as if hammered into the ground and watched as Mrs Coker slowly floated into the air.

'It's not very polite to run away without a thank you.'

The gentleman from the blue chamber was suddenly beside me and had hold of my wrist.

'Sir, let go,' I said, trying to pull free. 'You're hurting me.'

He wasn't losing me a second time. Desperately I looked

around, hoping that Pretty Poppet might once more come to my rescue, but she was nowhere to be seen.

'A lovers' tiff,' said someone in the crowd.

'No,' I said and before I could say a word more the wretch had picked me up and thrown me over his shoulder as if I were a sack of corn. This tickled the onlookers no end.

'Taking her to the Piepowder Court?' said one man. 'Let the magistrate decide your case.'

'Out of my way,' said the gentleman. 'I need no judge – I know the verdict in this case. The only way to deal with women is to give them a good hiding.'

He slapped me hard on the backside. My outrage was great as was my embarrassment at finding myself thrown over his shoulder and hanging upside down. The only view I had was of the muddy ground below me and the sight of shoes, boots and slippers that parted in twos to let us through.

'Help me,' I called out above the din of the fair. 'I'm being kidnapped. Please help me.'

No one took any notice of my predicament and all the while the gentleman held me maddeningly fast with one hand and with the other greeted all the ladies he passed, wishing them a good day with a great flourish of his hat.

For all my screaming I was royally ignored. We pushed against the sea of people who found the sight of me being carried upside down most amusing, as if we were a part of the entertainment. This scoundrel, whoever he was, knew where he was taking me. For all his swagger, he walked with a purpose. I caught a glimpse of carriage wheels and thought the game was up.

The carriage door opened and from within the voice of a young gentleman said to my abductor, 'What detained you?'

'She is a wanton baggage this one,' he said, trying to throw me onto the carriage floor. The man inside did his best to take hold of me but I had no intention of giving in so easily. I kicked and punched and fought like a she-cat, roaring at the top of my voice.

I was half in the coach, half out when the young gentleman said sharply, 'Keep quiet, you little whore,' and hit me hard across the face with his leather-gloved hand.

The gentleman who had carried me there said, 'Deal with her – we don't have time for this nonsense.'

It was then I heard Mr Crease's voice.

'Put her down,' he said.

Mr Crease was pointing a pistol at the gentleman inside the coach. He instantly let go of me and slammed the carriage door.

'Just bit of harmless fun – chasing a whore round the fair,' said the gentleman from the blue chamber.

There was a snorting of horses and before anyone could think to stop it the carriage began to move away. Seeing his means of escape fast disappearing, my abductor dropped me unceremoniously onto the muddy ground and vanished into the crowd.

I arrived at the fairy house decidedly giddy with all that had befallen me. Mr Crease left me to Hope's care.

～

She, seeing the state of me, covered with mud and worse, said, 'Oh, Tully, we have had a morning of such anxiety.' She backed away for I was no nosegay. 'There were reports that you too had been murdered.'

'"Too"?' I said in a stew of confusion. 'What do you mean by "too?"'

'All that matters is that you are home safe,' said Hope.

'Home' is a word that had never held any meaning for me. Milk Street was more a prison than anything. How strange that the fairy house should feel like home.

'Home,' I repeated for the novelty of it.

Hope put her clean white hand on my mud-caked face. 'That eye is going to be a very pretty picture unless something is done.' She rang a bell and told the footman to bring up a steak.

'I can't eat, not now,' I said.

'No, you ninny-not – it's to go on your eye. It will make the bruising go down.'

Mercy brought the steak. She swore she would dash the brains out of the villains who had done this to me. Hope calmly suggested that before anyone bashed anyone's brains out, I should have a bath and rest.

A bath was most necessary but, as for the rest, I felt there was no need. I wanted to tell Hope and Mercy what had happened but after the bath I was exhausted and, reluctantly lay down. Hope, with all the care of a nurse, placed the steak on my eye and to my astonishment I slept the best part of the day.

I woke at dusk, washed my face and dressed myself. Downstairs all seemed very quiet but then I heard raised voices coming from the rookery. I nervously knocked on the door.

A few minutes went by and I was on the point of leaving when the door flew open.

'Ah,' said Mr Crease, 'come in. I was about to send a servant to fetch you.'

Queenie kissed me and said, 'I could not have lived with myself if anything had happened to you.' She took me to the light to examine my face and I saw there were tears in her eyes. 'This will never do. You must see Doctor Ross.'

She rang a bell and gave instructions to the footman for the doctor to be sent for.

'It's not at all necessary,' I said. 'The steak improved it mightily.' But neither Queenie nor Mr Crease were remotely interested in the healing powers of steak. 'I'm so sorry,' I said. 'I didn't mean to worry you all.'

I was far from used to being the centre of their attention.

Mr Crease was standing in front of the unlit fire staring at me. 'Was it he?' he asked suddenly. 'Was it the gentleman who called on your father the day of the wedding?'

'Yes,' I said, disgusted at my earlier passion for him.

'Had you ever seen him before that day?'

'No – never.'

'Have you heard of the name Spiggot?' asked Queenie. 'Captain Ralph Spiggot?'

'Only today when I hid in Mrs Coker's tent. She read my palm and told me to beware of Captain Spiggot. I haven't a fig of an idea who he is. Why do you ask?' I didn't like the silence that followed and had a sudden thought. Perhaps Mrs Coker was another shadow? 'Please don't tell me Mrs Coker is dead and I saw her ghost?'

'No, you saw no ghost,' said Mr Crease. 'I heard that Mrs Coker was at the fair this year, performing as the fairy godmother.'

'What is all this about?' I asked.

I wanted to say 'nonsense' – what is all this nonsense about? But Mr Crease had his painted eyes firmly fixed upon my face. I felt unsteady and my complexion turned bright red. Queenie took my hands.

'You must be brave, Tully,' she said. 'I received some terrible news this morning – quite shocking. Mr Truegood has been murdered at the Fleet Prison.'

Perhaps a cow could jump over the moon after all. The idea of Mr Truegood being murdered was just as inconceivable.

'Wh…why?' was all I could stutter.

'A good question,' said Mr Crease. 'There was nothing of value left to steal. Mr Truegood had only some papers.'

'When did it happen?'

'Yesterday. The turnkey found him with his throat slit at about six in the evening.'

I was too stunned to speak.

'It seems that the last person to see Mr Truegood alive – apart from his murderer – was Martha,' said Queenie.

'His cook,' said Mr Crease, as if I might have forgotten that Cook had a name.

'Where is Cook now?' I asked.

'She has disappeared,' said Queenie. She paused then continued. 'Before I left Milk Street, Crease and I tried to find out who you had been married to. Mr Truegood told me it was his business and his business alone. I was furious that your prospects had been so recklessly thrown away. I demanded to know the name of your husband so that a court might free you – after all, the marriage has not been consummated.'

'No,' I said, 'and it never will be.'

Queenie handed me a piece of paper. 'This was found among Mr Truegood's papers.'

The script was elaborate, as if written by a spider with quills for legs.

Dear Mr Truegood,

Please forgive the abrupt nature of this letter. I have been in the navy too long and, deprived of the finer manners of polite society, become more accustomed to a Man-of-War than the drawing room.

Let me come straight to the point. I have long felt that it is nothing short of my duty to discover the name of my bride that my uncle in his undoubted wisdom had me married to when I was sixteen and she a child of twelve years. She being too young and too innocent to take up the duties of a wife it was thought expedient that I should make my way in the world and then return to claim my prize. My uncle, alas, becoming ill and his mind unmoored from reason, shortly before his death held a bonfire of all his correspondence and documents, including those relating to my marriage.

I recently have returned to England with the sole purpose of finding my bride and with the help of my associate, Mr Victor Wrattan, I have had some modicum of success. I now believe that your daughter, Miss Truegood, is the young woman I have the honour to call my wife.

I would dearly like the opportunity to meet with you and discuss the matter as I am sure that you are loath to part with a beloved child and I am equally loath...

'This is utter tosh,' I said, my insides tumbling. 'Surely this man cannot really be my husband?'

'Read on,' said Mr Crease.

... equally loath that she should be deprived of the role for which she was educated. To that end an amicable agreement which is beneficial to both of us can be reached. I assure you, sir, that I have no desire to have the marriage dissolved.

I am, sir, your humble servant,

Captain Ralph Spiggot

I was so stunned that I stared at the name until the spidery writing wobbled off the page.

'He can't be,' I said. 'He can't be the despicable man who tried to kidnap me at the fair.'

'The gentleman you first met at Milk Street? No, that was Victor Wrattan,' said Mr Crease. 'Mofty's husband.'

The horror of it slowly dawned on me.

'You mean... the young gentleman in the carriage – who slapped me across the face and called me a whore – he is my husband?'

Chapter Twenty

Newgate Prison

'You are to be moved,' Hope said, when she next came to visit.

'You look better,' I told her.

'You, my ninny-not, look ill.'

'I am troublingly tired.'

Hope busied herself round the ridiculously small cell as if it were full of furniture, and clothes that needed packing, when there was was just a bed, a table and a pile of ribbon-tied paper.

'Moved where?' I asked.

'To the prison governor's house. There, you will be better looked after.'

I couldn't help it, I laughed. To my surprise, Hope joined in.

'Is this the Duke of H's doing?' I asked, for I could think of few others who would have the power and money to buy me out of this cell.

'No,' she said. 'And it's not Queenie's either.'

'Then who? Is it Avery? Tell me, please. Have you heard anything of him?'

'No, not a word,' she said, adding quickly, 'It was Sir Henry Slater. It is surprising how much influence he has in unexpected quarters. And you will be glad to know that Mercy is improving. That at least is one grain of good news.'

'Yes. But still nothing from Avery?'

'Leave it, Tully. Pining for him will do you no good.'

She asked if she could take the manuscript. I had finished writing the first act of my story over a week ago. Now, I cannot write. Not by choice but because I have used all the paper and ink. I worry that I have hidden the truth of myself in the shade of naivety – not that it would matter as long as I was able to write more.

'I have something else to tell you – a solicitor will be coming to see you tomorrow, a Mr Attaway.'

'He was Lord B's solicitor. Why does he want to see me?'

'He will take over your case and make sure you have a good defence lawyer.'

'There's nothing to defend,' I said. 'I told the coroner that I shot Spiggot. I have no doubt that I will be found guilty.'

'Tully,' said Hope, 'only you can save yourself. I strongly advise you to choose to fight – to live.'

'Sadly, Justice, that dear, blind lady, might not give me the option,' I said.

Only when she had left did I realise she'd taken the manuscript. An Almond for a Parrot.

The walls in my cell chatter. It is filled with more voices than there are bricks – previous occupants muttering crumpled prayers to a God they've only just remembered.

That evening the jailer came, not with my dinner but to tell me I was to be moved on account of my pleading the belly.

'There are all sorts of stories about you,' he said, rubbing his hands on the sides of his trousers. 'They say you have a pearl hand that knows well how to rub a man's cock.'

I knew where this was taking him – I could see by the bulge

in his trousers. He closed the cell door and undid himself. His hard weapon sprang, loaded, ready to shoot. I doubted that it had given any woman much pleasure.

'Now, I was thinking,' he said, 'because I'm a thinking kind of man…'

'And with what do you think – your head or your lobcock?' I asked.

'You do me a little favour and show me this pearl hand of yours, and, in return, I will bring you some nice, pretty things – things you'd like.'

I felt a wave of nausea as he grabbed hold of my hand – the wrong hand – and put it over his weapon.

The image of Mr Truegood came to me and suddenly the jailer leapt back to the cell door.

'Who's that?' he shouted.

Mr Truegood had, for once, made a welcome appearance. True to his nature, true to his character, he had arrived with all his gore. He was never one to wear the scars of martyrdom lightly. He stood in the corner of the cell weeping. Not for me, for himself and for the injustice of all the ill fortune of his life.

The sight of the ghost withered the jailer at both ends.

'You're a bloody witch,' he said, his face white. 'A witch, that's what you are.'

He slammed the cell door behind him and turned the key.

Two constables moved me to the prison governor's house. The governor looked shocked to see the state of me. Perhaps he imagined I would be dressed in all my finery and able to entertain him with illicit stories and sexual scandals. I had been so long without a bath or anything that would own the name of gown or shift that I must have seemed a wild creature indeed. Nevertheless, I was taken upstairs and, to my surprise, there was water to wash with. The clothes laid out for me were not of scratchy fabric but of soft cotton. And that evening the meal was edible. For the first time I slept and dreamed.

In the morning a box arrived containing paper and ink. There was no one to ask who had brought it.

My door was firmly bolted and my windows barred, but through them came sunlight and a breeze.

Let the curtain rise, let the footlights shine. Take your seat, my love, and I will show you this short life of mine.

Chapter Twenty-One

Green Gooseberry Tarts

You may either use them whole, or make a marmalade of them with a good syrup. This last is recommended as the best method, for by this means you can judge easily how sweet they are, and ought to be, to please. For marmalade (if large) they ought to be cut in half.

The indigestible revelation that I bore the name Tully Spiggot kept me awake at night. I learned that the captain was twenty-two years old and resided with Mr Wrattan at Great Ormond Street. All that could be said in his favour, as far as I could tell, was that he had his own teeth and hair. Apart from that he was a known gambler and cheat. I felt more drained than the Thames at low tide. Why had this mudlark of a husband waited so long to climb out of the silt of the past to throttle my future?

The opening of the fairy house was only three weeks away and to make matters worse – or so it felt to me – two of London's most notorious courtesans took up residence. Hope and Mercy were delighted to be reunited with their dear friends and, by degrees, I became excluded from their *tête-à-têtes* and card games.

Flora Dingley was a small, doll-like creature. She arrived in a carriage bearing the arms of the Earl of Wellborne; her costume immaculate, her hair and gown studded with diamonds.

Bethany Goodere arrived shortly after. It was she who had been found with the footman, doing what his lordship's footman and his lordship's mistress ought not. The papers were full of the scandal. There were cartoons, and much ridicule of Lord Bagley who had sent her packing. Bethany was the most beautiful and the most terrifying woman. She wore her curly hair high and powdered grey, her skin was the colour of honey, her features hard except for her liquid, light-brown eyes that became darker with passion. It was with Bethany that my trouble began.

Bethany was given the finest suite of rooms the fairy house had to offer. With her came her maid and a hairdresser, a mole of a man called Signor Florentini who wore tiny spectacles perched precariously on the end of his nose.

I was certain that Bethany had taken a dislike to me the minute she met me and I'm afraid to say that the feeling was mutual.

When she heard that I was married to Ralph Spiggot, she said, 'Why, he is an abomination. It is said that he likes young girls and enjoys nothing more than humiliating them.' For the first time she studied me and, her curiosity satisfied, said, 'Oh fie, he will make a pretty dinner of you. How old?'

I told her I was near seventeen.

'He will whip you all the way to twenty and after that want no more to do with you. I have heard him boast on more than one occasion that he considers a woman over that age as being worthless to any man and better off dead. But I do declare,' said Bethany, laughing, 'once Ralph Spiggot has seen you, he will lose all interest. Those eyebrows are enough to make a bishop blush.'

I expected that at least Hope would defend me but she too laughed. Bethany had a cruel tongue and it near defeated my spirits that neither Hope, Mercy or Queenie ever came to my rescue. I did my best to keep out of Bethany's way but, a few days later, her maid came to my chamber and told me her mistress wanted to see me.

I found Bethany lying naked on her bed, propped up on pillows. Signor Florentini was leaning over her, examining her Venus mound with great care.

'Tully,' said Bethany. 'Come, sit beside me and tell me about yourself. You are a virgin?'

This was the exercise I had been dreading: she was determined to undo me, to make a fool of me. My eyes were fixed on Signor Florentini and my cheeks must have gone to fire for he had a barber's razor in one hand and in the other a soap mixture which he was lathering over Bethany's pretty garden as if very familiar with all its beds and furrows.

'What is he doing?' I asked.

'Oh fie! Don't you know? He's making sure the path is smooth.' She turned her gaze to my face. 'Those eyebrows. I do declare they need attention. Do you have hair elsewhere in such profusion?'

'Yes, but...'

'Show me. This is no place for modesty.'

I was not going to be bear-baited. I stood up and ran to the door but her maid barred my way.

'Sit,' said Bethany.

I hate to admit it but I did, with tears in my eyes.

'Where do you think you are?' she asked me.

'The fairy house.'

'And what is the fairy house?'

'A brothel.'

'And what is your role in it?'

'To assist Mr Crease.'

She had a deep, rounded laugh that made her breasts judder. 'You are a pretty, naive little fool.'

I sniffed and the maid brought me a kerchief. Signor Florentini moved Bethany's legs further apart and continued shaving.

'And I suppose you think Queenie keeps you here because she doesn't want you to be a whore?'

I said nothing. Bethany waved Signor Florentini away and her maid, too. When they had gone, her very mannered way of talking disappeared and her voice became low and musical with an unfamiliar accent.

'Listen to me, little Miss Innocent, Queenie says that to all her gals – you are no exception. I'll tell you this for a bag of nothing – there are three ways you can go: one, save that sweet maidenhead for your donkey of a husband and live with the consequences of slavery; two, find a convent – and live with the consequences of slavery; three, become your own mistress and learn, as I have done, to make a man pay. This, to me, is freedom, the best freedom a woman can have. I own my own money and no one owns me.' She slowly rose from the bed. 'Look at me.'

When I didn't she took hold of my chin and moved my face towards her. 'This is my gown, this skin given free when I was born. I have learned to wear it, be proud in it. Modesty is no whore's friend and it is the enemy of pleasure. So, I ask you again: do you have hair on other parts that Signor Florentini might attend to?'

I said nothing, so hard was the lump of rage in my throat. Cook always said I had a face as good as an open book that anyone could read without turning the pages.

Bethany laughed. 'I suggest you think about what I said. And this evening, join us for cards – but not with a face like that.'

Chapter Twenty-Two

Here lies Tully Truegood,
curvaceous and pretty.
She died an old maid,
More's the pity.

I determined to shake off my melancholy for it made a dull wit of me and I didn't like the notion that to Bethany I appeared a silly, half-grown gal, naive in the ways of the world. Hope was the only one I could confide in. I found her in her chamber, reading a letter.

She listened to all I had to say, then said, 'We should have been honest with you when you came to the fairy house, but Queenie, Mercy and me took you to our hearts and it seemed…'

'I don't want to live as Spiggot's wife,' I said. 'I don't want to go into a nunnery and that leaves…'

'The noblest profession of them all,' said Hope with a smile. 'Show me your wares, madam, and let us see if Bethany is right.'

I pulled my petticoats aside without a blush.

'Mmm,' said Hope. 'Yes, better by far that it all comes off, for you have pretty Venus mound and to lose it under such an ill-defined bush is, I think, a shame. The absence of it will add to your virginal qualities.'

She told her maid to prepare a bath.

With Hope I felt not the least worried to be naked, for she complimented me and assured me a thousand times that nakedness worn well is the height of elegance with which few gowns can compare. She gave me punch to drink and I think the alcohol helped in no small part to make me feel more confident about my body. I relished the warm water and Hope's sweet words.

It was only when I was dried and my skin smelled of rose water that Signor Florentini arrived. He said not a word while he methodically laid a cloth on the bed and arranged his razors and ointments neatly before him. Still not a word did he say as he indicated that I was to lie down on the bed. I did so, surprised to find that I did not feel at all shy in front of this man. He placed his small glasses on his nose, rolled up his sleeves and scrutinised me before sharpening his razors.

Hope looked on as Signor Florentini parted my legs until all of me was well exposed, then, taking his brush, covered my little garden with frothy soap. He gently moved the soft flesh of my purse with one hand while the razor in his other hand made sure that not one hair was left to spoil the view. The same he did with my legs and arms, and, rolling me over, parted the cheeks of my bottom. There was not a hair left on my body. He rubbed in ointments that were supposed to calm my senses, and didn't. When Signor Florentini was satisfied with his handiwork he moved his attention to my eyebrows. I was shocked that the plucking of such small hairs could cause such great discomfort. For all my begging him to stop, he carried on.

At last he stood back, studied me, and began to dress my hair. And what a palaver that was. He combed it out until – my oh my – it stood out as if I was a wild woman. He then powdered and pinned it moderately tight and by the time he was finished I had forgotten that I had no clothes on and was growing pleasantly comfortable with the sensation.

Signor Florentini took out a mirror for me to see his handiwork and at last spoke. His voice was so surprising that I thought someone else must be in the room. It was as high pitched as a young girl's, which sat oddly with his portly appearance.

'She is a beauty,' he said. 'If I may say so, far too much is made of clothes – a woman who is comfortable in her naked state is blessed indeed.'

Just when I was sure nothing more could be done to me, I was stood in the middle of the chamber while Signor Florentini blew powder all over me until I was china white. My nipples he dusted pink, as he did my cheeks, my lips he stained red. At last I was allowed to look in the long mirror. I could hardly believe the transformation. My face, which had been so overcast, now shone with light and there seemed to be more of it and it was better organised than when there had been thick eyebrows to cloud its expression. The white powder softened all blemishes and made one piece of me.

Signor Florentini packed his bag and, with a bow, left.

Hope found me a pair of stockings, shoes with embroidered heels and a small ruff made from silver lace that tied with a little black bow at the back of my neck. These were all I was allowed to put on.

'If I was a painter,' said Hope, 'I would make my fortune with your portrait.'

There came a knock on the chamber door.

Hope, taking my hand said, 'Quickly – go behind the screen and stay there until I call you. And then I want you to come out like a princess.'

The door opened and I heard Queenie come in with Bethany.

'If you can't find anyone for tonight,' Bethany said, 'you'll have to send out. Miss Jacqueline, I'm told, has some new girls in from the country.'

'I'm not using her,' said Queenie emphatically. 'All her girls are patched-up virgins. Hope, we are only hours away from this evening's entertainment and we are a virgin short. I'm at my wits' end. What would you suggest?'

'That you look no further than your own house, madam.'

I knew that if I didn't make my entrance then I never would have the courage to do it at all. I took a deep breath and, imagining myself to be wearing a gown fit for a queen, I appeared from behind the screen. For a moment there was silence.

It was Bethany who spoke.

'Signor Florentini's work, if I'm not mistaken,' she said. She walked round me. 'Flora had better see this, Queenie.'

'Oh, I can't be bothered with tonight's arrangements,' said Flora as she walked into the chamber. 'Surely you can...' She, too, stopped on seeing me.

If there was a moment to lose my confidence, this was it. No, I thought. I'd had quite enough of being left out of things and did not want to spend another night staring at a dead parrot.

'I could become quite jealous,' said Flora. 'Where did you get her from?'

'It's me,' I said. 'Tully.'

'Perfect,' said Flora and left the room.

'Can I come to this evening's soirée?' I asked.

'Yes,' said Queenie. 'Most definitely, yes.'

I spread my arms and span round and round, feeling myself to be as feathery as a bird. I heard Bethany's rich, dark laugh. I opened my eyes and found I had risen above the floor and knew if the room had no ceiling I could have touched the clouds.

Chapter Twenty-Three

Memory, I confess, is not always a faithful interpreter of the heart. It tends to forget all the little details in its haste to come to the point. But oh, my love – this night I can recall as if it has just happened. I go over it again and again, a charm to ward off the inevitable drudgery of greyness. A fog has descended over any hope of a future. Seven months is the most I can expect from this life – if I don't die giving birth or of jail fever then I have the hug of the hangman's rope to look forward to. If my child – our daughter – lives, Hope will bring her up. Memories are the greatest comforts I have. They keep the ghosts at bay, for even in the governor's house they're here a-plenty. The dead are often more vibrant than the living, unencumbered as they are by life, and only irritated by regret.

~

According to Queenie's wishes, I was to be dressed with virginal simplicity. The gown chosen for the purpose was a polonaise the colour of primroses, embroidered with white flowers. My stays were tight, so tied that my breasts sat unadorned, two soft peaches. The kerchief around my neck was of the lightest muslin, not hiding the fruit but making them appear all the riper.

It was Hope's idea that none of us should wear a hooped petticoat; without it, the fabric of my gown fell in a way that showed my figure to great effect.

When my maid had finished dressing me, I was told I must wait until called to the drawing room. Voices and music wafted up the stairs and I could not think what was causing the delay. In a vain attempt to calm myself, I walked back and forth, playing with my fan. I was trying to master it in an elegant manner when, without knocking, Mr Crease limped in. I stopped, quite prepared to feel the sting of his tongue. But as always, when I was certain he would say one thing, to my surprise he said another.

'Queenie tells me you rose off the floor this afternoon.'

I nodded and waited for the inevitable rebuke.

Instead he said, 'I will see you tomorrow morning in the long gallery.' He bowed. 'Goodnight.'

Shortly after, Hope came to fetch me. 'Are you ready?' she asked.

'Yes. Is Mercy in the party?'

'No, she is out. But don't worry, my ninny-not. Queenie has found you the most handsome gallant and I don't think you will be disappointed.'

The redecoration of the drawing room was complete and I was much taken by its elegance, by its windows in well-measured panes gazing lazily over the square. The chamber, lit with hundreds of candles, gave the occupants a golden glow. Music came from an antechamber, the doors of which were open, revealing three musicians seated with their backs to us.

Flora introduced me to her particular. The Earl of Wellborne was a grand man indeed, and older than I had imagined. He held a little glass to his eye and pronounced me delicious.

Bethany's gallant looked equally well bred and, like Bethany herself, not much interested in my arrival. He only once glanced in my direction before returning to concentrate on the charms of his new mistress. Hope's gallant was younger than the other two gentlemen and it was plain that he was already enamoured by her beauty. That left only an overdressed dandy wearing a wig that was parted in the middle, rising into horns on either side. He had the longest fingers and neck I had ever seen, was as tall as a willow tree and just as thin. His face was covered in patches.

I tried not to look disappointed when Queenie introduced me to Sir Henry Slater, for he appeared effeminate compared with the other gentlemen in the party.

'She is a picture, Queenie, I am sure,' he said, yawning. 'But not for me.' I was confused, for surely this was the man who was to bed me. 'I do like the gown, ma'am. No hoops – most radical.'

'Why, Sir Henry,' said Queenie, handing me a glass of champagne, 'I am flattered that you approve.'

She left me to talk to him.

'Are you come fresh from the country?' asked Sir Henry, taking a pinch of snuff.

'No, sir, I have always lived in London.'

'But you are really a virgin? Not just patched up for the night? My friend would not be impressed to find you have been overused.'

Queenie hastily returned to my side and swished Sir Henry's questions away with her fan.

'I don't deal in anything that isn't genuine, Sir Henry. Now, stop making the poor gal terrified.'

'Cards?' said Hope.

It was a suggestion that was greeted with approval by all except Flora, who said, 'I don't know – it will take the gentlemen's minds off pleasure. They will be more concerned with their wallets than our purses.'

There was laughter.

'Oh, what a wit,' said Sir Henry.

'Let us not gamble with money then,' said Hope.

'If we don't use money,' said the Earl, 'what, madam, would you suggest should be the token?'

'Why, clothes, sir,' said Hope. 'And the winner is the person who is wearing the most at the end of the game.'

This novel idea caused great delight and the Earl of Hatton put a twenty pound note on the table for the winner.

Sir Henry declined to play.

'No, by gad,' he said. 'I am on my way to my club and will leave you to your devices while I enjoy mine.'

He took my hand, kissed it and, making his excuses to Queenie, left.

I was somewhat puzzled and longed to ask Hope the meaning of his sudden departure. Had I done something to displease him? But she sat so far away at the other end of the card table that unless I had shouted she would not have heard me.

Queenie dealt the cards and, in all honesty, I was not paying much attention to the game, but I won the first hand while all round the table the other players were obliged to part with one item of clothing. When the clock struck ten I was the only one still dressed with a modicum of decency. Hope, on the other hand, was quite undone and Flora had on just her stockings. Bethany was enjoying the effect of her nakedness on the three gentlemen. Only their breeches remained to them.

'Enough,' said the Earl, kissing Flora. 'I have a need to be inside your pretty garden, my love. Miss Tully, as you are the least indecent of us all, this is your winnings.'

He handed me the twenty-pound note and left the drawing room, his arm round Flora's waist.

Bethany and her gallant were next, followed by Hope and her young stallion, who looked impatient to mount his ride.

Queenie glanced at the clock.

'Perhaps I should return to my chamber,' I said, gathering my clothes. 'I seem to have failed.'

'You're not thinking that Sir Henry was the gallant I had in mind for you?' she said. 'Why, my dear, he has no interest in the ladies unless they're dressed up like mollies. Come here.' She undid my stays, for which I was most grateful, and helped me back into my gown, tying it loosely and lowering my shift so that the two apples were well in view. 'Crease assured me he would be here,' she said, pouring more champagne. 'I can only think he has been detained.'

'Who?' I asked.

But before she could say another word, the footman announced Mr Avery Fitzjohn.

Chapter Twenty-Four

I hardly dared breathe, less by doing so the apparition would vanish. Was this my gallant? Could fate have dealt me such a winning card?

Queenie greeted him. 'Mr Fitzjohn, what a pleasure.'

He bowed most elegantly. 'Madam, I am sorry to be so unfashionably late. I have been dining with my brother, Lord Fitzjohn.'

'No matter, sir. It is a delight to see you. Let me introduce you to Miss Tully.'

I curtsied.

He studied me and then after a pause said, 'How very beautiful. Your taste, Queenie, is, as always, impeccable.'

'I'm glad Tully meets with your approval, Mr Fitzjohn.'

Shyness near overwhelmed me, for he was more handsome than when I had first seen him in the coffee house. His face in the candlelight was without fault as to its openness and kindness. For a moment we stood in awkward silence, more awkward on my part for he was taking me in and a quizzical look came over his features.

'I will leave you,' said Queenie. She wished him a goodnight and closed the door behind her.

'Have we met before?' Mr Fizjohn asked.

'No, sir,' I said.

'You remind me of someone, but it matters not.'

I didn't feel I could stay any longer being so scrutinised by him and, not knowing how to proceed, said, 'Shall I show you my chamber, sir?'

'After you,' he said, and with such a delicious smile curling across his lower lip, he picked up the bottle of champagne and two glasses.

Once in my chamber his eyes fell on Boozey.

'A very realistic, very *dead* parrot,' he said at last.

'Mercy gave him to me,' I said. 'He's stuffed – a new process, so I believe.'

I was regretting we hadn't stayed downstairs. At least in the drawing room there was music to divert us.

He poured the champagne and, sitting on the edge of the bed, handed me a glass and asked, 'Where were you born?'

'London,' I said, having no desire to tell him of Milk Street and Mr Truegood.

'Can you read?'

'Yes, sir,' I said.

'Are you a virgin?'

'Yes, sir,' I said again.

My hand was shaking and I dare not lift the glass to my lips less I spilt the champagne.

He gently took it from me and held it to my lips. I took a sip and he kissed me. Oh, such a tantalising kiss.

'More?' he said. I took another sip and he kissed me again, and I drank him in, amazed to feel my ache return with such uncontrollable force that my legs felt weak. He put his arms around me. 'I will be gentle,' he said, for I was shivering though it wasn't cold.

'I am just…' I said, and could not think what I was. 'I want this very much.'

His eyes danced as he took off my gown and undid my stays. I stood before him naked. He stroked my breasts, my stomach.

'You are exquisite,' he said and kissed my nipples. 'Skin as soft as peaches and just edible.'

He lay me down on the bed then stood and slowly undressed. I watched as each piece of his clothing came off. My, oh my, I swore that I never need eat again if I could feast my eyes upon him, for he seemed made to be the perfection of his sex. His chest was sun-kissed, his arms strong, his hands shaped like almonds. At last, he unbuttoned his breeches and the moment that had been the stuff of my fantasies had arrived. Before me, in an abundance of dark hair, stood a noble machine, upright and erect, the tip of it rose-red. I had indeed only ever seen poor specimens, for his was perfection.

He lay down beside me and, as he kissed me, my hand went tentatively to that pole of pleasure and found it velvet to the touch. He groaned and rolled me onto my back.

He sweetly caressed me, kissing every part until his hand found its way between my thighs, into my soft, wet purse. His fingers touched my quim then the fever by degrees overtook us. He parted my legs and, opening my purse, eased his way into the folds. Placing his machine on my tight slit, he made his entrance.

The pain was astonishing and I cried out.

Having gained a little headway, he said, 'Madam, it will hurt but with practice it will grow easier.'

'Don't stop,' I said. 'Please don't stop.'

Taken by a passion he advanced further, breaking all barriers that nature had put there against just such a glorious onslaught as this. Involuntarily, I cried out again and he pulled back a little and filled my mouth with his kisses. Such was the fire, so hard was his machine, that he was beyond the point of retreat and seemed resolved to conquer me completely. He gained the passage and I found myself battling with the oddest of sensations for, although it hurt prodigiously, there was much pleasure in his ownership of me. His majestic machine, stiff and hard, drove deeper and my body ached to receive more until I knew he had reached that moment in pleasure when all is a little death. Still inside me, and moving carefully so as not to lose his throne in these new-found places, he held me tightly.

'Forgive me for hurting you,' he said.

I, not realising it, had tears in my eyes. I assured him they were tears of joy.

'But I had all the pleasure,' he said, 'while you had only pain.'

I said it mattered not and kissed him, running my hands over his chest, kissing his neck, his cheek… and found, to my surprise, that he had again grown hard.

Without becoming separate, he moved me on top of him. Instinctively, I knew what my body needed and acted accordingly. Mercy had taught me well and I forgot all modesty. Regardless of the pain, I pressed down hard until I felt he was in my very womb. His hands returned to my hips and just when I thought I could take no more and would go wild, whatever was me, whatever was he, was lost in that perfect moment of rapture.

Chapter Twenty-Five

I woke in the morning to find Mr Fitzjohn had gone and on the pillow beside me was a small jewellery box. Inside were rose gold earrings set with red gems. I giggled, relishing the memories of the night. I had a lover, and the thought sent a delicious sensation through me. I was blessed indeed, for if Mr Truegood had had his way my virginity would have been long lost to the wine merchant and I would never have known such a tender, loving lord as my Mr Fitzjohn. Oh, what small steps can walk you into a different life. Avery. I said his name over and over again, even letting my imagination gallop ahead into forbidden places.

'Tully Fitzjohn,' I said to Boozey, laughing. He flew out of his cage and sat on the end of my bed, his head to one side.

I could smell Avery on my skin – such a delicious perfume – could feel where last night he had reigned in me. I sat up abruptly, wondering what hour it could be for it occurred to me that perhaps I had slept the whole morning, missing my appointment with Mr Crease. I dreaded to think what mood he would be in if that was the case.

Hope came in. Sweet Hope.

'Good morning,' she said, drawing back the shutters and letting in the lazy September light. 'Wasn't he the most hand-some gallant?'

'Oh my, oh my,' I said. 'Do you know, I think I could live with him inside me for ever.'

Hope laughed. 'Then you weren't disappointed?'

'No, he was perfect.'

I pulled back the bedclothes. The sheets were an unholy mess and standing felt peculiar for I was very sore. Hope said she had a remedy – which I was pleased to hear – and I quickly sat down again.

'You need to eat,' she said. 'All that lovemaking has worn you out.'

She ordered a breakfast of chocolate. We drank it and, while my maid bathed and dressed me, Hope told me about her gallant.

'Mr Fitzjohn left me these,' I said, showing her the earrings. With the eye of an expert she lifted them up to the light. I felt sure she was going to tell me they were paste and paint. 'I do not care a jot if they are made of papier mâché, they are most precious to me.'

'These, my love,' she said, holding the earrings out to me, 'are not fake. They are rubies and they look as if they cost a pretty penny.'

That they were real delighted me.

'I didn't think it was possible ever to feel as happy as this,' I said.

'Tully,' said Hope, 'don't fall in love with him.'

What could I say to that? Tell her the truth? That the kindling was laid the first time I saw you in the coffee house? That all you had to do was strike the flint?

'Remember, he is paying for your services and, in truth, is most probably married, or has a mistress, or just enjoys deflowering young virgins. Perhaps he is like Captain Spiggot and considers a girl over twenty worthless.'

I refused to give any thought to what Hope said. All those probabilities were distant clouds that had no right to be in such a blue sky as mine.

~

In the long gallery, Mr Crease stood looking out of the window. I said good morning, and without the bother of turning round he said, 'Did your groom speak to you at your wedding?'

'Yes. He said, "Marriage is murder."'

'Those are the precise words?'

'As far as I can remember.'

Still he stood with his back to me. 'Did you see his face?'

'No, we were both masked.'

I thought I would say more, and told him about the parson's wife. Mr Crease had the ability to be absent even though he was present and I wouldn't have been surprised to find that I had been talking to the wall. When I'd finished, he turned round.

'Interesting,' he said.

'What has happened to Mr Truegood?' I asked. 'I mean, has he been buried?'

'In a debtor's grave at the Fleet,' said Mr Crease. 'And with him is the truth of your marriage.'

'What do you mean?'

'I mean that there appears to be no record of it.'

'Then without a record Spiggot has no right to claim me as his wife.'

'Quite. Shall we start?'

That morning, everything Mr Crease asked of me I managed with ease. I rose off the ground again and again, not very high but enough to make an impression and, by degrees, I could hold it and stay there. At three o'clock, when we finished, Mr Crease said Queenie wanted to talk to me.

I remember wondering, as I went down the stairs, if she would tell me that tonight I would be expected to entertain another gentleman. The thought concerned me much but I needn't have worried – not at that time, at least.

Queenie informed me that I would be dining with Mr Fitzjohn in my chamber that night and my heart gave a skip of delight.

I curtsied, and was on the point of leaving when she said, 'Tully, you should congratulate yourself, for you have proved a great success with the young gentleman.'

I passed the rest of the day in the most glorious anticipation which, in itself, is an hors d'oeuvre to the main dish of love. I was quite unprepared when Avery arrived early. After locking my chamber door behind him, he took me in his arms and kissed me with unadulterated passion. I think he must have been dining all day on the same dish of longing as me. My petticoat and shift were pushed aside and, finding that I was moist, he dispensed with the inconvenience of undressing me, only unpinning my kerchief and gown, and swiftly loosening my stays so that my breasts were his to ravish. He kissed them until I started to tremble. He, too, was now overcome with agitation. His breeches were readily undone and I could soon feel the pole of him urgently burrow deep into the soft folds of me. He lifted me and I wrapped my legs around his thighs against his losing possession of me, then he pressed me against the wall and such was the force of him and such was my desire to own him once more that we both exploded together and tumbled onto the floor in a quantity of unwanted fabric. I burst out laughing at the swiftness of an act that had brought such pleasure.

I tried to make myself decent when our supper was brought to us, but Avery insisted that he would serve it himself.

Once more locking the chamber door, he said, 'We will eat, but I would prefer to look at you naked rather than in your gown, which detracts from your beauty.'

I stood and felt the liquor of him run down my thighs while he disentangled me from my clothes.

'Sir,' I said, 'it is surely only correct that you do the same.'

He took off his shirt, breeches, stockings and shoes, and stood before me. The sight of him made my body melt. I sighed, for never had a dish been more to my liking. He was so finely made, I was enchanted with my good fortune and like an unguarded fool said so. He ate with a good appetite and drank to my health. I was too full of longing to taste much and pushed away my plate.

'I think I could feast on you alone,' I said.

'Then, now, madam,' he said, 'I will be the dessert.'

Chapter Twenty-Six

At the beginning, we made love every night and let our bodies speak for us. Your caresses were love poems enough, my kisses sonnets to keep you satisfied. The truth of who I was, who you were, was lost in the flattery of lovers' words. My lie was that I never told you the truth. Did I believe you would not be interested? Or that it might devalue the mystery of me? It would have wounded my pride to call Ralph Spiggot my husband, but I was as certain as Bow Bells that I would soon be free of him. Whores are paid to be vessels filled with false promises and flowering lies. Truth was the last thing you needed to take to bed with you.

What little you told me seemed unrelated to the man who held me firm in his arms. Perhaps I was a coward not to question you further when you told me about your life in Paris, but I was a shallow fool who didn't want to hear your truth. I asked about frippery and fashion, only wanting to hear a fairy tale.

Avery had come to an arrangement with Queenie whereby I would be his particular while he was in London. In short, he paid handsomely for me to be his alone for the duration of his stay. I didn't think about the implications of this, only relished the notion that Avery wanted no one else to have me. For my part, I was all too eager to kneel at Venus's altar and

I told myself that if I had Avery's love – for three weeks, two weeks or even one – it would be enough and I could live the rest of my life on it. I see now I knew little of life's cruel blade.

It had been a week since we first met. Avery had not spent one night away from me, and I was as lovesick as any fool could be. I remember we lay on the floor by the fire, both of us naked, both of us unable to say what was truly in our hearts.

That day, Mr Crease had told me Captain Spiggot was bringing his lawyer to the fairy house, determined to claim me as his wife. I couldn't tell Avery. I didn't want anything so dirty to destroy the innocence we had. It sounds foolish but in all that we did, all that we enjoyed, there was a purity to it. To me, at least, it was simple: I loved him.

He suddenly said, 'You know, it is a heavy burden to carry a great name, one that you feel honour-bound to defend from stain.'

Having no name, great or otherwise to defend, I knew not how to respond and filled the silence with kisses. Then, quite unexpectedly, for he had never taken me out, he asked if I would accompany him to the theatre.

Such was my excitement the next day, it took all my will-power to concentrate on Mr Crease's instruction.

'Great seers...' He clicked his fingers. 'Are you listening?'

'Yes, yes, I am.'

'Great seers, and by that I mean mighty ones, can borrow the sight, but not the hearing, of an animal. There are advantages to this, for the animal can see what the seer should not.'

He said it so emphatically that I had no problem accepting it to be true and I agreed that would be a useful gift. It occurred to me that with the help of an obliging animal, I would be able to see Captain Spiggot, for that day he and his lawyer were to call on Queenie.

'But alas,' I said, 'my gifts are more humble.'

I was pleased with my reply for I hadn't used the word 'impossible', which more accurately described what I thought.

'Do you really believe it?' said Mr Crease, his painted eyes peering at me.

'Yes.' I hesitated. 'How is such a feat brought about?' I asked.

'Call Shadow,' said Mr Crease.

I did, and the little dog trotted in.

'Now ask to borrow his sight.'

Not wishing to incur Mr Crease's wrath, I knelt, and, taking the dear creature in my arms, whispered, 'May I borrow your eyes when Captain Spiggot comes to call?'

At twelve o'clock on the dot, Mr Crease stopped and called Shadow to him.

'I wish you would leave him here,' I said.

'I think he will be of more use to you in the parlour,' said Mr Crease, then added that he was going to lock me in the long gallery for my safety.

I sat down to wait, and in no small part to dream about my first night out with Avery. I had never been to the theatre – what an interior life I had led. I must have fallen asleep for I dreamed I was downstairs in the parlour. There was no colour to this dream. Two gentlemen were sat before me. One I recognised as Mr Quibble. He was dressed in a new suit of clothes, dark, with silver buckles on his shoes. It was not a comforting sight and his presence confirmed Queenie's suspicions of his purpose for visiting us in Milk Street. The other gentleman had a scar that ran down his right cheek from his eyelid in such a manner that the lid was pulled into a slant, giving his expression a permanent sneer. He sat with his riding boots stretched out before him, his hands stuffed nonchalantly into the pockets of his breeches. Mr Quibble took the lead, his tongue flicking back and forth, though I could hear not a word he or anyone said and could only guess what they were by the gestures they used.

This was the strangest of dreams for it had a logical order to it which none of my dreams ever possessed. I was able to study the young man with the scar and, as I did, from the folds of his red coat a boy emerged. His face, though unblemished, was already etched with the same cruelty that disfigured his older self even more than his scar. This boy appeared to be made of flame rather than flesh. Seeing Shadow, a look of glee spread across his features and he rushed at the dog, and must have pulled him by the tail for my vision abruptly shuddered. Perhaps it was that the young man caught a glimmer of the child he once was for something sparked his fury. I was quite unprepared for what happened next. His foot came towards me, the boy pulled a knife, and boy and dog found ourselves thrown across the chamber, the boy becoming dust, I descending into a sticky blankness that seemed to have glued my eyes shut.

Far off I could hear Mercy talking to me but still I could not open them. I woke to find her kneeling beside me, Mr Crease behind her.

'What is wrong with her?' Mercy's voice was trembling.

'Tully,' said Mr Crease. 'Tully, can you see me?'

I forced my eyes open and Mercy gasped.

Of course I could see him. I sat up, puzzled at their concern.

'Has the captain gone?' I asked.

'Yes,' said Mr Crease.

'I've been asleep,' I said. 'I had the strangest of dreams.'

'Can you see us clearly?' he asked.

'Look at her eyes,' said Mercy. 'I think you're working her too hard, Mr Crease.'

'What did my husband say?' I asked.

'Little of importance,' said Mr Crease.

Mercy took me to my chamber and I fell asleep again for my eyes felt better closed than open.

When I woke, Mr Crease and Queenie were looking down at me.

'Oh Lord,' said Queenie.

'They will recover,' said Mr Crease.

'Before Mr Fitzjohn arrives?' asked Queenie.

'What's wrong?' I said, and went to the mirror.

I looked as if I were dead. My pupils were white, all colour drained from them.

'What did you see, Tully?' ask Mr Crease.

'I dreamed that Mr Quibble came with the young gentleman and out of the folds of that gentleman's coat appeared a boy.'

'There was no boy,' said Queenie.

She sounded relieved and I would have been content to leave it there but Mr Crease said, 'Describe the young gentleman.'

'He had a scar down the side of his face. He stood up when he saw his younger self and kicked me – I mean Shadow – into darkness.'

Queenie looked frightened. 'Damn you, Crease. What black arts are you teaching?'

She made to leave but Mr Crease took hold of her arm.

'Wait,' he said. 'Tell her what Spiggot looked like.'

As Queenie described Captain Spiggot to me – the riding boots and the red coat – I caught sight of my ghost eyes in the mirror. My soul shook. The burden of my gift truly horrified me.

Chapter Twenty-Seven

Mr Crease concocted a potion. He tilted my head back and applied droplets to my eyes, and gradually the colour returned to my pupils.

'Please, sir,' I said to him, 'take this curse from me. I don't want it. Please, I beg of you, for I believe you have the power to do it.'

'I don't, Tully.'

'But these gifts, as you call them, are beyond my control. What if something of this nature should happen when I'm with Avery? He would think me a witch.'

'I told you long ago that you were no hen-hearted girl. Don't become one now.'

'What can I do?' I said. 'It's a curse, not a gift. It belongs to the devil.' Tears irritated my eyes and I gave way to them.

'I have been endeavouring,' said Mr Crease, 'to teach you how and when to use your second sight. But half the time your mind is elsewhere.

Perhaps, Tully, if you took a little more instruction you would find yourself better prepared for these events. Instead of them ruling you, you might have the wit to be their mistress.'

There was no sentimentality to Mr Crease, no softness in his approach.

I tried to recover myself.

'What do you intend to do?' he said. 'Hide your talents away for the rest of your life, pretend you're like everyone else? That way, madam, lies Bedlam.'

I took a deep breath. 'My husband,' I said, recalling all I had seen, 'sat with his legs stretched out and his hands stuffed in the pockets of his breeches. A violent-tempered, cruel man. Mr Quibble did most of the talking until the captain fell into a rage.'

'That is exactly right. Spiggot said that he spoke to you before the service, that he told you, "Marriage is murder."'

I nodded. 'I will never be persuaded to go anywhere near him. Can I be unmarried?' I asked.

'With difficulty. Your salvation lies in the power that has been given to you.'

'Salvation from what? From being the captain's wife? From being a whore?'

'I have no opinion on the profession. There is joy to be found in our sexual nature and all its manifestations. I have no argument with my conscience, no God to find me wanting. That is the prerogative of mankind – to be cursed with an unforgiving creator.'

He left me and I sat for the rest of the afternoon without moving, my mind oppressed by my thoughts.

~

Queenie had wanted me to look striking that night and I had a new gown for the occasion. By the time my maid and Signor Florentini had finished with me, it was time to leave. Queenie came to inspect to me.

'You are a credit to my house, Tully,' she said. 'Every eye in the theatre will be not on the players, but on you.'

'Miss Tully,' said Signor Florentini in his extraordinary, high-pitched voice, 'do you not want to see what you look like?'

'No,' I said. I couldn't think about my appearance. Suddenly, I had become aware of the clock ticking away precious hours and, in a matter of days, Avery would be gone. What then? The thought of taking another lover was abhorrent to me. 'Queenie, what will happen when Avery leaves London?' I asked.

'I will find you another gentleman.'

'And if I don't want one?'

'Then, my dear,' she said, and her voice hardened, 'there is always your husband, who seems eager to claim you. I need good whores, Tully, not reluctant girls. Now, smile, be enchanting – remember, you represent the fairy house.'

A carriage was waiting outside. Ned Bird, dressed in good clothes, opened the door and helped me in. His instructions were that he was not to leave me. Only when the horse set off did I feel a modicum of the childish thrill that a new adventure brings. I told myself not to think about Avery's departure, but to concentrate on the moment. If I wanted a reminder of the fate of girls who were not under the roof of a good madam then I only had to glance out of the carriage window. Covent Garden ladies were awake for business, brightly coloured fishes swimming alongside sharks.

The play, for the play was the thing, was a production of *Liars and Lovers*, which I now see was very apt. Avery greeted me with a bow. He was somewhat surprised to see Ned Bird.

'Do you need a bodyguard, Tully?' he asked, lifting my hand to his lips. 'I promise I won't kidnap you.'

'I don't think I'd mind if you did, sir,' I said.

'What is he protecting you from?'

'Myself.'

He looked so handsome with his clothes on. He wore a dark velvet coat with embroidery on the front, a duck-egg blue waistcoat, and a white stock at his neck. I felt proud to be with him. I knew we made a striking couple by the glances that came our way. My gown was far from being brassy and was more tasteful than many others. Some ladies wore their wigs high and their faces white, but when they smiled their teeth were yellow.

Avery bowed to the many acquaintances who greeted him but never stopped long enough for the inconvenience of introductions. He took me to a box that overlooked the auditorium and seemed designed not so much for one to see the play, but more to see the boxes opposite. Each box gave a miniature performance of its own; the fashionable gentlemen perched and pecked like cockerels, the ladies, painted parrots, fluffed out their feathers in mannered responses. Avery took my hand, squeezed it, and asked if I was comfortable.

'You look pale,' he whispered, his lips brushing my neck.

'I've never been to the theatre before,' I told him.

'You have already conquered it for you outshine all the fashionable ladies here. Tomorrow they will, no doubt, have their hairdressers copy your style.'

I laughed and, having improved the use of my fan, hid my blushes behind it. Avery sat close by me, his arm resting on the back of my chair. When the play started the lights stayed as bright in the auditorium as they were on stage – in fact, the whole place was so ablaze with candlelight that it was an invitation for the audience to continue talking. The actors were left to battle over the noise of London gossip.

I had been following the performance on stage so it was only at the interval that I realised, to my alarm, that we were being scrutinised by the ladies and gentlemen in the boxes opposite. At that moment, the door to ours burst open without so much as a knock and in came an incoherent drunk. His face was badly scarred by smallpox, his manners were appalling, and the only thing that could be said in his favour was he was exceedingly well dressed.

'So, this is your betrothed, what?' he said to Avery.

Avery's sweet expression changed to one of anger. 'Frederick,' said Avery.

Frederick helped himself to a glass of wine.

'Rather beautiful, by gad. I suppose she doesn't understand a word of English. I thought she was too grand to come over here and visit us *rosbif.*'

He laughed at his own joke and, having finished one glass of wine, helped himself to another. ''Ave you solved the leetle problem with your forthcoming nuptials?' he said, enunciating each word with an affected French accent.

Nuptials? I felt as if all the breath had been knocked out of me.

'The only way to make these frogs understand is to speak slowly,' continued his lordship.

'You're drunk, Frederick,' said Avery. Everything in him had tightened.

'I'll be as drunk as I want. I don't much care for sobriety, brother. Introduce us.'

The audience had become quieter and I suspected that we were the object of their interest.

'Frederick, may I introduce Miss Tully Truegood. Tully, my half-brother, Lord Frederick Fitzjohn.'

Lord Fitzjohn bowed unsteadily and would have fallen had the footman not caught him in time. 'Truegood? Not French then?'

I could see that Avery was on the point of losing his temper and I quickly said, 'Do you enjoy the theatre, Lord Fitzjohn?'

'Can't stand it,' he said. 'Makes me legs itch. The only good thing about it is you see who's here and if there's any new blood worth a mention. This season the place is full of horse-faced women. Have you noticed? You're the only beauty in the place, by gad, but, I'll wager you're not the bride-to-be.'

The door to our box opened again. I had never imagined that I would be so pleased to see Sir Henry Slater.

'Fitzjohn,' said Sir Henry to Lord Fitzjohn. 'I have been looking for you.' He took his lordship's arm. 'Come now.'

Lord Fitzjohn pulled his arm away. 'Slater, see what I've found: my brother being a naughty boy. Avery, what would the countess's family say if they knew you were entertaining this gorgeous jade? What whorehouse are you from, you delicious creature?'

I was caught completely off guard. 'From Queenie Gibbs' fairy house, sir.'

'Are you, by gad. Well, brother, when you've tired of the trollop...'

This time, it was Ned Bird who came to the rescue and did what Sir Henry had so remarkably failed to do. Lord Frederick

Fitzjohn was politely and firmly removed from the box, but the evening was ruined. I felt certain the whole audience had heard our conversation and now knew exactly who I was: a harlot from the whorehouse.

Chapter Twenty-Eight

I tried to pay attention to the play but all I could think was that Hope was right – I should have kept my heart locked up. Avery was engaged to be married and I felt as if all of me had come to a stop. There was a heaviness to my heart that I could not repress. As I watched the players, each actor seemed to be mocking me with his lines. I bit the inside of my cheek and tried to recover myself.

Avery no longer rested his arm on my chair, but sat upright and stiff. I didn't want to be in the theatre, not with every eye in the audience gazing in our direction.

I stood and, hoping my voice didn't give away my anxieties, said, 'Please excuse me, sir, I need some fresh air.'

Before he could answer, I left the box, followed by Ned Bird.

'Are you unwell, Miss Tully?' he said.

'No. I want to go home now.'

Avery came down the stairs after me and we stood awkwardly together on the steps of the theatre while Ned hurried off to find the carriage.

'I sincerely apologise,' said Avery. 'Frederick had no right to talk to you like that. He is an unmitigated fool.'

'It is of no consequence,' I replied. Then, unable to keep my jealousy in check, it bolted towards the precipice. 'Why did you not tell me you were betrothed?'

'It is my business and doesn't concern you. I will be gone soon enough and – '

I didn't let him finish. 'Do you love her, this countess?'

'No gentleman marries for love.'

'Then why marry at all?' I asked.

'Frederick has near ruined our family. I want my father's name to be restored to its rightful place.'

'I take it the countess is rich?'

'Yes, very.'

'And you're not?'

'Madam, I have yet to make my fortune, but the countess's dowry will enable me to rebuild my family's estate.'

It was the first time he had spoken to me with such a cold edge to his voice.

'I have no name of any value,' I said, 'so I cannot comment, though it seems to me that your business is all about property. And if a wife is of no more value to her husband than a sideboard, I think I would prefer to be a whore. At least there's some honesty in it.'

'Tully, let's not argue – I will be leaving in a few days. My anger is with the situation I find myself in, it has nothing to do with you. Will you not at least see the play out?'

Great was my anxiety to be gone and preferably never see him again.

'No,' I said.

Oh, how I hate tears, especially ones that are gaining the better of me, and I dispute anyone who says that they make a girl look interesting or pretty.

'Please dry your eyes,' he said, 'and return with me to the box.'

I curtsied, and without another word went out to the

carriage. Ned helped me in and we set off, a footman walking behind us and a lamp boy in front. I didn't look back.

By the time we reached the fairy house, I just wanted the solitude of my own chamber.

'Tully,' called Queenie, as I ran up the stairs. 'What is the meaning of this? Where is Mr Fitzjohn?'

I didn't reply and nearly fell over Mercy as she came out of her chamber.

'What brings you back so soon?' she said. She looked over my shoulder. 'Alone?'

The tears that I thought I had mastered overcame me at last. 'I never want to see him again,' I sobbed.

Mercy hurried me into her chamber. 'What happened? Did he hurt you?'

'Yes, he broke my heart. He is to marry a countess and his wretched brother called me a whore. All those grand ladies and gentlemen heard him.'

'I doubt that.' She wrapped me in her arms and I clung to her. 'Tully, you really must try not to fall in love so readily. Hush now,' she said, and kissed me tenderly.

'It was simple when I loved you. I wish we could be like that again.'

'Would you mind telling me what happened, Tully?' Queenie came into the chamber, her voice a sharpened knife. 'For there must be some reasonable explanation for your behaviour.'

I told her, and even as I said the words they seemed feeble.

'Let me be sure that I heard this correctly: you were insulted by Mr Fitzjohn's brother who called you a whore?'

'Yes, madam.'

'You found out that Mr Fitzjohn is engaged to be married?'

'Yes, and…'

'And instead of holding your head up high and showing London society the calibre of Queenie Gibbs' gals, you ran away. Who are you, pray tell me, to judge a gentleman who is paying handsomely for your services? Of course Avery Fitzjohn is engaged, you foolish, foolish – ' she slapped me across the face ' – numbskull!'

I had never seen her like this. She looked as if she could kill me, she was so angry. Mercy tried to stop her but Queenie's temper, once lost, was unrestrained.

'Do you wish to remain at the fairy house? Or have you changed your mind?' she said, hitting me with her fan. 'What do you think we provide here? Afternoon tea?' Her fan snapped as she hit me again. 'Your job is to pleasure your client, not to abandon him at the theatre.' My tears were making me shudder. 'He didn't pay for a new gown in order for you to ridicule him, and make me look a fool. I should have followed my instinct and left you at Milk Street.' She threw the broken fan at me.

'Queenie.' Unnoticed, Mr Crease had come in. He closed the door. 'Queenie – quiet.' He said it in a manner that burst the boil of her rage. 'Mr Fitzjohn is downstairs.'

'We should offer him Bethany's services by way of compensation,' said Queenie.

'He is adamant – he wants to see Tully.'

'Then she'd better go and apologise for her behaviour.'

I caught a glimpse of myself in the glass. I was shaking and my face was red and blotchy.

'Madam,' said Mr Crease to Queenie, 'would you leave this to me?'

Mercy took Queenie's arm and led her from the room.

'Sit,' said Mr Crease. 'And close your eyes.' I did, and when

I opened them again I felt completely calm, and my face had nothing to show where Queenie's rage had been.

'Come,' said Mr Crease. 'We are to go downstairs.'

It was on the landing that a thought came to me.

'Mr Crease,' I said, 'Mrs Coker gave me a pearl hand.' He stopped and looked at me with his closed, painted eyes. 'I don't know what it is but I'm certain that I should.'

'It will make a man reach the point beyond reason by the use of your hand on his machine. It might just be your redemption tonight.'

I stood outside the drawing room, my heart beating, the words, 'I am most humbly sorry,' on my lips, but the moment I entered, Avery came to me.

'You are full of passion,' he said, putting his arms round me. 'Your fire makes me seem cold, but I am not.'

'Forgive me, sir. I should have behaved with more decorum,' I said.

'Why should you?' he said. 'As I walked here I thought how I would feel if I found out that you were married. I was shocked by the outrage such a thought caused me.'

All my longing for him returned. I could no more be angry with him than with autumn for taking summer from us. I took his hand and led him to my chamber. We embraced as if it would be our last. He slipped me out of my petticoat and shift and took possession of me with such care that I reached that moment when all is lost and all is found again.

We fell asleep in each other's arms. I woke as dawn was breaking and, gently, I moved so that I might feast my eyes on his body. His sweet sugar stick was semi-hard, its head rising from its white shaft, his dark hair a forest curling round two baubles. As he slept I touched him and found that my fingers knew what was needed, where to press and where to release. There was excitement in seeing the effect my hand had on him for he became hard, so hard. He stirred.

'Tully,' he groaned. 'Oh, Tully.'

From his tip burst forth the dew of him and, having never tasted such liquor as this, I put my lips to it and kissed the moisture from him, salty and delicious.

He moaned again and, my hand never leaving that majestic machine, soon found the harmony of him and moved accordingly, my ache becoming desperate as my hand slid up and down, up and down until he exploded, crying out, a stream of white liquid shooting from him in a glorious arc.

In the peace that followed he whispered, 'Who taught you to do that?'

'No one. It was a wish.'

He looked puzzled.

'Did I do anything wrong?'

He laughed. 'Oh, Tully,' he said. 'You overwhelm me.'

Chapter Twenty-Nine

In those hectic days before the masquerade ball, I avoided Queenie. Her anger had sent a chill through me and I knew that if I let her down again I would be thrown out and forced to make my living on the streets. I had little sympathy from Bethany or Flora. I had never managed to make any headway with either of them. Both saw themselves as being at the top of their profession and me as nothing more than a silly girl. Due to my fall from Queenie's favour they felt free to unleash their razor-sharp tongues and their words cut deep.

'What will happen to Miss Prissy when Mr Fitzjohn leaves?' mocked Bethany.

'The streets,' said Flora. 'I can't imagine any good reason for keeping an unwilling whore.'

I had not the confidence to see that in part this taunting was brought on by jealousy.

I was sure that if I didn't prove myself with Mr Crease then their grim prediction would be fulfilled and I concentrated on my work as I hadn't done before. Mr Crease had a swing rigged up in the ballroom, far too high off the ground for me to reach.

'You will swing back and forth,' he said, 'and when I give the command, you will jump off the swing and float in mid-air.'

It was a truly incredible thought. I wanted to say, 'So that will be my end,' but Mr Crease had his painted eyes firm upon me.

'It will be difficult in all these petticoats,' I said.

'I suggest you take them off and rehearse in your shift and bare feet.'

I knew enough not to argue. I did as I was told.

'Good,' he said. 'I will leave you to practise.'

'But how do I reach the thing?'

'Ads bleed. You can rise off the ground, can you not? You will learn to rise to the height of the swing, that is all. Time is pressing, madam.'

By the following day I had only managed to rise a few feet at a time. Then I remembered the stairs at Milk Street that I had named the Coffin-Maker and Dead Drunk, and how I had once thrown myself down them and stopped before crashing to the floor. Why hadn't I ever tried to fly again? Because Cook had told me it was impossible. Perhaps Mr Crease was right. I believed it was impossible and impossible it became. I was contemplating this when Flora wandered into the ballroom.

'What are you doing?' she said.

I explained.

'Tish tosh,' she said. 'That is too rich.' She held her stays for she was laughing so much. 'You, oh fie, that is priceless, so it is. Really Mr Crease should know better. He might be able to do it – after all, he is extraordinary. But you... you are dull-witted and ordinary.'

Still giggling, she walked away across the ballroom. I felt a lump of rage so tight in my throat that I thought I might choke. While her back was turned from me, I closed my eyes and willed myself to rise from the floor, willed myself to be seated on the swing.

'This ballroom is dusty,' said Flora. 'Perhaps you would be better employed sweeping the...Tully?'

It was not elegantly done but I had mastered the feat. I had risen, grabbed hold of the seat of the swing and pulled myself on to it.

When Flora saw me she let out a scream which brought Mr Crease to the ballroom.

'She hasn't fallen?' he said.

Flora, her hand over her mouth, pointed up at me.

'Perfect,' said Mr Crease. 'Now jump.'

But first I wanted to acquaint myself with the sensation of being up so high and was surprised to find I enjoyed it. In fact, I would say it gave me courage to see Flora so small beneath me. I leaned back and leaned forward and by degrees the swing moved.

'When you are ready, jump,' said Mr Crease.

'No!' said Flora. 'No, Mr Crease, she will break every bone in her body.'

'What's going on?' Queenie had entered the gallery.

'Mr Crease wants Tully to jump. It's insane.'

Queenie looked unimpressed. I wanted so badly for Queenie to forgive me that I slid from the swing and fell like a stone to be caught by Mr Crease.

'That won't do,' said Queenie and turned to leave. 'Flora, your seamstress is downstairs.'

After that I practised every day, all day. I swung back and forth, a pendulum marking the passing hours until the time I would have to perform in public. Elevation was no trouble; the descent ruined the effect.

It was the nights that I secretly longed for. They belonged to Avery and Avery alone. We never talked of the countess again and, in those few days left to us, I tried and failed to harden my soft heart to the inevitable loss of him. I wonder how many lovers have longed to hold back time. I would have paid with my soul to stop the hands of the clock. I decided to give him a parting gift, something solid, and as time was so much on my mind I thought of giving him a pocket watch. Still owning the twenty pound note I'd won at cards, I asked Mercy if she would find one for me and have it engraved.

'You noodle,' she said. 'He is supposed to buy you gifts, not the other way round.'

'Nevertheless, would you do it for me?'

Mercy took the money. 'What should be the inscription?'

'"To Avery Fitzjohn from Tully".'

'You mean Tully Truegood,' said Mercy.

'No,' I said. 'Just Tully.'

~

The fairy house, which up to then had been only partially open, now showed itself in all its glory. The dust sheets were removed, folded and put away, chambers aired, beds fumigated against bugs, traps put down for rats. The stairs were polished and everything gleamed. On the ground floor, a vista of rooms opened into each other and beyond them was the ballroom, painted in a lush red with mirrors to reflect the dancers. At one end was a balcony where the musicians practised. Carpenters came and went, furniture arrived from Chippendale and Hepplewhite; food in vast quantities was delivered to the kitchen. An endless procession of tailors and dressmakers, weighed down by rolls of fabric and heavy books with all the latest fashions from the continent, passed through the hall.

Flora and Bethany virtually locked themselves away with their dressmakers to discuss the latest modes from Paris, how their hair should be coiffed and the quality of the masks they were to wear. All the while Queenie sat in her rookery with Mr Pouch, going over the books, making sure that nothing had been forgotten.

We were not the only house in the new squares of London to be engaged in feverish activity, for every butler and house-keeper worth their salt was preparing for the arrival of their master and mistress. The small, powerful elite of fashion-able London was returning from draughty estates and leaky country seats before the snows imprisoned them in perpetual boredom.

The invitations to the masquerade ball had been sent out long before. Two hundred people were expected. This was to be the first ball of the season.

'The most sought-after ticket in London,' so a newspaper reported, much to Queenie's delight. 'A masked ball always brings out the most extravagant fashions,' she read.

On the afternoon of the masquerade ball Queenie insisted that we all rested to look fresh. The house had never been so full of young gals, each personally selected by Queenie for their particular services, each obliged to sign a document saying that they would not get drunk and that they would abide by the rules of the house.

I went to my chamber, and was dozing a little when there was a knock at the door. To my surprise Avery came in.

I ran to him and threw my arms round his neck and kissed him.

'What are you doing here so early?'

He kissed me but at the same time untangled himself. I

looked into his face and asked if something had happened, for all the light-heartedness of him had gone.

'I must return to Paris,' he said. 'The coach leaves in an hour. I am sorry, Tully, I will not be able to attend the ball.'

'No,' I said, 'no, you must come! You can't be leaving, not tonight.' Then I stopped for it occurred to me perhaps an account of the incident at the theatre had found its way to the countess's family. 'Surely you could wait one more night?'

'It's impossible, my sweet. But I didn't want to leave without seeing you.' He hesitated. 'I wanted to tell you…' He stopped, closed his eyes and, shaking his head, said, 'It's of little consequence.'

'What's troubling you, sir?' I asked.

'You,' he said. 'You trouble me.'

'Have I done something to displease you?'

'No. Far from it.'

'Then what?'

'I cannot tolerate the idea of you being with another man and yet I can do nothing about it. I have not the resources to keep you. If I could, I would but…' He stopped. 'I thought when I met you that we… that I…'

'You are to be married, sir,' I reminded him.

He looked wretched. 'Yes, but not yet.'

I didn't know what to say. I knew what fabric must feel like when it is torn. But nothing, I told myself must overshadow the evening, even though my lover had chosen now, of all times, to tell me of his departure.

I pulled away. 'I thank you for your courtesy, sir,' I said, and curtsied, keeping my eyes to the floor.

And before I could say another word the door had closed

abruptly behind him and I was left with a heart less whole than it had been a few minutes earlier.

I needed my mind to be distracted before the reality of his going destroyed me. I knocked on the door of Mercy's chamber. She was looking at herself in the mirror. Signor Florentini had cut off all her hair.

'Radical, isn't it?' said Mercy. 'What do you think?'

'It suits you.'

She looked at me in the serious way she had. I bit my cheek, refusing to give in to tears. She took me in her arms and kissed me.

'Mr Fitzjohn has left, hasn't he?' she said.

I nodded. 'Tell me,' I said, 'do you know what it's like? Have you ever loved anyone?'

'Yes. I have – I do. But I would be grateful if you didn't tell Queenie.'

'I won't,' I said. 'Who is it?'

'Mofty, of course. I would willingly give up this game to be with her. There. You see, it's not only you who has a heart to lose.'

'Kiss me again and hold me,' I said.

A little later, her maid came to dress her.

'What is your costume?' Mercy asked me.

'A surprising one,' I said.

'I heard Mr Crease tell Queenie you are to be the star of tonight's entertainment.'

'I think not,' I said and was about to return to my chamber when Mercy said, 'Wait, I have something for you, although now it is sadly mistimed.' She handed me a small package. 'I thought it should be simple,' she said.

The pocket watch was plain in design but when I opened

it, I could see the cogs and small wheels turn and tick. It was engraved as I had requested. Mercy said, 'It looks a little odd without your surname.'

I clicked the watch shut. 'No, it's perfect,' I said.

I was saved from my misery by Signor Florentini. He came to my chamber, dressed my hair and painted my face. He hardly spoke and I was not in the mood for words. But he spent his time on me and, when at last he gave me the glass, I was surprised. My face looked more composed than it had before and I even saw a shimmer of beauty but whether it was me or Signor Florentini's workmanship, I couldn't say.

At seven o'clock, Mr Crease came to my chamber followed by a parade of footmen, one carrying a tray of champagne and two glasses, the others an assortment of boxes. Mr Crease opened a box.

'Put her in this,' he said to my maid, handing her a garment of cream gossamer that was more thistledown than fabric.

The bodice and skirts were one garment, worn without panniers or stays, made of muslin embroidered with small gold dots. My maid laced the flimsy gown tight at the back and at the front it was cut low so that that my breasts could all but be seen, but were beguilingly hidden behind a silk gauze. From another box came slippers of supple, gilded leather with ribbons that crossed-laced round my ankles.

When Mr Crease was satisfied, he ordered the maid out of the room and told me to concentrate, as I had in our rehearsals, on lifting myself from the floor. I did so and felt myself to be spinning. Once more grounded, I discovered that attached to my back were two tiny iridescent wings. Finally, he put his hands on my face and when he removed them I was wearing a simple mask with no ribbons to keep it in place. I looked in the glass again and saw an extraordinary being of Mr Crease's creation. What had I to fear? This was not me, this was not my face that so boldly stared back from the glass. This was a sprite of pleasure, a nymph of passion that not even gravity had the power to control. All care fell away and it seemed that Avery's departure had had no more effect than a sermon on Sunday.

I was intoxicated with excitement. I had a view of the square outside and could see that every other house there was ablaze with lights and the windows were full of people, an audience hoping to recognise the guests in their disguises.

It was a little after nine-thirty when Mr Crease, in a black domino and mask, came to fetch me. If ever a man looked more sinister I have yet to see him. He draped a cloak round my shoulders and took my hand.

'Come,' he said, 'let us dazzle London.'

Chapter Thirty

Fair Venus calls, her voice obey,
in beauty's arms spend night and day.

I have been told there are strange lands where live exotic
beasts, their heads larger than their bodies, birds of exuber-
ant plumage, and creatures that possess horns and resemble
men in all but nature. As I stood with Ned Bird, waiting to
make my entrance, the musicians playing in the gallery, I
thought that these creatures must have been washed ashore
here. They tottered about, holding tight to their papier-mâché
faces, mingling with others dressed from the Italian comedy,
with nuns and priests who belonged to no order other than
that of pleasure, with women changed into men and men
changed into women, with whores dressed as saints – the
world bedizened in borrowed gowns. The truth of who they
were was lost behind the array of masks. But I saw that from
the folds of their clothes, ghosts emerged, whispering shapes.
They needed no masks for they were here to haunt the living,
to niggle at their thick consciences in hope of driving them to
Bedlam for the wrongs they had committed. There she was,
Pretty Poppet, her arm on Queenie's waist. Seeing her made
me shudder. A bad omen, I thought.

'What do you think all those fine gents and ladies are hiding from?' Ned whispered.

'Ghosts,' I said.

I closed my eyes and, with all my being, willed the shades to be gone.

Gilded lights illuminated the ballroom's scurrilous paintings, a reflection of the delights that were on offer at the masquerade ball. Amid the collage of colour and the rising cacophony of chatter, still the dead clung, unforgiving, to the living.

Waiting for my cue, Ned and me watched the scene. When all the guests had assembled, the musicians stopped playing and everyone fell silent. The man in the hooded domino strode menacingly into the middle of the floor, parting the guests with a wave of his hand so that he dominated an empty space. He whirled round and round, faster and faster, and as he did his cloak disappeared to reveal a black and silver harlequin. He came to an abrupt halt and a loud cheer greeted the master of ceremonies.

'My lords and ladies,' said Mr Crease. 'For your delight and entertainment, we have filled our cellars with the wine of Bacchus and our kitchens have prepared a banquet fit for the gods. We have virgins and courtesans a-plenty, willing to share their innocent – and not so innocent – charms with you. We have gentlemen in need of lovers and lovers in need of gentlemen. Ladies, shake off all prejudice, for here is an opportunity to indulge your amorous inclinations without fear of interruption from father or husband. All we ask is that you leave your morals and virtue with your cloaks and swords.'

He picked out a man in the audience and, addressing him, said, 'If you, sir, happen to make love to your wife or to her maid, secrecy is the order of the night.' The ballroom rang with the raucous laughter of the guests. Mr Crease raised his hands and once more everyone was quiet. 'Be not ashamed of your desires. Relish your appetites and partake in all the dishes on offer. So, without another word, let the entertainment begin.'

Rose petals fell from the ceiling as I walked up to Mr Crease. He removed my cloak, nodded his head and raised his hands again for silence. I closed my eyes and began to spin up and up until I was on the swing, and set sail over the heads of the guests and ghosts.

I swung, causing my skirts to billow and the swing to go higher and higher until I could almost touch the naked lovers painted on the ceiling. The masked faces stared up at me in awe. Then I let go, throwing myself out, arms stretched, a flightless bird with nothing to stop me from falling. A horrified gasp rose from the guests. The ghosts vanished, hoping, no doubt, to catch me on the other side. But I was not to be theirs tonight.

As Mr Crease had taught me, I hovered, luxuriating in the audience's reaction, and for the first time I enjoyed the power my abilities had given me. I willed myself to slowly descend, and stopped about a foot from the ground where I floated until Mr Crease took my hand. I stepped down as if all along I had been standing on an invisible platform.

My performance was greeted by a cascade of clapping that only stopped when a footman brought the birdcage containing Boozey and put it on a small table. I took the cage, opened it, and walked round the ballroom, showing Boozey to the guests who all agreed that he was a very dead parrot indeed. I whispered to Boozey. He ruffled his feathers, spread his wings and took flight. At that moment, to a hushed disbelief, the black and silver harlequin transformed the ballroom into a jungle. Even the old sailor made an appearance, calling to his beloved bird.

Mr Crease clapped his hands. The illusion vanished, the sailor gone, the parrot returned lifeless to his cage.

The musicians started up again and the dancing began. Mr Crease and I were to give two more shows that evening. In the next one, I brought back Shadow and by the time Mr Crease and his dog had worked their magic with the fortune-telling alphabet cards, you could almost hear the heartbeat of those in the room who were desperate for fate to look on them kindly.

Queenie found us in an antechamber where we had escaped to take refreshments.

Mr Crease took her in his arms. 'Are you satisfied, my lady?' he asked. 'Yes, very,' she said and kissed him. She turned to me and put out her hand. 'Tully, you were superb. Quite enchanting. When you leapt from the swing…'

'Am I forgiven?'

'Yes, my dear. Where is Mr Fitzjohn?'

'He left this afternoon for France.'

'Then I will find you someone else to entertain.'

She stared at me and I didn't blink.

Feathers and dust. This was my world now, this was where I belonged.

'Why the hurry, madam?' said Mr Crease. 'Tully has more than proved her worth to the fairy house. She has value beyond that of any other courtesan.'

I left them to their own company. Pretty Poppet was waiting for me outside in the hall.

'He'll shackle you, that's what he'll do.'

'Who?' I said.

'It's you he wants. Come, I'll show you the cull so you can keep out the way of his cutty-eyes.'

Supper had been served and many of the guests now made their way to the drawing room on the second floor, which had been given over to cards. I heard whispering as I passed and comments about my costume. As I watched, outrageous fortunes were wasted on a roll of the dice, the play of a card.

A gentleman in a dusty-pink, striped Scapino costume came up and bowed to me. His mask seemed designed to revolt rather than please, being black with large moles upon it, and a bulbous nose.

'I do not know you,' he said.

'I do not know you,' said I.

Was he the reason Pretty Poppet had brought me here?

'I saw you on the swing, young fairy. How did you perform such magic? Wires, I presume.'

His voice was rich, buttery and far more seductive than the mask he was wearing.

'No, sir.'

'Come, come, my sprite. Surely you do not tell me that you can defy the laws of science? It is irrational.'

'If you find that irrational, then what, sir, are you doing in a fairy house?'

'*Touché*. Show me how it's done.'

'I will not, sir,' I said, laughing.

'Do you give private performances?'

'That depends,' I said.

It was then that I felt every bone in my body turn to lead.

Pretty Poppet was standing behind the chair of one of the gamblers, his costume was striped in yellows and reds, his mask dominated by a big, hooked nose.

Scapino saw that he looked in our direction and asked if I knew the gentleman.

'Never been keen on Punch,' said Scapino. 'He's too cruel for my liking.'

I didn't listen to what else he had to say on the subject because I did know the Pulcinella. With or without his mask, I knew Victor Wrattan.

Desperate to remove myself from Wrattan's orbit, I asked, 'Do you dance, sir?'

'I used to, but now I—'

He was interrupted by a very drunk lady whose clothes were in disarray.

'Kitty,' said Scapino. 'You look as if you have already been ravished.'

'Perhaps I have,' she said with a giggle.

This then was Kitty Lay, the notorious mistress of Lord Barbeau. I had become a student of the gossip of the day and in near every paper I read, Kitty Lay was described as a beauty. What I could see of her face beneath the mask did not leave me with that impression. She put her arms lazily around Scapino and turned to me.

'He's mine,' she said, confirming that I was correct in my deduction that the gentleman in the Scapino costume was none other than Lord Barbeau.

'Madam,' said Scapino, 'you are drunk.'

'And what other state would you have me in, sir?'

He muttered something in her ear.

'My lord, you are a bore tonight. I want to be extravagant.

Lend me some money for the cards and you can have me any way you want.'

She adjusted her dress, took the reluctant Scapino by the arm and walked unsteadily to the card table. Pulcinella stood up.

'Madam,' he said to her, 'please take this chair.'

'I would if I could,' she said. 'I will wait for it to come round again and then, if necessary, I will take it by force.'

She made to sit down, missed the chair and fell inelegantly onto the floor. In the commotion that followed I retreated to the antechamber that Mr Crease and I had used after the show, only to find there a rather portly gentleman, his pleasure pole well exposed, on the point of mounting an equally large lady. I quietly closed the door then jumped as I felt an arm round my waist and something sharp in my side.

'I have been looking for you everywhere,' said Pulcinella. He leaned his grotesque head towards me. 'You will walk with me out of here. You will look loving, and if anyone stops you, you will tell them I am your gallant for the evening. But if you make any fuss I will willingly put this blade through you.'

There was nothing I could do except hope that someone might see what was happening and would have the wit to ask where I was going. We had reached the top of the stairs to the hall and I could see the open front door and knew that once I had passed through it there was no return.

'Sir, where are you taking her?'

It was Ned.

'None of your business,' said Pulcinella, sinking his blade all too easily into my flesh.

'But it is,' said Ned, taking hold of Pulcinella's arm. 'Let go of her immediately, sir.'

Just then a Blue Pierrot with a white mask came up towards us. He looked at me and immediately blocked Pulcinella's way. I felt the knife pierce my skin and flinched.

'Madam,' said the Blue Pierrot, 'do you need assistance?'

I recognised his voice and my heart soared.

Chapter Thirty-One

Magic that evening lay in the power of Avery's voice, for the moment Wrattan heard him he pushed me away, ran down the stairs and escaped into the crowds of people who stood outside. Ned went after him. I tried to ask Avery how he came to be there, but the pain in my side overwhelmed me. I put my hand to my stays and found blood.

'What the devil happened?' said Avery.

Before I could answer, Flora came up to us. 'Where did Pulcinella go?' she said.

'Who?' said Avery.

'Victor Wrattan,' said Flora.

'Whoever he his, why would he try to take Tully away by force?' said Avery.

'I cannot imagine why,' said Flora. Seeing Queenie approaching, she turned on her heels. 'Tish tosh.'

'If I'm not mistaken,' said Queenie, 'it is you, Mr Fitzjohn. I'm very pleased you've come to our ball after all but you will have to excuse Tully – Mr Crease is about to start the third performance.' She stopped and put her hand to her mouth. Blood was seeping from my side into my gown. 'Oh, my! I will call the doctor.'

'It's not necessary, madam,' said Avery, his arms round me. 'I will attend to Tully.'

He carried me to my chamber, laid me on the bed and told my maid to bring warm water and bandages. Once she'd brought them, she was sent for wine and food and by the time she'd returned, Avery had played the part of an abigail. I was lying naked on the bed, my hair, which had been loosely pinned, had come tumbling down in thick ringlets. The wound wasn't deep but it did bleed profusely. Avery gently rolled me on my side, and cleaned and dressed it.

'You seem to know exactly what to do.'

'I have been attending to wounds since I was but seventeen. I was sent on the Grand Tour but, hating my tutor, I ran away from him in France and went to live in the household of a surgeon, a relative of my mother. He was a kind man and, as I didn't faint at the sight of blood, he made me his assistant.'

'And when you marry your countess,' I said, 'will you still practise?'

'I very much hope so.'

'I'm glad, for you seem well versed in human anatomy.'

'Are you acquainted with the man who did this?' One word, one lie and all is altered. I could have been honest with you then, except I had no desire to ruin the evening with the unpalatable truth. 'He must have been out of his mind, or drunk.'

'Probably both,' I suggested, and quickly changed the subject. 'Are you not supposed to be halfway to Dover by now?'

'I missed the coach, and I'm glad I did.'

'So am I,' I said.

'This, my lady,' he said, kissing me on the lips, 'is the best treatment for all wounds.' He placed his hand on my breast. 'These beauties, so white and firm, these nipples like rose petals…' He bent and took the tip of one in his mouth. 'It will be my pleasure to kiss every part of you.'

'Every part?' I asked.

'Yes, madam. It is the only cure I could prescribe for such an injury.'

'Then, sir, I am much in need of your medicine.'

He kissed my mouth, my neck, and down and down, and oh, the fire, it sent my body to flame. And my mind could only think of how he would feel inside me. When he reached my Venus mound, he kissed there the softest parts of the fruit, lingering until my juice flowed and I lost myself in the little death. His maypole hard, such a delight to look upon, to touch, he knelt above me, then, bending over, eased himself into the moisture of me until I could feel all of him and still want more. Our lovemaking that night had a sweet desperation to it in the knowledge that we would not meet again. Avery told me he was leaving at dawn and he could not miss the carriage. Not this time. We treated night as if it were day and let not one moment of it be lost in dreams.

I had a chance then to tell you my truth. It was on the tip of my tongue but the morning light flooded the chamber and you took me again. Why waste the last farewell with the dregs of the past? I gave myself to voluptuous lovemaking.

'Don't go,' I said, as I felt him ease out of me.

He bent and kissed my belly. Determined not to cry, I watched him dress by the dusty, autumn light.

'Wait,' I said, as if I had just found something in the wreckage to cling to. 'I was going to give you this last night.'

It was in a little cotton pocket and didn't look important.

'What is it?' he asked, taking it.

'A present.'

I was quite naked and, shivering, pulled the sheet off the bed to wrap round myself. Avery looked at me as he opened the present and I swear I saw a tear in his eye. He kissed me, said nothing more, and left.

When someone one loves is gone, one can almost bear the first few moments. I could still in my mind hear his voice, feel his touch on my skin. It was only as the minutes knotted themselves into hours that loneliness imprisoned me.

By the time all the guests had finally left, nine o'clock had passed and the fairy house had gathered itself in the silence, relishing the morning peace.

I went to find Mercy. Forgetting to knock – which was a bad habit of mine, especially where Mercy was concerned – I found her in bed with the nymph who possessed an abundance of red, curly hair.

I was on the verge of tiptoeing out again when Mercy said, sleepily, 'Tully?'

'I should have knocked,' I said.

'Yes,' she said. She sat up and pulled back the bedclothes. 'Come here.'

I climbed in and she held me in her arms and kissed me.

'Ned found his costume in some bushes. I brought his mask back. Perhaps I should nail it to the wall as a trophy.'

The woman with the red hair yawned and said, 'Who's this?'

'It's Tully. Tully, this is Mofty.'

'Is the wound deep?' asked Mofty, raising her head to look at me.

'Not too deep. I will survive.'

'You were fortunate. My husband is a vile, cruel man.'

'And he is in some way connected to my husband,' I said.

'Ralph Spiggot,' said Mofty.

'Alas, yes.'

'Spiggot was but a boy when Victor employed him. He is

probably the only creature my husband truly cares for. They are close, and together they are the very devil's disciples. You must take great care.'

Mercy put Mofty's hand on her breast.

We fell asleep. I woke to Mercy's kisses

Mofty said, softly, 'May I join in?'

'I would like it if you would,' I said.

Mercy rolled me over so that I was between them, and Mofty's mouth found mine. Such was their passion, so tender their kisses, I found myself much comforted. They both with such sweetness brought me to that moment when all is beyond reason and I let out a cry of joy. As Mercy went to Mofty I slipped out of bed and, silently closing the door behind me, I left them to the main dish that only lovers enjoy.

Downstairs the servants were still working and I was about to drift back to my chamber and sleep a little more when a footman arrived with a message.

'For Miss Tully Truegood, and no one else,' he said.

I thanked him, and thinking it was from Avery went upstairs shaking with excitement. Out of the envelope fell a key. Ignoring it, I hungrily read the letter – once to know it wasn't from Avery, again to understand what it was saying, and a third time to know what my future would be without him.

Madam,

Allow me to prostitute my pen and push aside all modesty. Let virtue go to church. My purpose as a shameful scribbler is simple: I am in pursuit of your sweet love. I have no illusions that it will flourish at first sight of me: my knowledge of such tender seedlings as love and desire persuades me that they need nourishment and time to grow. But first the seed must find a bed in which to lie.

I ask nothing more than that you accept my invitation to visit my garden at

Highgate. I designed it with the express wish of showing my mistress the tender way of my affections and how I would love her. The key that you hold opens the door.

Please, I pray, do not upbraid me. I am but a human filled with desire and loathing in equal measure, as are all God's creatures. In my youth my presence alone was enough to sway a lady's feelings. Now, in the autumn of my life and on this October afternoon, I beg you, my dearest of fairies, whose whole being has made me insensible to reason, to come to see the garden for yourself. You must be the judge. If my immodesty has offended, close the door, put the key under the stone, and think no more of it.

My carriage will call for you at one o'clock tomorrow afternoon.

I am, madam, your obedient servant,

Lord Barbeau

Chapter Thirty-Two

How could I respond to another man's touch so soon – too soon – after Avery's? If it was expected of me then I was bound to fail for I needed time to learn to breathe again in this less exalted atmosphere. I wished that I might conjure a magic spell to take away the leaden numbness that had crept through my body as if every part of my flesh knew my lover to be lost.

The one ray of golden light was the thought that now I could be called an adulteress, already on the path to ruin, Captain Spiggot might agree to end the marriage contract. Why would he wish to claim a whore for a wife? I was not rich, and every way I looked at the matter, there was nothing that would benefit him.

I lay in my chamber, listening to the bells of London and wondering where Avery was. By five o'clock I'd had enough of the tumult in my head and went in search of company. The house had undergone a transformation and the chaos of the night had been brushed, dusted, swept and badgered into order.

When I reached the hall I heard Bethany with Queenie and Flora in the drawing room. Bethany's voice was loud and angry. The door being open, I was about to go in when I realised that I was the cause of her fury. I stood in the shadows in the hall from where I could see the three of them. Queenie's expression was serene, but it was the serenity that saints wear in paintings and is not to be trusted.

'He belongs to Kitty,' said Bethany. 'You know that, I know that, the whole of London society knows that. And now, after a conversation of three sentences, Lord Barbeau throws her over in favour of Miss Whimsical. Tully knows nothing about the game – she's not educated – not in the art of pleasure, the art of conversation, or etiquette.'

Queenie's voice was as clear as the blade of a sharp knife and each word left its mark.

'Kitty's best years are behind her. She has let herself run to fat and is drunk more often than she is sober. I cannot abide drunks, they give a house a bad name and let in the wrong sort of company – dangerous company. Talking of which, tell me, Flora, why on earth did you invite Victor Wrattan?'

'Oh, tish tosh – he's an old friend,' said Flora, oblivious to what was building in Queenie, word by inevitable word. 'I didn't think he would cause any harm, after all…'

Bethany looked at her askance, her rage somewhat defeated by the realisation of what Flora had done. 'You invited him?' asked Bethany.

'There's no need to make such a fuss,' said Flora.

Bethany and Flora seemed quite unaware of how violent Queenie's icy rage could be. The air around her froze. I didn't have to be a seer to know what was coming.

'You are a guest in my house, Flora, and you pay very little for the privilege. I didn't see the Earl of Wellborne last night. Why didn't he come to the ball?'

'I've finished with him,' said Flora. 'He's so stingy. There are rumours that he's going bankrupt.'

'I will not have a spiteful whore in my house. I want you to leave.'

Flora looked stunned. 'Leave?' she said. 'Tish tosh! You don't mean it.'

'I was told,' said Queenie, 'that the Earl of Wellborne has found himself a younger courtesan, one who doesn't ridicule him and spend his money on frippery and presents for her other lovers.'

'You know I will take my clients with me,' said Flora.

'You will leave today,' said Queenie.

Flora gathered her words together and spat them out with force. 'You old bitch!'

Queenie stood. An unreadable smile crossed her lips, one that belied what came next. She went to Flora and slapped her across the face.

'You should have more care to the company you keep. You near put the whole of my enterprise in jeopardy last night by inviting Victor Wrattan. What your game is I don't know, but it's fortunate for you that Ned and Mr Fitzjohn intervened. Mr Pouch has your bill ready. Good day.'

Flora stormed out of the drawing room, knocking over a small table and shattering a figurine.

'That goes on your bill,' called Queenie, coming out to the hall as Flora flounced up the stairs. 'Ah, Tully, there you are. Come in, my dear.'

I followed her into the drawing room and stood as far from Bethany as I could.

'I didn't know,' said Bethany. 'Honestly, I didn't know she had invited Victor Wrattan or I would have said something.'

'Lord Barbeau,' said Queenie, not taking her eyes off her, 'is a man I respect. He has stood by Kitty but has been publicly humiliated by her once too often.'

'According to Kitty, he can no longer keep his maypole up,' said Bethany. 'It dances at half-cock and it's not her fault if she needs more satisfaction.'

'If every man in England could rise to the occasion,' said Queenie, 'and every women was pleased to greet him, then our profession would be redundant. Watch your step, my gal, you've already tripped once. Do it again and you're out.'

I moved to let Bethany pass.

'You are a witch,' she hissed at me. 'And you can go to the devil.'

'Sit down, Tully,' said Queenie when Bethany had gone. 'I'm very pleased with you, my dear. It seems you enchanted Lord Barbeau and he has quite set his mind on you. It may feel sudden, but this is the way the world of pleasure turns. He has asked that, if his garden is to your liking, he might take you to Bath.'

'Bath?' I said. 'You mean, leave the fairy house?'

'After what happened here last night, Tully, I realise I cannot guarantee your safety. It would be better for you to be under the protection of a man who Mr Wrattan and Captain Spiggot would never have the gall to cross.'

The small table was spinning and all the pieces of broken china floated before me an unresolved puzzle.

'The table, Tully,' said Mr Crease, limping into the drawing room.

I became aware of what I was doing and righted the table.

'And the figurine?"

I closed my eyes and willed it to be one. When I opened them again the unbroken figurine was in its place on the table.

Mr Crease had his painted eyelids on me. 'I wonder who your father was,' he said, with a rare smile.

Queenie examined the figurine. 'Not a chip on it,' she said. 'I will miss you, Tully.'

'Bethany won't,' I said, and immediately regretted how childish it sounded.

'You are just starting out on your journey. The others, they know how the circle goes. They also know that as time passes the circle becomes smaller and smaller.'

'That's what I adore about you, my love,' said Mr Crease. 'You are a philosopher, as well as the best bawdy-house keeper in the metropolis.'

~

The next morning, dressed in the finest gown that the fairy house had to offer, with silk stockings and silk shoes upon her feet and the prettiest of hats perched upon her head, this reluctant whore set out to see a garden.

Chapter Thirty-Three

Could I tell you where I was taken? I could not. Lord Barbeau's coach was grander by far than that of the Earl of Wellborne. Black with a gold crest on the door, two footmen at the back, the coachman and another footman at the front – all were turned out immaculately as were the four grey horses. If I had imagined that I would be able to sit back and enjoy the novelty of such luxury, I was much mistaken for it soon became apparent that Lord Barbeau's carriage caused heads to turn and children to run behind it.

My knowledge of London was so limited that I could have been in a different country. We bowled along, away from the tight-packed houses to where the roads widened and eventually we came to a stop by high brick wall. The carriage door was opened, the steps pulled down, a footman helped me to alight and there stood a man who announced himself as Lord Barbeau's butler. He bowed.

'Madam,' he said, 'it is His Lordship's wish that you wear a blindfold until we reach the garden gate.'

It seemed a strange request but then the whole thing had something of the unreal about it. I was already nervous and the blindfold did nothing to calm me.

The butler led me, giving instructions as we went.

'Madam, if you would lift your foot...here is a step...' and so on and so on until I felt gravel under my shoes.

At last, the blindfold was removed. The butler bowed and took up his position as a wordless statue beside a heavy, studded oak gate. The key that I held in my hand was thin and delicate and appeared incapable of opening a jewellery box, let alone such a stubbornly well-established door as this.

I turned to the butler for guidance. His face was inscrutable and, seeing that it was not in his remit to advise me, I pushed at the gate to find it well and truly locked.

'Feathers and dust,' I said and put the key in the lock. With a click the gate opened.

I'd had all the previous day and a sleepless night to imagine what this garden might be like. Hope told me of a duke who had shown her his magnificent grounds by way of seduction, and this I presumed would be similar. She described a formal arrangement of small box hedges planted in geometrical patterns, gravel paths ending in the necessary explosion of fountains – an illustration, if one was needed, of his grace's power and virility.

Instead of anything so formal, I was greeted by an arbour that hid the rest of the garden from view. I walked through an archway glowing with rosehips, and beyond it were herbaceous borders filled with autumnal flowering plants whose names I knew not, whose colours had such riches in them – reds and scarlets, a tapestry of russets. The sunlight, dipped in rose gold, threw long shadows across a maze of curved and winding walkways. The garden's very size, its intimacy, had a deeply reassuring quality, for I thought any man who could have planted such a garden must have a fine knowledge of women. A mist had begun to rise, a blush of modesty over such an immodest design. Beauty was to be found here in the dying of the year. Who would imagine that at the heart of green leaves burned such passionate reds as autumn brings, beauty defying death in all its finery.

In the middle of this voluptuous garden was an oblong clearing where trickled a little stream. Nervous as I was, I couldn't help smiling. Overlooking all was a bower where flaming leaves were falling and inside sat Lord Barbeau. Neither his costume nor his mask had served him well at the masquerade ball. I couldn't call him handsome, for he was more than that and not that at the same time. His eyes were grey, his mouth neither full nor thin-lipped, his features not chiselled but not undefined. He was extremely elegant, a fashionable man of the metropolis, and I didn't for a moment imagine the ruby and diamonds in his cravat were anything other than the finest, as were those in the buckles on his red-heeled shoes. His wig was of a dark grey, well fitted, and his three-cornered hat sat beside him. Both hat and master looked as if they had been waiting some time. I curtsied.

He stood, bowed, then, taking my hand, lightly kissed the tips of my fingers.

Two footmen appeared, one carrying a tray with two gold crystal glasses. While he poured the wine, the other helped me to my seat.

'Does my garden please you, my sprite?' asked Lord Barbeau.

'Very much, sir,' I said.

I made to lift the glass to my lips and found I was trembling.

'My dear sprite,' he said. 'I will not ravish you against your will.'

'Forgive me, my lord,' I said. 'I didn't expect the garden to be…like this.'

He leaned forward and looked at me with interest. 'And what kind of garden is this, pray?'

My cheeks were on fire. Surely there could be no mistaking its design. I chose my words carefully. 'I am told that gardens are designed to show off a gentleman's power and that they usually end in an explosion of fountains.'

'Yes,' he said, thoughtfully. 'It's rather predictable, all that rising water amid tight little beds of coiffed bushes. But I interrupt you – pray, continue. What do you think this garden says?'

'It echoes a secret that I would think few men understand, or have any interest in showing that they understand.'

'Go on, my sprite.'

'I think it's fashioned to be the inner part of the Venus mound, and we are seated at the spot of all desire.'

'Most delicately put, my sprite, most acutely observed.' He smiled, and leaned back. 'I have shown my garden to but a handful of ladies. When I was younger I needed nothing to go before me. Now I am older I must rely on my garden to win you.'

'Not at all, sir,' I said. 'You and the garden enhance one another. Which is more than can be said for the Scapino costume.'

Lord Barbeau burst out laughing and I too found myself in a fit of giggles.

'I looked ridiculous, did I not? That was Kitty's doing. If there had been a donkey costume, no doubt she would have insisted I wore it.'

It was twilight and I wondered how long we were going to sit there for soon we would not be able to see one another at all. I jumped. Suddenly the garden had become illuminated without a hand to help it.

'Do not be alarmed,' said Lord Barbeau.

'How do you do that, sir?' I asked.

He smiled. 'You are not the only person who can do the extraordinary, my sprite. But I rely on scientific inventions, which as you see, can be just as magical.' He paused, then said, 'Queenie told me you have just lost a gallant.'

'Yes, sir.'

'Was he your first?'

'Yes, sir, he was.'

'And I surmise that you fell in love with him.'

'How do you know?' I asked.

'My dear, intriguing sprite, it is written on that beautiful face of yours.'

Taking up his hat, he stood, and for a moment I thought he was about to tell me that it had been a mistake and he had changed his mind.

He gave a deep bow and said, 'If you wish to stay, take this path. If you wish to go, the carriage awaits you. The decision is yours. But whichever path you take, the other will be closed to you for ever.'

He took my hand and once more kissed the tips of my fingers. He bowed.

'Take your time,' he said and turned on his red heels and was gone.

I drank my wine and for a while contemplated my future. I didn't think I would ever love again but perhaps I could grow accustomed to Lord Barbeau. He made me laugh and he did have the most seductive garden. Weighing up my options, which were extremely few, I decided it was best to embrace what I was, a woman who enjoyed pleasure. I doubted that the passion with Lord Barbeau would be as it was with Avery. Perhaps that made the thought more bearable. Looking out at Lord Barbeau's garden, I was reassured that he was a man who loved women. Mercy once had told me that I didn't understand the true value of a vintage wine; she was right. It was a drink I would like to taste, and I knew then which path to take.

Chapter Thirty-Four

The house, like his lordship's garden, was elegant and far more refined than the fairy house, which hitherto I had thought the pinnacle of taste and sophistication.

A supper had been set out for us in his dining room amid candelabras, silver plate and crystal glasses. The dishes were served by white-gloved footmen while the butler hovered. Quite honestly, I had no idea how to make conversation with so many servants listening. I sat next to his lordship at a table that ran away from us into the darkened distance of the chamber.

'Must we be watched?' I whispered. 'I mean, sir, while we eat?'

Lord Barbeau laughed and waved his hand and, to my great relief, the servants silently left us.

'Is that more conducive to discourse?'

'Much more, sir.'

'Tell me about yourself, my little sprite.'

I thought an edited version of my life would be more appealing than the unexpurgated story and touched only lightly upon Mr Truegood and left out the account of my clandestine marriage. I was delighted when I caused Lord Barbeau to guffaw with laughter and, somewhat more confident, went on to tell him how I came to leave Milk Street.

'What I would have given to see you standing there in nothing more than your stockings and shoes,' he said.

Feeling a lot bolder, I said, 'With luck, sir, you might.'

'Are you flirting with me, my sprite?'

'Perhaps I am,' I said, blushing. 'After all, you have shown me such an intimate garden, it is hard not to.'

He leaned back and studied me. 'Do you enjoy making love?' he asked.

'Prodigiously, sir,' I said. 'But I am a novice in the art.'

'You make me wish I was still the young gallant.'

The wine was delicious and I had drunk a little more than I should have.

'You don't seem so very old, sir.'

'You flatter me unnecessarily, for I am well acquainted with the disadvantages of my age and not even your sweet words can remove the years from me.'

'Have you been married, sir?' I asked. 'Or are you married still?'

'My intriguing sprite, your ignorance of my life is wonderfully refreshing. I was married when I was twenty-four. It was an arranged marriage. My mother would have said it was to secure a great estate. I never expected to fall in love with my wife but, after a year, I was besotted with her. My days as a rake were behind me, or so I thought. Four of the happiest years of my life I spent with my angel.'

He was silent.

'Do you mind, sir, if I ask what happened?'

'I was in London when news reached me that she had fallen ill. I returned home to Chippenham with all speed but she died a day later. Her death undid me. I went abroad and sought consolation from every willing woman. I made love to many but never felt anything akin to what I had experienced with my wife.'

'That is so very sad,' I said.

'I haven't brought you here to make you feel sad, my sprite.' Rising from the table, he said, 'I look forward to welcoming you at my estate near Bath in one week. Does that suit you?'

'Yes, sir,' I said.

I curtsied, he bowed, and I left.

Queenie was delighted with this outcome. She told me that Lord Barbeau's solicitor had been there that morning and the terms offered for my services were generous to a fault.

~

His lordship required me to be well equipped with clothes for my stay. He specified sturdy shoes as well as the dancing pumps I would need for balls and attendance at the assembly rooms.

'It seems he has his mind set on showing you off,' said Queenie.

'But he hardly knows me.'

'It matters not an ounce. Win him over in the bedchamber – and don't be a fool like Kitty and lose him.'

It always astounds me how time has a habit of slowing to the pace of a slug and then, without warning, speeding into a gallop. That week was a whirlwind of dressmakers, shoemakers, and everything to do with lace, ruffles, embroidery and frippery. Then, before I'd even had time to think of the implications of what I was about to undertake, the morning for my departure arrived. I stood in the hall in my brand-new travelling gown and a jaunty hat, with Boozey in his cage and two well-filled trunks of clothes.

'You will write, my ninny-not?' asked Hope, fussing with the fur on my jacket.

'Yes, of course,' I assured her.

'Every week, I want to hear from you – not one detail is to go astray.'

'And you too – every week.' I turned to Mercy. 'Will you write?' I asked her.

She kissed me. 'Don't rely upon it,' she said.

Even Bethany, to my surprise, came down from her chamber to say goodbye.

'Have you made your will?' she asked.

'No – why?' I said with alarm.

'Ooh la la,' she said. 'You need to have made a will when you travel to Bath through those turnpikes.'

'Why?' I repeated.

'Because the roads are grievous full of highway men, out to snatch unnatural dead parrots from innocent whores. The most dangerous part of the Bath Road is the Maidenhead Thicket.'

I smiled, too full of excitement to be put off my journey.

'You don't believe me? Oh, fie. Tell her, Mercy. People put their trust in God when they take that road. Even those who have as good as forgotten his existence suddenly remember him well enough when they set off to Bath.'

'Stop it,' said Queenie. 'You'll frighten her.'

Everyone was talking at once and all went silent when the front door was opened and there waiting was Lord Barbeau's post-chaise drawn by four restless black horses. They were snorting steam from their nostrils and the two postilions were having trouble keeping them calm. The coachman secured my luggage, I was helped to my seat with Boozey's cage placed beside me, and, with a great waving of hands, the carriage set off at a mighty speed. I heard Queenie shout, 'Don't come back too soon!' and I sat back, wrapped in the luxury of upholstered seats and having perfect views from the front and side windows.

We must have made an impressive sight as we galloped through the countryside. The carriage overtook nearly everyone else on the road and each time we stopped, fresh horses were awaiting us. The following afternoon, with no mishap worth mentioning, we came to the rolling hills of the Avon valley, and here, in the village of Chippenham, the carriage turned down a private drive. It was lined on both sides by tall, autumnal trees and it wasn't until we'd rounded a bend that a spectacular house came into view. It sat in upright, square-shaped splendour and in the fading light looked as if it were made of burnished bronze.

The size of the house and grounds near overwhelmed me. I wasn't equipped to imagine anything quite so grand. We pulled up on a gravel drive and I was greeted in the hall by Mr Merritt, the butler who had shown me to the door of the secret garden. I hardly noticed which way we went for there appeared to be so many doors and galleries that I could well imagine that a guest having once become lost, might never be found again. Finally, we came to my chamber. It was beautifully designed, with a four-poster bed so large that five people could have lain there with no trouble at all.

'I hope it's to your liking, madam,' said my new maid. 'His lordship was most particular as to how the room was to be arranged.'

I stood at the window and, looking out over the distant hills, felt most ill-suited to the position I found myself in.

My maid had reset my coiffeur, which I wore unpowdered, when I spied on the dressing table a jewellery box with a note.

'A welcoming present for my sprite.'

It was a pearl necklace that tied with a pale pink ribbon and set my gown off to perfection.

'You look beautiful, madam,' said my maid.

I was indeed satisfied that I was a credit to the fairy house.

I found his lordship in the drawing room, the wolfhounds lying by the fire. They raised their heads sleepily when I entered then, sighing deeply, lay them down again.

Lord Barbeau bowed and asked if I had had a comfortable journey and if everything was to my satisfaction.

I curtsied prettily. 'Yes, sir,' I said, 'very much so. And I thank you, sir, for my necklace.'

'Excellent, excellent.'

I hadn't expected there would be guests and was surprised when a sombrely dressed parson entered, followed by a woman whose skin seemed to be scrubbed raw.

Lord Barbeau introduced me to his nephew, Mr Jonathan Ainsley, and his wife, who had arrived unexpectedly from Bath.

Mr Ainsley smiled a condescending smile. 'We were pleased to come and welcome my uncle to Bath,' he said in such a way that one would be forgiven for thinking that he alone held the keys to the city.

He regarded me with something resembling a sneer.

There was an awkward silence, which I had no idea how to fill.

At dinner that night, Mr Ainsley did most of the talking

while his lordship looked bored and drank his wine. I wondered if Mr Ainsley had ever seen his lordship's secret garden and doubted it.

'Who are your people?' he asked me suddenly.

I had so long been left from the conversation that I was lost in sweet reminiscences of Avery. I had to ask if Mr Ainsley would be kind enough to repeat the question.

'I asked about your family,' he said curtly.

'You wouldn't know them, sir,' I said. 'Our name is Truegood.'

'And in which county is their residence?'

'London, sir, Milk Street.'

'London – the capital of sin.'

I had a feeling that here was a man formed in the Smollett mould.

'I have heard,' he said, sniffing in the air, 'that a virtuous woman cannot walk in Covent Garden for all the abuse that the painted harlots might throw at her.' He took a breath and I feared we might be in for a sermon. 'What, I wonder, is this country coming to when every other woman in the metropolis is a whore?'

I shouldn't have said anything, but such foolish sentiments irritated me greatly. 'What, I wonder, do you suppose drove them to it?'

'Wanton lust,' he said emphatically.

'I disagree, sir,' I said, and the moment I had spoken, regretted doing so.

Mr Ainsley let out a snort which I think was supposed to be a sardonic laugh.

To my surprise, Lord Barbeau, with a mischievous look on his face, said, 'Perhaps you would enlighten us further, my dear.'

Oh, feathers and dust! Now I had done it.

'Women...' I said, and stopped and looked at Lord Barbeau.

'Pray continue, my dear,' he said.

'Women are the property of men. If they marry, all their worldly goods belong to their husbands.'

'And may it ever remain so,' said Mrs Ainsley.

'Amen,' said Mr Ainsley.

'But therein lies the problem,' said I.

'Madam, I do not follow,' said Mr Ainsley.

'Women have no money in their own right and many are subjected to the tyranny and cruelty of neglectful fathers and husbands. If a woman leaves this so-called protection, she finds the road to virtue closed to her by poverty and necessity. Her body is the only currency she possesses.'

'Oh, Mr Ainsley,' said Mrs Ainsley, 'I think I'm going to faint.'

'How dare you?' said Mr Ainsley. 'How dare you speak in such a manner in front of my wife? Uncle, will you allow us to sit here and be insulted by this... this...'

I felt my cheeks turn red and had risen to leave when Lord Barbeau said, 'Sit, Tully. Jonathan, Tully has spoken with great honesty and has made, I believe, a very valid argument.'

The parson was as purple as the port. 'Uncle,' he said, 'I had hoped you had at last discovered the path to godliness. But I find you are... you are the very devil!'

Lord Barbeau calmly asked Mr Merritt to have Mr Ainsley's carriage sent round.

As the dining-room door closed behind the parson and his wife, we could hear Mr Ainsley in the hall, delivering a short, angry sermon.

'And I'm damned,' he finished, 'if I will be preached to by a little whore.'

Lord Barbeau looked at me, his eyes sparkling, and we burst out laughing.

'My sprite,' he said. 'My sweet, clever sprite.'

Lifting our glasses, we drank to the future.

Chapter Thirty-Five

Lord B, as I came to call him, was one of the most honourable and generous men I have ever had the privilege of knowing. Up to then, my experience of older men had shown me little to recommend them. My father had been a drunken sop and a buffoon; Mr Smollett a licentious leek, the dancing master a milksop. Only Mr Crease could boast integrity, yet still he terrified me. I had no understanding of any of them. I soon realised that Lord B was in a different category altogether. Due to his patience and patronage, I grew from a noodle-headed girl into something resembling a thoughtful human being. He took a collection of unorganised thoughts and planted them in a bed of books. He watered them with encouragement, pruned their unruly stems and sprinkled them with praise until my learning blossomed into something approaching wisdom. But it took time and it nearly didn't take at all.

I had no idea what was required of me in the early days in that grand house with its large, well-proportioned rooms, its elegant windows with their eyebrows of drapery. Every night I expected Lord B would come to my bedchamber and, when he didn't, I began to wonder what his purpose was in bringing me there, and if he wanted me at all. After London and all the excitement of the fairy house, my new life was not what I had imagined it to be. We had no more visitors, or rather none that

Lord B wished to see. In the morning, weather permitting, we would walk together arm in arm through his various gardens and he would tell me the names of trees, of plants that relished the sun, and those that fared better in the shade. He took me shopping in Bath and, honestly, I could have become most terribly spoiled. I only had to glance at a bauble in a window of a shop and make some comment to find it was mine. I was very flustered by his generosity, especially as he seemed to want nothing in return.

'Sprite,' he often said. 'It is my privilege. I have the design and the means to spend money on you.'

I was worried we might bump into Captain Spiggot or Mr Wrattan, for I knew well that Bath was a place that made good pickings for gamblers and rogues.

~

As the weather grew colder, I spent my time exploring Lord B's library. He had a vast collection of books, some still with their pages uncut. I would sit in a wing-backed chair with a paper knife and slice them open; delicious wafer-thin food for the mind. When Lord B discovered that I had an interest in literature, he began to orchestrate my reading and we would often sit together, both of us lost in books. In the evening we would dress up and dine as if we had guests and he taught me how to play chess. But as for the reason I thought I was there, in that he showed no interest in me. Every night he would bow, say goodnight, kiss my fingertips and leave me to my slumbers. I admit to begin with I was most grateful. I told myself fortune had indeed been kind to me. Here was a man who enjoyed my company. I was fooling no one. I knew it wasn't enough, he had not paid so handsomely just for the privilege of teaching me French. As the days passed I became deeply concerned that I wasn't doing my duty by this kind man. I'd lain awake often thinking about going to his chamber but I never quite had the courage.

One evening we were called upon by a Doctor Gallicot, a gentleman whose features were permanently sucked in as if he had eaten something disagreeable. He was not tall, but stood ramrod straight, and an eyeglass hung on a chain from his waistcoat pocket. He bored my poor Lord B with a list of his ailments and supper was a lugubrious occasion that night.

'By your diagnosis, it is a wonder I am not dead,' said Lord B.

'My lord,' said Doctor Gallicot, 'it is in the express hope of avoiding that calamity that I am here.'

I wondered as I sat there if Avery would be as dogmatic once he became a physician and decided he wouldn't. Lord B drank more wine than usual and refused to listen to a word the disagreeable doctor had to say, but Doctor Gallicot continued with unsavoury prescriptions for his recovery.

'You should be in Bath, my lord, not out here,' he said. 'You must take the cure.'

'Along with a throng of fops who stink in their dirty shirts and tinsel, annoy the senses and offend the soul.' Lord B stood up and said, 'I've had enough of this. Goodnight, sir.'

I followed him into the hall. 'Please, sir, will you tell me what's wrong?' I asked.

He turned and looked at me as if he had completely forgotten who I was. 'I think it would be better that you returned to London. I am not fit company for you.'

I stood in the draughty hall, listening to the click of his

shoes on the stone floor as he walked away. I had no idea what I was meant to do.

The following morning Doctor Gallicot was back, accompanied by an apothecary who brought with him a collection of potions. The doctor's first prescription was that I was to be barred from his lordship's presence. He instructed Mr Merritt to make immediate arrangements for my return to the metropolis.

I was devastated and felt a complete failure – and dreaded what Queenie would say. I begged to see his lordship, if for nothing more than to say goodbye, but Mr Merritt told me it was impossible and handed me an envelope containing three twenty pound notes. I was outraged and refused to take it. I stormed off to my chamber.

My only solace was the arrival of a letter from Hope. Mine to her, written before Lord B became ill, had been dull for there had been so little to report. But I had confessed to my catastrophic failure to seduce Lord B and written that I had no idea how to remedy the situation. The reply arrived just when I needed Hope's wisdom most. After relating all the gossip from the fairy house, she wrote:

You must use your imagination. There are many forms of seduction and not all of them involve spring carrots – oh dear, I forget – what did Mr Smollett call the male root when under the influence of the female root? It still makes me giggle.

Seriously, my ninny-not, Mr Crease told Queenie and Queenie told me, that Mrs Coker granted you a wish. Mercy thinks it is all hocus-pocus, but I do not. If Mrs Coker did, and it is indeed, as Mr Crease said, a pearl hand, then I for one am green with jealousy. By the by, I simply have no idea why jealousy is green, do you?

But back to the matter in hand – or rather, pearl hand! There is an art in

it which, if used well, can save you a great deal of inconvenience and by that I
mean pregnancy and the pox so use it to your advantage, my dear.

   Do not, whatever you do, come back to London. Captain Spiggot is having
the fairy house watched and he has accosted Bethany, asking your whereabouts.
She told him she knew nothing – and told him more besides! That woman is
quite fearless.

Fortunately, my journey was delayed due to snow and, lost
in the library, with the wolfhounds, I was all but forgotten. To
keep me company I often took Boozey with me and read to
the dogs and the parrot. I loved hearing the words out loud,
their sound echoing before being sucked back into the books.

One afternoon, I was sitting in my usual chair with Boozey
flying about, when I felt an icy draught as if the door had been
opened. The dogs gave low growls and their hair stood up. I
looked round.

Her clothes were old-fashioned, her hair dressed in an
outmoded style, her face so sweet – I knew at once who she
was. The late Lady Barbeau beckoned me to her. I put down
the book, returned Boozey to his cage and warned the dogs
not to eat him. But they were snarling and wouldn't stop so I
picked up the birdcage and went to where she was standing.

I thought I knew the library well but Lady Barbeau pointed
to a book and I pulled it out to find the handle of a hidden
door. I opened it and followed her through to another, secret
library. Lady Barbeau had disappeared into the darkness and
I was thinking she had gone altogether when I jumped for she
had her hand on my sleeve, pulling me urgently towards to a
wooden spiral staircase. I climbed it after her. At the top she
put her finger to her lips and I held my breath for I could hear
voices coming from the other side of a curtain. Cautiously

moving the curtain aside, I saw Doctor Gallicot leaving Lord B's bedchamber with a bowl in his hand. Quietly, so as not to cause too great a shock, I went into the room to be greeted by the noxious smell of illness.

'My lord,' I said, putting down the birdcage.

'You shouldn't be here, my sprite. I'm a sick man. Forgive me, it was but a whim, a foolish notion to think I could...'

His dead wife was standing on the other side of his bed and I saw that she trembled when Doctor Gallicot returned.

'What, pray, is the meaning of this?' he said to me. 'I gave strict instructions that his lordship was to have no visitors.'

He had great authority to his voice, but I thought him no better than a butcher for he appeared to be bleeding Lord B to death.

'Madam,' said the physician, seeing that I showed no signs of leaving, 'please be gone immediately.'

'No,' I said. 'You will kill him if you continue with your leeches and your knives.'

The physician went to the door and instructed the footman to call for Mr Merritt.

Lord B said weakly, 'Come here, my little sprite.'

I went to him. He was too pale.

'It's wrong, my lord,' I said. 'He must stop bleeding you, he must.'

'And what, pray, do you know about medicine?' said the physician.

I looked round to see the spirit standing by my parrot's cage and an idea came to me.

I opened the cage and lifted Boozey out. 'Tell me, sir, is my parrot dead?'

Doctor Gallicot looked astounded. 'Of course it's dead,'

he said, as Mr Merritt entered the chamber. 'Take her away, Merritt. I have no time for cheap theatricals.'

I stroked Boozey and the parrot took flight. Doctor Gallicot paled.

'Tell me, Doctor Gallicot,' said Lord B, 'should I continue with your treatment? Or should I rely on the magic of my sprite?'

I could see that the man was shaken

'My lord, I have for many years been your physician, as I was that of your late wife. Are you are going to trust to some sleight of hand? We are talking about life or death.'

Boozey landed on the footboard of the bed. All animation left the parrot and he was once more stuffed and still. All the physician's composure vanished.

'This is witchcraft! My lord, she must leave…'

'I think not,' said Lord B. 'I will take my chances in Tully's care.'

'But I am your physician and I insist that…'

To my surprise, Mr Merritt said, 'You heard his lordship, sir,' and called for the footman to show the defeated doctor out.

'If his lordship dies,' said Doctor Gallicot to me, 'I will hold you responsible.'

My knees were shaking as I watched him depart with his leeches and bleeding bowls but I felt I had achieved no small victory. I looked about the chamber and the shade had gone.

Lord B put out a hand to me and smiled. 'Physicians can be the death of you,' he said.

Chapter Thirty-Six

The house fell silent, holding its breath, waiting to know how I intended to save his lordship. Mr Merritt stood before me, expressionless, and my courage wavered.

'Madam,' he said, with the steadfastness of a Doric column. 'What orders shall I give the staff?'

I imagined that this was how generals felt when commanding armies, except I was certain that Mr Merritt would oppose my strategy. But, instead, that afternoon he illustrated perfectly the absolute necessity of anyone retaining forty-one servants for without them little would have been achieved.

His lordship was removed to his antechamber and there I examined him, and was distressed to see that he was covered in bites. Fearing the bed to be infested, I ordered that the mattress be removed and burned, the drapes of the four-poster bed be taken away, the windows of the chamber opened and everything scrubbed clean. Lord B's valet washed and shaved his lordship and only when he was dressed in a clean nightshirt and cap was he carried back to his newly made bed. Comfortable at last, he sighed.

'My sweet sprite, this feels like heaven.'

Then seeing that new drapes hung round the bed, a frown crossed his face.

I knew what he was going to say: that this had been his wedding bed and he wanted nothing altered.

'If you are to recover, my lord,' I said firmly, 'the mattress has to be burned.'

'It's my fault,' he said. 'I'd always forbidden it because...' he took my hand '... because...'

I leaned towards him and kissed him on the lips, relieved that there was not a shadow of the winding sheet on my lord.

'It was long time ago, sir,' I said.

'Yes, a very long time ago.'

His two wolfhounds had been barred from seeing their master by Dr Gallicot and I allowed them into the chamber. They lay contented by the fire. I ordered Rhenish wine and a chicken broth to be made to my recipe. It was brought up by Mr Merritt himself on a silver tray and I fed his lordship silver spoonfuls of the nourishing soup.

I was reluctant to leave his lordship and sat in the chair beside his bed, the night bitter and my feet frozen. Around midnight he called my name.

I took off my gown and in my shift climbed under the covers, grateful for the warmth. He woke momentarily.

'Chilly feet,' he said, and rolled towards me, curving his body round my back for warmth and putting his arms about me, his hands on my breasts. Neither of us moved and we both slept peacefully till morning. A blueish light filled the chamber and there was the quiet that comes with the muffling of heavy snow.

Carefully, so not to disturb him, I turned towards him and found he was awake, his eyes upon me.

'Thank you, my sprite,' he said.

~

Mr Merritt informed me that for the time being we were cut off from the outside world, the roads being too treacherous to be attempted. He reassured me that we had more than enough provisions. For two weeks the great house sat adrift in a sea of windblown snow. Black crows cried out and I was grateful for the isolation for it was as if it prevented Death from galloping up to our front door.

We had a ritual of sorts. Every day the windows were opened to let in the fresh – albeit freezing – air, and the bed-linen changed. I was puzzled by the medicine Dr Gallicot had given his lordship and, on smelling it, decided that nothing so rotten could make anyone well and threw it away. I stayed with Lord B throughout every day, and every night I refused to leave his side. Finally, he began to show signs of improvement and, little by little, he regained his strength.

As his health returned to him he became restless.

'I'm not staying in bed with my legs growing weak,' he said. 'Enough, my sprite, enough. I am determined to be upright and dressed.'

There was one way I thought to keep him there.

'Could I change your mind, sir?' I asked as I undid my gown.

I gave him scissors to cut my stays, and took off my petticoat and my panniers. His lordship watched me with an amused smile on his face. I stood before him, naked apart from my stockings, which were held up by pretty bows.

'Perhaps,' he said, welcoming me into his bed.

It happened so naturally that I didn't feel it to be wrong. His kisses had a tenderness to them and were in their nature different to Avery's in every respect. Certain that the fire in him would have been transmitted to his maypole, I put my hand gently on that most tender of parts and was surprised to find that our kisses had not in any way awoken it. There it lay, sleepy, and I began by degrees to stroke it and tend to this most necessary part of all satisfaction. Gradually the member became harder until the muscles of it stood blood-gorged to attention.

'Madam,' he said, 'I have risen from the dead.'

I laughed and sat astride him. Naked, and with a longing in me that I never thought would show itself again, I eased him in to my little garden. I nearly had reached that melting moment when I felt the power of him wilt. I lay down beside him and put my pearl hand to work and instantly he regained his pose. He rolled me over and entered me that way, and then my lord let out the most glorious of cries. So unexpected was it that no doubt his servants thought that I had murdered him. Knowing him to be well enough for the main dish sent a thrill through me and I reached that moment that fails even the pens of poets.

Next morning he was dressed and, having eaten a light breakfast, went to his study to look at his post.

I had gone to tell Mr Merritt that we would be dining downstairs that day when there was the most terrible knocking at the front door. A footman opened it and, with a blast of snow and wind, in blew the irrepressible Mr Ainsley accompanied by another man wearing a three-cornered hat.

Mr Merritt followed me into the hall.

'Arrest her,' said Mr Ainsley, pointing his gloved finger at me. 'She is a murderess. God be my witness, my uncle died due to that witch's meddling in the black arts.' He turned to the man in the three-cornered hat. 'What are you waiting for, Constable.'

'I need to see some evidence, sir,' he said.

As the constable didn't take any action, Mr Ainsley took hold of me.

'Unhand me, sir,' I said, pulling away.

Mr Ainsley hardly drew breath before he continued. 'Merritt, from now on you will take your orders from me. Please be so kind as to show me to the chamber where his lordship is laid out.'

'Sir,' said Mr Merritt, 'I think you'll find his lordship is...'

Mr Ainsley bellowed at him in the manner of a fire and brimstone preacher. 'Did I ask for your opinion, Merritt? Remember your place! You are a servant here.'

It was then that Lord B came nonchalantly down the stairs, looking very well indeed.

'Most enlightening, Jonathan,' he said. 'So this is how you would conduct matters after my death.'

So surprised was Mr Ainsley to see Lord B that for a moment he was unable to speak. 'U-Uncle, I thought you were dead,' he said, weakly.

'Obviously. I take it that you have come out of the goodness of your heart to claim my body. Or is the truth that you are here to see what you might have inherited? I am sorry to disappoint you. It must be a wretched inconvenience for you to find that I am alive. Very much alive.'

'No, no, not at all, Uncle. No, it is joyous, most joyous.'

'Were the roads so treacherous, dear nephew, that you needed an escort?'

His lordship waved a lazy hand in the direction of the

constable who was looking none too pleased at being brought out on a fool's errand on such a cold day.

'I humbly beg your pardon, your lordship,' said the constable. 'I was informed...'

'Be quiet, man,' snapped Mr Ainsley.

'Pray continue,' said his lordship.

'I was told, your lordship, you had been as good as murdered by a witch,' said the constable.

'And when did you receive this startling information?' asked Lord B.

'Today, your lordship.'

'Jonathan, I wager Dr Gallicot informed you three weeks ago that I was ill?' Mr Ainsley gulped as if he was swallowing the psalms, page by inedible page. 'Yet you were only roused into action today?'

'The roads were impassible, sir, or I would have come sooner.'

'I doubt that,' said his lordship. 'Constable, you may leave us.'

'I'm sorry to have bothered you, your lordship. And you, my lady.'

'Lady? Lady?' hissed Mr Ainsley at the constable. 'She is no lady.'

'She don't look like no witch either.'

Lord B nodded to Mr Merritt, who handed the constable two sovereigns for his pains. He left, muttering to himself under his breath.

'Uncle, you misunderstand my intentions,' said Mr Ainsley, rolling his hat in his hands.

'It is one of my weaknesses,' said Lord B, 'that I never misunderstand. For the last two Sundays you have preached a sermon about a harlot who is living with a lord in the vicinity of Bath. The only thing you left out of your vivid description was my name. A rather entertaining cartoon was sent to me in the post. You see, Jonathan, the post has had no problem reaching my door, whereas you, who were so concerned that I was being murdered, were unable to come to enquire after my health.'

Mr Ainsley had opened his mouth to protest when another carriage was heard outside. The footman opened the door and Mrs Ainsely entered, followed by a servant with a trunk.

'I hope, Mr Ainsley,' she said to her husband, 'that you've had them air the beds and…' She stopped.

'Merritt,' said Lord B, 'show my nephew and his wife to their carriage. And, Jonathan, you need not bank on my leaving you so much as a penny in my will. Good day.'

When they had gone he turned to me.

'I think, my sprite, the time has come to set Bath by its ears.'

Chapter Thirty-Seven

Much that is written about me in the gutter press is exaggerated for the enjoyment of others and is more to do with salacious rumours, gossip and scandal – all the petty ingredients that go to make up the soup of human existence – than the truth.

It all started with Mr Ainsley's sermons. They did much to attract attention, for the idea that Lord Barbeau's mistress was a witch fascinated the bored inhabitants of Bath so when we eventually took up residence in Queen Square in March, I already had a reputation that the *Bath Chronicle* delighted in disproving. I was announced as being a great beauty and a credit to Lord B whose taste in all things was superb.

'What pomposity,' said Lord B when he read the piece. 'Money and a title, my dear sprite – not to mention a beautiful face – washes many a dirty sheet clean.'

It appeared that he was right for, far from being shunned, I was welcomed into the frivolous society of which Bath was composed and thus began one of the happiest times I can recall.

We had been settled in our new house about a week, and were late in bed one morning for his lordship was never an early riser, no matter how much I pleaded with him to be up to take the hot waters.

'No, sprite,' he said. 'The cure I rely upon is your loving –
better by far than the King's Bath where the water is pissed
in by incontinent old earls.'

I laughed. 'Do you speak this way to your society acquaintances, sir?'

'No, only to my beloved sprite,' he said. 'I saw a doctor
yesterday who said that the best cure that he knew of for my
malady is gambling. I presume he was working on the principle
that as I cannot take my wealth with me when I die I may as
well enjoy losing it at cards. Idiot!' I kissed him and felt the
fire in him return. 'Today, I want to stay in bed with my sprite.'

Later that afternoon as we lay sleepily together, he asked,
'What possessed you to refuse the three twenty pound notes
that I offered you when I was unwell? Kitty would have taken
them in a trice, demanded a post-chaise and have disappeared
in a cloud of lust to another lover.'

'Apart from the obvious, sir, that I am not Kitty, I felt I had
done nothing to deserve such generosity.'

'Do you feel you have done enough to accept it now?'

'No, sir,' I said.

'My dear,' said Lord B, more seriously than I thought the
subject warranted, 'I negotiated with Queenie to have you
for my mistress. Never did I imagine that you would become
my nurse.'

'Only a nurse?'

'My personal witch, then.'

'It matters not. The important thing is that you recover your
health. Please, sir, tomorrow will you…'

Before I could say another word he handed me a jewellery
box. I opened it and closed it almost immediately.

'Do you not like diamonds, my sprite?'

'These, sir, are worth far more than three twenty pound notes.'

'I hope so. I would be disappointed if they weren't worth ten times as much. My wish, sprite, is to drape you in jewels until you positively glimmer.'

Lord B opened the box, took out the diamond necklace and kissed the back of my neck as he did up the clasp.

I climbed, naked, out of bed to look at myself in the mirror. For the sheer joy of it, I spun round and round, rising until I touched the ceiling.

'Bravo,' said Lord B. 'My sweetest of witches!'

I landed and curtsied.

'I will have you painted like that,' he said. 'Naked, draped only in gems.'

'Would it be very wicked if I wore my necklace while you ravished me?'

'I always think,' he said, laughing, 'that a woman is most alluring when she keeps something on in bed.'

I fell into the pillows, wrapped in his arms, and, nuzzling into him, my hand found his maypole eager for the dance.

There are, as Hope told me, many ways to make love and I became well versed in making his lordship very happy indeed.

I could describe the King's Bath and the small alleys thereabouts, Wiltshire's Assembly Rooms, and the Pump Room. I could describe the numerous social engagements to which we were invited, the balls, the gambling and the folly of the *beau monde* at play. But it would be a sad waste of my ink and paper.

～

Lord B enjoyed giving small soirées at Queen's Square in the drawing room with its plastered ceiling of Greek gods and goddesses. It was on one such charming evening that he asked if I would show Boozey to his close friends. Doctor Gallicot's encounter with my parrot was the stuff of rumours, some malicious and some too full of folly for words. Merritt brought the bird to me. In the middle of the room amid the flickering candlelight, I stood and brought Boozey to life and let him fly round the chamber. Everyone clapped and wanted to know the secret of my trick. Not satisfied, they demanded more. Encore, encore!

'Come, sprite,' said Lord B, 'show my friends the true extent of your powers.'

It was then that she appeared. Visible only to me, the late Lady Barbeau, with such sadness, put her arms round his lordship's neck. He smiled an internal smile and put his hand to his shoulder. An irrational jealousy took me. I wanted her to be gone. She had no right to be here, now. This was my time, not hers. Without giving the wisdom of it a second thought, I rose in all my finery to the ceiling and stayed there until Lord B beckoned me down. But the sight of her had ruined my night and filled me with dread.

There was a routine to our lives, which in itself marked the passing of time. After much cajoling on my part his lordship reluctantly agreed that we would rise early and he would set out in his sedan chair for the King's Bath. An hour later, he would return home to dress before we both went to the Pump Room to meet with the sick and the sound, and drink three glasses of hot water that smelled of rotten eggs. Afterwards, the ladies went home for breakfast and the gentlemen to enjoy their newspapers at the coffee houses. Lord B had no mind to spend any time away from me so instead we would often have a private breakfast with his old friends and acquaintances.

It was the custom to then go to a service at the Abbey but, his lordship having radical views on religion, we went shopping instead. Lord B had decided to defy death with fashion, to blind the Grim Reaper with lace and *bon ton* and to that end we both dressed immensely elegantly and were much noticed as we took our afternoon promenade. I became bolder in my designs: if this was a matter of defeating death then surely we should be outrageous.

I must have been a success for, unlike Mr Ainsley, no one else bothered to enquire where my people were from. I developed a vagueness round the subject that proved to be worthwhile for, tennis for the tongue, the gossip went back and forth: I was a marquis's daughter, I was an earl's love child… and so on.

At that time there was an affectation in Bath for sprinkling French words into conversation, which led to the most marvellous misunderstandings. These were a constant source of mirth to his lordship who spoke French fluently and took much pleasure in teaching me the language. It became apparent to me that few people in society had any comprehension of what they were saying while we were able to converse without being understood by them.

His lordship's favourite comment was, '*Nous nageons dans un flot futile.*'

It was the folly of fashion that took me out early one August morning. I had become addicted to the shops of Bath, fascinated by all that glittered and all that was sold. The windows were full of everything that wealth and luxury could desire, arranged so beautifully to seduce the purse.

I had learned that a silk I had seen in a Paris dressmaker's book was now to be found in the fabric shop on Gravel Street. Usually when I went abroad, I was accompanied by Lord B, but that morning he seemed tired and I had insisted he stayed in bed to rest.

The weather being fine – or so I thought – I decided to forsake the sedan chair and walk, taking my maid with me. I was pleased to find that the mercer did indeed have the cloth I wanted. I had just made my purchase when my eye fell on some ribbons and I wondered if it would be too decadent to buy those as well. So consumed was I with the bibble-babble of my thoughts that I was at first unaware it had started to rain and that by degrees the shop had filled with people trying to avoid the downpour. Still contemplating the ribbons, I had sent my maid to find a sedan chair when someone whispered in my ear.

'They would become you, madam.'

I turned and found myself face to face with my husband. He was more handsome than I remembered, his scar less prominent than when seen through Shadow's eyes. Still, he had the same smug look on his face, certain that he had the advantage of me.

Before he could make his introduction, I said, 'Why, it is Captain Spiggot.'

He seemed momentarily nonplussed at my greeting him by name but bowed and said, 'Madam, it is a pleasure to see you. I was told you were in Bath.'

So this was my husband, the man my father had for some unfathomable reason seen fit for me to marry. A piece of pretty fluff with no more substance than a pasteboard actor on a cut-out pasteboard stage.

'And what,' I said, 'brings you here, I wonder? The company, your health – or the gaming tables?'

A flash of anger reddened his scar and had the effect of forming his thin lips into a sneer.

Ignoring my question, he said, 'I believe, madam, that we set off on the wrong footing and I would like to apologise for my previous behaviour.

'There, sir, you have the better of me for I have no recall as to how you behaved.' I curtsied and said. 'It has been charming, but if you would excuse me…'

The other customers, having nothing more entertaining with which to occupy themselves, watched us, spooling in the threads of gossip to stitch into rumours.

I was amused to observe that I had rattled him for he quickly glanced behind him for reassurance. I followed his gaze. Outside the shop was Victor Wrattan, staring in through the bow window, the glass distorting his face so that he appeared to possess more noses and eyes than any one devil should.

I wanted no more to do with Captain Spiggot or our stilted conversation and was relieved when my maid called to me, saying that a chair was waiting. I moved to follow her but my husband barred my way. As surprise had failed to upset me, he tried to take the high ground, this time with flattery.

'You are looking exceedingly beautiful,' he said. Quickly, he leaned forward and took my arm, pinching it tightly, then just as quickly he let go.

A cruel smile creased his lips. 'Good day. Until we meet again, Mrs Spiggot.'

Lord B was where I had left him, engrossed in the newspapers.

~

'Did you find the fabric?' he asked as I went to kiss him.

I could hardly remember the reason for my shopping excursion. 'Oh, yes,' I said and sat at the dressing table, trying to compose myself.

I had taken off my hat when my maid arrived with a new muslin gown that his lordship had ordered from Paris. The most delicate costume, beautifully embroidered, all it was lacking was Mr Crease's fairy wings. For a moment the sight of it almost made me forget what had happened that morning.

'Thank you, my lord. This is finer by far than anything I saw in the shops. Bath has nothing on Paris fashions.'

'Put it on for me, my sprite,' he said and kicked his left leg out from under the covers, letting it dangle there.

That was when I saw that death's winding sheet had begun to wrap itself round his ankle.

'My lord, we must find you a doctor,' I said. 'One that you trust.'

Ignoring my suggestion, he said, 'Let me read you this, it is the perfect illustration of the folly of Bath. "There was a fracas last night at Wiltshire's Assembly Rooms involving Lord Frederick Fitzjohn who accused one Captain Spiggot of insulting his waistcoat."' He looked at me over the top of the newspaper. 'Very pretty, my sprite. Do a turn…perfect!'

I cared not a fig about Lord Fitzjohn or my wretched husband. Let them blast each other's brains out. What mattered was my sweet Lord B. I felt that I was standing on the edge of a very high precipice and if he wasn't there, nothing would stop me from falling into the abyss. I went to him.

'A doctor – please, my lord…'

'I've seen fifteen doctors,' he said, 'and none of them do

I trust. Ironic, isn't it, in a city full of apothecaries, nurses, physicians, surgeons and quacks?'

'Will you not try again?' He put his hand to my face and I kissed him. 'It is pure selfishness, sir,' I said, 'for what would I do without you?'

'Tully,' he said, which made me sit upright as he never used my name. He sighed. 'My beautiful sprite. Call me an old fool if you will. I want you to marry me.'

Tears welled in my eyes.

'Is the idea so very unpleasant?' he asked.

'No sir, I would marry you...'

'Enough,' he said, 'it is as good as done!'

'...but I cannot.'

And I blurted out the unpalatable facts of my clandestine marriage.

'Your father,' said Lord B, 'in his wisdom, gave you away when you were but twelve years – to this Captain Spiggot?'

'So it seems. I only knew that I was married to a boy a few years older than me, and both sides gave their consent. My father was said to have the papers with him in the Fleet but when he was found murdered, there were none.'

'What an utter fool your father was,' said Lord B, and took me in his arms. 'We'd better have you divorced and be quick about it, for I am determined that you shall be my wife before I die.'

I kissed him and kissed him again. 'With any luck, Lord Fitzjohn will kill him.'

'Let us hope so. What about your new dress, my sprite?'

'Undo it, sir,' I said, for I knew of only one way to make him well. But that morning I had become aware that it wasn't enough.

Chapter Thirty-Eight

*The heart...is the beginning of life; the sun of the
microcosm...for it is the heart by whose virtue
and pulse the blood is moved, perfected, made
apt to nourish, and is preserved from corruption
and coagulation; it is the household divinity
which, discharging its function, nourishes, cher-
ishes, quickens the whole body, and is indeed the
foundation of life, the source of all action.*

WILLIAM HARVEY, 1628

I know of no recipe to heal the heart. Even love cannot persuade this most vital of organs to keep beating, no matter
how much one wills it so. I was under no illusions. Every day
the winding sheet crept up my lord's body. And every day he
refused to hear the word 'doctor' mentioned.

'Sir,' I said, desperate to know how I might change his mind,
'I have not asked you one favour since I have been with you
but now...'

'Now you are going to tell me that you are bored with
diamonds. I do agree that variation in all things is essential.
Perhaps you would prefer rubies? Note duly taken.'

'Your generosity is boundless, sir, but this has nothing to

do with jewels and well you know it. I want you to see a doctor – do not, I beg you, dismiss all doctors out of hand.'

The next day he was too ill to leave his bed and the pain in his chest was worse.

'Very well,' he said. 'As long as I am not bled.'

It was Mr. Merritt who found Dr Robert Thornhill. He had heard that the gentleman was of good repute: that he was a plain-speaking man, highly educated and did not believe in the practice of bleeding. I asked Mr Merritt to arrange for Dr Thornhill to pay a visit as soon as possible. The following day, his lordship refused to stay in bed, being determined to meet with his solicitor who had travelled from London to see him. I was certain that my marriage was the cause of this visit and wished it wasn't so.

The duel between Captain Spiggot and Lord Fitzjohn had resulted in both buffoons missing the other. Fate did not deal me a lucky card in that particular.

I took little notice of this solicitor and only saw him from behind as he went down the stairs, a thin man with a mincing step who wore a wig that age had turned yellow.

Mr Merritt said, 'Good day, Mr Attaway,' as he left.

The name I remembered, the man I forgot. I was relieved when Dr Thornhill arrived on time.

His lordship repeated to me that he would not see anyone who wished to bleed him. 'Neither will I be prodded and poked.'

'My lord, try not to be too cantankerous,' I said.

Dr Robert Thornhill had no interest in heaping false praise upon his lordship and, with simple courtesy, set about his examination.

I left them and paced outside the chamber until Lord B

called for me. I went in to find Dr Thornhill washing his hands in a bowl of water. He sat down opposite his lordship.

'Are you going to tell me the truth?' asked Lord B. 'Or are you going to lie to me? I'm sure you charge the same for both and I would rather pay for the truth.'

'So be it,' said the physician. 'Lord Barbeau, you have a disease of the heart, *angina pectoris*, and, unfortunately, the repeated bleeding has, without doubt, weakened you further. I will do my best but I can make no promises. You must help yourself and that means resting. I would suggest you return to your house in Chippenham and I will attend you there.'

'I'm not staying in bed,' said his lordship emphatically. 'I would die of ennui.'

'I'm sure, my lord,' I said, 'that we could find a way to keep you amused.'

'No!' said Dr Thornhill.

'You mean I can't even make love?' said Lord B.

'I recommend abstinence,' said the physician. 'And a plain diet and...' A smile eased its way across his face. 'And I can see, sir, that you have no intention of taking my advice.'

'I'm very glad we understand each other,' said his lordship. 'I will obey one of your instructions: I will leave Bath. I have had enough of these shallow waters.'

We left the following day. The carriage went so slowly it might have been in a funeral cortège. His lordship was grey by the time he was carried to his bed. I slept little for he had such a restless night of it and, in truth, even when he slept, I couldn't. The ghost of Lady Barbeau was ever present in the room, standing on his right side, her gaze never leaving him, waiting, waiting as she had for all those years.

When Doctor Thornhill arrived next morning, I walked in

the grounds. There was a little pavilion I hadn't noticed before, on the island in the centre of the lake. The sky was grey, heavy with thunder and the swans were alight with their whiteness.

'Ah, my sprite, at last,' said Lord B when I returned to his chamber.

I went to him and he took my hand.

'You must be brave, my sprite – and you are brave, I know. I have come to a decision: I'm going to live for the moment. And when I die I will go out in a blaze of glory. I have no desire to spend the rest of my days in bed waiting for the Grim Reaper. Boredom will kill me long before he turns up with his scythe. No, not a word. Have you ever seen fireworks, my sprite? I want my death to be a glorious display of light, a flame thrown against the darkness.'

For all his railing, Lord B had to admit that he felt better when in his bed. For the next month, falling into that morbid September, a nurse was employed to look after him through the night and I stayed with him in the day, reading aloud all the gossip and follies in the newspapers. We played whist and chess though he began to be impatient with the games and, more often than not, slept.

One evening, he said, 'She's here, isn't she? Grace is here.'

'Lady Barbeau? Yes, my lord,' I said.

'I think,' he said, 'she is standing to the right of me – just there,' and he pointed to exactly where she had been ever since we'd returned from Bath.

'Will you show her to me?'

'My lord, don't ask me to do that, I beg of you.'

'I know you can do it, my sprite. I have seen you often enough bring back your parrot. Let me see Grace – just once more.'

'If I do, she will take you.'

He held my hand.

'I had hoped to remain well long enough to marry you, but I don't think it will be possible. I am too weary, too fallen. I have done what I can to make provision for you but you must divorce Captain Spiggot first. Do you understand?' I nodded. 'When I am gone, you are to take all the jewels with you. I have a friend, a banker, who will look after them, and there is some money – don't go giving it to Queenie.' I tried to speak but he wouldn't let me. 'If you are in any trouble you must contact Merritt.'

'All of it means nothing without you,' I said.

'Come, come, my sprite, my sweetest one, let me go.'

I stood, and for the second time she looked at me, pleading. I couldn't do it. I wouldn't do it. My eyes filled with tears.

'Please, my sprite, I beg of you. Let me go to her.'

Shaking, I took a deep breath and willed her to become visible to him. He saw her, and reached out to her, and she lay down beside him, wrapped him in her arms and smothered him with death. I watched the years fall away from my lord until there on the bed was a handsome young man and the sight of him made me weep uncontrollably. Then all that was left was the shell of him, empty, soulless. I opened the windows in the chamber and called for Mr Merritt. Not one window in the house was left unopened for I wanted his lordship's spirit to be free to walk with her for ever.

Chapter Thirty-Nine

I remember looking at my shadow and wondering if it hadn't taken my soul from me, for never had I been more absent from myself than I was in the days following Lord B's death. The house that had vibrated with him felt abandoned, as if its very walls had no idea what to make of the silence. The wolfhounds dilly-dallied about and I could hardly think how to move one leg in front of the other. I wrote to Hope and then to Queenie to tell them what had happened. Their replies arrived on the same day as a letter from Mr Ainsley requesting that I leave his uncle's house immediately. I had expected nothing different. Defeated by the letter, I wondered if I shouldn't act on it straightaway.

Mr Merritt, steadfast as always, said that his lordship would have been most disappointed if I did not attend his funeral. We agreed that arrangements would be made for me to leave afterwards.

On the morning of the burial, my trunks were already packed when Mr Ainsley and his wife arrived unacceptably early, too early to be considered polite. They dismissed all the preparations that had been made by Mr Merritt and myself and complained that they had not been consulted. Despite the parson's insufferable whining Mr Merritt showed not a flicker of annoyance.

The funeral took place in the afternoon. The wind blew and leaves fell, golden tears to rest upon his grave. Lord B was buried in the family vault alongside his lady. Many came to pay their respects and Mr and Mrs Ainsley did their best to receive as many courteous condolences as came their way. Mr Ainsley purposely ignored me, no doubt hoping others would be led by his good example. No one thought it an example worth following.

Afterwards, with the help of my maid, I changed into my travelling gown underneath which I hid about my person all the jewels and the money his lordship had given me. I took a last look round the chamber and went down to the hall, carrying Boozey in his cage. The chariot had pulled up on the gravel drive at the front of the house and my trunks were already strapped to the roof. I was about to say my farewells to Mr Merritt and the other staff when Mr Ainsley came into the hall.

Not addressing me, he said to Mr Merritt, 'That is his lordship's carriage, is it not?'

'Yes, sir,' said Mr Merritt.

'Then what is it doing outside? Did I order a carriage? I did not.'

'It is for Miss Truegood, sir,' said Mr Merritt.

'That woman is quite capable of going by stagecoach,' said Mr Ainsley, still ignoring me. 'It is far more appropriate to her station. Send the carriage back to the stables.'

In exactly the same tone as he always spoke, his voice never rising or falling, his temper never wavering, Mr Merritt said, 'Until Mr Attaway has read his lordship's will, all the arrangements that were put in place before his lordship's death will be carried out to the letter.'

'Are you disobeying my orders?' asked Mr Ainsley, his lips pinched tight together, giving him the appearance of a rather ugly girl. He stamped his foot. 'You had better watch your step, Merritt.'

Seeing that Mr Merritt was unmoved by his threat, Mr Ainsley turned so red that I thought he might well burst.

'Witch,' he hissed at me. 'You should be burned.'

Mr Merritt took no notice and walked me to the coach, while from the safety of the house, Mr Ainsley shouted again, and louder, 'Witch!'

'I am sorry that he will be your new master, Mr Merritt,' I said. 'I think you would have fared better if Lord B had left his estate to his dogs.'

'My lady,' said Mr Merritt, bowing deeply, 'it has been a pleasure to know you.'

Biting on the inside of my cheek so as not to cry I was relieved when, with a jolt, we set off.

I suppose it was a dangerous undertaking, maybe even foolhardy, to travel with so much jewellery and money on my person. I should have been far more concerned than I was, but perhaps not caring a jot was, ironically, my greatest weapon for we were indeed stopped upon the King's Highway. It was approaching nine o'clock when the coach ran into trouble and the wheels became stuck firm in the mud. The footman helped me from the carriage and I stood on the side of the windswept highway while by the light of the postilions' lanterns, he and the coachman pulled the wheels free. I was so lost in my own thoughts that I was totally unaware of a horseman coming up alongside us. Only when I saw the rider did I realise we were in danger. He wore a three-cornered hat, a kerchief across his nose and mouth and held a pistol.

'Take down the trunks,' said the highwayman.

'No,' I said, emphatically. 'No.'

'Madam, I advise you to keep quiet if you want to live.'

'The trouble is,' I said, 'I'm not sure that I do. But I am positive that you will not take one shoe buckle from me while I am alive.'

The highwayman waved me aside with his pistol and again ordered the footman to take down the luggage.

'Leave it where it is,' I said and moved in front of the coachman, standing so that the highwayman would be forced to shoot me before anyone else.

'Madam,' pleaded the footman, 'he will kill us all if we don't do what he says.'

The highwayman hadn't yet dismounted, which I, knowing nothing about these robberies, took to be a good sign. I could see that I was proving something of a conundrum for he appeared uncertain how to proceed. I can well imagine that he didn't often encounter such determined resistance as mine – for I meant every word I said.

'Your ring, madam,' he said.

'No,' I said. 'The same principle applies: you will have to shoot me first. There's no other way you're going to have it or anything else of mine.'

The highwayman laughed.

I took that as a cue to make our exit. 'Is the carriage ready?' I asked the shaking coachman.

The poor man looked as if he was about to piss himself. 'Yes, my lady.'

'Then take your position for we are leaving.'

'If you move I will fire,' said the highwayman.

'Then I have the measure of you, sir,' I said, turning my back on him, 'for it shows you to be a complete coward. If you are to kill me, do it face to face.'

I climbed unaided into the coach and called to the coachman, 'Drive on.'

Suffice to say we were not shot at and the highwayman did not come after us. I thought it best to find an inn for the night so that everyone might recover their wits. It had begun to rain when we reached the next staging post. Another carriage stood in the courtyard. We entered to find that all the rooms had been taken by a French lady and her daughter, who were in the back parlour with a constable for they too had met with a highwayman. I left my coachman and went into the parlour in the hope that I might persuade the French lady to relinquish one of the chambers for my use.

She was a small, birdlike woman. Her clothes were in a sorry state and her face was caked in mud. In her hand she held her false curls; the young lady with her was clutching a rosary. She was deathly pale and her gown was torn.

'We were robbed. I lost everything – and my curls – look what the monster did,' said the French lady shaking her false hair at the constable. 'We were in fear of our lives.'

As she said most of this in French, the poor man understood very little.

'Please, madam, speak more slowly – and in English,' he said.

'We were in fear of our lives, *mon dieu*.' Turning to her daughter she said, 'This is a terrible country. We should not have gone to Bath – it is a dirty, provincial place with houses that look like hospitals. Even the baths themselves were dirty – like the English. This is a country of barbarians.'

She stopped when she saw me, and I curtsied and asked her

in French to explain what had befallen them. It seemed that the same highwayman we had encountered had collected a fair prize from this lady.

'We were robbed of everything, everything I tell you. I have nothing left.'

'Then, madam,' I asked, 'how do you intend to pay for all the chambers you have taken?'

The poor woman hadn't thought of that and it set off another bout of protesting that she wanted to be home, away from these savages.

'*Maman*,' said her daughter, 'calm yourself.'

At least she possessed some manners, which her mother was most decidedly lacking.

The innkeeper burst into the parlour. 'Is it true, madam,' he said to me, 'that you too were attacked on the highway?'

'Yes,' I said.

'And everything taken?' asked the lady.

'Nothing,' I said.

'Nothing?' she said, outraged. 'I don't believe you.'

'Whether you believe me or not, I need a chamber for the night and have the means to pay for it. As you have nothing, I'm afraid you will have to rely on my charity.'

Every inch of her bristled. I could see she was a woman who was rarely defeated. Her daughter was still fingering her rosary and muttering Hail Marys. I was too exhausted to be bothered further with their drama. They struck me as tiresome women.

The next morning, I breakfasted, settled my bill and that of the French ladies and, as soon as it was light, set off again. As we journeyed towards London on that sad October day, I had time to contemplate all that had passed and all that lay ahead. I had enough money to be independent of Queenie and the notion of renting rooms in St James's had a certain charm. I may well have been tempted if it hadn't been for the spectre of my ne'er-do-well husband, Captain Spiggot, who cast a long shadow over any hope of freedom.

London has a stench to it that floods the senses the minute you arrive; a perfume of which only those born in this cesspit of a city have any fond remembrances. A cold, autumnal nip was in the air and the mellow mist that journeyed with us from the countryside had, by the time we reached the metropolis, gathered itself into a grey, foggy veil, shrouding the city into a half-forgotten thing.

I arrived at the fairy house, having first deposited my jewels with Mr Little of Coutts in the Strand. With the departing of the coach the last ribbon that connected me to Lord B had been severed.

~

Writing of Lord B has brought on a great melancholy in me. I regret much that I never told him I loved him, for in my naivety I thought then that the heart could love only once. I see now that I have loved three people: none of the loves were the same and each is held in a different chamber of my heart. Mercy, Lord B. In the largest and least furnished chamber by far is the love I have for you. It has little more in it than a bed. How strange to have given you the lion's share of my heart when you have done so little to deserve it and I know so little of you.

Chapter Forty

So, with the death of Lord B, a new chapter of my life began.

Queenie was in the rookery with Mr Crease when I arrived at the fairy house and, seeing me, they rose as one. Mr Crease bowed, the striped fabric of his coat swirling about him. He closed his eyes so that his painted ones might see me all the better.

'What was I telling you?' he said to Queenie. 'And I was right.' I could only suppose that I had been a topic of conversation. Not bothering to explain the meaning of the sentence he carried on, 'You look remarkable, Tully: your complexion, your style, have a wit and gravitas that is much to be admired.'

All the while, Queenie was summing up my assets and, finding that they amounted to a lot more than they had done when I left, came to greet me.

'And I told you,' she said to Mr Crease, 'that Tully Truegood was going to be a beauty and I was right.' She paused a moment as if she had just seen a speck of dust in my eye that worried her. 'You haven't become puritanical in your grief, have you?'

There it was again: the old harsh Queenie, the voice that brokered no arguments. This was a whorehouse and I would be a fool to forget it.

'My circumstances wouldn't allow me to,' I said.

She waved her hand as if brushing such unpleasant thoughts

aside, and said, 'Lord Barbeau never bothered to teach Kitty Lay anything as far as I can tell. She remains, alas, as empty-headed as a bird's nest. You must have meant a lot to him.'

I nodded and said, 'I loved him, too.'

Queenie put her arms about me and kissed me on the cheek. 'A diamond in your heart, that's what his memory will be, to give you courage whenever you need it.'

I looked over her shoulder to where Pretty Poppet stood and thought that the girl was like a shard of glass in Queenie's heart, jagged and relentless.

Queenie returned to the safety of her chair, in fear, no doubt, that another uncontrolled emotion might inconveniently slip from her.

'You haven't come back a day too soon,' she said. 'Not a day. Bethany has as good as meddled with a hornets' nest and now we have a swarm buzzing about our ears.'

'Excuse me,' I said, 'what are you talking about?'

'My love,' said Mr Crease to Queenie, 'Tully knows nothing of this scandalous contest. But used to our advantage, it could bring about a meteoric rise in the career of a certain beauty that is standing before us. I hear the jingle-jangle of coins. Money, Mrs Gibbs, the shit of life.'

'Enough of this nonsense,' I said. 'Kindly explain yourselves.'

Mr Crease laughed. 'Listen to that, madam. There is the voice of authority where before there was only the bleating of a lamb.'

'Oh, be still,' said Queenie and sighed. 'Let me explain. Bethany, in what I can only suppose was misplaced wisdom, told her spark, a dull man by the name of Mr Spencer, that Mrs Coker had given you a pearl hand. Mr Spencer has a great weakness for gambling and he immediately bet Bethany five hundred pounds that Kitty's was still the only hand in the business worth mentioning. Like a complete idiot, Bethany took him up on the gamble. She can ill afford to lose five hundred pounds and I can ill afford unwanted tittle-tattle. Nevertheless, it was agreed that the contest would be held the day after you returned, when the thing could be proven once and for all.'

I laughed. 'And how are we to prove this?'

'Kitty has set down that the number of strokes necessary to bring a man to that delicate point is fifteen. If you have a pearl hand, you should be able to make a man reach the same melting moment just by resting it on his truncheon. And that is all you will be allowed to do.'

'Oh, feathers and dust,' I said. 'That's near on imp – ' I saw the look on Mr Crease's face and stopped. 'I have never managed such a thing. Cannot this folly be put off a little longer?'

'I think not,' said Mr Crease. 'The sooner this business is out of the way the better. I suggest tomorrow night.'

It made me smile to think what Lord B would say to such idiocy.

'*Nous nageons dans un flot futile,*' I said.

'French!' said Queenie. 'You speak French?'

'*Un peu,*' I said.

~

That first night in the fairy house, Hope and Mercy were both away and Bethany, knowing the trouble she was in, contrived to be absent when she heard I was back. I wondered how I might prepare for such foolishness and in the end decided to concentrate on my looks, for they would play the greater part in this exercise. Signor Florentini spent near the entire afternoon attending to every little hair and, when finally I was dressed, Queenie came to give her opinion on my appearance.

'Most *à la mode*,' she said. 'Though is not the kerchief unnecessarily modest?'

'No,' I said.

'Tully, we are not in Bath. This,' said Queenie, taking it away so that my nipples were on display, 'is far more what the occasion requires.'

My maid declared that the gentleman's heart would melt.

'I hope not just his heart,' said Queenie, dismissing her.

I looked in the glass and added some powder to my neck and breasts.

'There is, my beauty,' said Queenie, 'a rather special visitor here tonight for the first time. He heard of you in Bath and has a great desire to meet you.'

Sensing that I was not overjoyed at the prospect, she added, 'He has the way, withal, to elevate you in the world.'

For the purposes of my narrative, this gentleman will be known only as the Duke of H, for he was related to the royal family and the last thing anyone would want is that they be brought into this scandalous affair.

I had a feeling that Queenie had already negotiated my services. She patted my hand. 'Of course, Tully, you will meet him first and then make your decision. But I must remind you that without a protector you are far more vulnerable to the attentions of Captain Spiggot.'

The drawing room was to be used for the contest and a small stage had been constructed so that everyone there would be able to judge the competition for themselves.

I told Mr Pouch to call for me after Kitty had arrived.

By nine o'clock there was quite a crowd and the atmosphere was most jolly. I watched, unseen, from an anteroom as
champagne flowed, much to the delight of Queenie's regular
guests and those who were there for the first time. There was a
carnival atmosphere about the place – I had almost forgotten
how lush and loose these soirées were. Voices rose and fell
then swirled again on a wave of wit and a splash of drink. The
discussion centred on who the two gentlemen should be and
those who supported Bethany strongly disputed that either
of the participants should ever have enjoyed Kitty's services.

'That doesn't leave us much choice,' said one gentleman.
'Who here hasn't known that wondrous hand of hers?'

Finally, two gentlemen stepped forth. Both swore on the
Harris List that they had never had the privilege of knowing
Kitty's palm. There was a general agreement that the two
libertines were good for the sport and both were more than
willing for their appendages to be used to settle this most
unusual of bets.

'The one to the left,' whispered Queenie to me, 'is the Duke
of H.'

He was about five and thirty, with babyish features that
age would not be kind to. In truth, I was not taken with the
Duke of H, and I doubted that I ever would be.

Kitty was already on the stage, dressed in a garish costume
and with too much rouge upon her cheeks. She lifted a glass
of champagne high and then drank to the company. There was
no doubt that the gamblers in the room had already decided
the winner was a foregone conclusion.

'This,' she said, waving her hand, 'as many a gentleman
here could testify, is my speciality, and any of you who are

fool enough to believe that a cheap actress is able to endow a tart with a pearl hand is a real lobcock.'

There was raucous laughter and I wished that there was no need for this trite piece of theatre.

Mr Crease, who was acting as Master of Ceremonies announced, 'The one and only Miss Tully Truegood,' and it was then that I made my entrance. Kitty stared at me aghast. 'You are Tully?' she said.

Everyone had turned round and Hope, seeing me for the first time in a year, rushed up and gave me a kiss.

'Oh, my ninny-not – look at you!'

Mercy led the clapping as I took my place on the stage.

The two volunteers came up and were greeted by whooping and cheers.

Mr Crease put a screen between the two gentlemen so neither would receive any additional stimulation. He banged a gong, the gentleman on the right undid his breeches, his weapon already hard, well inflamed by the thought of what was to come. Kitty, with a pride that had to be admired, went vigorously to work. After what I took to be fifteen strokes, there was a sigh, and Mr Crease announced, to more cheers, that the point been achieved. Kitty stood and announced herself the winner, but Mr Crease declared that I was yet to play my part.

While Kitty had been employing her overused hand, I had taken the opportunity to look my gentleman in the eye. He was no more handsome close to than he was from a distance, puffy of skin, with more than a glimmer of arrogance about him, and I could see that he did not believe in such a thing as a pearl hand. He undid his breeches, seemingly proud of the fact that his weapon had not been so easily moved. The more I looked at him, the more I knew I had him, all of him. I saw him rising, could feel his cock yearning to be touched, just once. Still I kept my eyes locked upon him until the laughter had gone from them and something more animal, more essential had taken its place, and I knew he could not hold out any longer. It was then that I rested my hand upon that quivering engine. He let out a gasp of surprise and an arc of fluid that proved more sufficiently than anything else who the outright winner was.

The odds against me winning had been high.

Bethany came up to me. 'I knew you could do it. You see, I had faith.' And then she said, 'You have turned into one hell of a beauty, witchy woman.'

Kitty Lay bristled with rage and without another word marched out of the fairy house with her supporters.

Refreshments were served while musicians played, then the activities of the night began in earnest.

Queenie introduced me to the Duke of H, the gentleman with whom I had already become so intimately acquainted.

I curtsied.

'I have heard that a great courtesan can make a man explode just by looking into their eyes. And I can tell you that I would have shot my arrow even if you hadn't touched me.'

I thanked him for his compliment.

'I would like to have the honour of exploring your talents further,' he said, quite seriously.

I said nothing that would encourage him and nothing that would discourage him, and went to play cards. For the first time, I found that many young dandies wanted to partner me.

A little later, Queenie asked if she might have a talk. I followed her into the rookery.

'What do you think of the Duke of H?' she said.

In truth I thought little. He appeared to be a forceful bore, though I was wise enough not to say so.

Queenie saw immediately that I was not as enthusiastic as she thought I should be and said sharply, 'Perhaps you should see what else is on offer before you refuse him. Your husband has assured me that he will forgive your past if you return to him as a dutiful wife. He came here the minute he heard of Lord B's death.'

'Feathers and dust!' I said in disbelief. 'And you let him in?'

I felt an uncontrollable rage rise in me, a potent mixture of grief, hurt and the sense of betrayal.

'I run a whorehouse,' said Queenie, 'and…' Her hands went to her mouth, her eyes opened wide. 'Tully, don't… please don't.'

Only then did I realise what I had unconsciously done: every ornament, every piece of paper, every book – anything that couldn't claim the weight of gravity to hold it in place – hovered precariously in the air.

'I am merely trying to point out the merits of having the duke as a protector,' she said feebly.

'No, you aren't,' I said. 'You have already sold me to the duke for a handsome figure, haven't you? And now you are worried that you are about to lose face. I'd wager that it was at your invitation my husband came here.'

I was so furious that I would willingly have let everything crash to the floor.

'You are one of my gals,' she said, her voice querulous. 'Tully, don't go!'

I left her with her possessions hanging in the air. Why, I thought, should she lightly be forgiven?

At the card table I contemplated the options open to me. I could leave the next day, set up in my own rooms and wait for a gallant more to my liking. Or, find another madam to take me on.

I won well at Faro and when Hope leaned over to kiss me, it struck me that I would not leave the fairy house. It was home, the place where Hope and Mercy were, and Mr Crease and Ned Bird. Home was a word that I had never been able to use of Milk Street, and Queenie, for all her faults, was the only mother I had ever known. With a sigh, my anger vanished. Spiggot could go to hell – I would never be his. It was then that I knew that everything in the rookery had returned to its rightful place. Whether Queenie would forgive me was another matter.

~

It was around two o'clock in the morning when at last I retired to my chamber. I wondered if I could bear the attentions of the Duke of H and for the first time in a long while I remembered the nights I had spent with Avery, when I was innocent, when the world was so very wide, before it came to be no more than the reflection of the moon in a dirty puddle.

Chapter Forty-One

My maid had undressed me and I was in bed, pleased to be alone, the distant chatter from below a lullaby soothing me to sleep, when my maid knocked upon the door.

'I'm sorry, Miss Tully,' she said, 'there is gentleman here wanting to see you. He's very persistent.'

I told her to send the Duke of H away, for I was in no doubt as to who was pursuing me. 'Ask him to return tomorrow,' I said.

Hardly had I spoken when he pushed into my chamber and flung himself upon my bed. 'Why make me wait when I already adore you and have such longings that cannot be satisfied by your hand or eye?'

'Come now, sir,' I said, 'waiting surely adds to the delight of what is in store.'

'But I cannot wait, you have stirred the fire in me and I'm ablaze with a want of you.'

'Your flattery, sir, will not change my mind. Now, please, leave me in peace.'

My maid was still standing in the doorway, regarding the situation with interest. 'What shall I do?' she asked.

'Leave us,' said his grace.

'Please, sir, less haste, I beg of you!' I said, for the duke had already undone his breeches.

I could see quite clearly that there was no cooling of his ardour.

My maid returned, carrying champagne and glasses. 'With the compliments of Mrs Gibbs,' she said, and left again.

I smiled. I was forgiven, and more than Queenie's ornaments were back in place. The duke took my smile for encouragement.

'I am most sincere in my feelings, most sincere indeed,' said the Duke of H. 'I will be the tenderest of lovers.'

One look at him made me doubt that.

'I prostrate myself at your feet,' he said, his hand finding its way to my breasts. Then, hoping for no more resistance, he started to kiss my neck. 'Can you not tell I am in love?'

I doubted that too, for what he said had little sincerity to it.

He kissed me upon the lips with such force that his tongue near choked me. When at last he pulled away I was gasping for breath.

'Why such false modesty?' he said. 'Come, you are no blushing virgin.'

And before the inconvenience of any more words passed my lips, he kissed me again. I struggled to free myself.

'Your grace, please,' I said. 'Not tonight.'

'Yes, tonight it must be… it has to be… it will be… for tomorrow all could be ashes.'

A truer word he had not spoken, for no spark of desire ignited in me.

He stood up, abruptly, and took off the remainder of his clothes. I say took off, more he tore at them and revealed a prodigiously large weapon, the like of which I had not seen except on a donkey. It quite terrified me. I could only suppose that it must have previously remained half hidden and one touch had by no means allowed me to become fully acquainted with its size.

'Sir, will you not first have a drink?'

'No, no,' he said, hoarsely, and lay down beside me. 'This is the only nectar I need.' He slipped his hands between my legs.

'Sir,' I said, 'I would like to take a glass even if you will not.'

'This is torture,' he said, standing up again and going to the table.

He poured a glass of champagne. His pole stuck out alarmingly, but at least I had a chance to appraise him. He had a not altogether displeasing figure; he was well made in the quarters that mattered – perhaps too well made, for I was not certain that he would fit me at all.

He handed me a glass, I took a sip and that was all.

'I cannot wait any longer,' he said.

His weapon was fully loaded and desperately in need of being fired. He bunched up my shift over my thighs so that my Venus mound was well within his aim. There was little finesse in his manner. Having given me all that he felt was necessary to warm me to his desires, he thrust his point home far too soon, which immediately had the effect of cooling all passion on my part for he was not a good fit. Yet having once achieved the passage he cared little as to the pain given in the wielding of such an inappropriate weapon as his. I felt it tear through me and, all too soon, he released himself of his pent-up desire. He was not content with that. I had been used to Lord Barbeau whose strength in lovemaking had been much diminished by illness. This was, alas, not the case with the Duke of H and it was only in the light of a weary dawn that he did at last cease his assault on me and leave.

That morning, Queenie arrived with a tray of chocolate, full of smiles and fuss, to tell me that I had been greatly admired last night. Our wrangling forgotten, she was full of praise for my ingenuity at having captured the duke so quickly. I sighed. For the first time, I knew what being a whore meant, and I was disgusted with myself.

I never liked him, he never suited me. I tolerated him, that was all. It was his smell that I couldn't stand. He was a fussy man in everything pertaining to personal matters but it was the odour he released when aroused – sweet, sickly – that, by degrees, I came to loathe.

In the beginning I told myself that the old ache would return but it never did. When you love without love, you lose all joy. This was work that owed nothing to pleasure. Never once, when I was with him, did I melt away in ecstasy or find myself in that most extraordinary part of my being where all of me and all of my lover were one.

He paid handsomely for my services. My duties were listed: I was to be an adoring mistress, to be available for him at all times. I was to be immaculately turned out. I was forbidden from reading novels, which he stated were the ruination of women. If I became with child he would pay for me to have it abroad but would not recognise it as his. I was to have no other gallants while I was with him. This contract could be terminated by him at any time without obligation.

I never thought about being with child, or that it might be the natural consequence of these unnatural games. Yet in that I was very lucky, unlike Bethany, who shortly after winning the bet found she was pregnant with her third child.

Up to then I'd had no idea she had a child at all, let alone two. One, a boy, was farmed out to a family in Kent and Bethany paid for his upkeep. The daughter she'd had by a

Mr Fable, he had adopted, as his wife was unable to bear children. The price Bethany paid was her agreement never to see or contact her daughter. This time she would go to the country and come back once the baby had been weaned and found a home.

'I have beautiful babies,' she said.

The fairy house felt empty without her. Mercy was hardly ever there in those days; Hope told me that she'd rented chambers with Mofty and no longer had any interest in the game.

For the next three months I spent most of my days with Hope and my nights with the duke, while he pushed and shoved, pulled and gasped his way ever forward to the climax of his desire which always came a thrust too early.

Part of the agreement was that I had a carriage and four-in-hand for my sole use. Hope, and sometimes Queenie, would accompany me shopping or to the dressmaker's. I had a good eye, and, enjoying being ahead of the beau monde, I took to designing my gowns. I found that I could occupy myself for hours with nothing more than the frivolity of trimmings. How fluffy and foolish my mind became. My clothes and fashions were often the subject of the gossip columns, my fame all the greater through my reputation of having a mysterious pearl hand. By small degrees I became used to such indulgence, though not, alas, to the gentleman who paid for it.

Lord Barbeau had told me that salmon garner strength by swimming upriver. It is hard to imagine what good comes of being so excessively spoiled and not wanting for anything. To counterbalance the boredom that was an inevitable outcome of this way of life, I fed my mind with the buying and reading of the forbidden novels and, when I wasn't at the duke's beck and call or concerning myself with frippery, I spent my time lost in other people's imaginings.

I had confided in Hope that I had found myself pretending satisfaction with his grace when there was none.

'We all do,' said Hope.

He had no interest in me other than my body. Some conversation might have been enough to bring on some fondness for him, but there was none. He once told me it was better for a man to be in the wilderness than with a woman who had opinions and whose tongue was never still in the saying of them. He considered that a man was held in greater esteem if he had a beautiful woman at his side and delighted in the envious looks of his friends when we were together.

I find it hard to put flesh on the bones of such an engraving of a man as was the Duke of H. He appeared to me as nothing more than a plucked goose, all flesh and no feathers worth a mention. A caricature of ambition with little intellect to recommend him, he might as well have been drawn by the great Hogarth himself.

I knew that I meant no more to him than any other of his possessions, all of which he owned so that he might be shown in a favourable light. In the past my spirits would have risen on this hot air of folly, but they didn't, and I began to feel more and more like my parrot: dead, stuffed and still.

Chapter Forty-Two

Newgate Prison, the Governor's House

I had a visitor today – Lord B's solicitor, Mr Attaway. He came into my small chamber in the governor's house wearing the same yellow unpleasant wig and on his very thin nose a pair of spectacles that gave him a quizzical look, as if he could not quite remember the reason for his visit to this unholy place. He was accompanied by his clerk, Tubbs. Tubbs reminded me of a bee buzzing round a buttercup. The first thing he did was take hold of the chair on which the solicitor was about to place his learned bottom, and dust it vigorously before replacing it in position. Then he buzzed round the solicitor, bringing out sheaves of legal documents, tied with pink ribbon. It appeared that he was only able to stop buzzing if he could catch hold of his own arms and fold them under himself, with his legs twisted round each other. I was most entertained. If the pair had been on stage they would have received a round of applause for such a farcical performance.

'To what do I owe the honour of your visit?' I asked Mr Attaway.

The solicitor took off his glasses and handed them to Tubbs, who unwound himself sufficiently to clean them and give them back. Mr Attaway concentrated on the papers in front of him.

He cleared his throat and, keeping one finger on the relevant passage, said, 'Miss Truegood, as I am sure you are aware, I was retained as solicitor to the late Lord Barbeau. As you may not be aware, his lordship's wish was that the bulk of his estate should be left to you on his death. It is a most uncommon practice and not one I encouraged, yet on this one issue he refused to take sound legal advice. Furthermore, he instructed me to take care of your interests at the appropriate time.'

I looked at Mr Attaway, astonished, and tried to say something but I could see that once he had started he would not countenance interruptions until he had finished. He cleared his throat again.

'Due to your clandestine marriage,' he said, unnecessarily shuffling the papers, 'certain stipulations were put in place that had to be fulfilled before you came into your inheritance.'

'I think there is a misunderstanding,' I said. 'Lord Barbeau gave me gifts of jewellery and some money, but nothing more. I thought Mr Ainsley had inherited the estate.'

'Mr Ainsley?'

'Yes,' I said, somewhat impatiently. 'Mr Ainsley, Lord Barbeau's nephew.'

The clerk leapt to his feet and buzzed in the solicitor's ear. He rustled his papers.

'Ah, yes. You refer to the Reverend Jonathan Ainsley.' He sniffed as if there was an unpleasant smell coming from the ink itself. 'Yes, I have it here. Mr Ainsley was left two thousand pounds. He tried and failed to dispute the will. That is by the by. Back to the matter in hand. Your inheritance has been held in trust and the three trustees are myself, Mr Little of Coutts Bank, and Mr Merritt. They will continue to manage the estate until you...'

He ran out of words for there was little to say.

'…become the wealthiest whore ever to swing at the gallows.' I couldn't help it. I laughed out loud. 'Are you sure there is no mistake?'

Mr Attaway looked like a man who had never made a mistake in his life.

'As you are now unencumbered by a husband, you are the legal beneficiary of five hundred thousand pounds, in addition to his lordship's house in Highgate, his estate in Chippenham and the contents thereof.'

I was completely stunned. How ironic that, finally, I was my own mistress and richer than I could ever have imagined. There in all this gloom, a little crack of hope.

'It would seem, sir, that there is more than enough money for me to fight my case.'

'Indeed there is, madam,' said Mr Attaway. 'This murder is anything but straightforward. It is becoming increasingly necessary, especially in cases of felony, to instruct a defence lawyer on behalf of the accused. If you will allow me, madam, I will give the brief to Mr Gately, who is one of London's foremost barristers.'

'Please do, sir,' I said.

'Very good. I will make sure Mr Gately calls on you tomorrow.' He turned to his clerk. 'Have you written that down, Tubbs?'

I would imagine every word Mr Attaway had ever uttered was engraved on the clerk's heart.

'One moment, sir,' I said. 'If I have access to the money, then my dear friend, Mercy, must see the best doctor there is.'

'Is there anything else?'

'Yes, there is a woman by the name of Bethany Goodere. I want to help her…'

'Furnish Tubbs with the details and it will be done.' He paused.

'Would it be out of place if I made a suggestion?' asked Mr Attaway.

'Not in the slightest, sir.'

'Victor Wrattan should be investigated.'

'I agree, sir.'

He stood up. 'A man will be hired for the purpose. I will do my very best for you, Miss Truegood,' said Mr Attaway, taking off his glasses and handing them to Tubbs, who was already buzzing round in anticipation of being gone. 'Madam, my advice is two-fold: do not gamble, and…' he glanced at my belly '… do make a will.'

Thank you, my sweet Lord B, I thought as they left. I may hang, but at least my daughter will have a chance to be an independent woman.

Chapter Forty-Three

One evening in January, the duke and I were at the Rotunda at Ranelagh Gardens. It was a building that made me think, as we approached in the darkness, of an ogre's lantern, lights spilling from it as if it had been accidentally forgotten and one day it would be remembered and lifted up to light the way to the ogre's castle.

In the very centre of this vast space was a fireplace, a stone altar, surrounded on six sides by balustrades, and columns that rose to become armless, bare-breasted women before fanning out to the ceiling. Round the walls of the rotunda were two tiers of booths, a stand for the musicians, and high above them all were arched windows.

We were seated in one of the alcoves with his grace's friend, a young man, Mr Luckham, who was recounting how he had recently parted from his mistress.

'I took her to Italy,' he said. 'And one day we visited a palace where there was a lion in the courtyard. I paid for a viewing and we were shown into a chamber and from an open window had a good sighting of this most furious of beasts. When my mistress dropped her glove from the window, she told me that as I had often said I would do anything for her, now was as good an opportunity as any to prove I was sincere by retrieving it.'

The duke was finding Mr Luckham's story most amusing and it was while he was distracted that I noticed the French lady I had seen at the staging inn on the road from Bath. She was dressed in the most ridiculously tall wig that had in it a basket of blown glass flowers. With her was her daughter. A thin, startled deer of a creature, she was wearing a shepherd-ess's costume that made her seem very young. Then I looked again, for if I wasn't mistaken, they were accompanied by Lord Frederick Fitzjohn.

'Well, dammit,' said Mr Luckham. 'I went down to the courtyard with sword in hand and unlocked the gate. I stared that lion in the eye, and he backed off. I retrieved my mistress's glove from within a foot of the lion's paw!'

The French lady, her daughter and Lord Frederick Fitzjohn took the booth behind us. The French lady possessed a penetrating voice so that it was near impossible not to overhear every word she had to say.

'I have told you, Angelina, the engagement must be broken, *tout de suite.*'

'*Maman,*' said her daughter, 'let us not discuss it in the presence of Lord Fitzjohn.'

'*Pouf!*' said her mother. 'Who better knows the problems that we face than his lordship? Sir, do you not agree? This impediment to the marriage has been going on too long without resolution. It is ridiculous and makes us a laughing stock. I will not have it, he is nothing, he has no title, no fortune.'

'But, Maman, you know he is studying to be a physician,' said the girl.

'Your grace is right, by gad,' said Lord Fitzjohn. 'I shouldn't speak ill of my brother but...'

'Miss Truegood,' said Mr Luckham, seeing that he didn't have my full attention, 'would you demand the same of the duke?'

'I would not, sir,' I said.

'You see – here is a good woman. Do you know what I said to my whore of a mistress? I said as I returned her glove, "Madam, I have done this to show you that I am true to my word and henceforth I want nothing more to do with you." How could I have any feelings for a woman who put so little value on my life as to expose me to the fury of a lion for a paltry glove?'

'Well said, sir,' said the duke, who was laughing so much that he had tears in his eyes. 'Doesn't that amuse you?' he said to me.

I smiled but said nothing, for I was still in part listening to Lord Fitzjohn's annihilation of his brother's character.

'We will walk,' announced his grace, and what his grace wanted to do, we all did. We went round the Rotunda, ostensibly to admire the paintings by Canaletto, but really so that everyone might admire his grace.

We had reached the musicians' stand and a fair crowd had gathered round us when, to my horror, Lord Fitzjohn hurried up and for one terrible moment I thought he had recognised me.

But he gave a deep bow and said to the duke, 'It is a pleasure to see you, your grace, by gad, it is. And who is this ravishing creature?'

Lord Fitzjohn looked straight at me, his eyes resting impolitely on my low-cut dress, his indecent thoughts flashing clearly in his eyes. Finally remembering the party he was with, he introduced the French lady as the Duchess de Vauquelin, and her daughter, Countess Angelina.

La duchesse, a small woman made taller by the wig, was trying and failing to look down her nose at me.

Waving her fan, she said, '*Madame*, was it not you I met on the Bath Road?'

I curtsied. 'Indeed it was, your grace,' I said.

'Then I have to thank you for paying my bill. Are you the wife of his grace, *le duc*?'

'*Maman!*' said the young countess, sensing the question was inappropriate.

'No, your grace,' I replied, staring into her face.

She surmised the situation and moved to shield her innocent daughter from the influence of a fallen woman. Although I was better dressed than her and may have looked like a lady of quality, her nose had sniffed out that I was not. She called Lord Fitzjohn, who was deep in conversation with the duke, and he was reluctantly forced to return to his party.

I longed to leave, and just as I was thinking that the only comfort to be taken from this embarrassing scene was that Avery was not present, to my utter horror I saw him enter. Quickly, I turned away and went to stand with the crowd that was listening to the music, interesting myself in the programme, until the duke found me and reprimanded me for leaving his side without his permission.

'I have a headache, sir, and would like to return home,' I said.

'No,' he said. 'Not yet awhile.'

And we walked round the Rotunda with the unavoidable outcome of meeting Avery Fitzjohn. He was speaking to the countess when we neared their party. She had her eyes fixed on him and it was clear that she adored him.

Lord Fitzjohn introduced Avery to the duke, and the duke introduced me to Avery.

I examined him discreetly. He had lost the sparkle from those beautiful blue eyes that I once would willingly have fallen into for ever. It was as if something hung too heavy on him. A maudlin sadness overcame me as I remembered myself when I had first lain with him, the pleasure he had given me, the joy we had found in our lovemaking.

We walked in a party, round and round. To start with he was far away from me and Mr Luckham was telling the story of the glove and the lion to Lord Fitzjohn. As is the way with parties that walk in circles, eventually I found myself alongside Avery. The closeness of him brought on a physical ache. I longed to touch him, to tell him I loved him and I always would. Even though the remembrance of his kisses sent a delicious tingle through me I was saddened to know I had lost him. His voice, his manner, told me that his feelings for me had died.

'How are you, madam?' he said.

'Well,' I said. 'And you, sir?'

And so we took our places to commence the dance of false conversation, for everything I said there were a hundred other words I would have spoken, but such truths polite society avoids.

We left shortly after. I sat in the carriage with the duke, silent, which was the way he liked me best.

Suddenly, he said, 'You know, I think that silly fluff of, thing will in the end be persuaded by her *maman* to marry Frederick. He's far more suitable. The brother's damn good-looking but you can't base a marriage on looks. What was his name?'

'Avery, I believe.'

'No, *la comtesse* will marry Lord Fitzjohn if *la duchesse* has anything to do with it. His half-brother's had long enough to sort out the problem.

'What problem is that, sir?'

'I'm not certain,' he said and yawned. 'Some impediment to the marriage. God knows why anyone would want to marry. I hope to avoid it if I can. No, a mistress is much to be preferred. You can always hand her in when she grows too old; a wife you have until death. The law sticks you together and together you remain.'

'What impediment?' I asked.

Why are you interested?'

'I'm curious, that is all.'

'Like all women,' said the duke. 'I heard that old Fitzjohn put a clause in his will which resulted in his legitimate younger son being disinherited in favour of his illegitimate older son. Why the old fool would do such a thing, God only knows. His mistress – Frederick's mama – who became Fitzjohn's second wife, was one of the most scheming women I've ever had the misfortune of meeting.'

'Is she still alive?' I asked, staring out of the window, overwhelmed by sadness for Avery, and for myself.

'No. And I've had enough of this conversation. My mind is on other things.' The duke put my hand on his erect weapon. There it was, that smell that I loathed. 'Come here,' he said, pulling up my petticoats. 'Have you ever been ravished in a chariot?'

I thought of Avery, of the skill of his lovemaking, of the clumsiness of the duke's.

'Sir, I am not feeling well,' I said.

'Nonsense. I pay for you, remember? When I need you, I need you.'

His grace had already undone himself and he pulled me onto his lap so that his weapon found aim and quickly fired.

Chapter Forty-Four

I had, by the end of that month, moved out of the fairy house into more suitable lodgings, as the Duke of H put it, in Pall Mall. I had asked him if I could take Ned Bird with me but he wouldn't hear of it. I tried to explain why I needed him. His grace raised his bejewelled hand to silence me.

'No,' he said, firmly. 'All connections must be severed. I will it so and so it will be.'

Rich and fashionable society has, as far as I can see, little breadth to it and even less depth, being on the whole obsessed with itself and itself alone. Its sport lies mainly in scandal, its nourishment comes from gossip, and it is hard to imagine how society would pass its days without them.

Shortly after I moved, the duke commissioned a portrait of me by one of society's most eminent artists. It showed me in a white shift, leaning on the arm of a chair with my hands together, a string of pearls over my right shoulder and my left breast exposed. I stared out of the canvas with a soft smile on my full lips, my cheeks rosy, my hair pinned but not powdered. His grace was delighted with the results.

'There isn't another face like yours,' said the duke, who prided himself on being a connoisseur of everything fashionable. 'Don't you agree?' he asked his friend Sir Henry Slater, who I'd met at the fairy house the night I was still innocent, the night I'd first loved Avery.

'I declare,' said Sir Henry, 'even if Miss Tully were not a beauty, her style would always attract attention. As would her keen intelligence.'

To the fury of the artist, copies by good, bad and indifferent engravers were made and sold so my image could be bought in many sizes, some so small as to fit into a snuffbox. Now I was recognised wherever we went.

I found Sir Henry entertaining company. Unlike the duke, he had no desire for me to sit silently in front of him – far from it. Wit and conversation was what he craved. He once asked my opinion of what might happen if the Duke of H should become king.

Without too much thought, I replied, 'There would be a revolution.'

Sir Henry was the only person to lighten the ever-increasing boredom of the shallow life I now led. Gossip, bibble-babble. Fashion faux pas strangely held the same weight as the scandals that went on behind bedroom doors. The duke was forever recounting dull stories, embarrassing moments in society. These amused him no end.

One involved the Duchess de Vauquelin. He had been playing cards with her one night and she had lost badly. Her face aglow, she put her hand to her forehead and in doing so dislodged an artificial eyebrow made of mouse fur. Unnoticed by its owner, the eyebrow began, by degrees, to slide down the coating of powdery paint on her face.

'How we laughed,' said his grace. 'Including the duchess, until her daughter pointed out what had happened. She hasn't been seen in public since.'

I thought, this is what kills you in the end: mindless prattling, stupidity that eats away at your very soul.

Time passed and I became less sure of who I was. I saw myself more and more as an actress playing a part – the wordless part of a courtesan.

In April, a month that is neither governed by spring nor ruled by winter, the duke held one of his more intimate dinner parties at his house in St James's Square. It was for a small circle of his closest male friends. They had one characteristic in common: a great interest in themselves. I had hoped that I might be excused, for I hadn't had an opportunity to invite Hope to Pall Mall and longed to catch up with all the news from the fairy house. His grace, though, was insistent that I attend the dinner. Among the guests were Sir Henry Slater, Mr Luckham – he of the glove and the lion story – and Lord Frederick Fitzjohn.

He was hoping to become betrothed to the Countess Angelina.

'The damn countess would be mine,' he told us, 'if it was not for my brother. He is all that stands between me and a fortune.'

I wasn't acquainted with the last guest, a young rake who went by the name of Selway.

The duke's idea of an informal dinner party had all the informality of a state occasion. Under a crystal chandelier, the long table was laid with the finest glass and china, and footmen lined the walls. I, being the only woman present, was the first to enter that evening. I saw her standing on the table in her stockinged feet, wearing nothing but a shift. She was about sixteen years of age and around her neck was a noose. She was trying to attach the other end of the rope to the chandelier. I knew no one else could see her and wondered which of these gentlemen had unwittingly called forth this unhappy spirit.

As we took our seats, she looked wildly about and kicked a plate from the setting in front of Mr Luckham, sending it flying to crash loudly upon the floor.

'How strange,' he said, I didn't touch it.'

A footman hastily picked up the pieces and a new plate was put before the startled gentleman. As usual, I sat, not speaking, watching as more and more wine made its way round the table. All the while the girl skilfully tiptoed among the plates.

Mr Selway said, rather too loudly, 'I hear, Miss Truegood, that you have a pearl hand.'

I smiled and said nothing.

The ghost was unpinning her hair so that it fell over her shoulders. She now moved among the dishes that were being served and, to my amusement, rested her hand on the duke's wig. He shuddered and demanded that more coal be put upon the fire for the room had a chill to it.

The meal was over, and I had risen to leave the men to their port when Mr Selway said, 'You didn't answer me, Miss Truegood. Is it true? Do you have a pearl hand or is it only a myth?'

To my utter surprise, the duke said, 'Tully, why don't you show the sceptics here what you can do with just one touch?'

'I am sorry, your grace…' I said.

'Show them, woman. Come on, I demand it. Who wants to volunteer?'

There was a moment's silence and then I suggested Mr Luckham for the ghost was standing behind his chair. She looked at me and smiled.

'Very well,' said Mr Luckham. 'I'm up for the sport but I

wager you will have no success with me. I am made of firmer
metal than you, your grace.'

'I will bet ten thousand guineas that Tully will do it with
one touch.'

Mr Selway said, lazily, 'I will bet double that she cannot.'

The atmosphere had taken on a more serious quality. Such
hefty wagers brought with them a certain sobriety.

'Sir,' I said to the duke, 'this is not wise.'

'Not wise,' he repeated. 'And who, pray, asked you for your
opinion?'

I positively hated this man, and I'd had more than enough
of being thought of as nothing but an empty-headed doll.

The duke asked where I wanted Mr Luckham and if he
should be seated or standing.

'Seated,' I said, and pointed to a spot furthest from the table
where everyone would have a good view.

A footman duly put a chair there and Mr Luckham seated
himself. I knew what I was going to do and I doubted that it
would end well. If the fools wanted amusement, I would let
them have it. I stayed where I was on the other side of the table
and began to will the spirit to be visible to all in the room.

'By Gad,' said Lord Fitzjohn. 'How long does this nonsense
take?'

'Yes,' said the duke, impatiently. 'I don't remember having
to wait so long. What are you doing standing there? Go to
him, Tully.'

I didn't move.

'Come on, madam,' said the duke. 'You must...' He stopped,
for there she was, for all to see.

There was a gasp.

'Where the hell did she come from?' asked Lord Fitzjohn.

'Quiet, man,' said Mr Selway.

The girl knelt beside Mr Luckham and, speechless, he stared at her as if trying to remember just how much wine he had drunk. She undid his breeches. No one at the table dared breathe.

'It's a ghost,' said Sir Henry. 'How amusing.'

'Silence!' commanded the duke.

Mr Luckham, his voice trembling, said, 'Mary...'

The spirit began to sing:

> *Mistress Mary,*
> *Quite contrary,*
> *How does my garden grow?*

'You remember me,' she said, 'Your Mary.'

'Yes, yes,' said Mr Luckham.

'You remember...

> *With Silver Bells,*
> *And Cockle Shells,*
> *And so my garden grows.*

'You was going to marry me, you were. Remember all them fine words you spoke? Promised you did, if I would ride your cock horse. You ain't forgotten? And I, all innocent, believed you to be an honourable man.'

She took off her shift and stood before us in all her voluptuous beauty, then eased herself onto his erect pole.

'*Ride a cock horse*,' she sang moving up and down, '*we goes up to town to marry me, into the grave to bury me.*'

He threw his head back and groaned as she began to fade

from him. I walked to where he was sitting and put my hand once on his member. 'Mary,' he screamed, and exploded into the empty air.

There was a scraping of chairs for now the apparition could be seen dangling above the table from the rope about her neck, turning round and round, her face a skull.

Mr Luckham sprang up. 'Help me cut her down, help me someone, for God's sake…Mary!'

She vanished and all the candles went out.

~

'How did you do it?' asked the duke the following morning. 'Was she one of Queenie's girls? Or an actress? How did you smuggle her in?'

'Your grace,' I said, 'if I had done so, that would be supposing I knew what you were going to ask of me.'

'Mmm,' said the duke, being forced into the uncomfortable position of having to think logically. 'I am a rational man. There must be an explanation, for there is an explanation for all things.'

I said nothing.

'Madam, I asked you a question. Tell me how you smuggled in the woman.'

'I didn't, your grace.'

'Are you suggesting that this…ah…Mary was really a ghost?'

'Yes, sir.'

'Balderdash,' he said. 'We will speak no more about this. You are forbidden ever again to do such a thing in my house – or anywhere else – while you are my mistress.'

There became an even greater distance between us. One thing I knew for certain was that Sir Henry would spread the story of last night's events – spread it further than jam on bread.

Chapter Forty-Five

When I was eleven, there was an earthquake in London. The world shook, crockery fell off the shelf, windows cracked and people ran into the street, screaming that this was the punishment of the Lord. Childishly, I found comfort in the rumbling of the earth. The notion that there was a force greater than that of petty men and petty women pleased me. In the days that followed the earthquake, street criers announced that the sins of London were responsible for the terrible calamity and the end of the world was nigh. If I believed in a vengeful God, which I feel blessed not to, I might have thought that what happened next was, like the earthquake, perhaps just punishment for my sins.

I was at the height of my notoriety, for Sir Henry had embellished the events of the duke's dinner party and cast me in the role of sorceress. Avery was seen more often in London, in the company of the countess and her mother, and whether the story reached him I never knew, but I became aware that he avoided me whenever we met socially. On more than one occasion his seeming disregard for me almost stripped me of my confidence. It mattered little to me that near every man in London longed to spend a night with me if the one man I wanted made it clear every time we met that he had no desire to be in my company. No matter how I tried to approach him, he was always careful that we were never alone, and at the first opportunity he would make his excuses and leave. That he was so distant made the assemblies, balls and routs torture, for I was certain that whatever love he once had for me had turned to loathing. Many times I caught his eye and wondered what he was thinking, what those blue eyes saw. He didn't look at me with admiration as the other gentlemen did, more, I would say, with curiosity as if he was trying to find something in me he had lost.

~

Sir Henry Slater called most days while I was at my toilette, to relate all the gossip he had heard. One morning, a month or more after the dinner party, he said, 'My dear, you have to put an end to it – you positively do, I insist.'

'An end to what?' I asked.

'Don't tell me you haven't heard? Your duke is infatuated with a certain Dolly Kemp, a young actress, rather lusty in shape. If not elegant she has no noticeable defects apart from the largest bosoms ever to appear on stage. Black hair, fine skin and even finer arched eyebrows.'

'So you have met this Dolly?'

'Alas, yes. I went backstage to see Garrick and unfortunately I entered the wrong dressing room. My eyes are still recovering from the sight therein.'

'Tell,' I said.

'No!'

'Tell,' I said again, most amused.

'Miss Tully, it is serious.'

'I take it she is in the play that we saw last week at Drury

Lane. Come now, I can't fire my pistol at him without a ball shot of knowledge.'

'As you are so insistent, I suppose I must be candid. I found his grace already lost in her bosom and well mounted. She cried out, "Oh, sir, it's so big!"'

'What exquisite delight!' I said, giggling. 'Was it in pleasure or pain?'

'She looked to me,' said Sir Henry, 'as if she was well stretched in that department.'

What surprised me most about this revelation was that I felt not a flicker of jealousy, rather, I wondered when he would tell me that my position had been usurped.

So it was I set off that evening in high spirits, to meet the duke at Drury Lane. The roads being uncommonly empty, my carriage arrived ahead of time and I dismissed my coachman. I was on the point of entering the theatre when a woman approached me.

She was dressed in what looked like borrowed clothes. They ill fitted her slight frame. Her face was covered in a thick mask of white powder with two rosy cheeks painted on this blank canvas. A profusion of patches were spotted here and there.

'Tully, it's me,' she said. 'Have I changed so much?'

'Flora,' I said. I didn't know what else to say, for she looked as if all the silliness of her had been drained away through a sieve of cruelty.

'You're quite the lady,' she said.

Her vacant eyes darted this way and that. I thought she was drunk, for I could smell alcohol on her breath and, although there was a chill in the air, there were beads of sweat on her forehead.

'I have been robbed,' she said, 'and I haven't the means to pay for the hackney carriage.'

I brought out a coin and handed it to her. As she took it, I noticed her fingernails were bitten to the quick. I felt an overwhelming sadness to see the catastrophe of her life and how it had unravelled into this thin painted creature. I remembered her arriving at the fairy house in the earl's carriage, with diamonds in her hair.

'Please,' she begged, 'would you come with me and explain to the coachman? Tish tosh! I know it's silly, but he's in a terrible rage and the sight of one as famous as you might calm him down.'

I was wondering what to do when I noticed Avery Fitzjohn coming towards me with a party of friends. On his arm was a lady of quality. I was so startled to find myself in such close proximity to him that I couldn't even greet him. The lady lifted her nosegay and looked at Flora with an air of disdain. Avery bowed and seemed on the point of saying something to me when his companion pulled him away.

Flora was still waiting for me and so I walked with her to the hackney carriage, grateful to have a reason not to be in the foyer of the theatre with Avery and his disdainful lady. I thought little of where we were going, though I noted that beside the hackney carriage was a private coach, its windows blacked out. As I drew near to it, the door of the coach opened and I felt a blow that echoed through my whole body. Then was darkness.

I came to to find myself bound and propped up in the coach as you would a parcel. There was no sign of Flora, only my husband, Captain Spiggot, who sat opposite me with a self-satisfied smile across his face.

'Madam, we meet again,' he said, 'and this time, unlike in Bath, I am taking you, my whore of a wife, home.'

'I don't understand why you persist in this claim to me.'

'Because I want to consummate our marriage and share the joys of your inheritance which I believe are rightly mine.'

I laughed at him. 'Inheritance? What inheritance?'

'The legacy your grandfather left you – it was common knowledge among your father's cronies.'

Finally, it dawned on me why this blockhead had pursued me.

'My father,' I said, 'was like you – a braggart, a liar and a rogue. And my grandfather died penniless. Do you really believe, sir, that Mr Truegood would have sold me so cheaply if I was to inherit a fortune? You are a numbskull if you do. If I inherited anything, he would have made sure he spent every penny of it.'

Captain Spiggot's face slowly changed as he recognised the truth in what I had said. His eye twitched and his scar became more livid, and for a moment his face fragmented and became that of the spiteful boy. I regretted my hasty tongue, for his mood changed to one of fury.

He took a small vial from his pocket, grabbed hold of me and tried to make me drink from it. I managed to spit out most of the liquid and such was his rage that he slapped me round the face.

'If you do that again, my little harlot, I will severely punish you.'

This time the liquid made its way down my throat and after that I can honestly say that I remember not one single thing and had no idea where I was taken. I became conscious that I was lying on a bed, naked and cold, though a part of me was warm – uncomfortably warm. I was being rocked violently, back and forth. I tried to move and found my arms, like my legs, were tied to the bedposts. My head hurt worse than it had ever hurt before and my vision was blurred. There were three Captain Spiggots looming over me – one pushing forward, one pulling back and one in the middle. All were grimacing. Only then did I come to my senses. I was aware of what he was about and knew I had no way of stopping him. His weapon was well on its way to claiming me and I tried my damnedest to dislodge him.

He was at the height of desire, and my resistance fuelled it to such a degree that with a few more thrusts he had released himself and only then did these three disconnected images become a terrifying one as his pent-up fury spilt into me.

'Your cunt is too loose for my liking,' he said.

'You have no right,' I said.

'I have papers that prove you are my property, madam, and, as such, I can do with my chattels as I see fit. And I see fit to fuck you.'

He climbed off the bed, buttoned up his breeches and left the chamber.

There were no candles and the bedchamber smelled damp, as if the place wasn't lived in. I had a feeling that it had been borrowed for the occasion. I could hear voices, footsteps, the distant slamming of doors. In the darkness every noise made me tremble, and I was shivering by the time the door opened again. Captain Spiggot came in with a candle that he placed on a chair then stood at the end of the bed, examining me.

'How much does a man pay to spend the night with you?'

I didn't answer him, but said, 'Don't you want your freedom?'

'"What God hath joined together let no man put asunder."'

He unbuttoned and, without going to the bother of taking anything else off, climbed on top of me.

Even now I find it near impossible to write about. There are some things that make your whole being shudder in revulsion. I remember desperately hoping to free my mind from my body, to stand well away from it, to close my eyes and not see what was happening.

'I will break you as I break my horses,' Captain Spiggot said. In that pursuit he was brutal indeed.

I think my stillness and the absence of me made him wilt at the climax of this second assault. Or rather, I willed him to wilt and to my delight he did just that. He pulled out, cursing me, calling me every name that the vulgar tongue can think of. He went to where he'd left the candle, picked up something and came back to the bed. The shock of what happened next made me regret he had wilted at all. He held a riding crop.

'This is what I do when a horse throws me,' he said.

He gave me six lashes for my breasts, six for my stomach, and six on my thighs. I could taste the blood. All of me stung – a sticky, bloody kind of sting. As he picked up the candle to peruse his work, the door opened and in walked Victor Wrattan. With him was Flora.

'Is the deed done?' he asked.

'Yes, once. But the whore just now put me off my stride.'

'Naughty, very naughty, aren't you?' said Victor Wrattan. 'I remember you in your father's house, how much you wanted me when I put my tongue into your mouth and my hand upon your cunt.' Tears filled my eyes. 'You would have given yourself to me then and there, wouldn't you? She would have done, Flora, wet with longing she was. But I like resistance, enjoy breaking a woman. She was a young girl with no virtue, no modesty, a born whore. The likes of you debase your sex and in no small part our own. She was looking at herself naked in the glass – and longing for this.' He unbuttoned himself. 'You can watch, my love,' he said to Flora, who was shaking. 'You would like that, wouldn't you?' From what I could see she was terrified. He paused, looking at her. 'You wouldn't think she was once a beauty, would you?'

I wasn't the first and, alas, I won't be the last to be used this way, yet for all his savagery I knew he would never own the soft place in me. He would never find the pleasure garden, he would never know heaven in the eyes of a woman. The two of them would only carry the echo of their cruelty, nothing more. I closed my mind and words rolled over me. This small thing called flesh would recover, I would live. I would never take this man to ruin me, I would never take this man to humiliate me, I would never take this man.

They left me in that freezing room with no covers, tied down, my body raw from the use of the riding crop, the mattress sodden where I had pissed myself. There was one candle. I turned my face to the wall and it was in the light of that candle that I first saw the rat and the glint in its eye.

Chapter Forty-Six

The rat sat on a chair, cleaning its whiskers. And then it was as if Mr Crease was with me. He clicked his fingers.

'Are you listening?' he said. *'Great seers, and by that I mean mighty ones, can borrow the sight, but not the hearing, of an animal.'*

How had it worked with Shadow? Barely conscious, I fought to stay awake, to concentrate on the creature.

'Rat,' I said, softly, 'please…may I borrow your eyes?'

It stopped and looked in my direction. I stared into those gimlet globes and held the gaze until I felt it reel me in. The candle must have gone out for all was blackness. I became aware that my vision seemed split: one eye could see a shape stretched out on the bed, the other eye was watching the floor. The strangeness of the alternate views made my senses wobble. I had ignorantly believed that a rat would have clear sight, but I was looking at a greyish-blue, blurry abyss filled with indefinable shapes. Was that really me – purple, swollen? We were moving and I had no idea where we were or what we were looking at. Ahead was the glint of…something. I decided it must be a thimble, yes, a thimble, of that I was certain, and over there, a piece of silver brocade fabric. Out of it a spider emerged to scuttle on its way. There were more rats and there was nothing I could do; I was at the mercy of this creature whose sight I had borrowed. The rat might have lent me its vision but it had not lent me its will. Shadow was a spirit dog, susceptible to my thoughts. Not so this very much alive rat. How would my sight ever be returned to me? Where were we now? Behind the skirting?

I had to rely on my own hearing. There were sounds outside the chamber. I kept my body still as a soft tread approached. It must be Flora. I sensed she was near the bed.

'Tully,' she whispered. 'Tully…'

I was about to speak when I heard her scream. Then came a hard collection of military steps, they clattered up the stairs and marched to where Flora was. The voice of my enchanting husband echoed in the bare room.

'Shut your bone box for God's sake! What the…'

I heard him stumble back, a chair thudding to the floor.

'She is dead,' he said.

I kept my breathing as shallow as possible. Every inch of me waited for a rough hand to prod me. To my surprise there was none. The rat opened its eyes once more and we were back in the chamber. I could just make out foggy, grey objects. I tried to understand what it was that we were looking at and finally I saw a pair of boots. I felt the warmth of breath on my neck. Someone was leaning over the bed.

'Lord, she is dead,' said Wrattan.

A pair of shoes passed uncomfortably close to my host.

'She can't be,' said Captain Spiggot. 'Hell! What now, Wrattan? Are you sure she is dead?'

I expected to be discovered and punished further for this deception.

'Don't touch her,' said Flora. 'Just look at her eyes – they're white! Come away from her.'

'Quiet, you little bitch,' said Wrattan. 'I need to think.'

Flora fell to the floor, not far from the rodent. It scurried, unnoticed, along the skirting board, feeling its way with its whiskers to the other side of the bed.

'What shall we do with her?' said my caring husband. 'Bury her in a ditch?'

'No,' said Wrattan. 'No – let me think.'

I was becoming terrified that I might start to tremble but then the candle went out.

Wrattan shouted, 'Find another light, woman, and be quick about it.'

My host could see in the dark – not well, but enough to sense that the two men were now standing away from the bed by the wall. The light returned and with it a sheet. Flora screamed. I could see what was upsetting her. Other rats had emerged from the skirting.

'I can't look at her,' said Flora, laying the sheet over me.

'I suggest we leave her,' said my loving husband. 'We need not concern ourselves. I was once told about a man who had been found, eaten by rats, and no one to this day knows who he was. With luck, the rats will perform the same service here.'

Rain began to fall, tap-tapping the window pain. Wind rattled the glass and I heard a rumble of distant thunder. When lightning filled the room with its unearthly white light, the rat and I saw shapes hurry from the chamber. A clap of thunder merged with the slam of the front door. A key turned in a lock, a horse neighed and a coach pulled away. Then the only sounds were the rain and rats' claws scratching on the floorboards.

I lay there for what felt an eternity, tugging weakly at the ropes. It was hopeless. It was then I thought my wits would leave me as well as my eyes. Again I could see the shape – my shape – on the bed. I felt fur brush past me, up my legs, creep over my skin. I could see parts of myself, and an earthquake shook my flesh. I began to sob as I had never sobbed before. The more I cried, the more I became aware that my own sight was returning to me. I could see clearly a huge rat sitting not far from my face, gnawing the rope that tied one hand to the bedpost.

'Thank you,' I whispered, and gradually I anchored my mind.

I pulled that hand free, then the other, but I had lain so long spreadeagled on the bed that my lacerated body was stiff and I could barely move. It felt as if a day and a night had passed before I was even able to sit up and free my feet. With every sound the house made I thought Spiggot and Wrattan had returned to kill me.

In a great deal of pain, I at last stood upright, whimpering. The rats scurried away as I took the sheet and felt my way down the stairs, clinging to the banisters in the darkness. I wailed when the front door would not budge, but then a flash of lightning guided me towards a kitchen door. I pulled at it with what little strength I had and it opened. It was still raining heavily. Shoeless, and with only a sheet wrapped round my bare flesh, I hobbled down a gravel drive and onto a road.

Though my feet were cut with the stones I told myself to keep walking, one step after another, one step after another. Through the trees the sky was black, raw with rage and streaked with red. One step after another, and each was harder than the last.

Further down the road I heard horse's hooves approaching and I stopped as the silhouette of a rider came towards me.

It was too late, I thought. Wrattan has come again and now he will kill me.

So certain of it was I that I found myself once more weeping uncontrollably and I thought I cared little if I was dead, anything would be better than to be taken back to that house. The horse pulled up sharply, steam rising from its nostrils.

'Who's that?' asked a voice that did not belong to Wrattan.

'Help me, please!' I said, sobbing. 'Help me. I am from Queenie Gibbs' fairy house.'

What possessed me to say that I do not know and at that moment I did not care.

The rider dismounted. 'Miss Tully?' he said. 'Thank God.'

Was this a trick? How did he know my name? My eyes ran with tears and still I could not see his face.

He took off his coat.

'It's me, Miss Tully, it's Ned,' he said. 'Ned Bird. I'm taking you home.'

I thought I was hallucinating. Ned had come to take me home? How was this possible? He put his coat round me. I was in so much pain that it was hard to think where the hurt stopped and where I began. Ned lifted me up onto his horse then pulled himself into the saddle behind me. He turned the horse and we set off at a mighty lick. I lost consciousness, dreamed we were flying and felt the world was laid out before me. When I came to myself and saw the lights of the fairy house, I wondered if I was indeed dead, for it looked as if I had arrived in heaven.

Chapter Forty-Seven

I floated, the torn flesh of me falling away.

I wanted to say, 'There is no need for anyone to carry me, I'm as good as a seed blown on the wind.'

I was laid on a bed. There were other faces, there was Hope. She said, 'Oh, Tully, what have they done to you?'

> *I am raw meat.*
> *A lamb for the slaughter.*
> *I once lived in Milk Street,*
> *The brickmaker's daughter.*

My soul was becoming detached from my body, less concerned with the heartbeat. Let the clock stop.

There was Queenie. I noticed that she had a new cap. I was hovering near the ceiling and I could see every detail of the lace, it shone so white. She groaned.

'No, Tully, no!'

I looked for Pretty Poppet, for she wasn't with Queenie. Of course she wasn't with her, she was with me.

'Mr Wrattan,' she said, and put out her hand. 'He did that to me, what he did to you.'

I was about to take her hand. There wasn't much to return to in the bloody sack upon the bed. Nought but pain. But as I looked down at myself, there was Mr Crease, leaning heavily on his cane. And there was Avery.

Quite detached, I saw him touch me on my wrists, on my forehead, and with every touch there were filaments of light darting up to catch hold of me.

I couldn't think why he was there, couldn't make any sense of it. I watched, riveted, as he lifted the body of me. I was still in Ned Bird's coat and I wondered why Avery hadn't taken it off me. He couldn't. I had become stuck to it, glued there by my own blood. Mr Crease talked to Avery, words tumbled, somersaulting over one another, language losing its ties. All that kept me were the filaments of light that sprung to me from Avery's touch.

I was in water, watching as it slowly turned red; thin, wispy lines of blood running together. The sting and the shock of the warm water for a moment brought me down and I loomed above myself, closer to my body than before. I was washed out of the coat and the sheet, they floated away from me, Avery's hands healing, not intrusive, his shirt wet as he lifted me from the bath. He wrapped me in warm towels and gently dried me. I was on the bed once more and Avery tended to my wounds, his hands kind, urgent, determined to heal me, determined to keep me.

He said softly, 'Who would have done this to you, my love?'

My love. Had I heard him correctly? He said, 'my love' and I knew then that I couldn't leave my body behind, however tempting it was, for without it, how would I know if he meant what he had just said? There must, I thought, be a part of me that longed to have a reason to stay. Perhaps those two words were enough. My love.

Days slipped into nights, nights slipped into mornings, the

endless stitching of time. All the while, there was Avery, constant, caring. Little by little, word by loving word, I returned, eased back into my broken body.

Often in the nights that followed, I would wake, certain that Spiggot was in the chamber. I saw him emerge out of the darkness and come towards me. 'I will kill you,' he said. 'I will kill you.'

I always woke screaming, always thinking myself to be alone, thankful to see Avery who would put his arms about me, hold me tight, tell me to take a deep breath and another and another.

'You're safe, Tully, safe,' he said.

I knew the smell of him and, in that space before dawn broke, it was the greatest comfort there was.

Still the nightmares came without fail: Spiggot waiting in the shadows, standing over me. I dreaded sleep.

At night Avery took to lighting all the candles in the chamber and sleeping in the chair by my bed, but the image of Spiggot stood solid and haunted the dark places where the lights didn't shine.

I thought I might never sleep again. I was exhausted by the ghost of a living man. It's not the dead we should fear – their souls long to depart. It's the living that never leave us alone.

I often woke from the nightmare, drenched in sweat. One night, after Avery had had the bedlinen changed and brandy brought up, I realised that I had to sleep if I was ever to find safe harbour in my mind again.

I was shivering and Avery said, as he always said, 'No one will harm you while I'm here, I promise.'

And I thought, Should I judge all men the same as Spiggot

and Wrattan? If I do, what a small prison I would have locked myself into. I have the right to be free, to love and to be loved.

'It's the chill that sits in the heart of me that nothing can warm,' I said.

He took my hand and rubbed it, and I asked him to lie beside me, to hold me. I wanted to feel he was there, nothing more. For the next week we slept that way and at last I felt safe enough to dream.

~

Queenie came and asked to have some time with me alone. I didn't want Avery to leave me, but Queenie had on that face of hers, the one that would brook no argument.

The minute he had gone, she said, 'Do you think there isn't a whore, or, for that matter, a lady in this great city of sin, who hasn't been raped or abused, whether by a man she trusted, or loathed, or was married to? The real question is, how do you survive such an onslaught? Do you let it destroy you, send you to Bedlam? Believe me, I've seen some go that way. Or are you wise like Hope? She would tell you it is a hazard of the job. You, Tully, are wise.'

Queenie was standing in the middle of the chamber and I could almost see sparks of rage fly off her. The fury of the injustice crackled in her every word.

'I had a daughter – you know that. Pretty Poppet was her name. She was my little angel. I paid well for her to be looked after like a princess. She was brought up by a Mrs Inglis, who I believed to be a God-fearing, honourable woman. She ran a little school for girls. Too late, I found out what she was teaching and who the masters were. A gang, the cream of society, broke into

Mrs Inglis' house. They took each and every girl. But the one they gave special consideration to was my Pretty Poppet. She lived less than a day after that. And the worst part was that all those rich men walked free. After all, what are the lives of a few girls compared to the honour of such noble young gentlemen?'

'Wrattan killed her,' I said, and all Queenie's rage evaporated, and in its place were the cracks of grief.

She put her arms round me. I held on to her and we both wept.

'At least you're not with child,' she said after a while, 'and you haven't got the pox.' She took out a kerchief, blew her nose and took a deep breath. 'This, my gal, is your profession and you are at the height of your game. Make the most of it. It's the only way you will ever buy your freedom from such men as Wrattan and Spiggot. So stand up, show the bastards you are one of Mrs Gibbs' gals. You are the pride of this house.' She stopped and a stray tear rolled down her cheek. 'As Crease said, "You are no hen-hearted girl."'

'Why haven't Wrattan and Spiggot been arrested?' I asked.

'They both have alibis,' said Queenie.

'What of the coachman who drove us to the house?'

'He said he didn't know them.'

'So they still walk free?' I said.

'Yes. Yes, Tully, they do.' She wiped my eyes. 'Sir Henry Slater is your champion. He wrote a piece that was published in the London Gazette. He called it "The Great Injustice".'

She shook her skirts and dusted down her bodice as if freeing herself from any more unpleasant thoughts. 'This came from the Duke of H,' she said, producing a letter. 'Do you want to read it?'

'No,' I said. 'I can well imagine the pomposity of it. It ends our agreement, or rather his agreement.'

'And enclosed is fifty pounds,' said Queenie.

We both laughed. Laughter feels so much better than tears.

'I take it the big-busted Miss Dolly Kemp has moved to Pall Mall?'

'You are correct in every detail. All your possessions, including your parrot, were sent back.' She took my hand. 'There's so much to tell you,' she said. 'It feels an age since you were here. I now have one assembly a month, with cards, dancing and, of course, little sexual intrigues. Last month we had a full masquerade ball, with musicians and singers. It ended with everyone naked apart from their masks. Tully, you would have laughed at the sights! Lady Montgomery with that round tummy of hers – she nearly smothered skinny Mr Wescott. It was a sight to relish. That's what the art of pleasure is all about and the fairy house is the only one of its kind. You haven't seen the Chinese room – all the furniture is Chippendale. It's so beautiful, a work of art, that's what the clients say.'

'I want to know,' I said, 'how Ned Bird knew where to find me?'

'Mr Fitzjohn hasn't told you? Well, if it had been left to the duke I doubt whether we would ever have known of your disappearance. When Mr Fitzjohn saw that you weren't in the theatre with his grace, he was worried, especially as he had seen you earlier, talking to a hackneyed prostitute.'

'Flora,' I said.

'So I heard,' said Queenie. 'Poor, foolish girl. Anyway, he left the theatre and made enquiries outside. In Russell Street he found a flower girl who said she'd seen you bundled into a coach, and it had dark windows. Mr Fitzjohn came immediately to tell us what had happened. Crease and Ned went to Covent Garden and found the yard where the coach had been hired. The stable boy, after some...encouragement, remembered his master saying he was going to Enfield with two gentlemen. Ned spent the rest of the night and most of the following day touring the stews of Covent Garden and St Giles, and eventually heard of another gal who had been taken to an empty house up that way – and survived. She was able to tell him enough about the place for Ned to find it. He hired a horse, and the rest you know.' Queenie sighed. 'Mr Fitzjohn came again and again to see if there was any news of you.'

'Have you told him who Captain Spiggot is?'

'No,' said Queenie. 'Have you?'

'I can't bring myself to,' I said.

When she left I lay back on the pillows and remembered what Lord B had said when I told him about my clandestine marriage.

'Marrying in the Fleet is the beginning of eternal woe.'

Never had I felt the truth of it more. The beginning of my eternal woe was Captain Spiggot.

Chapter Forty-Eight

When sleep wouldn't come, I talked to Avery in drowsy words.

'Where do you think this hypocrisy began?' I asked one night.

'What hypocrisy?'

'The hypocrisy of a society that accepts it is perfectly right for men to be rakes, gallants and dandies and to enjoy the liberality of whores, harlots and courtesans, but expects women to stay pure when all they have to put their trust in are deceitful men, who hunt out virgins for their amusement but only want virtuous wives for the marital bed.'

'Is that what you think of me?' And before I could answer, he said, 'Yes, you are right. I was a hypocrite. I was prepared to marry the countess, who I didn't love, and willingly set you on the path to being a whore. It was the act of an unthinking man. I am not that. Could you forgive me, and believe me when I say I have changed?'

'What changed you?'

'In France, I heard people talk of freedom. They argue that it is not God given that women should be subservient to their husbands. I have heard speak of a new order that one day will come, when women will have equal rights with men. I don't want a passive wife, who doesn't enjoy the pleasures of *amour*, who has been educated to be ruled by the whims of society, rather than love and passion.'

'Do you think such a dream is possible?'

'I would fight for it.'

'What happened to the Avery Fitzjohn who said to me that he had the weight of a name, and...'

'I am truly sorry,' he said. 'I behaved badly. If I had been an honorable man, I would have taken you away with me after I had seduced you, and protected you.'

'If I remember correctly,' I said, 'you were betrothed and wanted a virgin – I suppose so that you wouldn't catch the pox.'

'Yes, that was the notion, but it didn't...'

'I think Adam and Eve would have much to answer for in a court of law.'

Avery laughed. 'I am being serious.'

'So am I. Adam was a coward – he wanted to taste the apple that his father had told him not to touch. What did he do? He tricked Eve into picking it for him. The snake is just a lie.'

'You didn't study the Bible?' said Avery, smiling.

'No. But I think the trouble began there.'

'And can you forgive me?'

'For what?' I asked.

'For being a hypocrite. I should have had the courage to tell you what I felt and I didn't.'

'What did you feel?'

'Don't you know? I fell in love with you. I think I fell in love with you when I first saw you in the coffee house in Covent Garden.'

'You knew?'

'I wasn't sure until you bumped into the street-seller. You

were so enchanting in your confusion. But when I saw you at the Rotunda, I hardly recognised you. Everywhere I went, people spoke of you and I thought I could offer you nothing, not even my name.'

I embraced him and that night, with his arms round me, I slept deep and safe.

When I woke the room was full of sunshine. Avery lay watching me.

'I have lost all sense of time,' I said. 'How long have I have lain here?'

'This is the sixth week,' he said.

'And you have been with me all this time?'

'Yes. I have had to leave you occasionally when you were sleeping but, if the truth be known, I have had no desire to be anywhere else. And, if you would have me, I would never want to leave you again.'

I ran my fingers through his thick curly hair and remembered the delights of our lovemaking when we first had lain together. Here was the man who had taken not only my virginity but my heart, and still was the keeper of it.

'I thank you, sir, for healing me on the outside,' I said. 'Perhaps, by the possession of me, you would heal me on the inside too.'

He kissed me, a timid kiss filled with desire. Nervously, I stretched out and his hands stroked my body. I took his fingers into my mouth.

'Oh, Tully,' he said as he kissed my neck.

I watched him undress, feasting on the sight, and by degrees began to tingle with anticipation. I trusted him, I wanted him – oh, how I wanted him. He was the most beautiful man, every part of him in perfect proportion, his noble member already risen to greet me. He took his time undoing my shift, kissing me all the while

'I have always preferred you naked,' he said. 'It is a gown that few ladies wear as well as you.'

I moved my limbs so that I was open to him. He kissed away the scars on my thighs, his tongue caressed my quim and I ached for him to be inside me. He kissed the scars on my breasts and I felt him urgent for admission, the delicious velvet tip begging to enter my pleasure garden. No aggressive movements, no violation in the ease with which he came into me, I could feel him stiff, pulsating with life, penetrating the depths of me until I owned all of him. It sent me wild, his eyes shone with love, his gaze never left me. I felt myself gather tight around his quivering arrow. Then it came on me, slowly at first, but with such unbearable ecstasy that I lost myself in the lush river of desire. He moved within me and we were one, I was he and he was me, there was no separation. My skin alight with passion, I was on fire and only to be soothed in the river of longing, carried on its ebbs and flows. I was near that moment of abandonment. He urged me on until I could hold it no more and felt myself explode into him. My climax brought on his and together we tumbled from a great height, into the roaring unknown. Our cries of ecstasy drove out the demon.

I had not before experienced such tender lovemaking, so different from anything I had known. It came from love, true love, a place to be treasured and, I suspect, rarely found.

Such were the delights we discovered that day that we both realised we were famished for more of the same dish. I touched that sweetest, noblest part of him that knew how to delight me.

He rose again and, taking my hand away, he said, 'I would rather spend my seed inside you, my love.'

And, oh, he did, he did.

At about two o'clock, he said, reluctantly, that he had to see a lawyer and would return that evening. As I watched him dress, my only consolation was that tonight we would have possession of each other once more. When he was at the door, he turned back to the bed.

'Would you marry me?' he asked.

'Yes,' I said. 'If I could, I would marry you tomorrow. But there is something I have not told you.'

He stared at me for a moment then took out his pocket watch, my gift to him.

He glanced at it and said, 'I must go now. The sooner I am gone, the sooner I will be back. And tonight we will tell each other all our secrets.'

I gazed into those blue eyes and thought I saw the future.

'I love you, Mr Avery Fitzjohn,' I said

'Then I am the luckiest man in the world,' he said as he opened the door to leave.

'Who is this lawyer who is taking you from me?' I called after him.

'A Mr Quibble,' he called back.

I haven't seen Avery Fitzjohn since.

Chapter Forty-Nine

The Governor's House, Newgate Prison

I have been in prison for only two weeks but it feels like a lifetime. Not a letter, not a word. In my mind I go over all that you said the afternoon you left, and have near gone mad imagining what could have befallen you.

Perhaps I misunderstood you. Perhaps you never loved me. Perhaps, perhaps, you lied to me. How lost am I. Still I refuse to believe that you would be so deceitful, for what would be the purpose in such deception? Or is love like sand, running elusively through the fingers?

Time hangs heavier than the rope that is waiting to hug my neck.

A Mr John Gately came to see me today, a solemn man with a face that would make a gravedigger proud. He bowed gracefully, flicked back his coat tails and sat.

'We haven't long to prepare. The case is due to be heard on fourth October.'

'Please, before we begin,' I said, 'there is something I must know.'

Mr Gately looked me straight in the eye. I could see that this was a man who believed in little. His disappointment with humanity oozed from every pore.

'I must know if Mr Avery Fitzjohn is alive.'

'Mr Avery Fitzjohn? The brother of Lord Frederick Fitzjohn?'

'Yes,' I said.

'Madam, he is dead,' said Mr Gately.

I could hear my blood thumping in my ears.

I must have had turned white for Mr Gately asked, 'Do you need assistance? Shall I call someone?'

'No one would come,' I said. 'When...when did Mr Fitzjohn die?'

Mr Gately had no interest in the death of Mr Avery Fitzjohn. It was an irritant, a distraction that he felt I could ill afford.

'Try to concentrate on the matter in hand, madam,' he said. 'You are accused of murder.'

Seeing that his words had no effect, he said, 'Perhaps it would help if you wrote down the events of the evening that led to the shooting of your husband, Captain Spiggot. I have the statements that you gave the coroner, but I would like to hear the truth from you.' He stood up. He had no patience with the humours of women. 'I will be here tomorrow morning and I hope you will be more in the mood for talking.'

'Wait, sir, please. What happened to Avery Fitzjohn?'

Finally, some part of Mr Gately's learned brain made the connection: Avery Fitzjohn mattered a great deal to this client and was the reason she was unable to concentrate. The lawyer sat down again.

'You haven't seen the newspapers?'

'I do not receive the newspapers.'

'Mr Fitzjohn went missing some eight weeks ago. He had an appointment with a lawyer, a Mr Quibble, but, according to Mr Quibble, he never arrived at the lawyer's chambers. Last

*week a body was washed up near Tilbury Docks. It has been
identified as that of Avery Fitzjohn.'*

'Who identified it?'

'Lord Fitzjohn. Mr Fitzjohn is to be buried in the family
vault.'

*The memory of Lord Frederick Fitzjohn, down in his cups,
swam before me.*

'The damn countess would be mine if it was not for my
brother. He is all that stands between me and a fortune.'

*These walls, which were used to hearing so much woe, were
almost comforted by tragedy. I felt dead inside. The only thing
alive in me was the baby, our baby.*

~

When Mr Crease showed me how to walk a tightrope, he said,
'It looks as if you are tiptoeing through air. But to balance
you need all your weight in your feet. It is weight that makes
the act possible.'

This letter to you is my only way of staying on the tightrope.
It gives me gravity, where otherwise I would fly away. I can't
think of you drowned, I can't think of you dead. Part of me
is sure that if you were, I would have known.

My lawyer wishes me to concentrate on the facts, without
embellishment, just the simple truth. And as I don't want to be
tried as a witch, the facts might serve me best. I had started,
this morning, to write them down when Hope and Queenie
arrived. My lawyer had sent for them, concerned that his
client did not realise the peril she was in or how severe were
the charges against her.

Perhaps it was because I had seen so little colour, but Hope *and Queenie, standing brightly dressed in my small cell, were parrots against the grey.*

Queenie gave me a hug and pushed my hair out of my face. 'You have to be brave, Tully,' she said. 'You have to.'

Rose petals. My knees weakened. Her perfume was so evocative of the fairy house.

'You can't let yourself be hanged. You have to tell the truth.'

'The truth is, I shot Captain Spiggot with Mr Crease's pistol.'

'You have to fight. You must plead not guilty.'

'How is Mercy?'

'She is getting stronger, day by day.' Hope was crying; Queenie was wearing the mask of determination. 'You're not to give up now, gal,' she said. 'You are with child and for that baby alone you'd better buck up your ideas. I hear that Lord Barbeau left you a very wealthy woman. Well, you have money enough to play a man's game. The one we play comes at a great price for when looks fade and the goods are damaged, whores are left to rot on the streets. I want justice for you and for Mercy, for Flora and for my Pretty Poppet. Hold up your head and fight like a she-cat, for if you are hanged, Wrattan will go free.'

'I will try,' I said. 'That's all I can do.'

'Hope, tell Mr Gately he can come in.'

The lawyer bowed as Queenie and Hope left.

'Shall we begin?' he said.

'Where shall I start?'

'What made you decide to leave the fairy house dressed as a boy?'

I told him the facts. The facts sounded logical. I left out the parts that would make a lawyer despair. Justice doesn't like the irrational. Mr Gately stayed for about an hour and wrote everything down.

Now I will write the true account of what happened the night I murdered my husband, for the truth is often stranger than the facts and the facts don't always tell the truth.

Chapter Fifty

When Avery didn't return that night I called for Mr Crease and asked him if he would send Ned Bird to look for him.

'Some calamity must have befallen Mr Fitzjohn,' I said, 'otherwise he would be here, I know he would.'

But as I spoke, I felt less sure.

Later, Mr Crease returned, carrying a box. He told me that Ned had set off to find Mr Quibble's chambers and make enquiries there. Mr Crease then asked if I would like to see the trick he was working on. I was about to say that I had too much on my mind to think of tricks, but Mr Crease looked straight at me with his painted eyes. Usually under such a gaze, I would turn away. It had never occurred to me to confront that stare, but, that day, I looked straight back at him and for the first time I could see into the soul of him in a way that his own eyes never allowed. I saw into the deep well of a kind man, wrapped in the crust of an ill-tempered skin.

'It involves proving the impossible possible,' he said, lifting the lid off the box.

He moved a side table and dusted it with his handkerchief before handing me a bottle of wine.

'Is there anything in this bottle apart from wine?' he said. 'Take your time.'

The glass was clear, the wine was white, the seal unbroken.

'No,' I said.

He took the bottle back, sat it on the side table, then brought out a candle which he lit, placing it in front of the wine bottle. From the box he took out his pistol.

'This looks most alarming, sir,' I said.

'Of course,' replied Mr Crease. 'Anything less would be a disappointment. The question is, do you think it's possible that by firing this pistol I can extinguish the candle, uncork the bottle and leave the bullet in the wine?'

'I would say that by all the laws of nature, no.'

He gave me the bullet for my examination. 'Can you see if there's a number written on it?' he asked.

'Yes. Nine.'

He took the bullet back and placed it in the pistol. With measured steps, he walked to the end of the room, turned and, with outstretched arm, fired. There was a loud bang. The candle duly went out and once the smoke cleared I could see that the bottle was indeed uncorked and inside sat the bullet.

'Pick it up,' said Mr Crease. He held out a basin. 'Pour the wine out.'

I did, and with it came the bullet.

'What is the number on it?'

It was a nine.

'That's impossible,' I said.

'Madam, I have proved my point. As you should know by now, nothing is impossible.'

'Then improbable,' I said. 'As improbable as Avery not returning.'

'On that we are agreed,' said Mr Crease. 'Let us hope Ned has news for us.'

But there was no news, not that evening, not the next day, or the day after.

Ned said, 'It's as if Mr Fitzjohn has vanished with the faeries.'

'If he had,' said Mr Crease, 'then at least we would a chance of finding him.'

By the time two weeks had passed I was near losing my mind. But I was feeling stronger and I called for Ned and told him I was determined to search for Avery myself.

'Miss Tully,' he said, 'that would be most unwise.'

'But you will come with me? I will dress as a boy and act the part of your apprentice.'

'You're not well enough,' he said, but seeing there was no way to dissuade me from what he considered a foolish notion, he sighed. 'You are very stubborn, Miss Tully, and I can tell there is no argument of mine you would ever listen to.'

Reluctantly, he went to wait for me while I changed my clothes. I knew for certain that it would be wise to have a weapon. From the landing I could hear Mr Crease talking to Ned in the hall below. Quickly, I made my way up to the long gallery where I found the box with the candle, the wine bottle and the pistol laid out on the table beside it. I picked up the pistol, checked that it was loaded and hid it in my jacket. It was then that I heard a cry. It filled the house with the sound cattle make when they are slaughtered. I rushed down the stairs and there in the hall with Ned and Mr Crease stood Mofty, her clothes covered in mud.

'He will kill her,' she was saying, 'he has taken her and I know he will kill her.'

'Taken who where?' asked Ned, his rough voice doing nothing to soothe Mofty.

Mr Crease said, 'Please calm yourself, madam, and tell us what happened.'

Mofty galloped, her words stumbled at the fences of comprehension and set off again at an even faster pace. Queenie emerged from the rookery.

'Oh, my Lord, what's happened now?' she said.

'Speak more slowly, Mrs Wrattan, I pray you,' said Mr Crease, and at last, at a canter, we began to understand.

I felt my heart become lead.

'Lately we have been receiving threats from my husband,' said Mofty. 'This morning we left London for Folkestone, hoping to escape to Paris. We were stopped on the highway by the driver of another coach. He was standing in the road, waving his arms, shouting that he needed help. Mercy ordered our coachman to drive on, but he said he knew the other driver and he was an honourable man. The second we came to a halt, we were done for. From the other coach sprang Spiggot and Wrattan. They tried to pull us from our carriage. Mercy fought and fired her pistol, and with the door wide open, our horses bolted, throwing her from the carriage. Our driver clung on until he had control of the reins once more and then he refused to stop. He wouldn't turn back but kept going until we reached a coaching inn where we raised the alarm. Wrattan will kill her, I know he will.'

Mofty crumpled to the floor and Queenie went to her.

Up to then all my thoughts had been of Avery, but, irrational as it may seem, I felt that somehow the fate of the two people I loved were wrapped together. I had lost Lord B, I might have lost Avery – I couldn't lose Mercy too.

Mr Crease picked up his cane, Ned checked his pistol. There

was no discussion as to where they were going. Queenie saw that I was set to leave with them and took hold of my arm.

'Tully, don't be a fool. They will kill you if they see you again, you know that.'

'I am going to find Mercy,' I said, and pulled free. 'And I'm not alone.'

I followed Mr Crease and Ned Bird out of the fairy house.

~

The best part of that afternoon we spent making enquiries in what felt like every tavern, coaching inn and stable yard in London. This time there was no obliging stable lad and the coach could have belonged to the devil for all the luck we had in tracing its owner.

At seven by the bells of St Paul's in Covent Garden, Mr Crease said he would go his own way, and suggested that Ned and me went to Molly King's to see if there was any gossip worth hearing. I felt suddenly exhausted, and was grateful for a seat at last. I stayed in the shadows, my head down, nursing a beer at one of the long tables. Ned sat next to me and asked questions of the other customers.

Then I saw Flora. I nudged Ned.

'What?'

'Flora,' I said.

'I can't see her.'

'There,' I said, nodding in her direction.

He looked straight at her and saw her not. She was a sorry sight indeed and in possession of the blackest eye that her white paint made worse. She looked desperate for a drink and was trying to get the necessary pennies together.

'Oi! Miss Flora,' he called. 'What's your tipple, girl?'

Seeing who it was, she seemed about to bolt but Ned shouted to the pot boy, 'Bring us a bottle of gin and a glass.'

A bottle of gin with its guaranteed oblivion was the worm on the line that reeled her in. She sat next to Ned and smiled at him. Two of her front teeth had been knocked from her head.

'That's good of you, Ned,' she said.

Her stare followed the bottle as it made its way towards our table. Shaking, she downed one glass and then another.

Ned put his hand on the bottle. 'Easy, gal. We have all night and there is more where that came from.'

Her eyes flickered this way and that round the tavern.

'Who is it you're afraid of?' asked Ned kindly. She didn't answer. 'Perhaps some food might settle your nerves.'

A dish of bread and meat was brought. She ate as dogs do when starved.

She took a swig of the gin to drown the food and said, 'How old do you think I am?'

'I couldn't say, Miss Flora,' said Ned.

'I am twenty-four. I look eighty.'

There was little to say to that truth.

'I have heard,' said Ned, carefully choosing his words, 'I have heard that Miss Mercy was taken today on the King's high road.'

Flora stood, ready to run, and made to grab the bottle but Ned caught hold of her wrist. 'Where is she, Miss Flora?'

'Thank you for the gin and the food, Ned, but now I must go.'

'Sit, Miss Flora.' Ned pulled her back down on to the bench. 'Where is Miss Mercy?'

'If I tell you, I am dead.'

'If you don't, you are dead anyway, by the looks of things.'

'Who is the lad?'

'My apprentice. He won't say a word.'

'Farringdon, at an inn by the Fleet River.'

'A tavern?'

Flora nodded. Ned poured more gin for her.

'Its name, Miss Flora?'

'Let me just lay my head down,' said Flora, 'and I'll tell you.'

'No,' said Ned, 'tell me now and then you can sleep.'

'You will be too late,' she said. 'It's all too late.' Her eyelids closed and she was gone into a stupor, the only kind lover left to her.

'You wait for me here, Miss Tully,' said Ned, getting to his feet. 'You look done in.'

As he left, I turned to Flora and nudged her to wake up.

I heard a sound so soft, no more than a candle being snuffed out. Her eyes opened and she looked at me, lifeless. A trickle of blood ran from her mouth. She was dead. And that was when I saw Pretty Poppet, waiting at the door, and I knew why she was there.

Chapter Fifty-One

By a half-cocked moon, we made our way steadily through the streets and alleyways of Clerkenwell. I stayed close on the heels of Pretty Poppet until we reached the banks of the stinking Fleet. There stood the Hedge Tavern, a hunchback building, its beams bowed by the damp from the river.

Pretty Poppet took hold of my sleeve as I went towards the door.

'Don't use that jigger. That's where they are,' she said, pointing at the roof. 'In the sky parlour.'

I followed her round to the back of the tavern through a midden of garbage, piled with empty barrels, where, clinging to the building, was a rickety staircase. I could feel Pretty Poppet's excitement; it fluttered from her as at last she neared her prey. Not a sound did she make on the steps. I took out the pistol and pulled back the catch as I had seen Mr Crease do when he fired it at the bottle. Now voices could be heard – not words, groans.

Pretty Poppet stopped. 'You have to show me to them,' she said.

'I will.'

I put my hand on the door.

'Wait,' said Pretty Poppet, and I watched as she pulled the flesh from her face so it was no more than a cloth covering her skull, her eyes floating in their sockets. She smiled at me. 'I brought my friends – the ones like me.'

I turned and behind me beamed three dead faces. One carried a doll and they all glimmered with the energy of revenge.

'They're here for the same reason as me,' said Pretty Poppet. 'Make us visible and don't fire that pistol until we are finished, 'cause we have waited longer than you for our turn in the dance.'

I heard the impatient tap of bone on wood, the victims waiting for the justice that no judge had seen fit to give them. I concentrated with all my being. If my gift was ever to be of any worth, this was the time.

'Let them be seen,' I prayed to the lord of chaos. 'Let them be seen.'

'Now,' said Pretty Poppet. 'Now, now!'

I pushed on the door. It was locked.

'Who's there?' called Captain Spiggot.

'It's only me,' said Pretty Poppet, 'and some of my acquaintances, come to kiss your arses goodnight.'

There came a breathy laugh.

'Go away, we don't need anything, not now.'

'Oh, but now it must be.'

We heard groans from behind the door and I thought that they were doing to Mercy what they had done to me. The noise grew into a duet of raucous grunts.

Pretty Poppet smiled at me and put a bone to her mouth. Her hand was webbed with skin that fell into small folds from her fingers. And then I felt a great pressure growing all around me, the noise of it grew and grew, the sound became a ferocious, whispering wind that rolled up the stairs with such strength that it blew the door open as if it were made of papier mâché.

Mercy was not there. My husband, his breeches round his ankles, was bent over a table, his hands gripping the edge, his fingernails digging deep into the wood. Wrattan was leaning over him and both were nearing the height of their pleasure. They looked up and slowly ecstasy was replaced by wilting horror.

Pretty Poppet flew at them and they pulled away from one another, Wrattan's weapon rapidly losing its power. Spiggot covered himself with his hands.

'What the devil…?' he said.

Wrattan, white with fear, backed away, Pretty Poppet spinning round him, pulling at his clothes.

'Mr Wrattan,' she said to him, 'don't you want to see Eve's custom house again?'

'No!' shouted Wrattan. 'No!'

His hair was tied back and she tugged at it, pulling chunks from his scalp. He yelled in pain.

'But I'm Pretty Poppet – you told me to dance for you. You said you wouldn't touch me if I danced for you. But you did, until I danced no more.'

'Victor, who are these fiends?' cried Spiggot, his legs giving way as Pretty Poppet's three acquaintances came fast into the chamber, on winds of retribution so powerful that the windows broke as the spirits whirled frantically this way and that. Their bony fingers pinched the men's faces, pulled at their clothes. They laughed as they spoke.

'You called me Chitty-Face,' said one to Wrattan. 'You jiggled me here – ' she pointed to the front of her ' – you jangled me here.' She pointed to the back of her. She turned over the table. 'You broke me, you choked me, and you didn't care.'

My husband's face glimmered with sweat. Urgently he pulled up his breeches, and shouted at Wrattan. 'Get my pistol – it's in my coat.'

'You called me Spider Shanks,' said another spirit. 'I was to cure you of the pox by my water fountain.'

And another said, 'You called me Gundiguts, Mr Wrattan. It didn't stop you taking me through the back door, your fingers round my neck. Don't ask me to breathe, I never will.'

As Wrattan took the pistol from Spiggot's coat, Spiggot was sidling round the room towards me.

'Fire that pistol,' said Pretty Poppet, baring her teeth at Wrattan. 'Fire it, for all the good it might serve you.'

The girls joined hands and danced round and round, faster and faster. Spiggot, I could see, was coming for me.

Wrattan lifted the pistol. A look of recognition came over his face as he pointed it. 'It's you,' he said. 'I'll fucking kill you, witch, if you don't stop them.'

Spiggot was nearly on me. I held Mr Crease's pistol with both hands and aimed at Wrattan. My pistol fired, as did Wrattan's, and, at that moment, Pretty Poppet pushed me out of the way. Spiggot stumbled forward and fell to the floor.

Finding myself unharmed, I shouted, 'Where is Mercy? What have you done with her?'

Wrattan's face was a picture of horror at seeing his friend wounded. He reloaded his pistol.

'I'm shot,' said my husband, incredulously. 'I'm shot.'

'It was her, that witch,' said Wrattan, pointing his pistol at me again.

Pretty Poppet whirled in all her grotesque finery and caught the bullet as you would a ball from the air.

'Victor,' moaned Spiggot.

Truly terrified, Wrattan ran from the chamber, Pretty Poppet in pursuit. She was not about to let him go. Her acquaintances, having taken their revenge, leapt out of the window and broke into a thousand specks of light, finally released of all earthly cares.

Mercy was not to be found anywhere in that labyrinth of chambers. I went back to the room where my husband had been left, and found him crawling across the floor, leaving a trail of blood.

'Help me,' he said. 'For God's sake, help me.'

I knelt beside him. 'Tell me where Mercy is and I'll help you,' I said.

'You bitch. I wish I'd killed you.'

'Where is she?'

His head dropped heavy on the floor and I felt a hand grab my shoulder.

Spiggot moaned. 'She shot me, my wife shot me.'

I still had hold of Mr Crease's pistol.

The innkeeper managed to find a doctor among his drunken sops of customers and although he had the shakes he seemed to know what he was about as much as any drunken doctor might.

'The two gentlemen kidnapped Mercy,' I said to the constable who arrested me.

'There will not be much mercy for you, my lad,' he replied.

It hadn't yet dawned on him that I was a woman. He took me downstairs and I held my head up for outside there was quite a crowd. They weren't staring at me, but had their eyes glued on the roof of the tavern where Wrattan was clinging to the chimney pots.

I said, 'You should arrest him for the crimes he's committed.'

The constable was not listening for he, like everyone else, was transfixed at the sight of Pretty Poppet who was standing on the edge of the roof while Wrattan clung to a chimney pot. I tried to break free, but the constable had me held firm. With a tug he pulled me away to a waiting wagon.

That was when I saw Flora. She smiled at me, her teeth gleamed white, none missing. Diamonds were in her hair and her beauty had returned to her, unblemished. The constable stared at her, open-mouthed. Flora said not a word but took hold of his arm and snapped it as if it were nothing more than a chicken bone. He was so shocked that for a second his scream was silent and by the time he'd let out a howl we were gone.

'Tish tosh,' said Flora. 'I have diamonds in my hair again.'

'Take me to Mercy – please, Flora, I beg you.'

'I drove in rich carriages and lay down on soft velvet. Come,' she said. 'I'll show you. And then I'm going home.'

She walked along the bank of the Fleet, her feet never once touching the water. By a warehouse not far away, she stopped.

'She's in there,' said Flora, and walked into the middle of the sluggish river. Whirling round, she threw her arms out and, free at last, dissolved into a myriad of diamond lights. I was alone, just me and the half-cocked moon.

It was an empty wooden structure. The moonlight shone through the slats on a shape hanging by a rope from a beam. Mercy's feet were balancing precariously on a chair. I ran to her and lifted her body so she wouldn't drop. Time stopped and all that had been, all that would be was no more than just that moment. If I let go, Mercy would die. I have no idea how long I held her, only that when at last Ned cut her down we fell together, willow leaves intertwined. I felt her hand flutter in mine.

'Live,' I whispered to her. 'Live.'

I was arrested for attempted murder of Captain Spiggot and the grievous wounding of a constable. Victor Wrattan was not arrested: he had been trying to save his friend from a vengeful whore. I was taken to Newgate and there was nothing more I could do but pray for Mercy, pray to a God who I doubt cares tuppence for whores like us.

Chapter Fifty-Two

Hope arrived early on the morning of the trial, weighed down with boxes. It seemed such a ridiculous sight and my cell was so small that there was hardly room for us to stand. Undaunted, she set to organising where everything should go. She had put a great deal of thought into what costume would emphasise my innocence and had settled on a petticoat embroidered with buttercups. The gown was of a liquid grey silk that caught the light when I moved.

'I think,' she said, 'considering the fabric, it looks modest and yet at the same time not without appeal.'

'It's perfect,' I said. 'How is Mercy?'

'Better,' said Hope. 'But it will take a long time for her to get her strength back. She told me to tell you to speak clearly, for only the guilty mumble their words.'

'I doubt that,' I said. 'Hope – do you remember the first time you dressed me? In Milk Street?'

'Yes,' said Hope. 'You were such a lonely little thing, so pleased to have sisters.'

'I still am.'

'Oh, stop it, stop it.' She blew her nose. 'This is hard enough without feasting on memories.'

She pulled my stays tight.

'Ouch,' I said, laughing. 'I'm pregnant and I must show it. After all, I am pleading the belly.'

She loosened the laces and concentrated on making sure the gown fitted me to perfection. My kerchief high, my hair modestly pinned, and at last I began to recognise myself. I was paler of face, that was true, but I still had a glint in my eye, a speck of determination.

Mr Gately had told me that he would not call me to the witness stand unless it was absolutely necessary. One small comfort was that the constable had dropped his charges against me and now blamed his injury on an unknown person in the crowd. It seemed he had thought better of exposing himself to public ridicule by admitting that his arm had been broken by a woman.

I know now that nothing can prepare you for a courtroom; the noise of it, the smell of it and how small the space is. Theatre at its most intimate, the play is performed without an ending or rather with one that is at the jury's discretion.

The moment I arrived in the dock a huge cheer went up mingled with booing. I was in a bear pit. The gallery was full to bursting and among the crowd, apart from Mr Attaway and Mr Tubbs, were Queenie, Mr Crease, Hope and Mofty, as well as Sir Henry Slater and, more surprisingly, the Duke of H.

A woman leaned over the rail and shouted, 'London should be cleaned of harlots.'

There was much jostling and among the faces leering down on me I was certain I spied Cook. I was trying to catch another glimpse of her when I felt an icy chill on my right side. I shivered. Pretty Poppet stood beside me.

'I ain't leaving you,' she whispered, lacing her bony fingers through mine.

The court rose as the judge took his seat. A small man, he was almost lost inside his ludicrously large wig. I remembered seeing him at one of Queenie's assemblies. On either side of him sat gentlemen in equally large wigs and imposing robes. I couldn't tell who they were, but all I knew was that they were intimidating, their well-fed faces lacking even a shadow of compassion. Above the judge's bench, square, dirty windows threw gloomy light on the proceedings. The courtroom was airless, the atmosphere made worse by the constant waving of burning herbs that smelled of ink and pen nibs rather than anything beneficial to the health.

My indictment was read out – not one word of it lost on its eager audience.

'Tully Truegood, of Queenie Gibbs' house in Lincoln's Inn Square, is indicted for the wilful murder of her husband, Captain Ralph Spiggot, on the first day of September, 1756. The incident took place in a certain chamber called the Club Room, belonging to an alehouse known as the Hedge Tavern. Here, it is alleged, she wilfully and with a malice aforethought did shoot the said Captain Spiggot. He was attended there by Mr Potts, a surgeon, and was then taken to Mr Wrattan's lodgings at Great Ormond Street. The captain lived for a week and died there.'

Mr Barrow, the prosecution counsel, stood up and called for Mr Potts. He looked only marginally more sober than when I had last seen him.

On being questioned by Mr Barrow, he said that he had found Captain Spiggot conscious and the captain had stated that the prisoner had shot him.

Mr Gately started his cross-examination. 'Is the accused here, Mr Potts?'

'No,' said Mr Potts, looking round the court. 'I can't see him.'

There was a roar of laughter from the gallery.

'Miss Truegood was dressed as a young man, Mr Potts.'

Mr Potts peered at me, unconvinced.

The cross-examination continued and Mr Potts became more confused with every question.

Mr Gately said, 'Would you say the bullet entered through the front or the back of the victim's body?'

'The back,' said Mr Potts. 'No, the front.' He looked round the courtroom for guidance. 'The front.'

The judge looked unimpressed and began to shuffle some papers that were set before him.

'I ask you again, Mr Potts,' said Mr Gately. 'Where did the bullet enter the body?'

I could see perfectly well that it meant nothing to the jury whether the bullet went in the front or the back. It made little difference. The facts were that I had shot my husband dead and all that they had heard so far had only confirmed their suspicion that I was guilty as charged.

Mr Potts looked in need of a drink and was relieved when no more questions were asked of him.

Next, Mr Barrow called the landlord of the Hedge Tavern, followed by the constable, who both gave fairly damning evidence against me, identifying the pistol I was holding when I was apprehended by the silver engraving on the stock. Mr Gately had no questions.

Victor Wrattan took the stand and I could see that the licentious libertine was relishing this public performance. Here was a man who was auditioning for a part in a play. Like the jury, he was certain of the outcome. He painted an elegant portrait of Captain Spiggot as a most honourable man who had tried to save his wife from the whorehouse.

'You are a liar, sir!' shouted Queenie from the gallery. 'A liar, a rapist and a murderer.'

Wrattan smiled. 'That is rich coming from one of London's most notorious brothel-keepers.'

A burst of laughter came from the court.

'Silence,' ordered the judge.

Victor Wrattan, seeing that he had the jury's full attention, continued. 'That woman,' he said, and pointed at me, 'manipulated a fortune out of the late Lord Barbeau, a sick and vulnerable man. By her wanton cunning she robbed Lord Barbeau's nephew, a penniless parson, of his rightful inheritance.'

The jury gasped in horror and there were cries of 'Shame on you!' from the gallery.

'Objection, my lord,' said Mr Gately, on his feet. 'This is immaterial to the case.'

Mr Barrow rose to his feet. 'My lord, Mr Wrattan is illustrating the nature of the woman who is on trial today.'

'Continue,' said the judge.

'My good friend,' said Wrattan, 'had a wife who was given to sudden fits of violent temper, a vicious and devious whore who…'

On he went, ending by saying it was in one of my rages that I had cold-bloodedly shot Captain Spiggot, and he, Wrattan, being afraid for his own life, had run onto the roof for safety.

The jury had enjoyed the performance so much I expected them to give Wrattan a standing ovation. On this testimony my case was lost. I was startled to find myself confronted by the prospect of my death.

'Do you have any questions, Mr Gately?' asked the judge.

'Mr Wrattan,' said Mr Gately, 'was there anyone with you when you were on the roof of the Hedge Tavern?'

This one question ruffled Wrattan's sleek feathers. 'I didn't see anyone,' he said.

'Let me help you,' said Mr Gately. 'There was, I believe, a young girl seen on the roof. Is that correct?'

'I didn't see anyone,' repeated Victor Wrattan.

Pretty Poppet squeezed my hand. 'Have the gentleman call me,' she whispered.

Mr Barrow stood up. 'Your honour, this has no relevance to the murder of Captain Spiggot.'

'It is relevant if there is another witness,' said Mr Gately.

Mr Barrow stood up again. 'Your honour, the girl was never found and has, therefore, never given a statement. This line of questioning should be dropped.'

'Mr Gately will concentrate on the facts of this case rather than hearsay,' said the judge.

My barrister changed his line of attack. 'Did Captain Spiggot tell you to take his pistol from his coat?'

'No,' said Wrattan. 'Captain Spiggot was unarmed that night. I had a sword.'

Mr Gately made little progress. Mr Wrattan was playing to the gallery. The judge dismissed Mr Gately's cross-examination, telling the jury that they should not consider it.

'You need me if you ain't to join me,' Pretty Poppet whispered. 'Make them see me and I will tell them what happened. When the occasion deserves it, I can dress myself as you do for society, in the habit of flesh and blood, well enough to deceive human sight. I won't let you down.'

~

The law stops to eat and I was taken down to a cell. I have to admit to being full of dread. I had been far too light-hearted about the notion that I might be hanged but it now looked a reality, and an unavoidable reality. Mr Gately came to see me. He told me to take heart, and that it would go better in the afternoon. I didn't think so.

'I want you to call Poppet Gibbs,' I said.

Mr Gately ignored my suggestion. 'I will call Mr Albion Crease next,' he said.

'I beg of you, call Poppet Gibbs.'

'Who is Poppet Gibbs?' said my lawyer, looking at me as if I was a complete numbskull.

'She is the girl who was seen on the roof of the Hedge Tavern and she is now willing to give evidence. I am paying you well for your services, Mr Gately, you will call her.'

The court reconvened after lunch and, just as in a game of chess, everyone took their places in the hope of seeing the queen taken by a knight.

'Mr Gately,' said the judge. 'Your next witness.'

'Your honour,' said Mr Gately, 'I call Miss Poppet Gibbs.'

What if she was to appear with her skin all ragged? What if she was not to appear at all? Mr Crease stared down at me with his painted eyes and gave me the courage I needed. I had never concentrated as hard as I did then on making a spirit visible. But she didn't appear. The call went round the courtroom again. I looked up into Queenie's face and I knew Pretty Poppet was there by an expression – a mixture of wonder and sadness – that came over Queenie's features. Poppet had not only garnered flesh but seemed to have taken advantage of the years that had never been hers. She wore them well and stood in the stand, rosy-cheeked and calm.

Queenie stifled a sob. Poppet, the grown-up daughter she'd

never seen, never known, smiled up at her. I could hear what she was thinking. Don't cry, Mother, don't cry.

'Your name?' said the judge.

'Poppet Gibbs, your honour, of Mrs Gibbs' house.'

Wrattan, who had stayed to see the rest of the trial, was lounging at the back of the courtroom, smiling to himself. I watched as slowly it dawned on him who it was who had taken the witness stand. All humour deserted him.

'Miss Gibbs,' said Mr Gately, 'where were you when Captain Spiggot was shot?'

'I was in the Club Room at the Hedge Tavern. I'd gone there with Miss Tully, looking for Miss Mercy, who that morning had been taken by Mr Wrattan and Captain Spiggot on the King's highway. Miss Tully feared that they would do to Miss Mercy what they'd done to her.'

'And what had they done to her?'

'Raped, and beaten, and near murdered her. I knew of the ways of Mr Wrattan for when I was thirteen Mr Wrattan and some other gentlemen broke into Mrs Inglis' school where I was a pupil, and four girls died that night due to those gentlemen's attentions.'

There was uproar in the courtroom and for the first time I felt a shift in the jury's opinion.

Mr Barrow stood up. 'That has nothing to do with the case in hand.'

'It has to do with Miss Gibbs going with the prisoner on the night of the shooting,' said Mr Gately

'Continue, Mr Gately,' said the judge.

'Miss Gibbs,' said Mr Gately, 'would you tell the court what happened in the Club Room at the Hedge Tavern.'

Pretty Poppet gave her testimony. She described exactly how

we had found Mr Wrattan and Captain Spiggot in a state of undress. She went no further, implied no wrongdoing, but at the same time leaving little to the imagination of the well-versed citizen of this city of sin. Speaking clearly, so that all her words could be heard, she ended by telling the court that she had stood on the roof of the tavern while Wrattan clung to the chimney pots, having left his friend downstairs, mortally wounded.

'He still had hold of Captain Spiggot's pistol, the pistol he'd shot his friend with. And the Fleet being only the other side of the chimneys, Mr Wrattan dropped it in the river.' She paused. 'I have come forward, sir, because I want justice for all the wrongs gentlemen like Mr Wrattan and Captain Spiggot do to women, to young girls who have hardly put away their dolls before they're thrown on the rubbish heap and left to become threepenny whores.'

It was the most impressive performance.

'Lies – it's all lies,' shouted Wrattan.

'But it isn't, sir, is it?'

The judge brought down his gavel. 'Order. Mr Wrattan, I will have you removed if you are not quiet.'

But nothing was going to keep Victor Wrattan quiet for he could see what few others in the courtroom could: Ralph Spiggot standing before him, the hole in his chest large and weeping.

As Mr Barrow stood up, Spiggot vanished. Wrattan, wild-eyed and sweating, leaned against the wall, breathing heavily.

'The problem, Miss Gibbs,' said Mr Barrow, 'is that all you have told us is hearsay. And the serious crimes that you have accused the witness of committing have no relevance to this case.'

I felt a chill run through me. I could not let Mr Barrow

demolish Pretty Poppet's testimony. With all my mind, I willed Spiggot to be visible to Wrattan again.

My dead husband appeared at the side of his friend and killer.

'I'm sorry, Ralph, I'm sorry!' whimpered Wrattan.

'Order, order,' called the judge. 'Will you be silent, sir.'

Wrattan desperately fought through the crowd, pushing and stumbling towards the courtroom door.

'Mr Wrattan,' said the judge, 'control yourself. This is the last warning I will give you.'

Mindless of the living, Captain Spiggot put himself between Wrattan and the door. Wrattan was frantic.

'We should have finished her when we had the chance,' he shouted. 'I meant to kill the whore, Ralph, I didn't mean to kill you!'

Spiggot leaned forward and kissed him on the lips. 'Say that again, Victor,' he said.

'Will you stay with me, Ralph?' cried Wrattan.

'Say it again, and we will never be parted,' said Spiggot.

Wrattan collapsed and the ghost disappeared.

'Ralph!' cried Wrattan. 'Come back – I didn't mean to kill you.'

The courtroom was brittle in its silence. From his own mouth, Victor Wrattan had condemned himself. Shaking and in tears, he was helped to his feet by two constables, arrested, charged and taken away.

The judge thanked Pretty Poppet for her testimony and, with her head held high, she walked from the court, never to be seen again.

The jury found me not guilty.

'The prisoner will be discharged,' said the judge.

It was all over.

Chapter Fifty-Three

I stood in the dock, unable to move. I recall a cacophony of noise and it seemed that the courtroom whirled around me; hands grabbing, faces grimacing. I had leapt the hangman's drop from guilty bound to innocent. There was a future, there would be tomorrows, and in my belly I felt for the first time a flutter of new life. Both of us were eager to live.

Mr Tubbs guided me from the courtroom. In the corridor, Ned was waiting, his face grey. He took my hand.

'Thank the Lord,' he said. 'Thank the Lord.'

We went up the stairs together to a chamber above the courtroom. It was a comfortable room with chairs and a desk, a safe harbour from the storms that raged below.

'I want to go home,' I said.

'By all means,' said Mr Tubbs, 'but first Mr Attaway wants to speak to you.'

I dreaded to think what the solicitor might have to say. I was impatient to be gone from this place less the truth about my witness be uncovered. Would I be re-arrested, retried? Was it possible?

Mr Attaway entered, his face solemn.

'Is everything in order?' I asked.

'Yes,' he said, in measured tones. 'The verdict stands.'

'Thank goodness,' I said.

Mr Attaway cleared his throat. 'Poppet Gibbs is dead.'

'I know that.'

'Dead and buried some fifteen years ago.'

'I know that.'

'She was murdered, along with three other girls, at Mrs Inglis' school. A group of men were arrested for the crime, charged and found not guilty. Among them, as I discovered, was Victor Wrattan.'

'I know that, too.' And I knew what he was going to ask me. I said, quickly, 'Will Wrattan hang?'

'It appears that he is more likely to be sent to Bedlam than to the gallows. At present he is in the cells, plagued by ghosts.'

The solicitor cleared his throat again but before he could question me, I said, 'Mr Attaway, there is really nothing else to say on the matter. All I ask is that you accept there is more to this world than most people comprehend, just as there is more to the law than I will ever understand.'

'I've seen many things inside a courtroom,' said Mr Attaway, 'but a ghost giving evidence – now, that is exceptional.'

'Perhaps not. Perhaps there were others you didn't recognise.'

A smile crossed the severe planes of Mr Attaway's face.

'Am I free to go?' I asked.

'There is nothing to stop you.'

'I'll fetch the carriage,' said Ned.

As he opened the door I heard Cook's unmistakable voice.

'I must see her, it's important.'

Tubbs looked questioningly at me. I nodded and Cook was ushered in. She was exactly as she had been when I'd last seen her, the day I left Milk Street with Mercy: pasty skin and raisin eyes. In her hand she held a roll of paper, tied with string.

'I'm Martha Longhorn,' she said to Mr Attaway. 'Longhorn's my married name,' she added, turning to me, as if that was all that was needed as an account of the intervening years.

'I have been trying to see you,' she said, 'but that busy legal gentleman – ' she pointed at Tubbs ' – would have none of it.'

'Madam,' said Mr Attaway, 'my client has had a long and trying day, may I suggest – '

'No!' said Cook, emphatically. 'I have waited too long as it is and things left too long go mouldy.' She sat down and adjusted her hat. 'Whoever would have thought it would come to this – that Poppet girl in court and giving evidence. You never seemed to like her much when she came to Milk Street.' She looked pleadingly at Tubbs. 'You don't have a drop of gin?' She moistened her lips. 'A little tipple would go a long way to easing the tongue.' Mr Tubbs poured her a glass of gin and she downed it in one gulp. 'That courtroom is a dusty place. The law gives you a right thirst, it does.'

She held out her glass for it to be refilled and, after she'd finished it, she continued.

'So I said to Mr Longhorn, "What am I to do?" Mr Longhorn is a man of determined principles.'

'Can we not talk at the fairy house?' I said. 'I am sure Queenie – that is, Mrs Truegood – would be pleased to see you again.'

'No,' said Cook. 'No, I can't go there. Mr Longhorn, being a religious man, has forbidden it. It was his suggestion, and his carriage brought me to the court, and that's as far as I am permitted me to go.'

'Mrs Longhorn,' said Mr Attaway, 'may I suggest you give the document you are holding to either myself or Miss Truegood.'

I was suddenly weary and could not for all the salt in the sea think what Cook might have to say that was so pressing that I should be prevented from returning home.

'Cook, where are these ramblings leading?' I asked.

'I saw your name in all the papers,' said Cook. 'Then – ' her voice dipped to a whisper ' – when Mr Longhorn said about you murdering Captain Spiggot and them calling him your husband…'

She still held fast to the battered roll of paper. I assumed it was my lost marriage certificate and, fortunately, no longer of any importance.

Mr Attaway said, 'Tubbs will take the document, Mrs Longhorn.'

I thanked Cook. 'I don't need it now,' I said. 'It's too late.' I rose to leave. 'It is my marriage certificate, isn't it?'

Cook held even tighter to the roll of paper. 'Let me speak without all of you flustering me.' I sat down again. 'I've been preparing these words and now they are well cooked and need to be said. You see, I'd put this paper in a drawer and then, when you got so famous and all, I showed it to Mr Longhorn and he read it to me. It has burned a hole in my conscience. I would have handed it over sooner, but I was in fear of my life.'

'Why were you in fear of your life?' I asked.

'That's what I want to explain to you,' said Cook. 'Mr Truegood sent for me when he was in the Marshalsea. Such a terrible state he was in. He gave me this here paper and made me promise that I would never show another living soul, and said that if I wanted to keep my giblets, I'd better stay quiet. He said if anything happened to him, he'd haunt me. I thought the old fool was playing a part, as was his way. Then, the very next day, I was told he'd had his throat slit. I was in no doubt who'd done the slitting.'

'Who?' I asked.

'That Mr Wrattan.'

'Why did you suspect him?' asked Mr Attaway.

Cook sighed. 'There are so many words and all of them need organising. Another little drop would help.' She took a second glass of gin. 'You know the master ran a gambling club?'

'The Hawks' Club,' I said. 'Yes, yes, of course I know. Please, Cook, I beg of you, come to the point.'

'I would serve wine and vittles and nightly I saw your father losing money at cards. A great deal of money.' Having started the story, she found that the gin had performed its miracle and loosened her tongue. 'One night, after Mr Truegood had lost more than any one man should possess, he was nearing his wits' end, for the debt had to be paid. One of the Hawks told him he had a friend who might be able to help. A gentleman came to see Mr Truegood and said there was a road out of his problems that didn't lead to the Marshalsea. He had a name that sounded like Dribble.'

'Quibble?' I said.

'That's it – Mr Quibble. Now, I won't say that I often listened at the door, though...'

'Please, madam, could we arrive at the crux of the matter?' said Mr Attaway.

'Well, the short of it is, I overheard Mr Dribble tell Mr Truegood that all his debts would vanish if he would agree to his daughter marrying his client's stepson. Mr Truegood didn't take much persuading, especially when he was told that the young gentleman in question was going abroad and, with any luck, you would soon be widowed. I took that to mean he was going to sea. You were married as agreed and Mr Nibble was true to his word. Your father's plate was full. But the old drunk didn't learn his lesson – once half baked, always half baked, I say. Then came the day, as certain as the day of judgement, when he hadn't a penny left to pay any of his debts so he cooked up a liar's pie. He told anyone who listened that when you were eighteen you would inherit a fortune.'

'Yes, I know that, too,' I said.

'One who listened well was that Mr Wrattan. I didn't like the look of him, or the smell of him – rotten to the core, he was – no amount of butter would make that man savoury. Mr Truegood owed him a great deal of money. But all the debts were paid off when your father married Mrs Gibbs.'

Cook had, as usual, left out half the ingredients that would make a good dish.

Out of impatience, I said, 'I have no energy for this story,' and again stood up. 'Please, Cook, give Mr Attaway the certificate. I am going home.'

Cook reluctantly handed the paper to my solicitor. He read it and his face became even more sombre.

'One moment, Miss Truegood. I advise you to look at this.'

I took the document to the light and read it. Then I read it again. The words began to dance, or rather my mind could make little sense of them. My husband's name was written in an assured, if somewhat wobbly hand. My writing was that of the child I was.

Tubbs caught me as I fell.

When I had recovered, Cook was staring at me. 'It's the shock,' she said.

'Explain yourself,' I said, anger welling up in me. 'Did it

never occur to you to send this to me? Have you any concept of the grief that was caused by your silence?'

'Like I said, I was in fear of my life,' said Cook. 'I was in fear of my life right up until today.'

'Mr Quibble,' said Mr Attaway, 'was Victor Wrattan's lawyer when he was accused of participating in the murder of the girls at Mrs Inglis' school. Mr Quibble, I see, is a signatory to this document. He was a witness at your clandestine marriage, Miss Truegood. I suggest that we investigate Mr Quibble's part in the murder of your father, and what appears to be a conspiracy to pass off Ralph Spiggot as your husband.'

'That's what I've been trying to say,' said Cook. 'They didn't want anyone finding that bit of paper you're holding. The master told me to keep it safe in case fortune should deal him a better hand. That murderer must have thought he'd have the marriage certificate amongst his papers at the Marshalsea. But he didn't, because he'd given it to me.'

~

My life had turned on a card when I was twelve. That one act had altered everything. How ironic that unwittingly Mr Truegood had married me to the man I have loved most. For my husband, as the wedding certificate stated, was Avery Fitzjohn.

Chapter Fifty-Four

Once I saw the spirits of the dead, but I have never seen your shade. Where are you, my love? Where are you? I see only the threads of memories that are too short to stitch our lives together.

~

I stayed at the fairy house after the trial was over. I had no desire to see anyone, go anywhere, do anything but lie in my bed, feeling our baby grow, watching the leaves on the tree outside my window turn red and fall. When they were all gone, I felt, so would all hope of knowing what befell you.

Queenie tried consoling then turned sharp as was her way. All words, kind or angry, were to me but a reflection of the weather. The days were windy, filled with fog and rain. Mr Crease called my melancholy the black dog of Newgate.

'A hound,' he said, 'with its teeth in your soul.'

My birthday came and went and still the black dog wouldn't let me go.

November arrived bitterly cold and near all the leaves had fallen. Only three clung to the one tree I could see. Two fell the night of the storm when the wind howled as loud as all the sorrow in me, rattling the windowpanes. In the morning, the morning of one leaf left on the tree, Sir Henry Slater arrived.

'I insisted on seeing you. Queenie couldn't bar me and Hope told me to try,' he said. 'My dear, you look like a tragic Venus rising from a cloud of counterpanes.'

'I am not good company, sir,' I said.

'No, but you are a delight for the eye to feast upon. Let me speak and you listen.'

My maid brought a tray of hot chocolate and its sweet aroma filled the room.

Sir Henry sat on a chair next to my bed and took a sip. 'I thought you would be amused to know that the Countess Angelina has unexpectedly cheated her mother and Lord Frederick of their designs and escaped into the arms of Jesus, becoming his bride in a convent of unfulfilled virgins.'

'I wish I could feel some pity for her but I cannot.'

'Indeed. But I haven't just come to prattle. No, I am here on a serious matter, one that is close to your heart. There is news, Tully. As you refuse to see him, Mr Attaway asked if I would try. He is in urgent need of instructions.'

'If it is about Lord B's estate, I have no instructions.'

'It is not.'

'Is…is it about Avery?'

'Not directly. But it concerns a certain Mr Quibble who might have some knowledge of his fate.'

I sat up. 'Tell me.'

'Mr Quibble has been arrested for fraud and debts, and taken to the Marshalsea where he is in the prison block awaiting trial. Mr Attaway thinks there is a good chance that if convicted he will be transported.'

'In the Marshalsea, you say?'

Colour must have returned to my face, for Sir Henry said, 'Ah-ha! So you are alive alive-oh. Mr Attaway wants you to know that he is seeing Mr Quibble this afternoon, and he thought, as a woman of strong opinions, that you might wish to join him and ask the lawyer yourself what befell Avery Fitzjohn. But if you are indisposed...'

I was out of bed. 'Of course I will join him,' I said. 'I have a black dog that needs to be returned from whence it came.'

'I don't see any dog, black or otherwise,' said Sir Henry. 'Is it a riddle? Let me solve it while you dress.'

I had no thought as to what I might wear and would have put on the first robe that came to hand if Hope hadn't intervened.

'This is the first time you will be seen in public since your trial. You must make an impression.'

I chose one of Lord B's favourites, a deep red gown, printed with peonies, my stomacher let out to accommodate my growing belly. Round my neck I wore a fur muffler. I looked in the glass and could see an outline of who I used to be. By the time I reached the hall I almost felt myself again.

I asked Ned to accompany me and the three of us set out in Sir Henry's carriage to Southwark. I could almost smell the Marshalsea before I saw it. All prisons smell the same but this one had the added perfume of the damp Thames air that clung determinedly to its walls.

Mr Attaway was waiting in his carriage in the prison court-yard. Tubbs was standing outside it, wrapping his arms about him and stamping his feet on the hard ground.

'The air alone here is murderous for a weak chest,' said Sir Henry.

'Which fortunately, Sir Henry,' I said as Ned helped me
down, 'you don't have.'

'*Touché*, my dear.'

Sir Henry stayed in his carriage, sniffing his nosegay for
fear of catching jail fever.

Tubbs bowed when he saw me. 'A bitter day, Miss Truegood.'

I left Ned with Sir Henry. It had begun to snow. The flakes
that landed turned grey, defeated by so much grime. I doubted
the building would ever be turned white by the magic of snow.

We made our way past the gatehouse and into the
Marshalsea, a place so full of the mists of ghosts that they
seemed to outweigh the living.

Mr Attaway pulled his scarf up round his face and walked
with purpose, unaware that, as he did, he fragmented the
spirits.

'There are a lot of people who want to see Mr Quibble,' said
the turnkey. He had a poxed and greedy face, and eyes that
stared more to the side than the front. 'A lot of people. People
with grievances, if you gather my meaning.' Mr Attaway didn't
answer and the turnkey took a new angle to the conversation.
'This is no place for a lady,' he said to me. 'Though we have
quite a few as inmates.' He glared at me when I too failed to
respond. 'You remind me of someone. I'm sure I've seen you
before.'

I pulled the veil of my hat a little further down my face.

We reached the prison quarters that were kept for serious
crimes. Here no prisoner was allowed out of his cell except to
be taken to trial. We walked down a long corridor with oak
doors either end and cells on each side. The turnkey opened a
cell door and we were greeted by the smell of shit, the chamber
pot having recently been used.

'Take that away,' Mr Attaway said, wrapping his scarf more tightly round his nose and pointing to the offending item. Tubbs handed the turnkey a coin, a necessary incentive. The turnkey and the smell retreated.

Mr Quibble was sitting on a low trundle bed. He showed no inclination to stand or even acknowledge our presence.

'Mr Quibble, you are acquainted with Miss Truegood, I think? We are here,' said Mr Attaway, 'to ask you for the truth of what happened to Mr Avery Fitzjohn on the day he disappeared.'

'I don't know and I don't care,' said Mr Quibble. 'Now leave me alone.'

'I have reason to believe you do know,' said Mr Attaway. 'That and more besides, for in my opinion you are implicated in the perpetration of fraud in connection with Miss Truegood's marriage.'

'I have not one word to say to you,' said Mr Quibble.

As he spoke, I alone could see the ghost of a monstrous man push urgently through the wall into the cell. He looked like a bully back such as would be employed in a cheap whorehouse. He went to Mr Quibble and rested his vast hand on the lawyer's head. Mr Quibble shuddered though he knew not what at.

'A lie is cheap,' said Mr Quibble. 'The truth is costly.'

'I will not give you a penny,' I said.

'Then you will never know the truth,' said Mr Quibble.

The ghost was watching me. 'He's mine,' he said. 'Leave the black box to me and I will make him sing.'

By the look he gave me I felt certain of it.

'We are finished here,' I said to Tubbs. 'Please call the turnkey.'

Huffing and puffing, the turnkey arrived. 'Leaving so soon?' he said. 'Does the smell of legal farts offend you?'

I turned to Mr Quibble who looked amused. 'By the time the oak door at the end of this corridor closes behind me, it will be too late, Mr Quibble. You will be left with the company of a spirit, a spirit that will terrorise you to the day you die.'

Mr Quibble trembled in mock amazement. As the cell door closed, I willed the ghost to appear to him.

'Perhaps, madam,' suggested Tubbs, 'it would be better if Mr Attaway saw Mr Quibble alone.'

'Knowing Miss Truegood, I doubt that it will be necessary,' said Mr Attaway, adjusting his spectacles.

'What is a black box?' I asked Tubbs as we walked slowly away from the cell.

'In the vulgar tongue, it means lawyer.'

'I thought so.'

'That lawyer will go to his grave without exercising his tongue,' said the turnkey as we reached the end of the corridor.

He had his key in the last lock and was preparing to let us out when we heard Mr Quibble scream.

'Come back! Madam, come back, I'll tell you everything. Don't leave me with him – come back, I beg you.'

The turnkey looked at us in astonishment. 'Blimey!' he said.

Mr Quibble was still screaming as we arrived at his cell door.

'You stay here,' said the turnkey. He unlocked it nervously for it sounded as if there was someone inside with Mr Quibble.

The lawyer was crouched at the back of the cell. His tormentor had a look of triumph on his face.

'Make him go away,' said Mr Quibble. 'Please, Miss Truegood, please.'

'What's rattling your dice box?' said the turnkey. 'There ain't no one here.'

Mr Attaway nodded at Tubbs who fetched three coins from his pocket and handed them to the turnkey. He took them with a grunt and left us, closing the cell door behind him.

'The truth, Mr Quibble,' I said. 'The truth.'

'It will condemn me,' he said.

The ghost moved closer to him.

'All right, all right,' said Mr Quibble. He could see the spirit as clearly as I and, never taking his eyes off him, he began. 'I was introduced to Mr Truegood when he was on the brink of losing everything. Unbeknown to him, he had…he had an asset in his daughter.' He seemed to waiver for a moment but started again, speaking fluently as lawyers do. 'My client, the second Lady Fitzjohn, was recently widowed and needed a simple soul to marry her stepson. Frederick, her son by Lord Fitzjohn, was born illegitimately but she was determined he would inherit his father's title and estate. Lord Fitzjohn had been persuaded by her to insert a clause in his will stating that if his legitimate heir, his son Avery Fitzjohn, married before he reached his majority, the boy would forfeit his inheritance in favour of his half-brother. It wasn't difficult to arrange. Ply a young gentleman with enough wine and he would marry a goat if you told him too. After the service, Lady Fitzjohn's brother assured me the boy was being sent abroad and was as good as dead. Mr Truegood was paid off and as far as I was concerned it was the end of the matter.'

'But it wasn't the end of the matter, was it, Mr Quibble?' I said.

The bully back moved closer to the lawyer, looming over him.

'Leave me alone – it's the truth,' said Mr Quibble.

'Tell the lady about that vicious grubshite,' said the bully back.

Mr Quibble flinched. 'Some four years after this,' he said, 'I renewed the acquaintance of an old client, Victor Wrattan.'

'Tell her where,' said the bully back.

'I don't have to,' said Mr Quibble.

Tubbs was alarmed for he could not see or hear the ghost, only the effect he had as he lifted up Mr Quibble and threw him against the wall.

'Tell her where!' barked the bully back.

'Do not concern yourself, Tubbs,' said Mr Attaway. 'Miss Truegood has the situation in hand.'

'I tell you, sir,' said Tubbs, 'the very devil is in this cell. I feel it, sir, I feel it.'

'At Mrs Morton's,' said Mr Quibble. 'She ran a molly house and engaged me for legal work.'

'And you kept a book of all them that practised sodomy, and you blackmailed them, didn't you?' said the bully back.

'Yes. Yes, I did.'

'Yes, you shit, you blackmailed me,' said the ghost.

'Did you blackmail Victor Wrattan?' I asked.

'Good Lord, no – I held my life too dear! Mr Wrattan is a violent man, ruled more by his temper than by reason. For all that, he was clever. He told me he'd learned that Mr Truegood's daughter stood to inherit a fortune on the day she turned eighteen. When I told him about her clandestine marriage, he suggested rather than see a fortune go to waste, we'd both profit if it could be proved that Miss Truegood had in fact been married in the Fleet to his friend Mr Ralph Spiggot. I had in my possession one copy of the original marriage certificate; your father, I assumed, held the other. He was heavily in debt again but couldn't be persuaded to hand it over. And he couldn't be relied upon to stay quiet so Wrattan called in a gambling debt and Mr Truegood was brought to this place.'

'And in this place, Victor Wrattan murdered him.'

'That was nothing to do with me,' said Mr Quibble, quickly. 'I only wanted the marriage certificate in my hand before I produced a false one showing you were married to Ralph Spiggot. But Wrattan couldn't find it.'

'You cockroach!' said the ghost. 'I should have lifted my boot and crushed you under it when I had the chance.' He pulled Mr Quibble to his feet. 'You stand up when you talk to a lady.'

'Go on, Mr Quibble,' I said, unmoved by his plight.

'My heart,' said the lawyer. 'I can't breathe.'

'Then let me pull you from yourself,' said the bully back.

'No, not yet,' said I, firmly.

'Miss Truegood,' said Tubbs, 'who is it you are addressing?'

'Quiet, Tubbs,' said Mr Attaway.

'To complicate matters further,' continued Mr Quibble, his hand clutched to his chest, 'Avery Fitzjohn, who I thought dead, reappeared, very much alive, wanting his clandestine marriage dissolved so he could remarry. Neither he nor Lord Frederick knew the name of the girl he had married in the Fleet. At this time, I was continually engaged by Lord Frederick to rescue him from the many scrapes he found himself in.' Mr Quibble, I could see, enjoyed recounting this part of his tale for some colour came back to his grey features and he let go of his chest. 'He never paid my bills. He came to me with a cock-and-bull story of how he was going to steal the affections of a wealthy French countess from his brother, marry her and restore his fortunes. The man is a piss-head with feathers for brains and any fool could see that the countess would never marry him. But Lord Frederick was immoveable. He wanted rid of his brother.' Quibble turned to me. 'There. I've told you the truth. Make this thing be gone.'

'When I couldn't pay you, you had me arrested,' said the bully back. Tubbs, for the first time since I had known him, had stopped buzzing and was still, white with fear.

'Tell her what she wants to know,' said the bully back. He pressed Mr Quibble to the floor.

In a whisper, Mr Quibble said, 'I, too, wanted Mr Fitzjohn gone. I sent a message to him, telling him I had discovered the name of his wife and asking him to call on me. Lord Frederick arranged for him to be accosted before he reached my chambers. I wasn't interested in what the thugs did with his brother as long they removed him.' Mr Quibble was on his knees. 'That is the truth – I swear I never saw him that day.'

'Because of you,' said the ghost, 'they hanged me.'

'Madam,' screamed Mr Quibble, 'make him go away – please.'

It was as if the core of me had turned to ice.

I said, 'Three times, Mr Quibble, you conspired to ruin Avery Fitzjohn, and twice your conspiracies came close to ending my life.'

'He is mine,' said the bully back. 'He belongs this side.'

I nodded.

We left the Marshalsea. The black dog had found its rightful master.

Chapter Fifty-Five

This, then, should be the end of my letter to you. A letter that has no address other than a family vault. Yet I cannot bring myself to let the ink dry on the final full stop. It would be as good as admitting that you are dead. I refuse to let you become a ghost; these words be your only flesh. I have travelled too far with you at the very heart of me. The love I have for you will last, it must last until I meet the ferryman.

This is the only way I can talk to you. Your voice is lost to me, your replies I will never hear. I often dream of the night I was taken to the Fleet to be married. I see you coming from behind the curtain.

'Marriage is murder,' you say and put your hands up to remove your mask.

I long to see your face but at the same time am filled with dread that all that is left behind the mask is a skull.

I loved you, I love you, and the love that was so precious to us had nothing to protect it. We were but puppets, our strings pulled by the desires of others, used for their cruel design alone. I will not easily let that love be devalued. I will not let go of my belief that you are alive somewhere. But where? And why don't you come to me?

~

I called our daughter Ava. Her birth changed me, gave my world a weight that it hadn't possessed since you vanished. The love I feel for this small stranger who looks like you and daily unwraps into a blue-eyed, curly-haired little girl surprises even me. When she smiles, you smile back at me. She has helped in part to dull the madness of desire.

Wealth and, I am told, my beauty, bring me suitors a-plenty, each believing emphatically that a rich widow must be in need of a husband to have and to hold such a fortune as she possesses. An expression of disbelief crosses the gentleman's face when informed that even if he was to become my husband, he would never have a penny of my money. How quickly pointless passion departs, how soon I am bored with the notion of anyone but you in my bed.

I spend most of my time in the house outside Bath. I really must call it an estate – after all it is one of the finest in the area. But, if the truth be known, I still feel an imposter and for a long time I imagined Mr Ainsley returning, accompanied by an army of constables to have me thrown out. It took me some time to comprehend the enormity of the generous gift Lord B had left me. It has enabled me to do what I want without the judgement of others. It is a treasure that I take great care not to lose.

My one extravagance is my gowns. It comforts me that I still possess such an appetite for satins and silks, for the folly of fashion plates. The caress of luxurious fabrics reminds me of your gentle touch, your long almond-shaped hands, the delight you took in undressing me. Here in a fold of silk, in the intimacy of petticoats, your touch holds firm.

Lord B loved to shock with his wardrobe and I, too, determinedly make a stir whenever I go into Bath. There is great pleasure in seeing duchesses and dowagers at the assembly rooms who have been busy trying to copy my style. Such folly never ceases to amuse me.

'*Nous nageons dans un flot futil.*'

The success of the estate and the management of the tenants and farms has more to do with Mercy and Mofty than me. Mercy calls herself 'Master Mercy', as do the tenants, and she and Mofty live in the dower house. Lord B would be so amused if he knew that the profitable upkeep of his property was due to the efforts of women. Dear, loyal Ned Bird lives here too. As for Hope, she has retired, and is the chatelaine of the Highgate house. She said that someone had to make sure that Lord B's secret garden never dies and I agree.

Queenie and Mr Crease keep up the fairy house in Lincoln's Inn Square, and occasionally give magical soirées. It seems to me that all the bows are tied, the cards played, and in a way everything has worked out, albeit differently than I had expected. But only a fool would expect anything from the future.

Ava turned three in the spring and it was mid-summer, a time of wasps and bluebottles, when I received a small package addressed to Lady Fitzjohn. Astonished to find myself thus enobled, I stared at it with something approaching dread before opening it. Inside was the pocket watch I had given you and a letter from Lord Frederick Fitzjohn. I read and reread it and thought the whole thing to be a garbled mess, his sentences bolting horses, his paragraphs upturned carriages. The gist of it was this: he was dying and wanted me to know what he had done as it was preying on his mind. He confessed to having sent his half-brother away on a ship that transported prisoners to the New World. He had paid the captain handsomely. The letter ended with the pathetic cry of all corrupt, dying men:

'God forgive me.' Not one word of any use, not the name of the ship, nor the captain, nothing that could be discovered. On an enclosed slip of paper, an unknown hand had written that Lord Frederick had died of the pox. The letter infuriated me. All avenues of inquiry closed in on themselves.

~

That night I slept fitfully. I was woken by a thud and, sitting up, saw that Boozey, who for years I had neglected, had fallen from his perch. Half his feathers were coming away and much dust had settled upon him. I gathered what remained of him, stuffing, feathers and all, and in my nightgown I walked barefoot down the stairs out into the garden, my parrot an offering to the morning. By the lake I stood, barefoot.

'It is not enough,' I said to the remains of my dead bird. 'It can never be enough not to know.'

My tears fell upon his feathers.

I felt a flutter in my hands and I stretched them out, holding Boozey towards the sky. I watched him gather his ghostly self, saw his wings embrace the air.

'Bring him home, Boozey,' I called. 'Bring my love home to me.'

My parrot dissolved into the sunshine of the new day.

Ava ran out to me. I picked her up and held her close. She told me there were water nymphs in the lake, that they were like fairies and could tiptoe on the waves.

'No, they can't,' I said, kissing her.

'Mr Crease told me so.'

Queenie and Mr Crease had been staying with us and, wherever Mr Crease went, Ava followed.

I had seen Sir Henry frequently, as he had taken a house in Bath. That morning he sent a message.

'*The sprites of summer madness are playing,*' he wrote. '*I have news the like of which you would not believe. All will be revealed this evening.*'

I smiled. We knew what he was going to say because Hope's letter had preceded his. Hers was short and to the point: Mr Sitton had returned from abroad and they had married last week. She ended by asking if I had received an earlier letter from her.

I had not.

'Married!' said Queenie. 'Oh, Crease. Hope married to Mr Sitton at last – and we weren't there.'

'Ads bleed,' said Mr Crease. 'Too much is made of weddings.'

~

As I was changing for dinner that evening, I stopped and picked up the pocket watch from my dressing table.

I said, quietly, 'This is still not enough,' and slipped it into my pocket.

Ava came in to watch me being laced into my silk gown. While my maid dressed my hair, Ava laid her head on my lap, looked up at me with those huge blue eyes and told me about the mermaids and sea dragons that lived under the water in the lake.

I said, 'You can stay up a short while to see Sir Henry, but you must go to bed when Nurse comes to fetch you.'

Hearing footsteps on the gravel outside, she ran to the window.

'Sir Henry must have arrived,' I said, without looking.

'No,' she said. 'It's not him.'

I went to join her and glancing out saw no one. 'Who did you see?' I asked, kneeling to be on her level.

'He has a sad face,' she said, then thinking a little more, added, 'He's lost.'

I wondered if she could see spirits where I no longer could. I stood and in the glass was nothing more than my own reflection. Ava took my hand and we went down together to the drawing room to greet our guests, my beautiful daughter dressed in her water-nymph costume.

Only when Mr Crease had performed one magic trick did she reluctantly go with her nursemaid to bed.

Dinner was served that night in the chamber with long windows that opened onto the garden. The air was still with the perfume of mid-summer. Sir Henry was so full of gossip – fragments of half-heard facts surrounding Mr Sitton's return – that he could hardly eat.

I found I was barely listening, all of me restless, every part of me on edge. Under the table I ran my finger over the inscription on the pocket watch: *To Avery Fitzjohn from Tully.*

'The very minute he learned his mother was dead and he was freed from the noose of her apron strings,' continued Sir Henry, 'he set sail for England. And damn near didn't make it!'

'Where had he been all this while?' asked Queenie.

'In South America. But he was taken ill on the voyage and was eventually transferred to a British ship which was reported as having an eminent physician aboard. Without the physician's care, I was told, he wouldn't have survived.'

I was about to ask Sir Henry if he knew any more about the physician who saved Mr Sitton's life when Mr Merritt quietly requested that I speak to Ava's nursemaid. I followed him into the hall to find her in tears.

'What is it?' I asked.

'Miss Ava is not in her chamber, madam. I put her to bed but...'

Mermaids and sea dragons...the ground seemed to give way beneath me.

. I ran out of the house towards the lake, then stopped. Walking towards me was Ava, hand in hand with a ghost.

'Mama,' she said, her face solemn, 'he is a magician. He can find a sixpence behind your ear.'

She reached out her small hand to show me the silver.

The world became silent and, in that silence, I searched for the sound of your precious heartbeat.

'Tully,' you said. 'I am not a ghost, I...'

I didn't let you finish but went to you and you took me in your arms.

I whispered, 'I have dreamed of this moment.'

'And I.' You smiled. 'She is my daughter?'

'She could be none other,' I said, your sweet breath warm against my face.

'I find, my lady, that I am married to the only woman I have ever have wanted to call my wife.'

You kissed me and in that kiss was the longing for a future near stolen from us. Once, you said we would tell each other all our secrets. Now, I promise you only the truth, for at last I can put down my pen and leave the blank pages for the years to come.

Acknowledgements

I first showed my idea for this book to Lisa Milton, who had the imagination to see its potential. It started life in one publishing house and ended very happily in another – with Lisa at HQ. I would also like to thank my agent Catherine Clarke, whose wisdom is infallible, and my personal editor Jacky Bateman. I am the luckiest writer in the world to have her on my side.

ONE PLACE. MANY STORIES

Bold, innovative and
empowering publishing.

FOLLOW US ON:

@HQStories